# THE TAPPING

*Death...All Things Before and After*

By

Howard J. Levinson

Copyright © 2014 Howard J. Levinson
All rights reserved.

ISBN-13: 978-1484047835
ISBN-10: 1484047834
Library of Congress Control Number: 2013908672
CreateSpace Independent Publishing Platform
North Charleston, South Carolina

# Acknowledgments

Quite a few people and a ghost or two were absolutely essential to the development of this novel. First and foremost, to my lovely wife, Sharon; thank you for keeping our life quasi-normal during this journey. I could never offer enough apologies or say I Love You enough to balance our account. To Jason, Sara, Tom, Jen and Aaron, thank you for understanding the nuances of your father as I grew up along with you. Many thanks to my mom, pop and my in-laws for their continued support, despite the quirky behaviors I often exhibited. To my blood brothers in law enforcement; Sergeants Gerard Johnson and Gary Wilson, to the riders of the LH Motorcycle Club and posthumously to Special Agent Richard Bauer and Sergeant Joseph Crump, thank you for the camaraderie, loyalty and laughs we have shared over the past three decades. Much appreciation to my friend and editor,Paul Wheeler, for his sharp eye and to Susan Sagarra and J. Sterling for their support on this project. To my publicist Marla Stoker, *Marquee Media and Marketing;* thank you for implementing the strategies that have made this novel so successful. To the image wizards at *Dean Eisenberg Photography* and *Kyle Stoker Graphics;* thanks for your patience and assistance with the cover. To Starbucks and Panera Bread Company, many thanks for the caffeine, pastries and carbs that are an invaluable life support system to writers and cops. And finally, to "Miss Z" and my ghosts; thank you for helping me believe in and understand the things that send chills down the spine.

The boundaries which divide Life from Death are at best shadowy and vague. Who shall say where the one ends, and where the other begins?

Edgar Allan Poe

# Chapter One

Solving the Wiley murder case was as much about me as it was those dead children. Ten-year-old Robbie Wiley, little sister, Taylor, and their father, Craig, were murdered on November 22nd.

I died that same day too. Morris Green, shot dead, in the prime of my life. Well, maybe a little past my prime. Our souls, or whatever you call that ethereal mist that leaves the physical body at death, met ever so briefly.

Some good people in the ER brought me back to this world, just as I had done for so many others. Of course that was when I was in the business of saving lives rather than taking them.

The Wiley clan was not so lucky. They stayed dead, almost dead.

In my day, I've seen many deaths and worked many murder scenes. The young, the old, the innocent, and the murders where the world is a better place because some piece of shit finally got what they deserved. Up until the Wiley murders, none of my cases touched me. I'd seen so much death and destruction as a medic, a doctor and a homicide cop that I had become immune, desensitized. Waffles are waffles, transmissions are transmissions, dead people are dead people. It's a coping strategy, distancing emotion and compartmentalizing. And I was an expert at it. My ex-wife Sheila, and our kids would certainly confirm that.

My physical injuries from the shooting healed slowly as the Wiley's remains steadily decayed at the cemetery. Their spirits, however, were free to roam about country. One thing I've learned about the dead, they have damn good memories. When it was time, the Wiley's found me and the tapping began.

I was good at being a cop. I was better at being the police than a doctor. But that was before I died, before the drugs and alcohol had their way with me.

Back then, I had the knack. The innate, intuitive ability to read people and crime scenes. It's something you just have. It develops into elegance and grace. And much like being an artist, you either got it or you don't. It can be a blessing or a curse-Michelangelo or Van Gogh, Thoreau or Hemingway.

The advanced forensic training as a physician certainly helped my police career. However, remaining in law enforcement even after earning a medical degree, was convincing evidence of my dysfunction that somehow we all denied for much too long.

There were other clues that I was a veritable cornucopia of psychological disorders defined within the DSM-IV, the Diagnostic and Statistical Manual of Mental Disorders. Raised in the bleak anonymity of 1960's suburbia by an absent father and physically abusive stepmother, I did not adequately develop the ability to express emotion or form trusting relationships easily. At least that is what the counselors at Juvie, the police department and, following my murder, my own shrink said.

And even before the Stoli and pain pills, I was an addict. My addiction was the rush. I could not be satisfied without regular infusions of risk taking and the accompanying infusion of adrenalin. I was unable to settle into the comfortable, predictable, sane life of a physician. No risk, no rush, no life. These flaws would eventually drive away my family and cause nothing but pain for nearly everyone that brushed by me.

# Chapter Two

Talk to enough cops and you'll discover that every one of us has that one case. The case that continues to pester us like a deep splinter or an ex-wife's attorney.

Over a lengthy police career, there are hundreds of cases. The people, the drama, the death and destruction. Multiple images replayed in the detective's mind, sometimes triggered like a migraine, by sight, sound or smell. Maybe they come to him in a quick flashback, or a nightmare. It's all part of the deal when you work murders.

But, it's the unsolved cases. The cases in which the grieving, disconsolate survivors call you on the anniversary of the murder asking the same fucking questions and expecting different answers that you don't have. It's the lingering doubts of what you did or didn't do that burrow deep foxholes into your anima. And if you let it, the toll of unsolved cases can be as damaging to a chakra as a club to a baby seal. It can get so that the coppery, iron flavor of blood forever loiters on your tongue, tainting every cup of coffee with just a hint of the kill gone unpunished.

There is always that one case.

The Wiley children were vigilant, patiently waiting for circumstances that obligated me to bring them closure. When it was time, they started the Tapping.

The dead children were found in the garage, in their father's well organized workshop. His tools hung neatly on pegboard above a workbench. Extension cords looped in tidy circles were stacked in a box labeled "Extension Cords". There were plastic drawer bins of nuts, bolts, washers and screws that looked right out of Home Depot.

Amidst the organization, was an unspeakable horror. The crime scene photographs of the workshop are indelibly etched in my memory banks like Homicide Hieroglyphics.

The petite, 7-year-old, Taylor, lay sprawled out on her back. Her left arm was casually draped over her forehead, as if she was blocking the sun while spending a summer's day at the subdivision pool. Jagged and bloody defensive lacerations were noted on the left forearm. She had been a fighter. A small, through and through .22 caliber gunshot wound penetrated the left hand. The wound edges were stippled with gunpowder indicating close proximity to the barrel. There were other stippled GSW's (gunshot wounds) located on her cheek and forehead.

Seven long, gaping wounds from a machete had split her cranial vault open. The blade cut deep into brain matter designed to last another 70 or so years. Blood stained her blonde, Shirley Temple curls, pooling under her head, matting it to her shoulders.

After she was moved by paramedics, a bloody image of her upper torso remained on the harsh concrete floor like a smeared Shroud of Turin. The medics said one bullet, which had apparently been lollygagging about in her oral cavity, fell out of her mouth onto the stretcher as they loaded her for a futile helicopter ride to the hospital.

Robbie was found next to his sister in a semi-seated position, wilting to the left against a lawn chair. He was dark haired and stocky like his father. He had been disemboweled from two barbarous, arcuate stab wounds. His stomach and intestinal contents had tumbled into his lap.

One of the crime scene photographs showed a roll of green and white nylon webbing and a rivet gun on the workbench amidst blood spatter. It appeared that someone had begun to add new webbing to the seat of that lawn chair. Who the hell re-webs lawn chairs anymore?

Mr. Wiley was found inside the house. He was seated in his recliner in the den, dressed casually in a navy blue polo shirt and blue jeans. A 12 gauge shotgun still loaded with two additional rounds of 00 Buck, stood barrel up between his legs. He had been decapitated by the first shell. Chunks of his face, skull and brain were scattered on the wall and bookshelves like a Jackson Pollock painting.

It's been several years since the murders. By now, Robbie would have discovered girls and cars, just like my son, Jake. Taylor probably would have had her first crush on some teenage boy-band idol, just like my daughter, Olivia. Craig Wiley would have wondered where the time had gone, just like I do.

# Chapter Three

On November 22nd by 8:12pm, the murdered children lay on narrow beds in the ER at St. Marks Hospital. The nurses neatly cocooned the dead children in clean white sheets, placing a top sheet over their bodies.

The paramedics had wrapped Taylor's face and head with so many layers of gauze to control bleeding that it looked as if she were a Mummy wearing a Turban. The boy's facial appearance was not all that distasteful. Having been disemboweled per machete, and dying almost immediately from a severed abdominal aorta there was no trace of the terror and pain.

Emergency room physician, Dr. Margaret Classa, had advised Grandma Cindy that Taylor had sustained multiple hatchet type wounds to her skull, lacerating the brain and that little Taylor had been shot several times in the face at close range.

"Mrs. Scalini," Dr. Classa said, "We've cleaned Taylor up, but the injuries are very significant and I want you to consider whether you want to see her in such a condition."

Cindy Scalini took a deep breath, "I need to say goodbye to both of my babies."

"I understand. Would you like me to go in with you?" Classa asked.

Grandma Cindy nodded as she wiped tears from her eyes with a tissue.

Dr. Classa put her arm around Cindy, who was dressed in a hooded, red velour track suit. Dr. Classa wore purple scrubs. She and Cindy, both full figured women, looked like two large crayons. Dr. Classa pulled the hanging screen open and they walked into the room. Cindy's knees buckled. Dr. Classa held her firmly. Cindy wobbled next to the bed for a few moments.

A barely audible "Why?" escaped.

Cindy took a deep breath in and stroked Taylor's cheek, the one without a bullet hole. Using her fingernails, she combed a neat part in Robbie's hair. After a few minutes, Grandma Cindy started into a symphony of deep, staccato sobs, realizing she could no longer claim the title of Grandma. Dr. Classa walked the shell of a woman out of the room to waiting family members.

A short time later, in the coolness of the morgue, blood seeped through Taylor's turban and congealed into Cherry Jell-O like globs onto the cold stainless steel of the autopsy table. A few red splotches like Dalmatian spots dotted the cover sheet over Robbie's abdomen.

"We'll just wait," Taylor thought. "Someone will come," and some did. Other doctors, police officers, the curious. The children watched as the visitors came in and out of the cold, quiet room.

Taylor and Robbie thought that wherever they were, it wasn't right. It was empty and hollow, like a house without furniture. And it was clumsy, uncomfortable and thick, like wearing dad's shoes and trying to run.

"Someone will come for us," she told Robbie. "I feel it. Grandma Cindy said all children have angels watching them. It must be an Angel who will come. Some Angel will come for us."

For the trapped souls of lost little children, who better than someone who had also lost his way. Who better than someone who was a daddy, someone who would understand, someone who had also been murdered.

As she had been promised, someone would come. It wouldn't be an Angel. It would be me.

# Chapter Four

**D**ying at the same moment was one of the few similarities between Craig Wiley and me. At the time of our death's we were both well into our fourth decade. We were both fathers of two children, ages 10 and 7.

Craig Wiley's marriage was in the shitter, as was mine. The similarities ended there.

Craig Wiley was a good father. He attended the PTA meetings and took the kids to the dentist. He was the parent his kids called for at night when they woke up afraid of the dark. He did his best. He had to.

If my kids, Jake and Olivia, woke up at night afraid and crying, I wouldn't be at home to hear them. At the time of our murders, their mother and I were divorced, after having been separated on and off for several years. I had been less than the ideal mate to the woman who had been our family anchor while I went off on my various career searches. I lived alone in an apartment, they stayed in the house.

We had separated due to a number of reasons. My drinking and the undercover life were the chauffeurs that finally drove Sheila and the kids away. I was living my life on the edge of a knife, and there was little room for the three other people I'd dragged into it. I was either working, drunk or passed out, activities not mutually exclusive. Every time I could have salvaged things, I chose not to. I had been turning left every time the road sign said right for as long as I could remember.

Even before our marriage, before my murder, I was predestined to battle demons.

Like so many WWII vets, my father Jack Green, married his high school sweetheart upon his return from Europe. They saved their money and bought a starter home. Within a few years they had two kids. I was first born. The next year they had Carol. Jack took a job as a traveling salesman, criss-crossing the country hawking the crap you buy at truck stop gift shops along the interstate. Things like snow globes, miniature spoons from the 50 states, Jesus and Elvis wall hanging plates, and bamboo back scratchers.

As the story goes, when I was six, our real mother Deborah, was playing poker with Jack and another couple. She had just won a hand with three of a kind, all Jacks. She was said to have winked at my dad and said, "I add you to my hand honey, and I have four of a kind. I win with Jacks." And then she dropped over dead, collapsing the card table. An aneurysm in her abdominal aorta ruptured at the ripe age of 25.

Six months later, Jack married Elaine Steinburgen, a widowed neighbor lady. Elaine had lost her high school sweetie in the Philippines during the Battle of Luzon. Elaine was not at all hesitant to let you know her true love was not Jack Green, or his offspring. She used a screech owl voice and her belt to teach Carol and me our lessons.

I took the brunt of Elaine's misery. In a classic example of displaced aggression, she abused the son in place of the absent, traveling salesman father. If I was especially bad, there was the box. She would lock me in the blackness of the storage area under the basement steps. I am claustrophobic to this day, and have to sleep with a light or TV on. Carol only got the box a few times, but she cannot step into an elevator without Xanax on board.

Jack and Elaine were both raised in observant Jewish homes, however they seemed to have lost their faith after the deaths of their spouses. If we went to the synagogue, it was only for high holy days, in much the same fashion and with just as much zeal as Christians who only went to church on Easter and Christmas.

The lack of a formal spiritual foundation, did not stop Elaine from being a Yenta bitch. Jack wouldn't be in the door two hours after returning home from a three week road trip before Elaine started in. "I pray to God Morris, that you won't end up like your father. A man who can't make a dime by rubbing two nickels together. Neither you or your sister will amount to anything if you take after him."

The Green household was always a battlefield of financial skirmishes. Jack never made any money to speak of. There were no family vacations unless someone from out of town had a bar mitzvah, got married or died.

I watched as my father lived a life of frustration and sadness. He had been a paratrooper and had seen combat but never spoke of it. My guess is that he, like so many of his fellow WWII vets, suffered from PTSD. His way of dealing was to compartmentalize and contain. He was quiet and distant. Elaine said he was like a car with a bad thermostat. It took a long time for him to warm up and he never really did to me or Carol.

As is often the case with neglected and abused children, I displayed oppositional and defiant behavior that worsened with adolescence. I fell in with the wrong crowd, and spent more hours in detention than I care to recall.

At about the age of 15, I found escape in two passions. I discovered running, the only positive addiction that continued throughout my life. My other passion, the Holy Trinity of sex, drugs and rock and roll.

By the time I was 21, I had dropped out of a pre-med curriculum that I was barely passing. I started playing guitar in a rock band and we went on the road.

I was in LA when Carol notified me that our father was dead. Jack had been killed somewhere outside of Phoenix. A tractor-trailer crossed the center line and crushed him between the steering wheel and a trailer loaded with Indian beaded key chains, corncob pipes and salt and pepper shakers with an imprint of all the presidents. I missed the funeral. The insurance settlement would later finance my Caribbean medical school adventure.

The band toured both coasts in an old Winnebago. There was a succession of smoke filled clubs, whiskey, white crosses, weed and groupies. With typical Green family luck, a record deal and the tour fizzled out after 18 months. With nothing else to do, I went back to college part time.

By chance, if you believe in such a thing, I started dating a rough and tumble girl who worked as a paramedic. Her stories of rolling up to horrendous car accidents and multiple victim gang shootings were as unbelievably exciting as our sex life. She said there was an electrifying thrill of intertwining with the human condition at its absolute worst. That often enough, you made the difference between life and death, God like. I was sold. I took night classes and in six months I was in uniform riding a rig as a paramedic. However, after a couple years of "Mother, Jugs and Speed" the luster and kick of fresh blood and guts wore off.

I tried on another career that seemed to offer an even better adrenalin rush. I put on a different uniform and became a cop for the Oakview Police Department. Oakview was a 90 man department about 25 miles outside the city limits.

In my first year, I tackled a gun toting hostage taker, was stabbed in the leg by a crack whore and I shot a burglar. The hours of boredom in routine police work were eclipsed by the magical moments of risk and mayhem.

I ended up at Oakview primarily because of the Chief of Police there, a meek mannered man by the name of Thomas Montileone. He liked the fact that I almost had a college degree and was a paramedic. But I think the primary reason he hired me was because I was a runner, a kindred spirit. The tall, rail thin commander of the Oakview PD was a distance runner in college and, like me, still ran nearly every day. In the early days of my Oakview police career, the Chief and I ran many a 10K, several half marathons and a couple full marathons together.

Montileone was always worried about losing his job and was easily manipulated by the Oakview City Council and others. The Chief's malleability served me well during my police career. It was Montileone that allowed me the freedom to go to a Caribbean medical school while keeping my job open at the department. However, the Chief's timidity would ultimately prove to be a failing trait, with tragic consequences.

In one rare instance of taking a right turn, I continued going to school while working as a cop. Our department had a liberal tuition reimbursement policy and within three years of being on the job, I finished my BS in Biology.

I saw an ad in a Paramedic trade journal that offered the opportunity to earn a medical degree while working. I effectively schmoozed Montileone. By working part time, using a lot of unpaid leave and vacation days, I attended a foreign medical school while still keeping my police commission. I got a great tan and earned an MD degree. I passed my foreign medical school graduate licensing examinations and finished an abbreviated residency program.

Despite being a doctor, albeit from an adobe hut Caribbean medical school, I still could not give up the craving for the rush. I had become addicted to the thrill of those life and death moments that present themselves in law enforcement. Rather than offering my new wife Sheila the opportunity to live the comfortable life afforded by a physician's income, I picked up a part time position as a family practitioner at a state funded community health clinic and returned to work at the PD.

I spent the majority of my police career assigned to specialized investigative units-Crimes Against Persons, Burglary and Homicide. I lived seven years as an undercover narcotics agent, assigned to the DEA's organized crime drug enforcement task force. Seven is supposed to be a lucky number. It was during this assignment, in the eleventh month of my seventh year that I was killed. Everything started on November 22, the day I died along with ¾ of the Wiley family.

# Chapter Five

The 911 call came into the communications center at 1614 hours on November 22nd. Dispatcher Chris Taney took the call. Chris Taney had been a dispatcher for 7 years. She was a 5'10" with a long brunette perm, 22" waist and a Dolly Parton chest.

"Emergency 911" Chris answered on the first ring.

The recorded line picked up a woman wailing in the background. The rectangular digital display above her desk revealed the caller's phone number and that the call came from 1003 Peachtree Circle, the residence of Phillip and Beverly Goldstein.

The other dispatcher on duty, Kimisha Jones, researched the address and learned that police had been to the Goldstein's home 8 months ago for a complaint of tall grass. Phillip and Beverly had been out of town for 10 days and a neighbor complained about the grass. Phillip apologized to the responding police officers and cut his grass. There was no history of violence at the Goldstein's.

"Emergency 911. What's your emergency?" Chris repeated.

"We have an emergency at 18 Wydown Lane!" Beverly Goldstein announced.

"What's the problem there ma'am?"

"Something has happened to the kids, Taylor and Robbie."

"What has happened, ma'am?"

"I think, it's their dad, Craig. Julie, that's his wife, the kid's mother. She says that he may have stabbed the kids and might be trying to kill himself."

"Is he there in the house with you?"

"No, No. This all happened at her house up the street. Julie got away and came down here."

"Where is he? Where are the children at?"

"They are at 18 Wydown."

The shrieking woman in the background is heard to scream, "18!"

Mrs. Goldstein, talking to the background affirms, "Yes, 18, I told them."

Chris typed a few notes on her keyboard and dispatched an ambulance to 18 Wydown Lane for 'possible child stabbing'.

"Where did you get this information from? Who is with you?"

"I have his wife Julie, here at my house. She said she got away and came down here."

"Ok, I want to make sure, 18 Wydown Lane, correct?"

"Yes. Julie and Craig Wiley's house at 18 Wydown Lane." Mrs. Goldstein answered.

"An ambulance is en route. Hold on, stay on the line with me while I get officers on the way over. Stay on the line with me while I get officers on the way, ok?"

"Yes. Just get someone over to their house, hurry." Mrs. Goldstein pleaded.

"Hold on."

Chris keyed her microphone.

"Oakview cars 3210, 3271, 3273, 3288 an assignment. I need you to respond to 18 Wydown Lane, 18 Wydown Lane. I have a neighbor on the phone from 1003 Peachtree Circle. The neighbor is stating that the female resident from 18 Wydown Lane is at her house on Peachtree. The female resident from the Wydown location escaped from the home and said her husband stabbed their children and is threatening suicide at the Wydown location. Meet the ambulance on the way to 18 Wydown Lane, children stabbed, suicidal subject."

"3271 en route."

"3273 also."

"3288 likewise."

"Ok, ma'am, I've got officers on the way over there. Are you Mrs. Goldstein?"

"Yes."

"Ok. Mrs. Goldstein, tell me what is going on there."

"I don't know. I mean Julie is really upset. I don't know what the heck she is saying half the time."

"What do you know about the injured children?" Chris asked, calm and professional.

"Julie is just beside herself, I don't know what is going on. First thing I did when she walked in here is call you guys."

"Can I talk to her?"

"Yes, good idea. Hold on, hang on." Mrs. Goldstein says.

"Can you talk to the 911 dispatcher?" She asks Julie.

Julie Wiley is heard to say, "I'll try," and lapses into hysterical sobbing.

Kimisha Jones turns to Chris, "Damn, I can hear that through your headset. What is going on there Chris?"

Chris shrugs her shoulders and continues, "Ma'am, I need you to help me."

"Oh, please, help me!" Julie croaks through coughs.

"We have officers and an ambulance on the way."

"Help me, help me. He, he tried to kill me, the kids. He stabbed, I am so scared."

"Ma'am, tell me what happened. Where are the children?"

Julie Wiley's wailing increased, rivaling a Baptist wake.

"Please ma'am. I need you to tell me what happened."

Ten second pause.

"Ma'am?"

"I don't know, he wouldn't let me see them, I barely got out of the house without being killed."

"Ok, what kind of weapons does he have?"

"He has a shotgun in the house, and he said he strangled them, like he tried to do me and then he said, uh, he said he stabbed them."

Chris keyed her microphone, "Officers responding to 18 Wydown Lane, be advised that the subject in the home may be armed with a shotgun."

Chris Taney continued her line of questioning.

"What happened? When did this all start?"

Julie gasped for air a few times. "After they got home from school. I was in bed. I mean, I was sick, and I was in bed, He must have found them coming up the street from the bus stop, brought them home and did it."

More sobs. "Please help me?"

"We have officers on the way and an ambulance."

"Please help me, help, help them. Oh my God."

"Car 3210, I am responding," Oakview Sergeant Martin Weingart advised.

"3210, you are responding at 1616."

Chris turned her head towards her fellow dispatcher, "I wonder what took the leader of the Aryan nation so long to let us know he was en route."

"You are so right. Oh my God, he's such a hater," Kimisha said. "We had that meeting last week at Oakview about the calls for the black and Hispanic gang activity in the apartment complexes and he actually looked at me and said 'you people need to get your act together.' Like all black folks are graffiti spraying, color wearing, gun toting gang members. He's a real piece of you know what."

"Don't I know," Chris nodded. "He hates everybody, Jews, Mexicans, Asians. An equal opportunity bigot."

Dispatcher Taney kept Mrs. Wiley on the phone as the two officers, #3271, #3273 and their Sergeant, #3210 blasted through intersections.

"Ma'am, I know this is really hard for you right now, ok? I need you to tell me what happened."

"I can't go back in that house, please tell them not to make me, I can't see them like that."

"Ma'am, we're not going to make you do anything. I am just trying to find out what happened. What did your husband do, what did you see him do to your children?'

"I, I didn't see him do anything to them. He came into our bedroom and tied me up and put duct tape over my mouth and tried to strangle me. I've got his fingerprints on my neck," she said accompanied by sobbing, followed by gagging and retching.

"Ma'am, can I talk to Mrs. Goldstein?"

"Hello?"

"Is this Mrs. Goldstein?"

"Yes, what do you need me to do, I just saw the police cars go by."

"Just try to keep her calm, I can't get much out of her. All I got is that he tied her up and tried to strangle her, stabbed the kids, but she said she didn't see it. So I'm not sure what's going on."

The responding police interrupted.

"3271, 10-23-on the scene."

"3273, I'm also on scene."

"3210 likewise."

"Units on the scene at 1619 hours. All officers, be advised, only emergency radio traffic. Possible armed resident, possible injured children."

Chris returned to Mrs. Goldstein. "Do you think she needs an ambulance?"

"She has some red marks on her neck, but nothing serious. I'm a nurse, um, she's pretty hysterical. She may need to be medicated."

"OK. I'm gonna send an ambulance to your house to check her out."

"Good idea. Do you want me to stay on the line?"

"Yes. I may need to speak to Mrs. Wiley again. I'm sending an officer to your home too."

"Thank you."

# Chapter Six

Following the only semblance of standard police protocol that would be exhibited that day, the responding officers arrived tactically turning their emergency lights and sirens off as they pulled off the main road into the Wiley's neighborhood. They parked their patrol vehicles two houses down and approached quietly on foot. Sgt. Weingart sent Officer Nelson Williams, #3288, a black officer, to the rear corner of the home. The back of the bus, in Weingart's world.

Sgt. Weingart asked Dispatcher Taney to phone the home in the event the homeowner would answer.

"3210, I have called the home twice. No answer. I'll call again now. Stand by. Be advised there may be injured children inside."

Weingart knocked on the front door of the residence.

"Oakview Police, Oakview Police. Come to the door now!" His deep voice boomed.

There was no response.

The front door was locked. Half of a wooden barrel sat in front of the concrete steps leading to the front door. The barrel was filled with straw, corn shucks and a dehydrated pumpkin. The pumpkin was no longer the scary jack-o-lantern that perhaps it had been the month before. Someone hadn't bothered to switch holiday decorations from Halloween to the approaching Thanksgiving.

"Dispatcher, we've heard the phone ring at least 10 rings. There's no answer at the door," Sgt. Martin Weingart said.

# Chapter Seven

For all his shortcomings as a bigoted dickhead, Sgt. Weingart knew the basics of high risk building entry.

"We're making entry into the residence," he told Dispatcher Taney.

"Emergency radio traffic only, Oakview officers making entry," Chris said, as she pressed a button which produced a two second, high pitched tone, emphasizing the high risk emergency to all officers on duty.

The overhead garage door to the residence at 18 Wydown Lane was open and a black Chevy Suburban was backed into it. Weingart and Officer Tom Pischoch, #3271 entered the garage. Officer Bill Telling, #3273 covered them, watching the front door and front of the residence. It was a late afternoon November day, and there was minimal daylight sneaking into the garage. Weingart and Pischoch kept flashlights in one hand, their 40 cal. Glock pistols in the other. Each man entered on opposite sides of the garage. Using hand signals rather than talking, they conducted a near silent, quick sweep through the double car garage.

An 8' extension ladder hung horizontally on the wall next to the Suburban. A garden hose wrapped in a nice circle, a push broom and a squeegee hung neatly on hooks on the far wall. A blue plastic bin labeled "OIL DRY" stood next to a door leading to a storage area. The empty parking spot had been swept clean. Someone kept a tidy garage. Someone else didn't bother to change holiday decorations.

There was a storage area at the far end of the garage The door to the storage area was wide open. Pischoch and Weingart shined their lights in there, noting shelving units and a ping-pong table on its side. They didn't notice the door beyond the shelving unit that led to a workshop.

"We're clear here Sarge," Pischoch whispered to Weingart.

The service door into the residence from the garage was open about 6". They stood outside the door listening for about 30 seconds. Except for the sound of the furnace kicking on, they heard nothing.

Weingart and Pischoch positioned themselves on either side of the door.

The service door moaned as it opened. They found themselves in the foyer of the split level home. The men noted steps that led down to what appeared to be a den and up to a living room and kitchen. Wooden banisters with widely spaced, black wrought iron posts framed the stairs and upper level balcony.

"Telling, you stay on the landing here and cover us. We're going upstairs first," Weingart whispered.

Pischoch's Glock led the way up. A child's nylon pink windbreaker was draped over the balcony railing at the top of the stairs directly ahead. An empty *American Girl* box was lying on the landing at the top of the stairs.

A little girl had hurriedly taken off her coat. She had torn open the box to play with her new *American Girl* doll and left the box wherever it landed. The doll, Caroline Abbott, did not make a new friend for very long that day.

Weingart and Pischoch swept through the small kitchen. They noted an open loaf of bread, the bread tie lying aside the deflated end. Three plastic Solo cups and several small dishes with pizza crusts were on the counter. A silver cardboard crown from Burger King and two crumpled Burger King bags lay on the kitchen table. The sink contained several dirty dinner plates and a Teflon pan filled with congealed grease. Dark stained French doors led from the kitchen onto a deck. Pischoch whispered, "Deck and kitchen clear."

Pischoch crouched low and stepped into a short hallway leading to a large, open living room with cathedral ceilings. The room contained a dark leather couch, a matching loveseat and a glass topped coffee table. An arched, brick fireplace, took up an entire wall. The fireplace was framed by 6' artificial palm trees. The two officers swept the room. "Living room clear."

The hallway overlooked the den on the lower level. Pischoch shined his flashlight into the den and noticed Craig Wiley in a recliner.

In hushed tone, Pischoch notified Weingart, "Sarge, dead guy in a recliner downstairs."

Weingart looked at the bloody, decapitated man in the recliner. His thoughts were like bingo balls in a rotating bingo drum. Weingart stepped closer to look into the lower level. "What the fuck Pisch. I cannot believe this bullshit! For Chrissake, we're in Oakview, white bread yuppie land. I had enough of this crap when I was in the city."

"3210 to Dispatch. Send an ambulance, we've located one adult victim. He's, uh, decap, uh he's DOA and for sure a closed casket."

Chris looked up, raised both arms in the air and shook her hands in supplication, "Oh my God. What an asshole. To say that on the air? Really? Now, everyone with a police scanner or a smart phone app for one knows that we have a dead, decapitated resident."

"Yea, but you know Montileone doesn't have the balls to say anything to him. Weingart won't catch any heat for it," Kimisha said.

"3210, clear, ambulance should almost be on the scene," Chris said.

Weingart motioned to Officer Telling to join them. "Search this fucking house, find those fucking kids. You guys search this level. I'll go check downstairs."

Telling and Pischoch went down a hallway and approached the first room.

The door was open. Pischoch entered the room and turned right painting the room with his flashlight and Glock. Telling looked left and their lights met at the far wall. It was a little girl's bedroom. Taylor Wiley's bedroom. And it was anything but orderly.

The new Barbie doll leaned against the far wall next to a pink and white plastic play crib filled with stuffed animals. White wooden bunk beds were situated along the wall across from the door. A dingy white bedspread, laced in pink, was rumpled and gathered at the end of the top bed. A pillow without a pillow slip was crumpled against the headboard. It appeared that Taylor slept on the top bunk.

The bottom bed was a bare mattress and served as a catch all. Clothes that had been washed were lying in several piles on the mattress. Any evidence of folding was long gone.

An unfinished pine bookcase and matching nightstand completed the disorderly set. Two of the four dresser drawers were open and contained crumpled girls shirts, shorts and pants as if they arrived by free throw shot. Telling took a quick peek in the closet. It was sloppily filled with more toys, clothes and shoes. "Damn, what a pig sty," he muttered.

No suspects, no victims, the officers moved on.

Telling and Pischoch continued down the hall to the next room. Four foot high navy blue wood wainscoting lined the walls. Robbie Wiley's walls were papered with sports logos. Shelves along the far wall displayed an orderly collection of toy cars and animal figurines, primarily dogs. A wooden hat rack with baseball caps from the Cubs, Reds and White Sox stood next to a twin bed that was neatly made. A 24" X 36" framed print of a regal looking German Shepard police dog hung on the wall above the bed. There were no open dresser drawers or strewn clothes.

"What a difference man. This could be a room in a friggin display home," Telling said. The room was cleared and the officers moved down the hallway.

In the next room the officers noted a corner desk upon which was a computer and a brass banker's lamp with a green shade. Shelves on either side of the desk were filled with paperback and hardbound books, some Jackie Collins, James Patterson, Tom Clancy, Scot Turow, Richard Marcinko, stacks of Readers Digest, Mademoiselle, and People magazines.

Telling and Pischoch cleared the office, the bathroom, the utility room and hall closet.

"Son of a bitch. Watch yourself Tom," Telling whispered as he nearly stepped in 2 small piles of dogshit on the hallway carpeting.

"Where are the dogs then?" Pischoch whispered back.

"Where are them damn children is what I wanna know." Telling said as they kept moving.

Telling and Pischoch crept down the stairs and met Weingart in the den. He was standing by the recliner.

"Nothing in this room but the dead guy," Weingart said. "He did a number on himself for sure. That Lazyboy will be going to the dump. One of his damn eyes is on that bookshelf over there watching us. Watch your step boys. There's pieces of this fucker's skull and brains scattered all over the floor too. There's more rooms down there," he said pointing down a hallway. "We gotta find those fucking kids. Go down there next."

The hallway was lined with dark, wood paneled, sliding closet doors. Each door was opened. There were no children, just miscellaneous household crap. The end of the hallway led to a master bedroom where they noticed an open suitcase on the floor filled with clothes. The bed was not made and the maroon sheets were stained with dark splotches that looked like oil. A sweep of the room and accompanying walk-in closet and bathroom failed to locate the children.

"3210," Weingart called in to Chris Taney.

"3210," go ahead.

"We've searched the residence. Can you ask the caller if she knows where the kids could be?"

"Hold on, I have her on the phone."

Chris returned to the phone and asked Bev Goldstein to put her neighbor on the line.

"Mrs. Wiley?"

"Yes, yes. What. Please help me, please."

"Ma'am, do you know where the kids are?"

"I, I think, I think they may be in the workshop."

"Where is the workshop?"

"It's, behind. It's the back part of the garage."

Chris keyed her microphone and gave Weingart the information.

"Tom, you and Telling go back to the garage," Weingart advised. "See if there are kids in a back room, workshop or something. I'll stay here with the dead guy."

Chris Taney notified Weingart, "3210, the ambulance is outside if you need them."

"Tell them to hold off until we find the kids. The dead guy doesn't need anything."

Chris and Kimisha rolled their eyes and shook their heads in unison.

Pischoch and Telling returned to the garage. Telling flipped two switches and fluorescent light bathed the garage in a whitish haze.

"Shit! Me and Sarge should have come farther in this storage area and we would of seen them other rooms."

They walked past shelving units on which there was a set of golf clubs, neatly arranged pairs of rollerblades and ice skates. Pischoch entered the workshop room, followed by Telling, each leading with a Glock pointing at opposite walls. As they approached, Pischoch spotted a gold glint on the floor and recognized it as several shell casings. He and Telling immediately stopped and crouched to look closer.

"Spent shell casings, looks like .22 caliber," Pischoch said.

"Yep. A shotgun inside and a .22 out here. What the fuck?" Telling added.

Lying on the floor, along the far wall, they saw two crumpled and bloody, motionless children. A long, ovoid track of blood slipped away like volcanic lava from the blond locks of an impish little girls head. A boy with dark curly hair, his lower body in a torque position, was nearly disemboweled.

Pischoch keyed his microphone, "Dispatch, we need ambulance now. We've got two children in the garage. Get the medics in here now!"

# Chapter Eight

A t the time of my death and the Wiley murders, I was assigned to an under-cover narcotics drug enforcement task force. It was composed of detectives from the county and several municipal police departments. My partner was Tom Reynolds, an officer from the Kirkland PD a municipality just north of Oakview. Over the past 18 months, we'd infiltrated an outlaw, 1%'er motorcycle gang involved in methamphetamine production, chopper thefts and murder. The case had recently culminated with the indictments of 19 shitheads.

Our drug unit had a successful track record with convictions or guilty pleas in nearly all our cases. Before November 22nd, we'd only had one case that went south when a mid level meth cooker pulled a gun on us. Tom and I had to shoot him. It was ruled a good shoot by the prosecuting attorney's office and we both got meritorious service commendations for killing the bastard.

A narcotics task force partner can be much like a spouse. It helps to share some common ground. Like most narcs, we rarely socialized with anyone other than cops. We both rode Harleys and had taken trips together to bike rallies in Sturgis, Laconia and Daytona. We rode with the same group of guys, all of us undercover, all of us working for either a task force, the state police, DEA, FBI or ATF.

Tom and I also shared the fact that we both had other lives that were more normal and sensible than the work we chose. We both had livelihoods that didn't require placing ourselves in danger every day, but neither of us would give in to the need to feed the rush.

The Reynold's family has farmed and ranched 500 hundred acres for well over 100 years. When Tom was not fighting crime, he was looking for missing cattle or rigging a temporary fix to a hay baler. The Reynolds farm made money when the crops and cattle were good. The police salary helped when the weather didn't cooperate. But it was the rush that kept Tom at Kirkland.

And of course, I was the adrenalin addicted doctor.

There were some distinct differences between us too. Physically we were Laurel and Hardy. I am non-descript with an average look. 5'9" 165lbs., shoulder length brown hair, deep set blue eyes and a Dustin Hoffman nose. For the most part, I blend.

Among other personality defects, I have the classic long distance runner's persona. I was a one time, 3:25 marathoner. I liked nothing better than to be left alone to suffer the pain of a long steep, anaerobic hill. When we were married, Sheila used to say I was like a car with a bad thermostat. I rarely warmed up to other people, and if I ever did, it took a long time. Apparently, I come by that honestly.

Tom, on the other hand was a big, ol' country boy. 6'5", 240 lbs. of Hank Williams listening, Carhart wearing, cowboy boot stomping, hell raising. He had grown his hair and beard long and scraggly over the past couple of years. He could have been on a ZZ Top or Charley Daniels album cover. Tom would stand at the bar and talk to a stranger with skin flaking psoriasis and a hacking cough. Although he bitched about everything from his piece of shit truck, flooded back roads and piss poor police pay, he always had a smile and hearty laugh ready to break through the surface.

Tom was a Baptist who drank, danced, cursed and smoked. He and his wife, Bethany, took their three boys to church nearly every Sunday. Tom figured he could give at least one day to the Lord as long he could give the other six to the devil.

Unlike Tom Reynolds, I gave all 7 days to the devil. Given what I'd seen as a paramedic, a doctor, a police officer and detective, I had little faith that there was a benevolent God.

"What kind of God would allow the shit that happens to people to happen?"

My lack of faith in anything was just another wedge between Sheila and me. Sheila had been raised as a Catholic and despite being married to a Heathen, she raised our kids to believe in the Holy Trinity and not the sex, drugs and rock and roll one. They still attend mass more often than not, and I am sure she has said the Rosary more times than I have tipped a cocktail.

The former Mrs. Morris Green is a nurse, working in Obstetrics at Ballantine Memorial Hospital. She's been there 18 years and is known as Mother Sheila, since she has ushered more babies into this world than 1000 Octomoms.

Sheila is also a devotee to yoga, apparently another coping mechanism she picked up along the way.

In the early days of our ill fated marriage, she tried her best to interest me in yoga, meditation and the Tai Chi she practiced regularly. She even urged me to go to temple, try Judaism or Buddhism, find anything that would fill the dark hole she recognized expanding inside of me. I told her long distance running was just as good, and eventually it was. Sheila ran a long distance away from me.

I have to give her credit. She did a Tammy Wynette and stood by me for nearly a dozen years. She stuck with me through the police and medical school whirlwind, a residency, clinic hours, police department rotating shifts and then the assignment to the drug task force and DEA. I would be gone for days at a time leaving her at home with two small children, and she put up with it.

Despite the regular practice of relaxation techniques and meditation, Sheila still wore her worry like a second skin. Towards the end, she said I was an anchor pulling her and the kids to the bottom of a pit.

The crowning blow came with telephone death threats and the firebombing of my truck in our driveway, following a case I had worked against a group of Skinheads. Sheila reached her limit and we split up.

The move was unsettling, but not altogether unexpected. I had been accustomed to pushing the envelope with everything. Family was no different.

Back then, I usually started my day with a red beer, Budweiser and tomato juice. Then I'd head to the community clinic where I was Dr. Morris Green. I wore a pair of Dockers and a collared shirt. I'd pull my long hair back in a ponytail, put on a white lab coat and treat the parade of the pitiful.

Notables at the clinic were Medicaid patients who'd rather spend their money on Old Crow than insulin. COPD'ers who came in the office smoking non-filtered Camels and Congestive Heart Failure patients who drank a 12 pack of Falstaff a day.

We saw a lot of cancer patients for pain management as well as the terminally ill on hospice care. At some point during the Wiley case, it became one pain pill for them, one for me and a balancing act with the clinic narcotics log and prescription pads.

Up until the time of my death, I was a man living a lonely, dangerous life. I was an addict, without faith or family. I had a fucked up past, a tornadic present and a shaky future.

# Chapter Nine

On November 22nd, the day of my death, Tom and I conducted a briefing prior to a buy-bust drug deal. We held the briefing in the squad room at Oakview PD. Tom and I stood adjacent to the podium in front of the rows of chairs normally occupied by patrol officers at the beginning of their shift.

We had developed a strong case on a particularly vile, mid level heroin supplier, Bryan Brown aka BB. We had arrested BB in possession of several guns and a ½ kilo of black tar heroin. He was looking at serious jail time and rolled over on his source for the heroin, a Mexican family by the name of Estrilla.

Carman Estrilla was a known commodity in the dope world. He was one of the main suppliers of Mexican black tar heroin in the Midwest. DEA analysts reported that the Scalini organized crime family was involved in transportation of the heroin to the Midwest and East Coast. They were said to control distribution in this area. We could put a serious dent in the heroin supply if we could get into the Estrillo organization.

Because of the volume of heroin, the connection to a Mexican source and a crime family, the DEA had 'adopted' the case. The US Attorney's office designated it as an "Organized Crime Drug Enforcement Task Force" (OCDETF) case. To our team, OCDETF meant that we were federally deputized as DEA agents when working the case. We coordinated with ATF and FBI. And we received federal overtime pay.

Hoping to reduce his jail time, BB cooperated. He made some recorded calls to his contact, "Jorge" and set up a deal for a several pounds of heroin. BB told "Jorge" that he was dealing with outlaw bikers who were expanding their inventory from methamphetamine to include heroin. It made decent business sense.

BB set up the deal at an apartment. He told Jorge it was his girlfriend's place and very safe.

Truth be told, BB wouldn't be meeting anyone, He was in a cell in county lockup. Jorge would have to deal directly with Tom and I, and BB's girl's place would actually be our undercover apartment in Stonehaven, a cheesy, Section 8 government housing complex, on the south side of Oakview, along Interstate 55.

It was the kind of place where seasonal landscapers and roofers from Guatemala live, 12 in a two bedroom apartment. It was the place where the asphalt drive is pocked with car swallowing potholes and the dumpsters always have mattresses sticking out of them. In the summer, kids bounced on trampoline box springs and shot basketballs through milk crates nailed to telephone poles.

It was a simple buy-bust. Jorge would show up with the drugs. We would arrest him and try to get him to take us up the ladder to his source, hopefully an Estrilla or maybe a Scalini.

Our team included Patty Klos, an undercover detective from the Fairwind PD. Bill Taylor and Nacho Perez, county detectives assigned to our team, and DEA Special Agent Rickey Henry. A couple other DEA agents, Dennis and Jose would be there for added muscle if needed. Chief Montileone was sending Will Newsham, one of the Sergeants from my department, along with plain clothes detective Lawrence Johnson, to assist with surveillance of the apartment complex.

I started the briefing, "There is a packet for everyone with pictures of the bad guys and the location. It's gonna be a buy-bust for 2 kilos of black tar heroin. We are doing this in the Stonehaven UC pad. Sorry Bill, but we have to use your apartment for some business."

Bill Taylor had taken over the UC pad as kind of his own personal crash pad. Bill was 52 years old, twice divorced and drank Scotch on the rocks from dusk on. He was Don Knotts skinny with male pattern baldness. We rarely saw Bill during any fish, fowl, or mammal hunting season, but he had bagged a 10 point buck last weekend and had returned to work.

Unfortunately, child support and alimony was taking about 40% of his paycheck. He had moved into his mom's house in the country some 70 miles away, and stayed at the UC pad better than half the time to control gasoline expenses.

"Jesus Bill," Tom added, "There were clothes, pizza boxes and about a dozen Red Box movies all over the place. You couldn't hardly sit down from all the crap. I hope it won't bother you Billy boy, but we cleaned up the place a little."

"And where did the fucking claw foot bathtub in the living room come from?" I asked.

"Yea, well, I've been meaning to take them movies back," he said in his cowboy drawl. "Oh yea, the bathtub. Man, she's a real classic, a little cleaning up and that puppy will be worth something. City people love that kind of antique crap. Damn thing was a real hassle getting it in the apartment. Heavy as a drunk fat girl in a wheelbarrow."

I shook my head trying to figure out when he may have pushed a fat girl in a wheelbarrow.

"Thanks for decorating with so much style," I said. "We moved the tub behind the couch so we have some room to move around. I guess we could make a coffee table out of it in the meantime."

"Yea, that'd work just fine with me. I'll bring a piece of plywood back with me from the farm."

I continued, "The first photo is of Jorge Estrada, Hispanic male, 30 years of age, 5'8", 140 lbs, brown eyes, black hair. Jorge will probably be arriving in his blue over black 1990 GMC Blazer. Last we checked, it had Temp tags on it. The analysts tell us he is Carman Estrilla's nephew from a first wife. Not the closest relative unfortunately. We've kept BB's arrest close to the vest and we're operating on the assumption that no one knows anything about it. BB's last taped conversation with Jorge sounded fine. Nothing in Jorge's voice indicated that he was hinked up. It sounds like Jorge wants to start moving some weight to go up the Estrilla/Scalini corporate ladder. So the story about BB's new bad ass biker customers wanting to buy volume is pretty good bait."

Tom took over. "Jorge hangs with Daniel, last name believed to be Gonzalus. We don't know much about Daniel except that BB says he's Mexican, mid twenties, tall and skinny and quiet. He usually just stays in the background when they delivered the shit. No photo available. We figure Daniel is probably an illegal fuck, some kind of protection, gunman, maybe a relative, we don't know."

"Rickey," I said, speaking directly to our DEA representative, "It doesn't have to be a buy-bust. This would really work better if the government would let the money go, actually buy the heroin and let the Mexicans walk. It would get us closer to Estrilla, maybe buy us some real credibility. We could do a buy-bust on the next one for 5 kilos or something like that."

Bill chimed in, "Hell Doc, you know the government ain't never gonna do that. Cheap bastards never let the money loose. So, we have to risk our fucking necks to get this done."

DEA Rickey responded, "I asked the Special Agent in Charge about that. It's a lot of money, but I explained it could get us really close to Estrilla and Scalini. But Bill is right. The SAC won't let the money go. He said something to the effect that we can't be lining these dope dealers pockets with that much money."

Heads shook and we all grumbled about how fucked up working narcotics was.

I continued the briefing. "The bad boys are set to show at 5pm for the deal. We'll tell them BB is running late, and when he doesn't show up we'll just do the deal without him."

BB says the big packages are usually brought in a gym bag," Tom added. "So look for that when they get outta the car. We hope to have this done in less than 10 minutes. They may want to wait longer for BB or to count money, so who knows for sure with these Cans."

"We'll do the deal, and if it goes well, the bust signal for when they are getting ready to leave the apartment is, 'It is a pleasure doing business with you.' They walk out the door. Patty, Bill and Nacho swoop in on them. If anything goes bad in the apartment, I will say, 'Sorry, we can't see eye to eye on this, and you guys come in and arrest all of us."

"Or we'll say 'Oh shit!' and you'll hear gunfire," Tom said, followed by a few chuckles.

I wanted my people on the arrest team. If something bad happened, at least I could trust we would all agree on a story to be told. Whether it was the truth or not, wasn't all that important as long as it was consistent. I couldn't count on DEA Rickey or his people to lie for the right reasons.

I lifted a black and hunter orange backpack from under the table. "The money is in this. You can't miss it. It's all photocopied and I signed for it. After the arrest, let's make sure we get this back or I'm fucked for lining the dope dealer's pockets." A few more snickers from the crowd.

I continued, "After their arrest outside, Dennis and Jose, you guys storm into the apartment and cuff Tom and me. Walk us out. I want those boys to see us arrested too. They can think BB ratted us all out. Patty and Dennis will put the Mexicans in the van. Jose, since you speak the language, you ride with the suspects, in case they start talking amongst themselves."

"The van can then take off," Tom said. "Make sure someone has the cutter so one of you can uncuff Doc and me. We'll gather up the dope and money and we will all meet back at DEA. If we get mileage out of being arrested great. If not, Doc and me can be part of the interrogation team as they start to claim it was all a mucho misunderstanding."

Tom looked at his watch, "It's 1330. How about we all meet back here at about 1500. We'll get on our gear and saddle up to be in place about 1630. We're missing a meal boys and girls. Anyone feel like BBQ?"

Sgt. Newsham and Detective Johnson from my department say they have something to do back at the station. Everyone else goes to Bandana's BBQ. If Jorge and Daniel flip, we could be working for a couple days straight. The general consensus is that they will probably tell us to fuck off and that we can probably make happy hour somewhere.

I had forgotten that I was supposed to get hold of Sheila. I shot her a call from Bandanas. Sheila heard the background noise and immediately assumed that I was day drinking. It was a reasonable deduction.

"No, we're just having lunch. We got something going on in a little while," I said, squeezing the lime into the Corona.

"Dammit Morris," Sheila said. "Didn't you tell me that you'd go over to my dads and listen to his lungs tonight. He has that God awful cough he gets every November and he'd rather have you look at him than his doctor. You know what he calls Dr. Hsu, don't you?"

"Yea, he calls Steven Hsu a 'slanty eyed, slope headed, greedy bastard' and he never fails to mention that he dropped bombs on Steven's relatives. And Steven is the nicest guy, and is a great doc. And he's from China for Chrissake. Your father, Archie Bunker, gotta love him, but that's why I'm calling. I may be running a little late."

"Morris, my father's had this cough for a week and you keep saying you're going over. But something always keeps coming up dammit. So, can you go over there or not tonight?"

I imagined that her face was crimson and the veins in her neck were distended. The Hulk turned green, the Irish in Sheila took over when she got angry.

"We're doing a buy-bust at 5 and then some interviews. I can't imagine it will take more than a couple hours. Tell your dad I'll be over at 8:30, at the latest. You and the kids going to be there?"

"They will. I won't. I'm going out tonight for a little while. I'll tell my dad you'll be there. You just make sure you are, dammit!"

"I will be there. Scout's honor,"

"You got kicked out of Boy Scouts for lighting fires."

"I'll be there. Where are you going?"

"Just out with some friends."

"Well tell him I said hello," I hung up.

I gulped down my Corona and waved to the blinged out waiter to bring another.

"Problems doc?" Tom asked.

"Sheila's been dating the same guy for a while. I think it's getting serious."

Tom shook his head, and looked up at the ceiling. "So what. You guys are done. She's good looking, two great kids, a house paid for by you. What do you expect? She's a catch buddy. Just because you're not dating anybody, don't mean she can't?"

"I know Tom. I don't know why I get upset about this."

"Guilt, my Hebrew friend. You have the guilt."

Tom was correct. I was a shitty husband and father and was angry at myself for it.

I wondered whether Sheila had kept count of the number of times I promised something and didn't keep my word. Like, when I said I would be home or I said I would be home sober. Or I said I would be home early and came home early, but it was early the following day. That I promised I wouldn't get hurt, or killed. Each broken promise carving a small crease in Sheila's heart. Each time, my choices, my actions, exacting a levy on our marriage that eventually fractured it.

# Chapter Ten

I have always found the 'gearing up' process immediately prior to a buy-bust a dichotomy of anxious exhilaration accompanied by a sober and serene calm as we prepare to engage the enemy. It takes place with diligence and awareness that more than just a few friends have died shortly after the exact same preparation. But we temper any worry with an irrational denial that it will never happen to us.

The team returned from lunch and were busy getting ready. The plastic connectors on their webgear, the black, lightweight nylon duty belts, were clacking and snapping together, nearly in unison. Their .40-caliber Sig-Sauer semi-automatic pistols positioned low in thigh holsters for rapid draw. They pulled their bulky, tactical Kevlar vests over their heads. The vests held 4, high capacity Sig-Sauer clips, 2 handcuff pouches, 6 flex-cuffs, pepper spray canisters, and flash-bang pouches. Dennis and Jose carried Bushmaster .223 fully automatic assault rifles in short slings hanging in front of their vests.

Tom and I wore no protective gear. On the day of my death, I had on a dark blue, long sleeve Henley shirt, a pair of worn out blue jeans and a patch covered, black leather biker vest. Tom was wearing farm attire, tan canvass Carhart bib overalls with an insulated flannel shirt over the top.

Like the winning baseball pitcher who wears the same underwear, and puts his shoes and socks on in a specific order while on a no-hit streak, I have an OCD process prior to a buy-bust. Until that day, the process had been successful in warding off the bad juju of injury and death.

I wore the wire on this one and dropped the cigarette pack sized body wire deep into the inside left leather vest pocket. I snaked the microphone up.

It peeked out behind a stitched hole in a "Ride to Live-Live to Ride" patch over my left chest. It was invisible.

My stainless CZ-75, 9mm semiautomatic pistol with the 3 ½ inch barrel, was tucked in my waistband, close to my right hip. The rubber handgrip barely rose above the belt line and was hidden by my shirt and vest. A leather sheath sown into my left boot held a 10", straight blade K-Bar knife. I had gutted many a deer with this knife and it always kept a sharp edge.

The final piece of my ensemble was a flash-bang stun grenade. An unlikely weapon for undercover work since it is a bit bulky and about the size of a small summer sausage. I stuffed the grenade in my crotch, as I had done on a number of previous buy-busts. It was uncomfortable, but part of the OCD routine that I had to follow. If you looked close, you'd think I had a package like Tommy Lees.

A flash-bang grenade is a non-lethal explosive device. When the pin is pulled there is an Armageddon bright flash of lightning and smoke accompanied by a Ten Commandments, God awful loud bang of thunder. If you don't know it's coming, and you don't cover your ears and eyes, you become disoriented, temporarily deaf and blind. I've seen blood running from the ears of bad guys if they were near it when it went off.

My crotch flash-bang was the smoker's cigarette in that box that says, "Break glass in case of emergency". If I have to go to the flash bang, it is a bad day, but it is better to have and not need than need and not have.

Tom was armed with a short barreled .40 cal Glock he concealed in his front pants pocket, a 6" switch blade in his left boot, and a two shot .22 derringer in the right boot.

Everyone finished gearing up.

I adjusted the flash-bang to the left and glanced at the wall clock. "It's 1530. Tom and I will ride over to the apartment and set up the video. Any last questions?"

"I may need to take a crap, the BBQ is rumbling things down there already," Dennis said as he patted the rifle hanging over his belly.

"I hate when that happens," DEA Rickey said, empathizing with his pal. "You put all the stuff on and have to take it all off to take a shit."

"Dennis, it's early," I said. "We have time to take care of all our bodily functions. Tom and I will head over now. Give us a call or text when everyone is in place and we'll test the wire. Let's be safe today. I got something I have to do afterwards. After happy hour, that is."

Tom and I saddled up on our Harleys and rode over to the apartment. We parked in the designated spaces. I carried in the government fund backpack containing the cash.

We set up the room and cracked open a couple of longnecks while we waited for the team to show up. We tried to relax although we were both a little edgy. Tom turned on the stereo. He chose some Bob Seger, but kept the volume low so as not to interfere with the audio transmission. We listened to "Against the Wind" unaware of the fear and pain we were running towards.

# Chapter Eleven

had guzzled down my first beer and Dennis was wiping his ass at the station, when Jorge and Daniel were dropped off in front of the apartment. No one was in position yet to notice the arrival of our targets. Their vehicle had a bad exhaust and I just happened to look out the window in time to see a rusty, primer-colored, 4 door Chevy piece of shit occupied by two roofer looking Mexicans drive away.

The God that I had little faith in was one funny character.

There was a knock on the door.

"Holy fuck. They're here, someone just dropped them off," I said.

Tom jumped to his feet and looked at his watch, "Jesus Christ, who would've figured these would be the only early Mexicans on the fucking planet. Shit, no one is here yet."

Three more raps on the door.

"This doesn't feel right Tom," I said.

I peeked through the drapes. Jorge was the bigger of the two and he was clearly no bodybuilder. As advertised, he was all of 5'8" and 140lbs. He looked much older than 30. His ruddy, cocoa complexion was cracked and pock marked. He had gone a few days without shaving. He wore a buzz cut, black jeans and a grey hoodie, zipped up to the neck. A few dark lines of ink crept upwards out of the neckline. He stood eerily still, a black Adidas gym bag hanging from his right hand.

Daniel was a couple inches taller than Jorge, skinny as Gumby with coal black hair slicked back with something, baby oil, Vaseline, maybe Quaker State. It shined and looked as if it was painted on. He was wearing a tan khaki shirt and matching tan pants. Daniel was doing the Mexican sway, rocking his head and shoulders from side to side as he knocked.

"They got a bag with them, the heroin. If they get spooked, I don't know if they'll come back Tom. Maybe we won't get a second chance. Son of a bitch."

Tom peaked out the other window, "Hell Doc, they're little fellers, let's just do it. Our guys will be getting here soon. Turn on your wire, they'll hear what we're doing."

Sealing our fate, I agreed. "Alright," I said, ignoring that little voice in my head that was screaming to call the troops and stall for time.

Tom opened the door, gave Jorge and Daniel a once over and with a head nod, motioned for them to come in. He looked up the street hoping to see the surveillance teams pulling in. He saw no one and shut the door.

The four of us nodded to each other and stood in front of the couch paired off like prizefighters.

I spoke first, "I'm JD. This is Tom."

"Where is BB?" Jorge asked.

"You're early. You know how fucking niggers are, don't you?" Tom says.

Jorge nodded slowly. More of the ink from around his neck peeked out. "Si, do you have the money?" foregoing any further pleasantries.

"Do you have the product?" Tom replied.

"No lo se. No conocemos. Um, we do not know you. BB confia un ustedes, he trusts you, but this," Jorge said in halting English, pointing at us and glancing around the apartment, "This is a risk we do not take."

"Then why don't you come back in a fucking hour when BB's fat, black ass will be here," Tom said reaching for the door, stalling for the team. The two Mexicans did not move.

"I guess BB told you that we've been doing business with him for a while," I said. "We've had a few problems with him and his fucking gangster friends. A lot of bullshit. Too many young punks who think they're tough guys. They don't understand this is a fucking business."

"Si," Jorge agreed, nodding, relaxing his stance a bit. A little more ink appearing around the collar. BB's amigos, um very young. Usted tiene el dinero. Show us the money!" Jorge demanded.

"Is the product in the bag or what? Show us that you have the shit!" Tom said, role playing a bad ass, impatient biker.

"Hey man, we don't know you either. Let's just wait for BB," I said hoping to buy some time.

Tom spoke to Jorge. "We have the money, it may be here. Or, we may have to call for it once we know you have, what you were supposed to bring."

"Yes, yes mi amigo, we have what we were suppose to bring," Jorge said coolly with a wry smile. He unzipped the gym bag. I watched Jorge as the bag opened.

Daniel shifted his position. Tom glanced up as Daniel made the proverbial furtive move by suddenly reaching behind his back. This move is as universal in cop speak, as putting the hands to the throat when choking. It sends an "OH SHIT" message to all cops.

Tom received the message and before waiting to see a weapon, he yelled, "Gun, motherfucker! Doc, gun." Tom reached into his pocket for his Glock.

My attention was momentarily drawn to Tom's yelling, as Jorge reached into the bag and grabbed what turned out to be a Tec-9, a high capacity 9 mm assault pistol.

The front sight on the barrel of Jorge's Tec-9 snagged on the bag. Jorge began yanking up on the weapon. I grabbed Jorge's arms and hands clamping the weapon to the bag and we began a World Wrestling Federation routine.

Daniel brought a revolver out from his waistband and fired off a couple rounds. Tom wiggled his Glock out from his pocket and dove to the floor returning fire. He continued to shoot at Daniel as he rolled like a secret agent in a movie. Daniel shot a couple more times. Acrid smoke and the odor of gunpowder filled the room.

For a 'little feller', Jorge was one strong motherfucker and was successful in pushing me off balance. I fell backwards onto the couch. I focused on Jorge as he continued yanking on the assault pistol, finally freeing it from the gym bag and leveling it at me. I did a Nadia Comaneci and pushed back with all the energy in my runner's quads, catapulting myself backwards over the couch. A stream of shots followed me as Jorge fired the fully automatic Tec-9.

There was nothing graceful to it, nor was there any good way to land when you're trying to outpace lead traveling at 2200 feet per second. I ended up inside Bill's claw foot bathtub. The bullets pierced through the couch and struck the tub. Pieces of ceramic and cast iron splintered off the tub. Shrapnel slapped me in the face. I had landed on my right side in the tub, on top of my pistol making immediate return fire impossible.

It was time for Plan B. Break the glass, get the cigarette.

I reached in my crotch and pulled out the flash bang, pulled the pin, and yelled "FLASH" for Tom's sake. I tossed it over the couch and hunkered down in the tub. I put my fingers in my ears.

The explosion of lightning and thunder rocked the room. Even protected by the tub, the strong concussive pressure rattled my brain. It took a minute to recover.

As I rose slowly, I was met with grey smoke and heat. I left the security of the tub and rolled over the edge onto the ground. I became acutely aware of pain in my left shoulder. I glanced down and noticed that the black leather of my vest glistened red.

"Holy shit, that motherfucker shot me. I'm fucking shot!"

I crawled to the end of the couch, peeking around the claw feet and sofa legs. Daniel was lying prone on the ground moaning. Jorge was coughing and struggling to get to his hands and knees.

I noticed that my field of vision was wrong, limited, one sided. I could not see out of my right eye. It felt hot and it stung.

"Tom!" I yelled.

Tom answered, his voice weak, "Doc, I'm hit. I can't move my legs. I think I'm spine hit. Fuck!"

I wanted revenge. I wanted someone else to bleed. As I crawled towards Jorge, I was Charles Bronson and Freddy Krueger.

I tried to stand. As soon as I raised up, a searing pain shot through my right eye. I instinctively put my palm to it and blood filtered through my fingers.

The stun grenade had landed within a foot of Jorge. He took the brunt of its effect and had rolled over on his back gasping for breath and coughing from the smoke.

I stood over him bent like an old woman with a dowagers hump. It felt like someone had shoved BBQ embers into my eye and shoulder. Blood was dripping from my face pocking the carpet.

With a resplendent knee drop, worthy of any WWF match, I dropped onto Jorge's ribcage with all of my weight. Jorge's chest caved in and made that crunchy sound and feel that only multiple broken ribs will make.

The sudden movement caused a brutal glass shattering pain inside my head and chest. I rolled to the floor in agony. Jorge and I lay side by side for a minute, wheezing and grunting with each exhalation.

Jorge coughed and choked, spitting out blood. I recovered enough to free the CZ from my waistband. I slapped the side of Jorge's head with it to get his attention.

"You gonna rob us you fuck! Kill us and rob us!"

"Fuck you, policia," Jorge gasped.

"Policia?" My mind sped around the corner and did a 360 in an attempt to grasp the fact that somehow Jorge knew who we were. That Jorge and Daniel were there to murder us because we were cops. Kill the cops and take their money.

"You motherfucker," I said and then retched several times. My head felt as if it were splitting in half. I gasped for air.

"Doc, my legs," Tom yelled as he tried to drag the lower half of his body across the carpet. A tire track width stream of blood followed behind him.

"They tried to fuckin kill us. I'm shot too Tom. They knew we were cops. Where is our fucking damn team?"

"I don't know. I'm getting sick, I'm gonna pass out Doc," Tom said, abandoning his attempt to slither further.

"Stay awake Tom. Just stay awake, stay here, with me here," I said, blood dripping from the corner of my mouth.

"Ok, Ok, Ok," Tom said, his breath heavy. "Get em to tell us who ratted us out. If it's BB I'll kill that nigger dead," anger and hate strengthening his voice.

I jammed the barrel of my pistol into Jorge's flail chest segment. He screamed and gagged, gurgling air and blood, a frothy pink mist geysering out of his mouth. Then he settled, panting with small choppy breaths.

I whispered into his ear, "You're drowning in your own blood motherfucker. I can get some help or break a few more of your ribs. Tell us you fuck! Who set us up!"

Jorge turned his face towards me. "Fuck you!" he said and spit a mouthful of his blood into my face.

Rage took over any sense I had. "No, fuck you asshole," I whispered this time and put the barrel of my pistol under Jorge's chin and pulled the trigger. The back of Jorge's head peeled back and red mush sprayed the floor.

"Holy shit, Doc. Holy shit. What happened? What happened?" Tom asked, hearing the shot.

"I shot the fucker Tom. He spit his blood in my face. Fuck him."

"Good. Fuck him. Good," Tom panted. "Doc, I can't move nothing now doc."

"Just stay still. They'll come get us Tom."

Daniel had rolled over on his back in time to see me execute Jorge. He grabbed the couch and pulled himself up, balancing on one knee. He made an attempt to stand. His tan khakis were bloody wet and stuck to his legs. Tom's secret agent roll was successful. He had hit one of Daniel's thighs and it was fractured and bleeding badly.

Daniel fell onto me swinging fists and elbows and knocked my pistol away. I tried to protect myself with the one arm I could use. We tussled briefly. Neither of us had much left to give.

Daniel rolled on his back, huffing from the minimal exertion.

I pulled my Buck knife from my boot and stuck it under Daniel's chin. Daniel's black eyes widened.

"Nombre. Give me a name of the motherfucker who told you we were police!"

"No lo se. No lo se, please, please," Daniel started to heave and cry.

"Nombre, motherfucker! Who ratted us out you fuck?"

Daniel vomited blood and something that looked like Hamburger Helper. I pushed Daniel's chin sideways with the tip of the blade, turning his head to keep him for choking. The tip of the blade went through flesh and dug in his mandible. He screamed and reached towards the knife. I pulled the knife away and pushed the tip in between two ribs, just puncturing the skin. He screamed again.

"A fucking name. Who said we were cops?" I asked with a hoarse voice through more of my own coughs and blood.

"No lo se. Policia. A Capitan. A Capitan," Daniel coughed and started to cry. "Jorge, tiene conexiones con la policia. Policia. Here. They tell Jorge. No lo Se. Por favor!"

Daniel had become a few shades lighter. Except for the slick black hair, he could have been Caucasian even Scandinavian.

"If he don't know nothing, fuck him," Tom said, his voice hollow and fragile.

I whispered in Daniel's ear, "That's the guy you shot you piece of shit!"

Taking the same path I had used countless times as a paramedic to perform intra-cardiac injections of epinephrine, I plunged the K-bar blade upwards under his left costal arch, directly into the left ventricle of his heart.

He screeched like a crow. His eyes widened with surprise then squeezed shut with pain as his face turned lavender. Daniel exhibited a small shudder as his life escaped the suction of his body. He made a final grunt and laid still.

"Both of them are dead Tom."

"Good," Tom said.

"Yea, good," I said as the lights dimmed and the sirens came closer.

# Chapter Twelve

Cindy Scalini had been on the elliptical machine when the phone rang. She was trying to lose that stubborn 15 pounds which clung to her thighs as closely as her grandchildren. She was wearing a red velour track suit with a pink doo rag for a sweatband.

Cindy Scalini received the phone call from Bev Goldstein's house that chased her life away at 32 minutes into the workout. She called her husband, Anthony several times on his cell phone. He did not answer. She left frantic messages in his voice mail for him to call her immediately. She had been the first family member to arrive at the hospital. She had been the first to speak to the chubby ER doctor.

She found her daughter Julie lying on a cot in a screened-in emergency room cubicle softly sobbing and asking, Why? Why me?" Julie did not want to see her children so Cindy made the identification of her dead grandchildren. She called Anthony again and left another message.

Oakview Police Officer Herbert Davidson had ridden in the ambulance with Mrs. Wiley from the Goldstein's home. He was at the hospital waiting with her when Cindy arrived. Officer Davidson asked Cindy a few preliminary questions trying to determine what may have led to, what he delicately called the 'incident'. Cindy told Officer Davidson she had no idea. She told him that she had spoken with her son-in-law Craig, earlier in the day. She said he seemed like himself and had said that Julie and the kids were fine. She said he sounded perfectly normal. Cindy told Officer Davidson that the whole thing was unreal and that Craig loved those kids more than life itself.

Dr. Classa released Julie Wiley from the ER with a prescription for Alprazolam, instructions to take the medication and call their family doctor in the morning.

At Officer Davidson's request, Cindy followed him as he drove her daughter to the police station to speak to a few detectives. He said the detectives just had a few questions that wouldn't take long. Cindy sat outside the interview room. She called Anthony again. This time he answered.

"Cindy, what the fuck. I got back in the cabin and the fucking phone shows eight calls from you. I'm checking deer trails and deer stands for Chrissake. What the fuck do you want?"

Cindy conducted her own symphony of sobbing for Anthony. In between gasps and coughs, she told Anthony what had happened.

"Jesus fuck! What the fuck!" Anthony said, his bulky mass deflating into the nearest slat back chair.

"Alright, I'm leaving now. I'll be home in less than two hours. What the fuck happened? I can't believe Craig could do that. Are you sure? Jesus Cindy, he was more attached to those kids than Julie. You know how she is. Oh my God! What the fuck! What the fuck! Jesus Christ." Anthony took a few deep breaths before continuing.

"Fuck Cindy! No, no, there's more to this than that fucking story, I can tell you that."

"Just hurry Tony. We're at the police station now. Julie is talking to the detectives and..." She nearly dropped the phone because of the scream from Tony's end.

"She's what! Oh, motherfucker, get her out of there! Call Chatham. Fuck, fuck, fuck me! God damn it! She can't talk to the cops! There's no way of knowing what the fuck she'll say. Get her out of there and call Chatham as soon as I hang up. Even better, you just get her the fuck out of there and I'll call Chatham." Tony's breathing was choppy. He pinned the phone between his shoulder and ear. He was standing, talking and quickly changing out of his camouflage coveralls.

"Shit Cindy." Tony's voice was elevated. Cindy felt the anger in his voice. "Take Julie home. Neither of you talk to anyone until I get home. Do you understand?" His voice now garbled as the SUV started bouncing down the gravel one lane road leaving his property.

"Tony. Christ! Our babies are dead! Do you get that you asshole! Don't be so Goddamn worried about cops and lawyers for once damn you!"

"Don't fucking start Cindy! Don't start. I'm worried about our daughter for now and what she could say. Or what maybe what she fucking did!"

"Don't you for a minute even think that Julie was involved in any of this, don't you even, you prick!" Cindy yelled.

"Shut the fuck up Cindy! Get Julie out of the police station and go the fuck home!" He blinked his eyes, flipped through the contacts and called Chatham Newsham's personal number. It rang twice.

"Chatham Newsham."

"Chatham, It's Tony," His voice was a little smoother as he pulled onto a two lane state highway.

"Well, hello Tony. How are you? What can I do for you?" Chatham asked.

"Oh shit Chatham. Shit, man. Big fucking problem Chatham. Julie's husband, Craig, remember him? The dog trainer. He apparently went nuts. He, I think, I think he killed my grandkids and then killed himself. I can't believe what I'm fucking saying here. Fuck. Julie got out, escaped, some shit like that, but she's at the police station."

Tony paused, trying to make sense of it all and collect his thoughts, two diametrically opposed actions.

He continued, "Fuck, I don't even know what police station she's at. They live in Oakview, maybe there. I have Cindy getting Julie out of there and taking her to my house. I don't know if they consider her a suspect or what. I'm an hour and a half away at my place in the country," Anthony paused for a breath and Chatham took the opportunity to speak.

"Oh, Tony, I am so sorry. My God. I've been watching the news about two children and their father in Oakview. Oh my God, terrible, just terrible. I had no idea it was Craig and the kids, I'm so sorry. Oh my God," Chatham said, momentarily cupping his hand over his mouth and shaking his head in disbelief.

Chatham Newsham immediately morphed from concerned friend to attorney, "Call Cindy and make sure Julie asks for an attorney right now Tony. Whether they think she is a suspect or not, does not matter. She needs to stop talking to the police immediately," Chatham cradled his cell phone as he got his London Fog from the closet.

"I will head over to your house to meet Julie and Cindy. Tony, I am so sorry. Oh my God. I'm so sorry. I cannot imagine how you and Cindy are feeling." Chatham took a few seconds with which his legal neurons were connecting and organizing what had happened.

"Thanks Chatham. Please hurry over there," Tony said his heart pounding.

"Tony, please don't take this the wrong way, but Julie is, well, she is," Chatham paused, searching for the right adjective that would describe Tony's daughter without disturbing him.

"Chatham, she's a friggin witch, I know it. She's always been a little spoiled brat. Partly my fault I guess. Fuck, Chatham, Last week, we were over there and she got fucking unhinged when Taylor spilled her milk. She threw a roll of paper towels at her like a 90 MPH fastball, screaming at her to clean the fucking mess up."

Tony gripped the steering wheel hard, his knuckles blanching as he pictured his granddaughter dodging the paper towels. "Julie is like her mother Chatham, they are both fucking crazy. And you are God damn right Chatham, Julie is a loose fucking cannon."

"Yes, yes Tony. She could pose, well she could be well, challenging and could be a problem if words were put in her mouth or the police misinterpreted what she says. Or, God forbid, if she was involved in some way. I don't even want to think of that. Tony, I can't believe Craig could do such a thing to his own flesh and blood. We could never even imagine. I mean, a father couldn't. It is still unbelievable. And from what I knew, he was a good man and a good father."

"He is an OK guy, I mean, well, he was anyway. That's why it's so unfucking believable. He wouldn't. He loved those kids. I tell ya, something else is going on," Tony said.

"And that is what we need to talk about at your house. Call Cindy, get Julie home ASAP and call me when they are clear of the police station. Do you want to call your father or shall I?"

"I'll call him. I'm sure he'll come over to the house with mom. It's going to be bad Chatham, really bad. Hell, they saw Taylor and Robbie several times a week. Shit, they saw those kids more than I did. What with Craig traveling for work and Julie, doing who the fuck knows what she does, my mom babysat a lot. Mom was close to those kids. It's going to be really fucking bad." Thinking of what the scene at his house would be like brought a sense of dread as heavy as midnight cemetery fog. Tony blinked several times clearing tears.

"Yes, I know," Chatham closed his eyes tightly and ran his fingers through his thick white hair. He hung up the phone and immediately called his eldest son, Spencer. Spencer was a partner at their firm, the Newsham Law firm.

Spencer Newsham was playing tennis at the Fairwinds Tennis Club when his mobile phone rang. He apologized to his partner, dressed without showering and drove directly to the Oakview Police Station.

Sgt. Kenneth Murphy-Quinn, known around the station as MQ was reviewing reports at the front desk when Newsham arrived. He was a little disheveled, and still sweating from the doubles match.

He slid a business card in front of Sgt. Quinn and pronounced, "I am Spencer Newsham of the Newsham Law Firm. We represent Julie Wiley. I would like to speak with her right now and she is to undergo no further questioning by the police."

The Newsham Law Firm had a reputation well known to law enforcement. They had taken advantage of loop holes, police errors and used astute legal maneuvering to keep more than just a few suspected organized crime figures, drug dealers and an assortment of nefarious characters out of jail.

"I suppose you are Will's brother then, huh?" Murphy-Quinn said, not bothering to look up from his paperwork.

"Yes, yes I am. But that is not pertinent. I would like to see Mrs. Wiley right away. She is not to undergo any further questioning."

"Mr. Newsham," MQ said, as he put his pen down and glanced at Spencer. "You don't look much like our Sgt. Newsham. Will has dark hair and is rather corpulent. Husky, I should say. I think I would call him a full-figured kind of guy."

Spencer was lean, muscular, and blonde with a strong jaw. "A perfect Nazi," Sgt. Murphy-Quinn thought.

"Yes. Well, we are brothers. Now, about Mrs. Wiley."

"Mrs. Wiley left about fifteen minutes ago with her mother," MQ said as the desk phone rang. "Excuse me, I have to get this."

"Thank you Sergeant," Spencer said as he walked out the door, dialing his father's phone number.

"Asshole. Just like your brother," MQ muttered just before he picked up the phone.

# Chapter Thirteen

I was alone in a damp and foggy place. Streetlights snaked along both sides of a road emitting a yellowish haze. In the distance, they came closer together and then disappeared into blackness. There was a one story, weather beaten and dilapidated building to my right. It looked sinister, like a place I wouldn't want to enter. I found myself standing on a platform. Everything was tinged bronze and tan as if the place was in sepia tone. I was wearing a Nike windbreaker. The wind picked up and blew my jacket open. My breath fogged. I hugged myself trying to warm my hands in my armpits. There was no warm, comforting bright light summoning me home to heaven.

Out of the blackness, a solitary pinpoint of light approached. The sphere of white light burned through the damp fog. The light increased in size as it came closer.

The noise was deafening. Metal on metal, screeching, sparks, smoke, an electrical burning smell. If this light signaled the presence of the Lord, it was certainly not the soothing consolation I had expected. The pressure in my ears increased as the headlight, from what turned out to be a train, slowed as it neared the platform. The locomotive pulled one passenger car. Harsh fluorescent light filtered through the mist from the passenger car windows. The light bathed the platform and erased the sepia tone, changing the surroundings to black and white.

Through the fogged windows of the car I saw the figures of a man, flanked by two children as it crept by. I was shaken by a violent and sharp spasm in my back and chest that pulled me towards the train as if I were iron filings and the train a magnet. The white light was replaced by the train's rear amber and red running lights. Dragged after the train, I fell off the end of the platform into nothingness.

As I woke up, the world of black and white dissipated and I took in the new scenery. The all too familiar furnishings of an ICU. Subdued lighting, cloth curtain, IV and drainage tubing, infusion pumps, blinking monitors, an oxygen mask, Betadine stained sheets.

"Wait! Train! Who are? What?" I mumbled.

"Morris, Morris!" Sheila said loudly.

"Sheila. The train." I said, still partially confused, drugged and dazed. My voice was hoarse and weak. "Wait," I said, continuing to take in my surroundings. "I was somewhere else. I don't know. Where am I? What the fuck is going on?"

"You're in the ICU. You're at Ballantine Memorial," Sheila sobbed.

"What the hell?" I asked taking a minute, gradually focusing and trying to remember. "Where's Tom?"

"Tom is in surgery," Sheila stopped right there and started into a cacophony of crying.

"What the fuck Sheila, what happened, what's happening?"

"Dammit Morris. I got that call from Patty. That you and Tom were shot. You fucking died Morris and they brought you back."

"Oh shit. Oh yea. The Mexicans. Oh fuck. Yea, I know, I know,"

"You don't know, you jack off! You don't know how much this is killing me, and the kids too. God damn it Morris. You're a God damn doctor for Christ sake. And you got killed today for what?"

The human brain is fascinating. It is nothing short of amazing how many thoughts a man that was clinically dead just a short time ago, can process in a split second. So I am a selfish prick who must have regularly spaced, life risking experiences to feel alive and I don't care who I hurt to get my fix. That easily sums up a page or two in the DSM IV. I have damned near been murdered, and while lying in the ICU, my Catholic, Taoist wife is giving me Jewish guilt."

If nothing else, I am the king of avoidance behavior. Like a master switchman, I changed tracks to back off from whatever heady conversation Sheila may have been steering towards.

"I can't move my left arm Sheila. It feels like there is a knife stuck between my shoulder blades. I can't see out of my right eye and it feels like my head has been beat with a sock full of nickels. How long have I been here? Sheila, what are my injuries? My right eye. Am I blind?"

Sheila dabbed her eyes with a tissue and sniffed. She looked at her watch, "Close to six hours now. You were shot Morris. A bullet went in at a weird angle. The doctor said it glanced off a rib and lodged near your thoracic spine, T 5. Fortunately, no spinal cord involvement, but they didn't want to remove it. And you were hit with a bunch of chunks of metal from a bathtub? I don't know. He said something like that, cast iron chunks, something. A few pieces hit you above your eyelid, in your neck, and several in your scalp. You almost lost your eye. You were in surgery over three hours."

I reached up and felt the bulky dressing over my forehead, dragging the cord from the pulse oximeter across my face.

"You lost enough blood that you coded."

"I died, I fucking died?"

"Yea, Morris you died. They did CPR and the whole works," her words were hard and bristly. "You went into V-fib. They shocked you a few times and got you back after a couple of minutes."

"Holy shit," I mumbled and coughed, which ignited fireworks inside my head.

"They think you may have damaged eardrums from the flash grenade. I didn't see your eye, but the nurse said the globe is intact. Your cornea is scratched. Some of the underlying muscles are damaged. They called in someone from plastics but she won't be here until tomorrow. The nurse did say you won't have a right eyebrow."

"I'm sorry Sheila, it wasn't supposed to go like this."

"Yea, it never is, is it Morris?" she said with that accusatory tone I've well deserved the hundred times she's delivered it.

"What about Tom?"

"Tom's still in surgery. All I know is that they called in Dr. Kannandy. He's the top neurosurgeon here. Patty said she heard Tom's spine was damaged. I don't know any more than that."

"Shit!"

"From what I am hearing, your angels were looking out for both of you and it's a miracle that you're both even alive," Sheila scooted a chair up to the bed and sat. "Seeing as we're part of the hospital family system here, they're watching you pretty closely. Remember Willy Davenport, the nurse in the ER? She was working when they brought you in. She told me to make sure those 'white divas' upstairs take good care of that crazy man," Sheila did the best Queen Latifa imitation she could muster.

I smiled, "Willy's probably saved more souls than Jesus in her 20 years working in the emergency room here."

"She saved yours, if you have one," Sheila said as she took my hand. "Willy started your second IV, and took care of your eye when they first brought you in. She said she would come up and check in on you later tonight. Oh, and Chief Montileone is here somewhere too."

"I bet it's a friggin' circus."

"Yea. There's a lot of media people downstairs. Some guy in a suit from DEA is here talking to Rickey. There were a few other guys I don't recognize that have FBI lanyards around their necks. Sheila leaned close to my ear and whispered. "There are two Mexican guys in the apartment that are dead and they're all wondering how that happened."

I closed my eye and blew out another breath through puffed out cheeks. "Man, what a clusterfuck. What the hell. What does it take Sheila, am I a mess or what?"

"Damn right you're a mess," She paused and stared at me with eyes that were overstocked with an inventory of tears and hurt. She pulled a Kleenex from the box on the nightstand.

"I'm sorry I'm so fucked up Sheila."

"No argument there," she said sniffing back a tear, gaining resolve. "Buddha says, 'the way is not in the sky, the way is in the heart.' You're always somewhere in the sky Morris. Searching for something other than what you have. Like a damn shark, constantly on the move. This is what ruined our marriage Morris. I'm just not enough for you. We're not enough. This job, this craving you have for thrills or danger, or whatever it is. It's eating you up. We are secondary. You rarely see the kids. Sins of the father, you're Jack Green reincarnate."

"Bullshit. I see the kids."

"Give me a break Morris! You see your kids less than Jack saw you and Carol. And what's worse, you live 15 minutes away. You're not a traveling salesman on the road. And you had a great family to come home to. You chose this path. But you just don't see it for what it is. Maybe you will someday, but it's getting later and later for us to be there when you finally do," Sheila paused, tears forming again.

"Yea, I know. You're right, you're right. But I have a splitting headache and just got not dead. Can we talk about this later?" the master switchman said.

# Chapter Fourteen

It was just after 10:30pm. Leno was jabbering out a monologue on the 60" flat screen in the background. Chatham Newsham stood in front of the black marble bar in Anthony Scalini's great room. Anthony had poured them both a Scotch. The walls and 12' arched ceilings were pearl white that reflected sharp, angular rays from several sets of long stainless track lights. Each set was directed at art prints. On one wall, framed copies of Picasso's *Guernica* and *The Kitchen*. The adjacent wall held DaVinci's *Mona Lisa*, Raphael's, *A Portrait of a Young Man* and Titian's, *Venus of Urbino*.

A massive natural stone fireplace with an 8' dark oak mantle bore 3 lead glass vases filled with a collection of silk flowers. An ornate brass stand held a set of fireplace tools that could easily have been used as Medieval battle weapons. Across from the hearth was a wall of sliding glass doors that led out to a massive white, plastic wooden deck.

Three black marble pedestals situated in the corners of the room supported life-size statue replicas of the Bernini's *Apollo and Daphne*, Michelangelo's *David*, a *Venus de Milo* and Danaid's *Three Ladies Pouring Water*, complete with live running water. The room was too bright and ostentatious given the circumstances.

The great grandparents to the dead children, Ruth and Francis Scalini, sat on a long, white leather couch. Ruth was dressed simply in a loose floral smock dress. Her long grey hair was pulled up in a bun. Her skin seemed ghostlike. She wept continually.

Cindy sat next to Ruth, also sobbing. She held her mother-in-law's hand and offered words of comfort, as useful as losing lottery tickets.

Julie Wiley was sitting by herself on an adjacent love seat. She appeared casual, knee over knee, hands folded neatly in her lap. Chatham noticed her sweatshirt was inside out and her wavy blonde hair was a chaotic mess.

Chatham thought to himself, "How can this woman look so normal, detached and unemotional? Her husband just killed her children and then himself for God's sake?"

Francis Scalini, Patriarch to the Scalini crime family, a man accustomed to violence, spoke first. His voice was clear and crisp, despite his 77 years. He'd spent years in the church choir as a boy, followed by decades of singing along with his favorite artists, Sinatra, Kelly, Puccini and Pavarotti. It had kept his tone youthful.

"We died today along with our beautiful children. Ruth and I, we both," his Italian accent still heavy. Francis paused, uncharacteristically emotional. That strong voice finally cracking under the strain of lost innocence. "We cannot stand the thought of what happened. Dio ci aiuti."

Francis stood and paced the room, unable to sit any longer. He left Ruth for Cindy to manage. Cindy put an arm around her and pulled her close.

Francis circled the room, as if waiting for clearance to land somewhere. Anthony poured him a drink and handed it to him. Francis took the tumbler, his hand shaking, the Scotch stippling the white carpet. He placed it on the bar without a sip.

Francis turned to Julie. She looked up, peering into the eyes of her grandfather. His eyes were steel blue. They had always reminded her of Paul Newman's eyes. But her grandfather's eyes did not have the hint of softness that Paul's eyes carried. Grandpa's eyes were always firm, direct, unyielding like a strict school disciplinarian.

Still, this was the same man that gave her horsey back rides when she was little, the man who showed her how to churn home-made ice cream and bought her too many bicycles to mention. This was the man that gave her his full attention when they were together. Grandpa was a much better man than either her father, or her husband.

Francis Scalini leaned against the bar, closed his eyes and wept. Julie watched as he appeared to crack and crumble like a dried Saltine.

Francis Scalini took in a deep breath, cleared his throat and repositioned his posture, standing firm and straight, "Julie, come with me. Anthony and Chatham you come too. We need to talk." His voice, once again, was strong and determined. Ruth and Cindy stood. Francis shook his head. They sat down like tandem Olympic divers.

Julie, Anthony and Chatham sat at the kitchen table. Francis stood behind Julie. He put his hands on her shoulders, "Julie, Julie, so difficile. So, difficult. But you must tell us what happened, all of it. No matter what it is. We have to know. We have to know now."

"Grandpa, I can't, I can't," her head shook from side to side. "I am so afraid to say, it's horrible, just horrible."

"La mia famiglia mio sangue. You are my family, my blood Julie. Don't be afraid. I am right here. We must know. We must know," his voice remained quiet and steady.

Francis took a seat across the kitchen table from his granddaughter. A small and wiry man, his thick, dark, hair was slicked back with Brylcream, Gray strands from his temple frayed loose as he continually ran his fingers through, in an attempt to soothe his nerves. His sharp Sicilian face was rough as creek rock with acne pits and several scars racing down his cheeks and chin like snakes, from a lifetime of battle.

Francis asked himself how something like this could happen to his family. His, his, grandchildren viciously murdered. In other families, yes, he read about such tragic things, but not his. His thoughts went to his wife Ruth, weeping in the other room. She was aware that their business had a dark side. He tried to insulate her from the worst aspects of it, the necessary violence. Somehow, it had stolen into their home, the angello della morte, and taken their precious children. How could this happen?

Francis had built his organization over the last 50 years with violence and intimidation. As soon as he had gotten the call from Tony, he immediately wondered whether this was retaliation for something he had done. What had he done that would provoke such personal violence? Never, never once in his entire life had he ever ordered any of his men to ever touch, or even threaten a child of an enemy. There were rules, "Omerta" the code. This was barbaric. How could this happen? Someone would pay dearly.

He reached his arms across the table and took hold of Julie's hands softly.

"Julie, look up at me. Look up here child," he said as Julie continued to sniff and hyperventilate. Francis looked through the glass tabletop and noticed Julie's knees bouncing up and down like pistons.

"Chatham, get her a glass of water please," Francis asked calmly.

"Honey, you need to tell us what happened. I know it is hard, but we have to know. We are your family and we love you. We will help each other get through this."

Chatham handed Julie the water and she gulped down a few swallows, water dripping down her chin and onto the table top. Francis pulled his handkerchief from his pocket and dabbed her chin and wiped the table.

"Just like I used to do for you when you were little, ey," he said. "Okay, better?"

Julie nodded and leaned back, slumping in the chair. She folded her hands in her armpits.

"Grandpa, I just don't know what to say. How he, how he," she stammered.

"Ok, Ok. I know this is hard Julie, but you can do this. Just tell us what happened."

In between sobs, Julie sputtered out the beginning of her story. "He, he, Craig, he came home and he went crazy. He tried to kill me, choke me. And then he, he did it, he did it." She curled into the fetal position and was rocking back and forth.

Anthony knelt next to her and gently pulled her back so she was sitting upright again. He kept his arm around his daughter to hold her up in the chair. "Please Julie, tell us what he did, what happened, what did he do?"

Julie bristled at her father's closeness. She pulled and tried to lean away but he held her tight. She gagged and coughed, remembering the too many times this man tapped on her bedroom door at 3 or 4 in the morning, smelling of nasty cigars and beer. Mom was always asleep, or so she thought.

She tucked that girl away, that girl who did those things. That girl who did not scream or fight, was stored in some dark recess of her mind. Until the next time, she tucked that girl away. That's what she did, how she handled things. This would be no different.

She closed her eyes, clamped her jaw muscles down with resolution to get through this.

"I don't know. I don't know. He just came home. He, uh, he said something about how we couldn't be a family anymore and that we should just all die." Julie coughed and started to crumple again, but her father kept her from closing into herself. Her head went chin to chest.

Francis met Anthony's eyes and then looked over to Chatham. Chatham had taken his legal pad out and was taking notes.

Francis asked, "Craig, he went crazy. That is what you're saying? Craig, he killed his own kids. He did this? Perche Julie? Perche fare questo? Why would he do this? Why he would do this Julie?

"I don't know Grandpa, I don't know," Julie said hugging herself and looking at her feet.

Francis reached across the table with one hand and lifted her chin off her chest. His palm was flat and his fingertips touched lightly under her chin. He held her chin as if her head were on the platter of his hand. He looked directly in her eyes. "Julie, Julie. We need to hear it from you." His voice had changed.

"What happened. You need to tell us. It is very important for all of us Julie. You tell us now." There was a difference in the timbre of his voice.

Chatham and Anthony had been at any number of meetings where this tone, honed by decades of brutality, had emerged. They knew immediately that Francis was reaching a limit. Family or not, he wanted to know now. He wanted to take action. Francis Scalini was not one to wait.

Julie felt the change in her grandfather's voice and she feared it. It was something she hadn't seen in him. He was always just Grandpa to her, not the Don of the Scalini Organized Crime family, just Grandpa.

Her father, on the other hand, was quite different. He was the stereotypical cartoon goombah. Anthony Scalini was a big man, well over 6' tall and a good 50lbs. overweight. He used his size and position in Grandpa's company to push his family around just like he did anyone who got in his way. Her father had told her things, bragged about things he had done. She remembered some, other things she had tucked away.

She had seen him and her mom fight. She had seen her father push her mother through their sliding closet doors. She had helped her mom patch drywall on more than just a few occasions.

She had seen her father pull a man through a car window and beat him unconscious in what could only be classified as terminal road rage. She had seen him leave the house at night, and return as she was on the way to school in the morning, his clothes torn and face and arms bruised and bleeding. He would say, "You should see the other guy kiddo," and laugh it off. Her mother would nurse his injuries, and her own.

She had never thought of Grandpa in that way.

She kept her head up when Francis pulled his hand away, but it was too difficult to look him in the eye. She closed her eyes and spoke in a hushed voice, "I, I don't know where to start Grandpa. Please, don't make me say. It's awful, it hurts, it hurts so much."

"God dammit Julie," Anthony said. "We all lost something, we're all hurting. We're a family and we handle things as a family. And God dammit you're part of this family and we, take care of each other. But, this, this is, I don't know what the fuck this is. And I want to know. We all want to know. Now you, you are the only one who knows and you have to help us understand. We're all going to get through this and you're going to help us!"

Chatham Newsham stood at the butcher block island table paying attention to the drama, trying to stay ahead of the game as lawyers are accustomed to do. He had been the Scalini's lawyer for nearly 50 years and never had there been anything that remotely approached this intimate level of violence. There had been quite a few suspicious deaths and disappearances of adversaries, but never children.

Francis sat upright, slapped the top of the table with his hands, "Julie, tell us what happened. Now! Julie, Now!"

Chatham winced as Francis demanded that Julie tell her story, "Jesus, the woman just lost her children and husband," he thought. However, Chatham was not one to question Francis Scalini. Francis had become what he was, by being a shrewd and astute student of human behavior. He noticed everything and he anticipated, planned and took decisive action. This tragedy would be handled no differently.

Chatham was well aware of how petty and self centered Julie Wiley was. His firm had dealt with a few issues in which Julie had acted out, drawn attention to herself and the Scalini name.

When she was in high school, a classmate flirted with her boyfriend. Julie knocked the girl down, and while the girl was dazed, she used a pocket knife to cut off chunks of her hair. A few years later, a neighbor asked Julie not to park so close to her mailbox. Julie slapped the poor woman in the face with an umbrella and broke her nose.

Chatham's firm diligently took care of the victims of Julie's wrath with money and promises. Julie's short temper was a well known liability in the family. They all had hoped she would settle down once she married and had a family.

Chatham was also aware that Julie would never be considered for mother of the year. She had abandoned her first born for about a month, refusing to take care of Robbie, clearly in the throes of a post-partum depression. Craig stepped up and filled in as mother and father.

Chatham had spoken in confidence with Craig on a few occasions. As recently as a month ago, Craig had called Chatham in confidence, to get a feel on what he could do in the event he and Julie divorced. He said Julie was having terrible mood swings, spent money like no tomorrow and some days wouldn't get out of bed. He told Chatham that Cindy was giving Julie some Prozac to see if it would help her daughter's mood. Craig feared that his wife was going crazy. His canine training business was starting to make some real money and he wanted some protection for the business and the kids.

In light of today's events, Chatham thought it very telling that Craig had said at the time, "Mr. Newsham, I would have to get custody of the kids. She couldn't raise them."

Julie stood up, wriggling free of her father's grasp. She took her glass over to the sink and emptied it. She pushed her glass under the ice dispenser, opened one of the refrigerator doors and poured a glass of apple juice. She wanted some sugar and gulped deeply. Facing away from everyone, she stood at the sink, looking out the window. She closed her eyes, looked up and began.

"I stayed in bed all day. I wasn't feeling good at all. I'm on my period and was cramping. But I still got up, and got the kids." She paused for a few deep breaths and took another gulp. "Craig left early to go to the gym and work out, so I got the kids off to school and went back to bed. He, um, he said he had a few things to do with the dogs. He had to meet a potential client, something like that. I don't know for sure.

Later in the morning, he came home and brought me some herbal tea and a couple of capsules of something he said he got at the supplement store. He was always trying to get me to take some of that crap he was taking. Vitamins, supplements, herbs. He said the tea settled stomachs.

I took the capsules and drank the tea. It was easier to do what he said than argue with him. I don't have much faith in that stuff, so I took a couple Somas too. I know those work. Most of the stuff he brought home from the health food store never did anything. But, he wanted me to take it so I did. The tea was pretty minty and he had mixed in a lot of honey since he knew I like it sweet. He left and went to his meeting or to doing whatever he was doing. I napped a little and woke up with a headache. I took a couple Benadryls to put me back to sleep."

Chatham was taking notes. Francis had also stood up and was now leaning on the sink counter top next to her, watching her profile and listening. Anthony sat at the table alone.

"Go on now, Julie. What happened next?" Francis asked, his posture and voice softening.

"Craig stopped by again and woke me up. It was around lunchtime and I told him I was a little hungry. We had a pizza the night before, so he heated up the leftovers. He fixed me another cup of minty tea and gave me a couple more of the herb capsules. He had a movie he had borrowed from one of our friends. Craig, um, he said he had some time, so he got into bed and we watched the movie. It was, what was it? Something about cars. I was sleepy so I dozed off and on during it. My stomach was feeling better. Maybe the pills and tea worked after all. After the movie, he got up and put on a clean shirt because he said he had a client meeting. I was afraid I wouldn't wake up, so I told him to pick up the kids at the bus stop. He said no problem and he left again," she paused.

"God Dammit Julie. Get to the point already. What about the kids, what the…" Anthony blurted.

Francis interrupted his son, "Go ahead child. What happened next?"

"The next thing I remember Grandpa, uh, is him coming down into our room. He must have come home with the kids while I was sleeping. I asked him if everything was alright, alright at school. He said everything was fine. He said he told the kids I wasn't feeling good. That they, they should be quiet and stay upstairs."

Julie started to weep and sniffle. Francis handed her a handkerchief. She dabbed her eyes and blew her nose.

"Thank you Grandpa."

"Go on with what happened Julie," Francis said.

"Craig, he came back in the room. He had this look in his eyes, like I never seen before," she paused. "I can't say this Grandpa, I just can't." Julie sniffed and sobbed.

"Yes you can honey. Yes. Yes you can. And, you will. The story, Fini!" Francis said, his voice changing from soft to stern and demanding. Anthony stood and took his place beside his daughter, putting his arm over her shoulder. Chatham wondered how many people had been led into a remote area flanked by these Scalini men, never to be seen or heard from again.

"It's personal, Grandpa, really personal and embarrassing," Julie said.

"Jesus Christ Julie," Anthony said. "There is no such thing as embarrassing at a time like this. Finish the God damn story!"

Julie tensed and she wriggled out from her father's arm. Anthony stepped in to regain his grasp. Francis patted his son's arm, shook his head and nodded towards the table. Anthony returned to his chair.

Julie took a breath in and paused, puffing her cheeks and exhaling. Her shoulders dropped as she started to speak. "Craig, he, tied me up. He, he tied my feet to the bed and my wrists together. I couldn't fight him, I was still groggy from the pills. And, and then he left the room. He came back a few minutes later." She slouched, still breathing choppily.

"God dammit Julie, stop fucking around. Get to what happened to the kids," Anthony slammed the table with his fists. "What the fuck happened to the kids?"

"Antonio," Francis said, his voice harsh. "Let her go on."

Anthony nodded his head, "Sorry, sorry. You're right pop, sorry. Julie, go on, you know I get my temper sometimes. Go on, please. Like Grandpa says."

Julie started weeping. Francis once again reached under her chin and rotated her face towards his. His penetrating steel blue eyes squeezed her brain. He didn't say a word.

"He came back and I told him to let me go, untie me. He didn't say anything. And, um, I asked where he had been. He didn't answer Grandpa. He wouldn't tell me. Then he got on top of me. And all of a sudden he put duct tape over my mouth. I couldn't breathe except through my nose. I tried to yell, but it was no use. Then he put some lotion on my back, on my back end. And then he put his hands around my neck. And then he forced himself into me, into my uh, um into my rear. It hurt and he was choking me and pushing my head into the pillow. I couldn't see or hear anything around me. I was scared he was going to kill me."

Anthony was shaking his head back and forth mumbling, "Oh Christ."

"I couldn't hardly breathe. The tape, it came loose and I turned my head to the side and said, Craig, Craig I love you. Please stop. Please don't kill me, please Craig, I love you. It was a mistake, everyone makes mistakes. I was begging him not to kill me. Begging him Grandpa. It must have gotten through because he let go of my throat. I was coughing and I just continued to tell him over and over that we could work this out and begging him to untie me." She paused again, "Grandpa, I need to sit down."

"Of course," Francis said through tightly clenched teeth. He led her to the kitchen table. "What did Craig do next?"

They assumed their positions at the kitchen table.

"He, untied me and then he went into the closet and got out a shotgun and put bullets into it. He had this crazy look. Like a monster. His eyes were bugging out. It was, it was like a horror movie. I asked him what he was doing. He said he couldn't take care of his family the way he wanted to. He said he couldn't have sex the way he wanted and that we all had to die."

"I can't fucking believe this shit. I can't fucking believe this is happening, Anthony said, looking for agreement from his father who remained stone faced. Chatham showed nothing either.

Francis steeled his gaze at his son. Anthony understood that he was to shut the fuck up. "Go ahead, what happened next Julie?" the old man said flatly, like Joe Friday in Dragnet.

Julie blew her nose into her Grandpa's handkerchief and wiped a small drizzle of snot from her upper lip. "I got off the bed. I begged him. I begged him not to kill me and that we could work it out. And I was like backing out of the room to get away. He told me to stop and he blocked my way out. He said it was too late for us. And when he said that, I remembered that he had checked on the kids. I asked him, Craig, Craig did you hurt them? And he just said it was too late for them. I asked him, what did you do? What did you do? He just said it was too late for them." She paused.

"Go on, go on, finish the story," Francis urged.

"He, told me I had two choices. I could shoot him, or he would shoot me and then himself. I told him I couldn't do either. I begged him, begged him to please put the gun down and to let me go. He, he told me to get out. I pulled on some clothes from the floor. I backed out of the room, up the steps. I kept telling him I loved him and we could work this out. He followed me, pointing the gun at me the whole time. Telling me to be quiet, be quiet and, to just get out. I got to the garage, got into my car and drove as fast as I could."

Anthony stood up and leered at his daughter. A menacing, angry glower rolled over his face. "You left the goddamn house without knowing what happened to your kids? What the fuck were you thinking?"

Francis looked up at Anthony and again his look was sufficient to sit him down and shut him up. Chatham took notes, circling his lawyerly scribble, "How does a mother leave the house not knowing?"

"Where did you go Julie, where?" Francis asked.

Julie just wanted to finish the story. Her speech quickened. "I drove down to Bev Goldstein's house at the end of the block. Our kids go to school together. I banged on her door and told her. I told her that Craig had killed the kids, that they were in the workshop and that he, he was going to kill himself and that I needed help. Bev called 911 and I went into the bathroom and threw up. She gave the phone to me, and I spoke to the lady at the police department telling her that we needed help at my house and to hurry."

Chatham continued to jot notes down. "How does she know the kids are in the workshop?"

Francis steepled his fingers and put his chin atop them. He was stunned by what he recognized in his granddaughter.

Francis looked over at Chatham.

Chatham noticed that the fierce confidence that had always bracketed his friend's face was absent. The old man's eyes were wide and cluttered with pain. Chatham had never seen this barren look in his friend's eyes. Francis was momentarily frozen in between confusion, disbelief and knowing. It was a condition unbecoming and dangerous for such a powerful man. There was no more life in him than the statues in the living room. Chatham offered comfort with a nod, as much empathy and compassion as a lawyer can muster.

No one spoke.

Chatham broke the silence, "Julie, I understand you went to the emergency room?"

"Yea, I did Mr. Newsham. An ambulance came to Bevs, and they picked me up. A nice policeman rode with me the whole way and stayed with me the whole time."

"Son of a bitch, fuck. Fuck. Fuck," Anthony grumbled through clenched teeth.

Chatham continued the line of questioning. He could see that Francis was still stuck in a blender of emotional turmoil.

"Julie, what happened at the hospital?"

"They put me in one of the rooms and I sat a long time. A nurse checked on me but it seemed forever before a doctor came in to see me. They'd brought the kids there too. A doctor came in and told me that they were doing everything that could be done for them. She examined me, they took some of my blood and some pee. And then, the doctor, she came back and told me that, she told me that the children were gone." Julie stopped and hugged herself, sobbed and shook in a display of anguish.

The sound of a chiming Grandfather's clock entered the room. By the time it had finished, Julie had regained her composure. "The doctor gave me a pill to help me and then Mom got there. She had to go in and make the identification, I couldn't go in and, see them like that. I couldn't do it. And now Grandpa, maybe, I wish I did, cause, I didn't get to say goodbye to them," Julie sobbed and blew her nose.

"Your mother tells me you went to the police after that, and she got you from there. That right?" Anthony asked.

Julie nodded.

"Mother of God. You're children and husband are dead, and they want you to talk. Bastardos!" Francis had returned. He looked over at Chatham who was still taking notes.

"Why did you have to go to the police? What did they want? What did you have to say?" Francis asked in a series of short, breathy exhalations.

"The policeman who stayed with me in the emergency room, he said I had to. He said I was a witness. I needed to give a statement. He said it was routine and that it wouldn't take long. He was nice Grandpa."

"What did you say to the police?" Anthony asked in a terse and accusatory tone.

"I don't know. I just told them what happened. Just like I just told you, just now. The story. They were detectives. They were nice too. They asked me if I needed anything, got me soda. They asked me to start with what happened in the morning and go on like I did here. And that's all really. And I guess I told them what I just told you."

"Julie, did they read you your Miranda rights before they talked to you? And did you write a statement," Chatham asked.

"Um, yes, yes they did read me the rights thing. But I didn't have to write anything down on paper. They said they would get a statement at another time and that was when mom picked me up."

"How long were you in with the detectives Julie?" Chatham asked.

"I don't know. It's all a blur. Not all that long," Julie said.

Francis stood and walked behind Julie, once again putting his hands on her shoulders.

He spoke over her looking directly at Chatham, "Julie, I think maybe you better go back in with your mother and grandmother and let us talk for a little while. Maybe you want to lie down."

Francis helped her up and walked her back to the grievers in the other room where Julie took a seat between her Grandma and mother. Francis whispered in his wife's ear and she responded with a nod.

He returned to the kitchen and let out a series of hushed Italian words that were easily understood as the equivalent of "Fuck, damn and holy shit!"

Both Francis and Chatham took seats at the kitchen table. "What are we to do?" Francis asked, looking from his son to his consigliore. He steepled his fingers again. "What she said, you heard it. It is not, it is not right."

"Pop, she is fucking lying. I don't know about how much, but that cockamamie story she gave is bullshit. What the fuck do the police already know from her? Jesus Christ, why didn't she call?" Tony stopped, realizing that he was at his place in the country checking his deer stand, not to mention that she never called her father anyway, except to borrow money.

Francis may have well have been finishing his son's sentence as he said, "Julie, that one, she never calls for anything but money," he paused, shook his head and looked into his son's face. "Money, which is the only thing she was good at, that one. No? She kept the books good for you, what? For a few years. Did a good job no, Tony?"

"Yea, she was good at keeping things straight. You know with the accounts from the construction company, the money from the south, the BullPen, and the stuff off shore, she was sharp, keeping things straight. And that's one of the main reasons I'm worried pop. She knows things." He nodded his head, pointing an index finger to his forehead, "Sa dove il denaro e nascosto."

"She knows some things. Something, non tutto, Tony," Francis said, waving his index finger.

"Maybe it wasn't the wisest thing to do, having her help with the books pop. But she, she said she needed the money. What do you do but help your kids?" Tony said.

"My Julie, she knows better. She wouldn't talk about family business. At least, spero e prego," Francis said, crossing himself.

"Yea, I hope and pray too pop," Anthony said.

Francis crossed himself again. Always the pragmatist, Francis Scalini looked to his consigliore. "The damage, if any, is done. It is what we do from here on. Chatham, you have been listening and taking notes."

Chatham looked from father to son, "Tony and Francis, I am so sorry for your loss. I wish I could do or say something that is of some comfort."

"We appreciate you being here with us Chatham," the old man said. "We have watched each other's families grow over the years. You are like family and I know you feel loss too. But we must attend to the matters at hand. Please, what do you think about all of this?"

"You can be confidant that your accounts, all transfers, the BullPen, all shell companies, everything is well shielded and protected. Spencer has been handling all of that and can provide you with the necessary assurance if you are concerned. But for now, I have to tell you, I am, let's say, I am uneasy with the story Julie just provided. It carries a number of questions any rookie investigator would have noted. First, any normal parent, or should I say, well there is no easy way to put this, but any loving parent, would do everything in their power to save their children from harm, or die trying."

Francis grimaced and closed his eyes momentarily. Chatham paused, knowing his friend was in pain.

"As I listened, it sounded like Craig was attending to her needs. Somehow and without reason, he suddenly turned into a homicidal rapist?" Chatham asked, seeking no answer. He continued, "Of course people can snap and kill. No doubt about that. And maybe that is what happened. And that is probably how we will have to spin this."

Chatham knew that no one in the room believed Craig snapped, but he said it to be tactical.

Chatham continued, "She is alleging a rape by a man who just brutally murdered his children, yet he unties her and lets her go. She makes it sound as if Craig was intent on killing his family and then killing himself. Francis, in murder-suicides, as the name implies, no one survives. So, the fact that she survived is a controversial hole we will have to fill." Chatham looked directly at Francis as he spoke, "There's enough for the police to conclude something is not right. We'll just have to deal with it in some fashion. I am also concerned about what she said and how she acted at the hospital. The doctor or the staff there may have found her actions to be unusual or inconsistent with the circumstances. And they took blood and urine samples. Did they do a rape kit? Will they do a tox screen? She said she took Benadryl and Soma. God knows what else."

Chatham flipped back a page in his legal pad and tapped his pen on the page. "That's not the most problematic though." He looked directly at his friend of nearly 40 years. "How did she know the kids were in the workshop? In her story, she did not say she left her bedroom."

"I heard her say that. I don't know Chatham," Francis said. "Come ella sa? How did she know? Jesus help us," His words filtered through the steepled fingers in front of his mouth.

"I know pop. She's fucking lying. Let's get her to tell the truth!"

Francis continued to shake his head. He deflated and slumped in the chair, "No, not tonight Tony. Basta abbastanza. Enough is enough."

Chatham continued. "There are a number of problems here that we will have to deal with. A lot will depend on what we determine, is the truth, and what we decide to reveal, as the truth."

Francis and Anthony sat in silence, absorbing what Chatham had said. It was a confirmation of what they had been thinking, a confirmation of the known.

The father and son, were decisive, harsh and brutal men in their family business. Had this not been of their own flesh and blood, decisions would have been clear and concise. Whoever was responsible would die, but this was a wobbly and opaque uncertainty.

Francis spoke, his words grey and listless like a sunken battleship, "We lost two today, we cannot lose three."

Chatham spoke softly with genuine concern, "You both have a lot to do in the next few days. Ruth, Cindy and the rest of your family will need you to be there for them. Let me work on this. At least for the immediate time, you attend to your families. Spencer and I will put together a strategy. I'll have to sit down with Julie and go over this again and make sure she understands what we have to do and say. The sooner, the better. So, if she gets some rest tonight, I'll come back in the morning, say, 10am?"

Francis nodded his head in approval.

Chatham continued, "I think it better if neither of you are here. She will probably speak more freely."

Again, Francis nodded and looked to Anthony for a head bob which promptly followed.

"It goes without saying that if the police want anything, anything, call me. Remember, my youngest, Will is a Sergeant with the Oakview police department and I will get him involved in this."

Tony nodded his head, "And of course, we have the Chief over there too."

Chatham made a note in his notebook. "Yes, Chief Montileone will help as he always has. He'll be no problem. I'm certain we will be able to find out what, if anything, Julie said in her interview that could be a problem. Will's a good boy and he'll take care of whatever we will need. He's keeping me abreast of the other situation that happened today."

"Yea, that's pretty fucked up too. Shit. Thank you so much Chatham, for all of this," Anthony said.

"Yes," Francis added. "The next few days are going to be very difficult. Thank you, for being a good friend."

The three men rose in unison from the kitchen table and returned to the living room.

Cindy went to the closet, retrieving coats.

Francis and Ruth gave their granddaughter a hug. They gave the expected assurances, "We'll work through this and we love you."

Francis shook hands with Chatham, gave him a hug too.

Chatham, Francis and Ruth left Anthony's house at the same time.

Cindy gave Julie another one of the pills, Dr. Classa at the ER, had provided. Julie went upstairs to her old room. Cindy went with her daughter and sat at the end of the bed until Julie's choppy breaths settled into a soft and steady rhythm. Anthony was already snoring heavily from their bedroom.

Cindy Scalini took off her shoes and softly stepped down the stairs. She stood on the last step and looked into the empty living room. Her knees gave way. She grabbed the banister to keep from crumpling to the floor. Her butt slid down two steps. She drew her knees up to her chest and stifled her cries, heaving with ratcheted gasps. Her grandchildren would no longer run barefoot on the carpeting, or slide down these stairs. She stared into her living room at the stark whiteness. The splash of the water from the fountain was the only sound. Her gaze drawn to the gaudy and bizarre collection of artwork Tony had that goomah of his hang.

"How have I lived in this house? It looks like a God damned display model for some bordello. How the hell have I lived with this man, this family, this long? Those kids were all I had keeping me here."

Cindy pulled herself to her feet. She went behind the bar and grabbed a new bottle of Three Olives Vodka and went into the kitchen. It was empty and cold like an operating room.

She sat at the kitchen table drinking and chain smoking Tony's cigarettes until dawn.

# Chapter Fifteen

Chatham chose his dark blue, pin-stripe, Hart-Schaffner and Marx suit along with a crisp, white shirt, blue silk tie, and his onyx cufflinks. There was a decent probability he would be along for a perp walk with Julie Wiley today if things went south. He wanted to be prepared for the eventuality.

He arrived at Anthony and Cindy's just before 10am and pulled the cream colored XJ6C Jaguar up to the front door. He'd bought it new in 1975 and he pampered it nearly as much as he did his children. He only drove it on dry, temperate days. This day was cool and sunny, a perfect day for motoring. Too perfect to do what he knew was in store for him today.

The Jaguar's in-line 6 cylinder shuddered briefly. "Time for a tune-up," he thought. It's motor ticked as he grabbed his briefcase from the backseat and stepped on the cobblestone drive.

Cindy was standing in the open doorway, leaning against the door frame. She was lighting a cigarette as he came towards her and she looked like hell. Eyes sunk deep, her skin pallor not too many shades brighter than the statutes in the living room. She obviously had yet to sleep and hadn't changed clothes since yesterday.

"Hi Cindy," he gave her a peck on the cheek and a hug. She turned without a word. He followed her into the kitchen.

"I thought you quit smoking Cindy," Chatham said, immediately recognizing his error. "I'm sorry, that was insensitive of me."

"It's alright Chatham. I'll be lucky if I don't start smoking crack. It is still so unbelievable." Cindy sucked in a deep drag on the cigarette and exhaled slowly with an audible huhhhhh.

"I'd forgotten how good these taste. What the hell do I have to worry about? Dying of lung cancer? My babies are gone Chatham," Cindy started to sob. She stopped herself.

"Come on, I've got coffee. I'll get you a cup and go get her. A dash of milk in yours right?"

"Yes, you have a good memory Cindy. I haven't had coffee here in quite some time."

"Yea, but back in the day, you were here a lot," she said, lighting another smoke.

"That I was, that I was," Chatham said as Cindy left the kitchen to get her daughter.

Chatham settled into a chair at the kitchen table and waited for Julie. She came into the kitchen followed by her mother. Julie looked as fresh as grocery store produce.

She was wearing a mauve knit sweater and loose fitting black slacks. Her hair was clean and brushed, pulled back into a ponytail. Chatham noted that her makeup appeared to be skillfully applied. Pink lipstick, eyeliner and a bit of blush on her cheeks. Chatham noticed other details. There were no scratches, bruises or skin irritation indicative of being duct taped or choked. Her fingernails were intact.

"Good morning Mr. Newsham," she said with a flattened monotone.

"Hello Julie. Did you get some rest?"

"A little. I took some medicine."

"Do you feel up to resuming our conversation?"

"I suppose."

"Cindy, can we go in the other room by ourselves?"

"Chatham, take her in the den. It'll be quiet. I'm gonna go take a shower."

Anthony's den was a typical man cave featuring a red brick and stone fireplace that was every bit as massive as the one in the living room. Above the hearth were two stuffed deer heads, a 10 and 12 pointer. A rough hewn Oak wooden bookcase along another wall was filled with books Anthony had probably neither bought nor read. Two overstuffed, chocolate brown leather couches with matching recliners, faced another sixty inch big screen TV and a wireless Bose surround sound system.

Chatham directed Julie to one of the recliners. He sat adjacent to her on the edge of the couch.

"Julie, I've known you and your family a very long time. Your grandfather and I go back to the days when we were young men, younger than you are now.

We were just starting out in life. He is more than a client. Francis is a very good friend and I think of you all as family. I remember, when you were little, we all got together sometimes. You probably remember my boys, Spencer, Mark and Will"

Julie interrupted, "Yea, yea, I remember Mark and Will. I haven't seen either of them in ages. I think the last time I saw Will was when I was just out of high school. I remember running across him, at the airport. He was in uniform, in the military or something like that. I remember thinking I never figured him for a military guy. You know he was always so, well, um, easy going."

"Yes, well he went into the reserves after high school and, anyway Julie, what I'm leading to here is that I want you to trust me and know that I am here as your friend. I am here to help you and your family through this difficult time. How do you feel about trusting me?"

"I trust you Mr. Newsham. My dad and grandpa have always said you were like part of the family. That he could always call you for advice and help. And you took care of a few things for me when I was going through a phase."

"Thank you, I'm glad you feel that way."

Chatham took a sip of coffee. "Julie, we have to discuss what happened last night. I know you told us a version of what happened. But, I must tell you, and I'm being honest as a friend should be, I have some concerns about whether what you said, is completely accurate. It seems like there are some missing details that would better explain some of the questions and concerns we all have."

"That, what I said last night, I swear to God that is what happened. I swear," Julie said looking down at the carpet and rocking the recliner.

"You were under a lot of stress. And sometimes stress makes our memory less reliable. Julie, I believe there are some parts of what you said that are accurate. But, there are other parts that we need to talk about. We don't have a lot of time to figure out a plan to help you. The police will be asking more questions very soon. They will be comparing the physical evidence they found at the house. They may use forensics, trace fibers and hairs, maybe even DNA testing. I need to know exactly what happened in order to respond to whatever it is they determine. And of course, I have to know what you said when the police interviewed you yesterday. Can you see the importance here of letting me know exactly what happened so I can help all of us through this?"

"What will happen if the police want to talk to me again?" Julie asked.

"They won't, not without me being there with you. I am advising you to avoid all contact with the police for now. They may view you as a witness to a terrible tragedy, or, if they have any reason or suspicion, they may treat you as a potential suspect. That could lead to interrogations. With hard questions in a less than friendly atmosphere, even with me as your lawyer. And Julie, listen to me very closely here," Chatham paused, he put his hand on her knee, and leaned towards her to emphasize his next few words.

"Your future, potentially your life, could depend on what you tell me really happened. I mean really happened. And how we turn it into something that assures you are seen as nothing more than a victim of unspeakable tragedy."

Julie looked up, but avoided eye contact. The rocking stopped. She sat still, considering his words.

"A victim of unspeakable tragedy," she thought, "I like that." A minute passed as she shifted positions in the chair sinking deep into the bolsters. She softly chewed on her lower lip.

Chatham's hand fell away from her knee. He sifted through his briefcase for a legal pad of paper.

"Mr. Newsham, you can never tell my grandpa or anyone what I am going to tell you. I'm really trusting you, more than anyone I've ever trusted in my whole life. You have to promise me. You have to," she pleaded.

"Julie, here is what I want you to do. Give me a dollar."

"What, what are you talking about, give you a dollar?"

"By giving me payment for my legal services, you are hiring me. I will be your lawyer. Not your fathers or grandfathers. Yours. Everything we say will be bound by what is called attorney-client privilege and cannot be disclosed to out-side sources. That is, without your approval."

Julie rifled through the slacks she'd gotten from her mom's closet, "Wow, here's a five. It's my lucky day."

Julie didn't see the fleeting cringe on Chatham's face. He tossed the five into his briefcase.

"I'll get you change later. Now, you are officially a client and anything you say is protected by attorney-client privilege."

A brief smile passed over her face, "Alright, so, some of the stuff I said is true. But, there is, there are some things." Her voice trailed off as she settled back into the bolsters.

"It'll be easier if you start at yesterday morning and tell me what happened in a chronological order. Start from when you awoke to when you left the police station. I need to know everything."

Julie shifted in the chair and crossed her arms over her chest. The chair rocked slowly.

"Please Julie, please don't be ashamed, embarrassed or feel like you can't tell me something, well, explicit or otherwise racy. I've been an attorney for many years, and I have seen most everything. I have had clients charged with a variety of things, from homicides to bank robbery, arson to rape."

"Mr. Newsham, I, just don't know, I…" she paused.

"Julie, trust me, you won't embarrass or shock me and it will stay between the two of us."

"Mr. Newsham, it is so hard," Julie sniffed and sobbed.

Chatham handed her his handkerchief, "I know. But it will be okay, trust me."

She daubed her eyes. Chatham noted that her eyes were clear and dry.

"Ok, so here goes. Like I said, I was sick yesterday morning with my period. I got the kids up and off to school and went back to bed. Craig came home later in the morning and like I said, he gave me some herb capsules and that tea. He said he had to meet a potential client, somebody. I don't know who. He didn't tell me a lot of stuff like that. Anyway, he said he had to go out of town and would be gone all day, but he would be back in time to pick up the kids at the bus stop, so I should just sleep in and feel better. He left me a few extra herb capsules and some tea packets and told me I should take them again when I woke up. And like I said, I took a couple Benadryls and went back to bed." Julie took a breath and brought her knees up to her chest embracing them with her arms.

She glanced at the stairs before she started. She spoke quietly, "I've, I've got a, I've been having an affair," she paused, waiting for Chatham's response, expecting some type of disapproval. There was none. He nodded, urging her to continue.

"For a little while now. Craig and I were having some problems and I found someone. It's not like, well, it's not like, Craig never did anything. I know he screwed around on me. It was several years ago. The kids were real little. I found out and he promised he wouldn't ever again. So I forgave him. I always suspected that he had a few one night stands whenever he would be gone for a couple weeks, you know in Mexico, or Bosnia, Thailand or wherever he goes to deliver and train their dogs. So, it's not like I'm the only one in the marriage who, you know…"

Chatham nodded his head, "I understand."

"So, me having a friend, I didn't think it was that much of a big deal. Even if he found out. I could say now we were even. And once I had my friend, I figured, who cares what he does."

She paused. Chatham said, "Please go on."

"This is where, you promise, you're my attorney, whatever I say stays here and you help me stay out of trouble. This is our secret, no one will know but you and me?"

"That is how it works, attorney-client."

Julie took a breath in as if she was preparing to dive into the deep end of the pool, "After Craig left in the morning, my friend came over. Since Craig was going to be out of town for most of the day and the kids were in school, we figured it was clear. He works a lot of evening hours on his job, and with the kids and Craig, it was hard for me to get out at night, so mornings were good for us."

She paused, "And I don't want to bring him into this, so let's get that down straight, alright?"

Chatham was certain that he would have to find out who her lover was and have a talk with him. He wanted her to continue so he avoided her demand, nodded and side stepped, "Please go on Julie."

"He came over. I had told him I was cramping and he brought over some pot, figuring it would settle my stomach. You know they use it for cancer patients who have nausea. We smoked a little and I was feeling good, relaxed, like all calmed out from the weed and the Bendryls. Oh yea. I did take a couple Somas too, just like I said last night. So, my friend, he was massaging my back with some baby oil and it felt really good. Before I knew it, my friend had slipped handcuffs on my wrists. And I said like, Oh, so we're gonna play are we?"

Chatham noted the corners of her mouth curl towards a smile and his stomach twisted.

"You see, it was him and me watching the movie, not Craig. Craig and me, we never played games in bed. My friend, he got me into it."

"There are many, many couples that play games in bed, perfectly acceptable. So it was your friend who restrained you?" Chatham asked.

"Yea. We use some clothesline and handcuffs. I guess you get the picture," Julie said.

Chatham noted that her voice had become eerily bright as if the story elevated her emotional barometer.

"You're alone in the house with your lover enjoying each other's company in an adult manner to which you both agree," Chatham synopsized.

"And since I was on my period, we had sex, the other kind," Julie paused again, looking for any reaction from the lawyer.

Chatham wore his poker face and jotted a few notes. "Go ahead Julie, I'm just trying to keep a timeline of events on paper." His voice carried no trace of judgment.

"The weed was good, the sex was good, We'd taken some Benadryls and Somas and we just passed out. The next thing you know, Craig came home. Must have been 3 or so because he had picked the kids up at the bus stop," Julie's breathing became choppy. She tucked her knees tighter and rocked back and forth in the chair.

"I can only imagine. Quite a shock. Craig showing up. What happened next?"

"Well, he came home and he must have fixed the kids a snack or something and sent them to their rooms. We didn't hear a thing. But he came down to our room, opened the door and there we were, my friend and me laying on the bed sleeping. We were naked and I mean, I was still tied up Mr. Newsham. Craig went crazy, I mean crazy. I mean, I guess I would have too, seeing what he saw. He was yelling about how could I do this, in our house, like in our bed."

"It must have been very disturbing Julie."

"Tell me about it. Like we planned on falling asleep and getting caught. Anyway, Craig grabbed my friend." She started nibbling the tips of her fingers.

"It's alright Julie. Please continue."

"He grabbed my friend, and they started fighting. I mean to tell you, Craig is strong. He grabbed him off the bed and threw him against the wall and hurt him. My friend was kind of, knocked goofy for a minute. He was kind of on his hands and knees, just leaning up against the dresser shaking his head. And Craig went to the closet and got the shotgun out. He loaded it, and pointed it at him and yelled at him to get up."

Julie sat upright in the chair and leaned forward. She used her hands as she spoke, making the motion as if she had a rifle and was pointing it. "Just like her grandpa, talking with the hands. The Italian in her," Chatham thought.

"I started screaming at Craig to put the gun down and don't kill him! And telling Craig that it was all a mistake and I was sorry, and that I really did love him and that I was sorry and that it was just a mistake I made, and that please, please put the gun down.

Craig turned to me and pointed the gun at me and said that he ought to kill both of us. He called us both a bunch of really bad names and stuff. And I kept telling him I was sorry and that if he could only forgive me we could work it out, that we could work anything out because I really loved him and to please put the gun down. But Mr. Newsham, I was still tied up, I couldn't move or do anything to help.

My friend came to, while me and Craig were screaming at each other and Craig wasn't paying any attention. My friend grabbed one of Craig's dumbbells and smacked him in the head, hard." Julie pantomimed the action.

"I mean it made a crunching sound. Craig went down to the floor and his head started bleeding. My friend kicked the shotgun off to the side."

Julie stopped abruptly. She stood up and walked over to the fireplace facing away from Chatham.

Chatham took the opportunity to scribble a few notes without disrupting Julie's flow, "Craig threatens with gun." A seedling of the legal defense planted.

"Craig threatened to kill you. Please go on."

Julie put both hands on top of the mantle and kept her back to him. Her voice softened and her pace slowed.

"Mr. Newsham, the kids ran into the room about the time that my friend hit Craig. They saw their daddy fall to the floor and they saw the blood. They started screaming. And I was screaming too. 'What did you do? Jesus Christ, you killed him!" She paused and Chatham noticed that she was gripping the mantle with her fingertips.

"Mr. Newsham, I was still tied to the bed. I couldn't do anything. I was squirming, trying to get my hands loose. I was screaming at the top of my lungs for somebody to get me loose."

Julie turned to face Chatham. Her eyes were bleary red. She held her wrists together as if she was still handcuffed. "Untie me, untie me. I was screaming at anybody to untie me. And, Robbie and Taylor saw me naked on the bed, and my friend was naked too, holding the dumbbell in his hand and Craig was on the ground bleeding," she started to sob and cough.

"My God Julie, I am so sorry. It must have been awful for you, so helpless," Chatham said, offering counterfeit words of sympathy hoping they would prompt her to continue.

"Taylor jumped on the bed grabbing at me saying 'Mommy, Mommy, Mommy' and I was so oily she couldn't get a hold on me and she was like wierded out by the oil." Julie sat down on the brick hearth.

"What happened next?"

"Robbie ran to his daddy and shook him. Craig moaned but he didn't wake up. And then Robbie started screaming at my friend, 'You hurt my dad, you hurt my dad!' And then he started kicking at him, and just out of reflex, James backhanded him and knocked him against the dresser."

Chatham wrote, "Lover's first name is James. James strikes Robbie. She calls it 'out of reflex'"

"I was yelling for somebody to let me go, and Taylor was going nuts screaming about her daddy and looking at me and rubbing her hands with the oil and screaming about how Robbie was hurt."

Julie closed her eyes and shuddered. She hugged herself, as if the temperature in the room had dropped to below freezing. Chatham rose and put his arm
around her, led her back to the recliner and sat her down.

"Relax Julie. We can get through this. We're just talking through it."

A few minutes passed as Julie rocked back and forth and composed herself.
She picked up an Esquire magazine off the coffee table and stared at the cover
silently.

Chatham wrote, "Potential use of the boyfriend as protector. Response to
chaos in bedroom seems legitimate, probably close to truth." He quietly waited
and hoped she would continue.

"Please Julie, go on. What happened next? What happened to Craig and the
children?"

Chatham listened to Julie's monotone story for the next five minutes. She
kept her head down as she spoke, slowly flipping through the magazine as if she
were narrating from the glossy pages. The chair was silent and still as she told her
story.

Chatham Newsham's hands were moist and trembled as he jotted down a few
notes. Chatham was glad he hadn't eaten as he was sure he would have vomited.

He recalled what his friend of many years said last night. "We lost two today,
we cannot lose three."

Chatham would do everything in his power to honor Francis Scalini's words.

Julie put the Esquire down. She lit a cigarette and a grey haze surrounded
them both.

Chatham wiped the nervousness from his hands on his trousers. He stood
and paced a few steps back and forth in front of the hearth as if it were a jury box.
He knew the worst of it now. He'd heard what was probably 90% the truth. Now
it was back to business. "We lost two, we cannot lose three."

"I know you don't want to, but you need to tell me about your boyfriend. I
need to know more about him. I need to talk to him. How much do you trust
him? How do you know him?"

"I said no! You work for me. I won't bring him into this. I don't have to!"

Chatham heard the 13 year old spoiled brat he had gotten out of trouble
more than once. He knew all too well that they would find out the identity of the
boyfriend. Whether Julie helped or not was immaterial. It would just be easier if
she cooperated with her own defense, but they would find him. If this man had
anything remotely to do with the murders of Francis's grandchildren, his lifespan
would be shorter than a housefly's. Even if this man had nothing to do with it,

he would suffer, he would remember for the rest of his life whose family he had screwed with. If not death, a cracked skull or broken legs were the usual fare. The Scalini's responded definitively. The man would either disappear or end up in a hospital.

"Precisely correct Julie. Because I work for you, I need to know everything about everything to protect you and your family. Your friend, he's party to this. He is potentially a liability. It depends on a number of factors we do not know at this time. I'm sorry, but I'm going to have to talk with him Julie."

She pointed her finger up at him. "No. No you're not Mr. Newsham!"

Chatham crossed his arms over his chest. It had become a pissing match, "How about this. Julie, you can set up the meeting with him. It will be entirely between us. Only the three of us will know we met and talked. I promise you that. I will not tell your father or grandfather."

He pushed his glasses down to the tip of his nose and stared down at her, "My priority is to keep you safe, and to protect the Scalini family. And that I will. I always have. You know that very well. We will meet, and we will develop a plan that protects all of you, including your friend."

Chatham returned to his seat. Julie abruptly stood. She brushed past Chatham. The smoke from her cigarette snaking past him, slithering under the mantle before fading.

Chatham waited.

Julie took one last drag and flicked the cigarette in the fireplace and sunk back in her chair.

"I met him about 6 months ago. He's a cop in the city. He works with the drug unit and they needed a dog. Guess who they bought it from?"

"I see," Chatham said.

Chatham scribbled brief notes as Julie provided the history of her relationship. "City cop. Ask Will if he knows him? 6 month affair! Was this a premeditated plan to get rid of Craig and the kids??? Any witnesses to the affair?"

Chatham looked up from his notepad. Julie was working an Emory board on her fingernails.

"So you see Mr. Newsham, we've been together a while. And I have, well I have feelings for him that I didn't have for Craig. Not just sex either."

"If you are in love with this man, then that is all the more reason that we protect him too."

"I don't know if it is love, but," Julie picked up a buff pad and shined her nails. "I mean things were so bad with Craig. With him, it's like being able to breathe for the first time in a long time. Craig and I were arguing all the time. We were like cats and dogs."

"What were the arguments about?" Chatham asked.

"About money. About the kids. He wanted me to be a maid and a nanny. No. Really he wanted a slave. Take care of the house, the kids, the yard, the bills, while he went doing his dog training in all those places. A week in Mexico, a week in Thailand, a week here, a week there. I wanted to do something too, not just be some kind of housewife."

Chatham jotted down a few more notes. Julie's defense was coming to form. He wrote, "Money problems, Craig was emotionally abusive to kids and her. Demanding, distant, uncaring."

"He'd come home from a trip, we'd immediately argue if there were dirty dishes in the sink or laundry not done. He'd slam doors and put his fist through the walls. I threw a few plates at him, I'll tell you that. The kids, they saw it all."

Julie stopped her buffing and threw the pad on the coffee table, "It hasn't been very nice."

Chatham scribbled more notes, "Domestic violence"

"Did he ever threaten or hurt Robbie or Taylor?" Chatham asked. Just mentioning their names brought a lump of bile to the back of his throat. "This is the worst thing I have ever done," he thought. "May God forgive me."

"Oh heck no. Those kids were his little angels. They could do no wrong. He always brought them home a toy or trinket from wherever he went. Stuffed animals, that kind crap. What did he bring me? Not a God damn thing."

"How long had this arguing and fighting, breaking walls. How long had that been going on?" Chatham asked.

"I'd say at least a year. Although the last couple of months, it seemed to get better. I don't know if it was because I was doing something for me, rather than always just him and the kids, but it got a little better around the house. Craig seemed to be easier going. He wasn't so mad all the time. He was like, a lot calmer about everything. I don't know, but he seemed like, he was happy for the first time in a long while."

"What do you think brought about Craig's change?" Chatham asked.

"Who knows. Last week, I even asked him if he was taking something to relax. Weed, Xanax, downers, whatever. Everyone always thought he took, you know steroids, for all those muscles, but he never took a one. If it wasn't vitamins or protein shakes, he wouldn't take it So, I thought maybe he got some kind of herbal valium shit from a medicine man in South America or something like that, but he said no, that he was just trying to take it easy and be more calm, not let things get to him as much. I didn't really care what it was. Whether he was meditating, or masturbating, or had a girlfriend, I didn't care. Either way, he was easier to deal with, and I was glad of it. I mean, until, well, until,"

"Until yesterday. Yes. I understand," Chatham said.

He scribbled on his pad, "Boiling point reached. Spin the steroid use? Money problems. Did Craig have girlfriend?"

Chatham laid his notepad upside down on the couch and stood. He walked to the mantle and turned to face her.

"Listen to me Julie. We're going to develop a strategy for your defense."

He noticed her stare deepen, lines formed across her forehead and her lips pursed.

"That is, Julie, if we need one. Here's how we are going to handle this," Chatham paused, not sure how to define what he was about to do. He had compromised his values plenty of times over the years, but this was much different. Children were involved.

Chatham held out his notepad and dictated a story from his notes, his voice uncharacteristically anemic. "Craig was emotionally distant and abusive. He had used steroids and drugs. He had been cheating on you. He was violent at times, broke things, punched walls. He threatened you. You were afraid of him. He often threatened to hurt you and the kids. He didn't want a wife, he wanted a slave. He was no longer the man you married. You told him you were going to leave him."

Chatham narrated the remainder of the defense strategy with a growing acerbic taste in his mouth. His chest burned, a flare up of chronic acid reflux, the result of a lifetime of defending evil deeds. He cursed the damned loyalty he'd forged so many years ago with Francis Scalini and vowed to himself this would be the last. He would do his job. This would be the last.

As Julie listened to Chatham's plan, her face relaxed and a faint smile appeared. She picked up the buff pad, "That sounds nice."

# Chapter Sixteen

As soon as I was physically able, I grabbed a wheelchair and made my way to an elevator and down a long hallway to Tom's room, pushing the IV pole ahead of me with my feet. Tom Reynolds was lying in bed, the cover sheet crumpled at an angle across his protruding belly. Droplets of blood speckled his sheet. A large splotch of what looked like pink lemonade, a mixture of blood and IV fluid, settled next to his leg. The IV pump alarm was howling and blinking it's red eye. Various other monitors paid no attention as their green, yellow and red lights softly blipped and chimed. Some of these machines would be Tom's companions for some time to come.

Tom looked up as I pulled my chariot bedside. His straggly beard hung down over the tubing from his oxygen mask. He pulled the mask off.

"Bunch of bullshit is what this is."

"Jesus Tom. Fuck."

"Those motherfuckers tried to take us out Doc."

"Yea. Yea they did a pretty good job too. I'm sorry man, really sorry. I just wish we would've done something different. I wish we would have waited. I wish we would have fucking waited. God dammit Tom."

His chest and abdomen were wrapped with white bandages. A drain tube poked out from a bandage over his left Ilium. Pneumatic compression leggings sighed on and off.

"Me too, Doc. Ain't this the shits?" Tom said, looking down at his feet and shaking his head. "Least I'll be saving money on boots."

Tom pointed to my turban and covered eye. "It doesn't look like you fared so well there cyclop boy," Tom's IV tubing hung from his arm dripping blood and saline, expanding the pink pond.

I couldn't help it and started to cry albeit from one eye. I snorted snot and tears back. I coughed, which caused a small explosion inside my head, a small price to pay for two working legs. I wanted to talk to Tom, but could not find the words. My guilt meter was ringing with more bells than a Swiss clock shop at noon. I just wanted to get out of there and escape from the gnarling incrimination and responsibility that was hammering my head and my stomach.

I blinked away the head pain as well as it would allow and fought the urge to pivot around and wheel away. My eye tracked the leak from Tom's arm, "Jesus Christ Tom, your IV is out. I'm so sorry Tom. This is all my fault. I should have never. We should have waited. I'm sorry Tom."

"Enough of that pitiful bullshit Morris. It is what it is!" Tom said with a surprisingly substantial voice, overcoming the ringing of the IVAC. "My old lady and my preacher says we should be thankful we're still alive. I reckon they're right. So you cut the whiney ass crap. It ain't your fault anymore'n it's mine." He shook two fingers at me dribbling more red and clear fluid. "The good Lord got us into that clusterfuck, he'll get us out of this one."

I sniffed back more snot, reached in between Tom's side rail and inserted the tubing back into his IV and hit the reset button. The pump quietly settled down to business.

Apparently Tom felt that we needed to do the same.

We sat in silence for a couple of minutes. I stared at the ceiling and the dry erase board with the date and nurse information.

Tom broke the silence, "So we gonna get our story together on how them 'Cans' met their maker or what?"

I mustered a terse smile. Over the next 30 minutes, we devised a tale that somewhat followed the events of the day. A good lie always has some measure of truth within.

The story became that as soon as the Mexicans entered the apartment, Daniel pulled a gun and started shooting. As Tom fell, he was able to shoot Daniel, thus the gunshot wound to Daniel's leg. Ballistics and forensics would bear out these facts. Tom went into spinal shock and had no recall of anything after being shot.

Jorge screamed out "Fuck You Policia" and began firing an automatic weapon. I jumped for cover, ending up in the bathtub. I lobbed the stun grenade. Jorge must have fallen into some furniture after the detonation of the concussion grenade and broke his ribs. He dropped the TEC-9. I stumbled out from the tub having been wounded by a glancing TEC- 9 round and shrapnel from Bill's cast iron tub.

As I came around from behind the couch, Jorge was on the floor reaching for the machine gun. Jorge and I wrestled. I was able to pull my gun out and put it under his chin to end the struggle. Once again, forensics would support this account.

As soon as I had ended the threat from Jorge, Daniel jumped on me and knocked my pistol from my hand. We rolled around on the floor. I was able to get to my knife to end the attack from Daniel.

No one else would ever know the variance from the actual events, not wives, girlfriends, or therapists. No one.

We discussed any possible weaknesses in the story. Fortunately the body wire microphone had been ripped out when I fell into the tub, so there was no audio recording and we had not turned on the video. Tom and I agreed that our account would work. We sat in silence for several minutes. I focused on the dry erase board and ceiling again.

"It seemed to be the right thing to do at the time Tom. But now, I can't shake the feeling that it was wrong. That I crossed a line. I shouldn't have killed them Tom. It was wrong."

"Fuck that doc. Those motherfuckers, they needed killing. If you hadn't of done it, and I was able, I woulda killed both them sons of bitches 10 times over if need be."

"You know I've done my fair share of bad shit Tom. Hell we both have. Planted dope on somebody who needed to go down, slept with informants, lied on search warrants, the usual bullshit every narc has done at one time or another. We shot that meth tweaker dead when he pulled a knife on us, and that didn't bother me much. In fact, I never mentioned it, but I was supercharged after that fucker went four paws up. I felt the best I had ever, the most alive. You know I'm no panty waist Tom. But this one, this one was different. I should've cuffed them and we could have found out who the rat was. Then they could've rotted in jail. We're not supposed to be the judge, jury and executioner."

"With pieces of shit like that? Fuck we're not. If not us, then who? If they're gonna kill two cops, who the fuck won't they murder. Kids, whole damn families?"

"I know, I know," I said, my voice lowering softly, "I just didn't think I would ever flat out murder anyone, much less two anyones."

"Two dope dealin Mexicans ain't anyone Morris. They're horseshit. Saved our lives is what you did Doc. I know you don't believe much in the Lord and whatnot, but you did a good thing and he'll see it thataway. You rid the world of some evil. Those were some evil motherfuckers. Just like in the good book, you smote their asses Doc. And God'll love you for it."

"Yea, I really feel the love, don't you?" I blinked away a few tears. "Either way, you're right. It is what it is. Just another one of our little secrets, except this is a pretty big one."

"Doc, I think it was Benjamin Franklin said, two can keep a secret if one is dead, but you know I'll die before I say a word."

I put my hand on top of Tom's and gave him a squeeze, "I know. I know. Thanks."

I stopped at the door and wheeled around, "And by the way Tom, Franklin actually said, 'three can keep a secret if two are dead'."

"Fuck you smart ass," Tom replied.

To this day, we have kept the secret.

Evil or not, with or without God's love, I had murdered two men.

# Chapter Seventeen

I was in the hospital for 11 days. I suffered with piercing hot pain that traveled like a bucket handle from my left shoulder blade around my chest. They said it was the result of nerve and soft tissue damage from the bullet fired out of Jorge's pistol that remained inside me, adjacent to my thoracic spine.

Even though Bill's tub saved my life, I developed shredding migraines from the whacking my skull and eye took from the cast iron shrapnel. They were the kind of headaches that cause you to vomit and force you to lie still in a dark room for hours. I was often dizzy and unstable on my feet.

Jim Farrar, my neurologist, said I had suffered a MTBI, a mild traumatic brain injury from the impact of the chunk of bathtub metal against my head. He warned me to watch for signs of PTSD-post traumatic stress disorder, including flashbacks, nightmares, anxiety attacks and insomnia. I was familiar with both entities, having treated a handful of patients with one or both. MTBI and PTSD are some pretty fucked up things to have. Ask any Iraq or Afghan war veteran. I wondered whether I would be able to resume my pre-shooting/murder life.

Since Sheila worked at Ballantine, she was able to spend time with me before and after her shift. Even though I was part of the hospital family, the nursing care was pretty shoddy once I left the ICU. I was thankful for the help Sheila provided.

At first, I couldn't walk without assistance due to the dizziness and visual challenges and I relied on Sheila to get around. As we strolled through the hospital complex, nurses and other doctors stopped us and asked how I was doing and wished us well. The rumors were plentiful. All the previous suppositions that Morris Green was more than just a few bubbles off plumb were reinforced.

That there was this doctor at the People's Clinic...Dr. Morris Green, who continued being a cop even after med school and had been shot in a standoff with Mexican drug lords. That he'd lost an eye, but had cut the throat of one of the drug dealers and blown the head off the other.

Dr. Detective Morris Green, one-eyed, cop of the Caribbean, was the talk of the hospital for a little while and the well deserved recipient of awkward glances.

Sheila brought me home from the hospital to recover. It was nice to stay in my old house.

The following weeks were chaotic. There were multiple doctor visits and follow up visits with surgeons. My right eyebrow was indeed history, replaced by an angry 2" scar. I wore a patch for several weeks and had some serious problems with vision in the right eye. I saw half of the world through a pink tinted film.

One of the only good things to come from the shooting was that the Green family spent more time together while I was recuperating than we had in the past two years. Jake and Olivia were great home care aides, making sure I was drinking Gatorade and ice tea, instead of Vodka or beer. We were almost like a family again.

Sheila accompanied me to a meeting with Dr. Farrar at his office in the Ballantine Medical Complex. Jim Farrar and I were about the same age. That's about where our similarities ended. Jim had gone to the Washington University School of Medicine in St. Louis and had done his neurological residency at Johns Hopkins. No surf and sun Caribbean schooling for Jimmy. He'd never considered any career other than that of being a doctor. Dr. Farrar had that George Clooney look, a real lady slayer, had never married, and always dated beautiful women.

We sat in uncomfortable chairs across the desk from Dr. Farrar.

"The bullet is stable Morris. It will not injure your cord, but as you know, you will develop more scar tissue around it that will probably cause additional discomfort. We'll handle that with meds and future surgeries if needed. Now the head injury, that's a wild card. The symptoms of the MTBI and PTSD can be cognitive, behavioral and emotional and may be more debilitating than your physical injuries. Nightmares, persistent headaches and problems with balance are common, as well as having a short temper. Some memory loss is common. My hopes are that these symptoms will diminish over time," he stroked his chiseled chin.

"I couldn't remember shit before the shooting," I said interrupting him. "It's going to get worse?"

"Morris, everyone in their forties and fifties have memory problems. Pay attention to whether there is a progression in memory loss. If your memory problems worsen, let me know. You may also experience a diminution in focus or difficulty in concentration. You may find activities such as multitasking difficult."

"Fuck Jim, multitasking is about all I do, all I have ever done. What the hell?"

Sheila cocked her head to the side and added some deserved sarcasm, "And that is and has always been part of your problem isn't it Morris? You can't do just one thing." She turned her attention to Dr. Farrar, "So, how do we treat this Jim?"

I spoke first. "Medication, medication, medication. And if that doesn't work, more medication. Most of what I am taking now isn't doing shit. I either feel like a Zombie or I am wound up like an 8 day clock, or I get constipated. Like I said, it isn't doing shit."

Dr. Farrar turned to Sheila, rather than his ranting peer.

"Sheila, for now, Morris is correct. But, over time our goal will be to progress to the point where his reliance on meds is minimal, if possible."

"You can wean me off the SSRI's but leave my Alprazolam and Oxycontin alone," I said sharply.

Dr. Farrar rolled his eyes, shook his head and stared at me. "Jesus Morris. Give the attitude a rest will you?" He flipped through my chart. "I will see you once a month for follow up. I notice that you're seeing Louise. You're in fine hands with Louise Brandeis. She trained in Jungian psych before med school and still uses some of the techniques in therapy. She's my choice for shrink of the decade. In addition to monitoring your progress, you and Louise will be getting into what makes Morris Green tick, your past, and probably some dream analysis." Dr. Farrar paused and glanced over at Sheila, "From what I hear, you've had some rather intense dreams?"

I raised both arms, looked up at the ceiling and castigated my ex-wife, "Jesus Sheila. Jim is my neurologist, not Joseph with the Amazing Technicolor Coat. You're discussing my sleep habits with Farrar? Who else are you sharing my fucking impairments with?"

"Lighten up Morris," Sheila said. "You think I want to keep waking up, hearing you scream. I look in your room and watch as you thrash around in bed, drenched in a cold sweat, screaming about a train?"

"It's alright Sheila," Jim said. I noticed that he was nodding at her and that a fleeting smile crossed his face. I glanced at Sheila who was smiling back at Jim, the kind of naughty and sweet smile she'd given me when we were together. I wondered if he was screwing her and whether I was fodder for their post-coital talk. The hairs on the back of my neck bristled.

Dr. Farrar continued, "I asked Sheila about your sleep habits and she answered. That's all," he said with a soft, soothing tone that I am sure he used with the intention of assuaging my outburst.

"God dammit. Dammit the two of you anyway," I said, settling back into my chair.

"You see what I am saying Morris. The temper? Anyway, I expect Dr. Brandeis will work you through the dreams." Jim said. "Do us all a favor and keep a log of what's going on in that head of yours. Monitor your symptoms. Keep track of any changes. Use a notebook or a laptop, just keep track will you please Morris?"

Dr. Farrar turned, his chair squeaking loudly and squared with my ex. "Sheila, we both know he won't, or it will only be a marginal attempt. So, I'm asking you to keep track of his behavioral and physical symptoms. Try keeping a date and time log of his outbursts, or when he loses something or can't remember something important, or he has a disabling headache or starts having anxiety issues."

"Hey now. I'm in the room here. You can talk to me. I'll do my part," I said, trying to defend myself with little success.

Dr. Farrar turned back to me, "Thank you Morris. We'd really appreciate that."

# Chapter Eighteen

Shortly after I got out of the hospital, we held a task force team meeting at my department. I closed the door and shut the blinds concealing us from the inquisitive eyes of the other officers and administrative staff. The purpose of the meeting was to put together an AAR, an After Action Report. It's a debriefing of the event and summary report. Patty and Bill were going to write it. Since there were no other witnesses, the AAR would be reliant on what Tom and I reported. Tom was still in the spine unit and was unable to attend in person, but he phoned in.

Neither Patty nor Bill would ever know what really happened.

"I tell you what Doc," Bill said, "that place looked like a Comanche raid on settlers." The top of that one beaner's head was splayed back like he'd been scalped and the other one had your K-Bar sticking out of his chest like a damn flagpole."

"I'm sure it was a bad scene, but thank you, thank you, thank you Bill, for putting that bathtub in the living room. It saved my life."

Bill grinned, "Yea. I told you city folks would like it."

Tom and I went over the story as we had discussed in the hospital and the team wrote up the tale as told.

The county prosecutor was satisfied that the killings of Daniel Gonzalus and Jorge Estrada were justified. No charges were filed and the case was closed.

The Supervisory Special Agent in Charge of DEA, the man who said we didn't want to be lining the dope dealer's pockets, gave me three kinds of hell over doing the deal before everyone was in place. Maybe he was right. All I could do was nod. Had we waited, perhaps none of this would have happened.

There was no heroin. There was nothing in the Adidas bag but Jorge's gun. Obviously, Jorge and Daniel had been sent to assassinate us. We were supposed to die that day. I actually did and the life Tom led before the shooting was also dead. I would soon learn that mine was too.

If there truly was a source in the department, a Capitan, as Daniel had whispered, if there was an insider who tipped off the Mexicans that we were cops and had to be erased, their identity remained a mystery.

The man made of jello, Chief Thomas Montileone, denied that anyone in his command could act in such a traitorous manner. "We don't even have the rank of Captain in Oakview," he said in answer to the accusations. "If there was a leak, it would have to have been someone at DEA, city or county. Not my men."

Not surprisingly, DEA, city and county police circled the wagons. Each conducted an investigation of their own agency, finding no leaks.

Montileone said that these things are part and parcel of narcotics cases. In a newspaper article, he was quoted as saying, "The suspects use drugs and are all paranoid. It was just a robbery, plain and simple. A drug rip-off. Happens all the time. Unfortunately this time, it happened to our people."

I urged the Chief to polygraph all of the command staff, Sergeants and Lieutenants anyway, just to be sure.

"Now Morris," the Chief said, "I know you want to cover all the bases and I appreciate that. But, look here. There is no real proof that a leak in intelligence existed. Just one lying drug dealer telling you what you wanted to hear. I won't put my people through the stress and process of polygraphs. It would look bad to the media and would lower morale in the department. And we certainly don't need that, do we?" Chief Montileone held a couple press conferences and within three weeks, we were old news.

Tom and I got meritorious service for valor awards. Tom accepted his award from retirement and the department bought him a top of the line powerchair. He received a generous disability. He had enough years in service and was also eligible to get his pension.

Our drug team built the Reynold's family a ramp and poured concrete pathways to the house, barn and machine shop. Due to headaches and left shoulder pain, I wasn't much help, so I bought beer and manned the BBQ pit.

I was off work nearly 6 months during which time I underwent several surgical procedures to my right eye and a radiofrequency ablation to the nerves in my left upper chest. The ablation procedure was supposed to kill nerves that were causing me trouble. The procedure was only marginally effective in relieving the left sided chest and back pain. My 4 X a day doses of pain meds moderated the intensity but never totally relieved it. The migraine headaches and the dizziness became less intense. My pre-existing tinnitus, a remnant of years playing guitar in front of a stack of Marshall amps got even louder and became a constant, high pitched hissing, like locusts on steroids blowing whistles. The pain meds were my friend and my doctors supplied an ongoing prescription.

I visited Tom a few times at the Reynold's ranch. Tom seemed to have found peace with the loss of his legs and his retirement from the PD. Maybe Tom was onto something with religion.

I asked God what to do a few times and waited for a reply. Maybe he was still pissed at me for slewing a couple of his Mexican creations. He never answered any of my prayers. I returned to my long held belief in not a fucking thing. I had not yet figured out that the good Lord had already answered. He'd apparently sent Jorge and Daniel, setting in motion a carousel of events that would lead me to the Wiley case.

I reluctantly agreed with Sheila, and Jim Farrar that I probably should not return to a lifestyle that included undercover work, long night hours, stress and danger. I begrudgingly considered that perhaps I could be a one career man. Maybe I could settle in and be satisfied as a GP at the clinic.

As fate would have it, or as plans in the ethos were being formulated for Morris Green, Chief Montileone called. He asked if I was interested in coming back to work as a general assignment detective rather than a narc. The department statistics for solved crimes were sagging and the Chief thought my detective skill sets could help. It was one of those increasingly rare moments when Montileone made a decision on his own.

Chief Montileone told me that I would be partnered with Sgt. Kenneth Murphy-Quinn, affectionately known as MQ. Sgt. Quinn was built like a Hobbit and was known to have a very sharp wit. We were contrasts in ways other than physical appearance and attitude.

I had enough career hats to fill Captain Kangaroo's hat stand. MQ had one hat. He had always been a cop. His father was a city cop and his grandfather was a town marshal in the 1920's. MQ said it was a genetic inheritance.

Despite being a few years younger than me, he has a haggard look that adds a decade. MQ is 5'5", stocky, like a fireplug, coming in just under 250lbs. At this point in his life, he pontificates that "Fitness is an exercise in narcissism for those too weak willed to accept their genetics." His round face is tattered and peppered with lumps and scars from 8 years in the Golden Gloves. The nightly Bushmills he drank painted a rosacea road map that butterflies across his broken and bent nose and cheeks. At the time we partnered, MQ had been an Oakview Sergeant for 17 years and had been running the detective bureau for about 4.

MQ has a wonderful command over the English language. He often uses a symphonic vocabulary even in petty conversation. It is a delight, although sometimes aggravating, to converse with him. There is always a dictionary or thesaurus on top of the toilet tank in the detective washroom.

MQ's police intuition is as finely tuned as an angels harp. He is nicknamed "Sol" as in King Solomon, due to his innate ability to solve problems and cases. That is, everyone's problems but his own, at least the misery he conjures up for himself.

MQ lives his entire life waiting for the sky to fall. He is constantly worrying about getting fired, despite the fact that he has received a number of awards and commendations for service to the community. He worries that his wife will leave him, even though they have been married 22 years and she is about as devoted to him as Mother Theresa was to the lepers. He complains that his daughter will probably marry some tattooed, nose ring wearing, punk rock freak. Never mind that she is on the cheerleader squad, in the National Honor Society and spends more time in a library than Stephen Hawking. He fears that the next rain storm will turn tornadic and blow his house down and that the engine in his car will suddenly seize up.

Kenneth Murphy Quinn is pre-diabetic, his cholesterol is in the mid 300's, yet he'll start each day with a trucker's breakfast and complain about how he wished his doctor would get off his ass about his weight and the gout. MQ blames all the impending personal disasters on his physical stature. "I am transfixed in this nugatory existence because short and fat people cannot garner respect from a world obsessed with tall and thin automatons."

Sheila was downstairs halfway through a hot Yoga video. She had a fire going in the wood stove and the blower on high. She was wearing black spandex tights and a skimpy white tube top that barely held her breasts. She looked like a model, one of those beautiful, tall and thin automatons. I watched her sweaty body proceed through a few poses and considered how lucky I was, or had been.

I sidled up next to her and joined her in a Warrior pose routine. I told her about the Chief's offer and asked her for an opinion.

She quickly came out of the pose, "Holy shit Morris, you're asking me, rather than telling me what you've already decided to do or have already done? The therapy or the drugs must be working on you. At least that's something." A passing smile crossed her face, replaced by the strain as she returned to Yoga.

While she moved from Warrior 1 to Warrior 2 to Reverse Warrior, I said I was considering the option. "I figure that a detective bureau position with regular hours, and a suit and tie could serve as a stop gap, a gradual move towards a normal life".

Sheila came out of the pose again and squared off with me. A cute drop of sweat dripped from the tip of her perfect Anglo-European nose. "This is your opportunity to retire your badge and gun, Dirty Harry. You can work at the clinic full time, or open a practice. You don't have to go back to The Job," she said, putting finger quotation marks around the job. Your kids are finally getting to know their dad again. We're even getting along a little. Why screw this up Morris?"

"I'm just not ready to let it all go just like that Sheila. I've been a cop almost my entire life. Granted, along with other things for sure, but I think I need to ease my way towards becoming a regular citizen."

Hers eyes narrowed and her lips pursed. "You are so full of shit. A citizen? Like cops are not citizens, regular people. There are thousands of cops that lead normal lives Morris. It's just that you become some kind of larger than life, cartoon cop."

She grabbed for a water bottle and her towel, "Dammit Morris. I know how you are. Every time you get some police assignment, it turns into something right out of Miami Vice, CSI or Law and Order and whatever it is, it consumes you. All of you. And then, we're not part of that life that you lead. We end up just being along for the ride. And the last time it nearly killed you. I am not putting my kids through that again. So this is it Morris Green. If you go back to the department, you can also go back to your apartment." Sheila threw her water bottle at me, hitting me in the chest. She turned away and flicked off the wood stove. I stood in the hotbox all alone.

# Chapter Nineteen

My apartment was in a commercial and residential area only a couple of miles from the house. I'd moved there when Sheila threw me out for the third time, figuring it was temporary. It turned out that the third time was a charm and permanent.

There is a strip mall with a Starbucks, Nail Salon, Dominos and Massage Envy next to my building. Most of my fellow apartment dwellers are young professionals. There are lots of BMWs, Saabs and Subarus in the lot. Each townhouse came with a dishwasher, washer and dryer and access to a nice pool and fitness facility. That was a draw. Jake and Olivia came over to swim now and then and I used the free weights and machines.

A few days after moving back into my apartment and before returning to work in the detective bureau, I had another of those bizarre dreams.

It was another train dream. Harvey Keitel and I were standing on a train platform. Maybe he was in it because I had recently watched one of his early 1990s movies, *Bad Lieutenant*. Not to mention, there was a bad cop somewhere that got me killed, and in this movie, Keitel is as corrupt as they come.

In my dream, he was immaculately dressed in a tight fitting black suit, a crisp, starched white shirt with silver dollar sized, sterling cufflinks. He had on black wingtips that were so finely polished that they were like mirror. He wore a white Fedora, cocked to the left. I was wearing the black leather biker vest and blue jeans I had been killed in.

He put his arm over my shoulder. "Those two burrito eating, drug dealing fucks, their deaths are not important Morris. Not in the least. They were messengers, that's all, plain and simple like Western Union. Just messengers my friend."

A loud gust of wind cut through my vest like motor driven icicles. A metal trash can rolled past us as if it were a tumbleweed in a New Mexican desert. I started to shake like a wet dog. Harvey raised his voice and came closer to my ear, "Don't worry about killing those fucks. Bad people should fucking die. Remember that Morris. Bad people should fucking die!"

"What the fuck are you talking about?" I heard me ask him.

"Say it Morris. Say it. Bad people should fucking die!"

"Say what? What the fuck are you talking about?"

He jumped down onto the tracks, "Get down here out of the wind. I don't want to lose my hat, and it's messing up my hair, plus we can't talk. Don't just stand there, come on!"

I followed him and we walked between the rails. The only sound was the pea gravel crunching under our feet. He stopped abruptly, stepping in front of me. He grabbed the lapels of my vest and pulled me close. His face was within an inch of mine, like a Drill Instructor at Boot camp. I felt the spray of his spit.

"And you watch for the God damn train Morris. The fog, the train, the passengers. You pay attention and watch for that fucking train." He shook me and yelled, "And you say it Morris! Bad people should fucking die. God Dammit, Say it!"

"Alright already. Bad people should fucking die!" I said.

I looked down the tracks, a small point of white light approached, growing larger and larger, brighter and brighter. It was suddenly right on top of us. I tried to break loose from his grasp but could not move. I awoke screaming, my heart racing and lathered in sweat. "Sheila, holy shit! Sheila!" I focused on my surroundings and remembered where I was. I got out of bed and paced my empty apartment like a man on strike.

"Holy shit. What the fuck was that about. Bad people should die? Harvey Keitel?. The train?

It was 3:00am. I watched the clock and infomercials about rubber-sealant spray, weight loss programs and Ginsu knives until a haze of daylight came in through my blinds. I started coffee and headed out the door into the sultry air for a run.

The sweat stung and burned as it dripped into my bad eye. There was a heat warning for today. The morning meteorologist said it was going to be an Orange air quality day. I didn't care. I love the sweat and the burn when running in the heat. The elbow pumping required to attack steep hills was one of the only activities that seemed to mitigate the pain in my shoulder blades. At the summit of Hester Avenue, I stopped at the QT.

Verdell was behind the register. "V" had been the day shift manager for the past year. I waved to him as I hustled past the counter and the half dozen customers waiting to buy hot pockets or cigarettes. I headed towards the bank of coffee, sodas, icees and smoothes. I re-filled my water bottle and grabbed a couple of napkins, wiping my forehead and face, and stuffed the soggy paper into the trash. "Keep it cool doc," V said, flashing a peace sign as I left the store.

Re-emerging into the morning air that was every bit as warm and wet as a steam vaporizer, I continued on down Hester road, turning into Blessed Sacrament Cemetery, the halfway point. The path around the graveyard was an even 1.2 miles. It was 2.5 miles to get there, 2.5 back. In total, an even 10K. Most days I was able to be back at the apartment in an hour. Not too bad for a worn out old man.

Is there such a thing as coincidence? After Sheila and I split up, I moved into an apartment just up the street from Blessed Sacrament. My runs would take me there, past the well manicured graves of the ghosts who would eventually drive me to the very edge of sanity, nearly to my death for the second time.

# Chapter Twenty

A t the time of the murders, Julie Wiley's paramour, James Paul Patrick, was 37 years old and had been a city police officer for 15 years. He had worked in the Patrol Division for ten of those years where he had distinguished himself. He worked drug interdiction on the interstate and had made numerous, large drug seizures. He had the knack.

James had also gotten in trouble a few times. Allegations usually centered around the use of excessive force during arrests. The charges were always dropped when the claimants and any witnesses either disappeared or withdrew their complaint.

His reward for the drug successes and the aggressive attitude led to an assignment with a specialized crime control squad, the Street Safety Unit. The SSU was responsible for clearing street corners of drug dealers and any other type of criminal element that attempted to contaminate a neighborhood. They were successful and had received a number of commendations from the police chief and citizen groups which overshadowed the denouncements from the local ACLU concerning their tactics.

Much like my old team of narcs, the members of the SSU were a cohesive band of brothers. They routinely rolled up on armed groups of drug dealing gang members who had nothing to live for. These were kids who didn't care about dying or killing, especially if it was the police doing the dying. Five years of day to day battle in that environment built a strong allegiance between members of the SSU. Like my team, they worked hard and they partied hard. Aside from the murders I'd committed, my transgressions in the name of justice, paled in comparison to the SS unit.

The members of their street unit made alliances with the black and Hispanic gangs moving a lot of product through certain city neighborhoods. For a share of the profits in cash, or for pot, coke or heroin, the SSU offered protection and a blind eye to thugs who were left alone to prove that capitalism works. They also routinely busted competing gangs attempting to move into the area under their control.

James Patrick and his compatriots often resold the drugs they confiscated. Usually, only about a third of the cash or dope at the scene of a bust made it into evidence. It was in this role as cop and criminal, that James developed an alliance with the Scalini organized crime family.

Vincent Scalini was a young, up and coming gangster. He was old man Francis Scalini's grandson, and Anthony's nephew, which also made him Julie Wiley's cousin. He was a good earner in the Scalini organization. He needed a source within the law enforcement community to insulate and protect his interests on the street.

A mutual friend introduced Vinny to James and a few of the SSU members. Vinny and James began a friendship and an alliance involving drugs, prostitution and pornographic movie production that was profitable for everyone involved.

The summer, before the murders, James had been given the task of finding a new narcotics dog. Craig Wiley's dogs had been recommended by another police agency.

James was tall and thin, 6'1", 170lbs. Despite the rough lifestyle, the alcohol and drugs, he'd stayed in shape. He played in softball and hockey leagues. Five of his teammates were SSU members. They worked hard and they played hard.

He wore his sandy hair shoulder length, and grew either a full beard, or sported a moustache and goatee. He often wore a college baseball cap and kept his hair pulled back in a ponytail. He could pass for a grad student.

James parked his unmarked unit, a dingy white, 1998 GMC Yukon in the driveway. The unit had seized the anonymous looking SUV earlier in the year. He walked up to the front door of the Wiley house and rang the bell. Julie Wiley answered a minute later looking blonde, tanned and fresh. She was wearing a blue and white striped tube top and a pair of Daisy Duke cut offs. James was impressed as he shook her hand, flashed his badge and introduced himself.

"Hi James. I'm Julie, Craig's wife. He told me you were coming over for a demo of what the dogs can do. Come on in, he's in the back. Oh, don't mind these girls," she said, pointing at the two hyperactive Pekingese swirling around her feet like dust bunnies. "They're my little babies. This one is Willy and this one is Nilly." She turned. James and the two dogs followed.

"Can I get you anything to drink?" Julie asked.

"A Coke would be great if you have one and it's no trouble."

"No trouble. I'll be right back."

James watched Julie's ass as she went up the stairs. He was paying close attention to her smooth butt cheeks just peeking out from the Daisy Dukes. The two rat looking dogs followed her. Craig Wiley came into the room at the same time.

"Great ass, huh?" Craig said.

"Oh shit, sorry man," James said. "I didn't mean to be rude or anything."

"It's alright. I don't think I could trust a guy who doesn't at least look. Or one who doesn't drink," Craig said with a grin.

"Guilty on both counts. James Patrick. I'm with the street team," he said extending a hand.

Craig shook James's hand with a pincer like grip. "Craig Wiley, dope dog man. I've got some terrific animals that will make your job a lot easier and more fun. Ever work with drug dogs?"

"Yea, we have a few that we call out on searches from time to time. You're right. It is pretty cool to watch the dopers when you bring the dog in. They get scared shitless, especially those bad ass thug gangsters. They call out for their mama like little babies when that dog is on their ass. It's fucking funny." Both men chuckled.

Craig assured him that his dogs were from quality lines. "These dogs have been trained in the Schutzhund trial fashion," he explained. "They are excellent at narcotics detection, tracking and protective services. All my dogs score high on the trials."

James didn't know what a Schutzhund trial was and didn't care. His mind was still thinking about that fine ass of the dope dog man's wife. He followed Craig out through a rear garage service door to the back yard. There were three kennels with concrete pads and grass runs surrounded by 6 foot chain link fence panels.

As they came outside, a couple of 100 pound German Shephards exited their dog houses and approached the fencing. They looked at James and started to bark.

"Ruhe," Craig said, and the dogs quieted. "Sitz," each dog sat, tongues wagging.

"They're gentle and playful when not working. Julie and I have two kids and two little house dogs. These animals are good with children and other pets as long as you train them right." Craig opened up one of the kennels and leashed 'Masha', one of the Shepards.

"They speak German. I'll give you the commands when you buy the dog. We provide quality after the sale service." He brought Masha out into the backyard. "Masha is here for some training and grooming. He goes back next week to one of the alphabet agencies, but we can use him as a representative example of my dogs. What would you like him to find?"

"I hid some dope in a couple places in my ride," James said.

"No problem whatsoever dude."

Julie returned with a Coke and handed it to James.

"What, nothing for me?" Craig asked.

"I didn't know you wanted one."

"Never mind," Craig led the dog out to the driveway. "Let's show him what you can do Masha."

Masha proved as capable as Craig had described. He indicated on the hood of the car. James opened the hood. Masha jumped up on the front of the car barking at the engine. Craig placed a bench in front of the car allowing Masha to get closer to the engine. Masha pawed at the air cleaner where James had placed an ounce of pot. Masha then found the gram of meth under the front seat, and soon was pawing at the purple Crown Royal bag containing an eight ball of cocaine in the trunk.

"Fucking great dog you got there Craig," James said. "Write up a bid. I'm duly impressed."

"I'll fax you our standard bid and contract later today. I'll be out of town with Masha for a couple days, but you can leave a message with Julie if you have questions."

The two men shook hands and Craig led Masha back to the pens.

James upended the Coke and handed it back to Julie. "Thanks."

"Anytime. I look forward to seeing you again James."

"Sure thing."

James turned and walked back to his car. It was already stuffy from the heat. He cranked up the airco and looked in his rear view mirror as he drove away from the Wiley's cul de sac. Mrs. Wiley was watching as he drove away.

"Man that dog might be good, but that girl is superfine. I hope I can do some quality service after the sale with that little honey. She'd be great in the movies."

# Chapter Twenty One

Ten days later, Craig's bid for supplying a dog to the narcotics unit was approved. James called the Wiley home and left a message on the answering machine, giving his office number. A short time later, Julie Wiley called. She said she was just leaving to pick up Craig. They were going out for happy hour and dinner at a restaurant near the airport.

"James, I'd, we'd, really love to see you again. Why don't you meet us at the restaurant and bring the paperwork?"

James agreed. On the drive over, he thought of Julie Wiley's firm ass hugging those short shorts, her long blonde hair, soft lips and ample tits not entirely contained by the tube top. She just looked damn good, healthy, a farm fresh MILF. She probably didn't have a drug habit or a history replete with half a dozen assorted STD's. She was so different than his usual fare, girls from the BullPen.

The Bullpen

Years ago, the Scalini family opened an upscale restaurant/bar in a massive three story, turn of the century Victorian. They called it the Bullpen. A masculine term that brings to mind sweaty, muscular men firing baseballs at 90 MPH or bulls penned in, fertilizing cattle. The name fit the place.

The Bullpen was, from all outside appearances, an elegant and modish restaurant and bar. It's dark and quiet atmosphere, tuxedoed staff and valet parking, for those that didn't arrive by limo, offered a marvelous dining experience at an average of $700.00 for two. The society pages included blurbs of who was seen there with who and often more importantly, who wasn't there.

The first two stories were covered in white clapboard siding, the third in weathered, brown shake. There were three chimneys jutting out of the strongly pitched roofs. The front porch extended the entire 55' length of the home. Each level sported a meticulously detailed porch with ornate spindles and thick railings. On busy spring and summer evenings, the decks were filled with diners waiting for tables inside.

The upper level windows were tall and arch topped with stained glass churchlike patterns. It was quite a paradox, given the nature of the activities within. Brilliant copper guttering snaked around the eaves reaching to the ground at all four corners.

The kitchen, bar and five star restaurant took residence on the first and second floor. A mirrored and red velvet lined elevator, always staffed by a petite blonde in a French maid's uniform escorted patrons between floors.

A discrete elevator off the kitchen went underground. The basement was transformed into a fantasy land. People of money and power came to the Bullpen for drinks, dining and to be seen. Those with special proclivities found their way to the basement where they could be restrained with leather straps, ball gagged, handcuffed and whipped with feather boas or a cat o' nine tails. The services ranged from simple prostitution to bondage, sadomasochism and sexual torture.

It wasn't unusual for patrons of significance, Washington politicians, influential business playmakers, and those from the society pages to be tied down to a metal cot in a jail cell setting, with their dick squeezed in a cock ring while a spandex clad, gorgeous Scandinavian Scalini 'employee' in silver lame' gloves, screamed obscene names, smeared them with baby oil and worked them over with a bullwhip.

The Bullpen was known by the elite few as the Loch Ness monster of super sexual shit. The powerful could be made to scream like kids on the playground while paying high dollar for the experience. Manager Vincent Scalini assured confidentiality to these powerful men. They expected their secrets to be kept secure. Until an occasional need arose, the secrets were secure, stored on a hard drive with a cloud based back up. Vinny kept DVR copies in a wall safe.

Aside from serving whippings and fine food, the "Bullpen" also functioned as a money Maytag. With a legitimate clientele whose cars and watches could pay off a good sized chunk of the national debt, large quantities of Scalini cash from drugs and prostitution were routinely filtered through the Bullpen books.

Vincent utilized a forensic accounting firm, run by a cousin, to assure that any money subject to scrutiny by the government would not be contaminated with even a trace of dope or cum.

The upper level, third floor of the building was devoted to the "VJ Productions" studio, Vincent and James. The two men had parlayed some of their fortunes from the dope game to finance their interests in porn movie production. The better looking Bullpen girls starred in the films along with various male 'actors' from the Scalini family crews.

Well before my soul was epoxied to the Wiley's, VJ Productions had filmed a porno video with a plot that would later become all too familiar.

A bored, stay at home, suburban housewife is depressed and tired of her daily routine of cleaning house, doing laundry, driving the kids all over and living with a cold, distant man. She survives by pills, pot and alcohol.

Her doldrums are relieved by a plumber who arrives to fix a leaky faucet. Of course, the lonely housewife is built like Pamela Anderson and the plumber has a huge faucet. The husband is not expected to return home anytime soon.

But, this lame story included a twisted plot for which VJ movies were known, sex with graphic violence. The husband comes home early and bloody mayhem follows.

James had his pick of the movie starlets for years. And the girls from their movies were certainly hot, but they were all cut from the same cloth. Julie Wiley was certainly different.

As he drove towards Ombardino's Restaurante', James let his imagination run. Perhaps in the middle of dinner, Craig would get called and have to attend to some dog crisis in a far away land. He and Julie would be left to their own desires. His fantasy was nearing completion when he pulled into the restaurant parking lot.

Craig and Julie were already sitting at a table in the bar when James arrived. Craig was wearing a Navy blue polo shirt with a gold emblem over the left chest and a similar patch on the right shoulder. He had on dark blue military style fatigues, his pants bloused into shiny black combat boots.

When they first met at the Wiley residence, James had noticed more about Julie and the dogs than about Craig Wiley. He did not recall much about Craig, except to note that Craig shook hands like the Hulk and was damn lucky to have a smoking hot wife.

Today, James noted that Craig was powerfully built with a triangular form, a thick neck and defined arms. He was no stranger to moving iron at the gym.

James approached their table. Julie noticed him and waved, the smoke from her cigarette trailing. She spoke quietly and stuck her hand out before Craig said anything, "Hi James. Please have a seat."

He smiled at Julie and shook her hand softly, making eye contact. She wore a silver lame blouse cut down the middle and a black, frilly leather vest buttoned once that just barely kept her tits from falling out. She was stunning. James thought if burning embers of coal were ever azure blue, that was how he would describe her eyes. He felt a sizzling coolness, a rush through his head when their eyes met and he withdrew his hand slowly from her smooth touch.

"Hey, how's it going man," Craig said standing up. Craig's firm grip snatched James from the fantasy he wanted to complete. The two men sat down. James handed Craig a folder containing the contract and procedure for completing the sale.

Craig flipped the pages, signed twice and closed the folder. "Tell your people thanks. I'm glad you guys decided to work with me. You won't be sorry. Your dog will pay for itself in drug and money seizures in less than 3 months."

"I have to tell you man, you weren't the lowest bid."

"You can't get the best on the cheap dude. But thanks again. Hey, so much for business. Let's get a buzz going. I've been out of the country working some long ass hours. You know, working with one of those three letter federal agencies. The ones that don't do what they do, and aren't where they really are. I was working with a few of their agents and a handful of some cocoa colored friends. Well, they're friends this decade anyway. Man, it was all work, 10 hour days or longer, hotter than shit. They never use good hotels and I always feel grimy, no matter how many showers I take. But, it's good money, ain't it Jules?" Julie smiled and nodded. Her blonde bangs partially covering her face.

James was sure she was looking at him through her bangs.

"I could use a few cold A-B products," Craig said, waving his bulky arm to catch the waitresses' attention.

Julie locked eyes with James, "James, you guys are really going to like Craig's dogs. They are cute and cuddly, when they're not working. We have young kids, and the dogs are so gentle with them."

"You'd love for all the dogs to sleep in our bed if I'd let you. It's bad enough those little rats are in our bed. They're dogs Julie. Dogs, not people. They need to know that."

Julie ignored Craig's haranguing, "You have kids James?"

"No. Divorced once. Fortunately, no kids from that train wreck."

Julie nodded her head and stared into him like she was doing an appraisal.

James returned her gaze, sensing something. He felt some kind of connection was forming with this woman. They ordered the first of several rounds. Craig and James drank Buds, Julie finished off several Cosmopolitans.

Craig continued to chat about his company and some of the interesting clients he had. He had worked for several former Soviet Union republics, helped train NATO canine troops in several European countries and supplied dogs to the Argentinean government's organized crime drug task force.

James believed about half of the bullshit Craig was saying, but if half was accurate, Craig was an impressive and formidable character.

"I'll be back in a minute. Potty time," Julie said. Her body brushed by James as she left the table. Her perfume lingered, leaving a hint of a fresh island breeze.

Craig continued to ramble about his most recent travels to South America. James acted attentive but his mind was processing Julie Wiley as a friend or foe.

James decided that fucking this guy's wife would be more trouble than even a snapping pussy was worth. Spurning the beer buzz that often put his other head in charge, and despite the fact that he was inexplicably drawn to Julie Wiley, James made a conscious decision to leave her alone.

He decided it was time to go.

"I think I'm gonna get going. We've got an early search warrant."

"Alright man. Thanks again for the business. You guys will be happy, I guarantee it," Craig said. Both men rose and shook hands. "I don't know where fucking Julie went. She's probably still putting on makeup or some shit."

"That's alright. Tell her I said bye. I'll talk to you soon Craig."

James turned and headed towards the door. He smiled to himself, proud that he had won the war over his penis. However, his bladder was talking loudly and he decided he'd better take a leak before hitting the road.

Ombardino's restaurant was an old shotgun style building, about 50 feet deep and 18 feet wide. The restrooms were at the end of the elongated room. The narrow hallway leading to the lavatories served as storage for booster seats and a steam table for buffets.

James took care of business and exited the restroom to find Julie in the hallway. Once again her eyes found his. James smelled her again. That freshness massaged the inside of his head.

As if choreographed, each stopped. She stepped into him. Her breasts rubbed against his chest. She lifted her head and whisked her tongue around his ear. She blew lightly on the damp spot. James pulled her close with one arm and pulled the back of her hair down, tilting her lips up. He kissed her gently at first. Julie responded with a moan and he French kissed her forcefully and grabbed each of her ass cheeks, pulling her hips toward his. He already had a full erection.

Julie kissed back with a lusty vengeance fueled by the Cosmos and unmet desires. Wet, sucking, open lips, she drew his tongue into her mouth, biting harder than he expected.

She reached between his legs and rubbed him. James pulled his mouth free and thought of Craig not all that far away, "Hallways are not the best place for me."

Julie squeezed his crotch. "It doesn't feel like hallways are all that bad for you."

James pulled her in close and slipped his hand between her legs. He found her wet and warm as she moaned. "Mmm, James, we have to get together. Craig will be going out of town soon. I'll call you. I will call you," she said with a shudder.

# Chapter Twenty Two

James thought a little too often about Julie and where this relationship with her could go. His intuition, that police sixth sense, the knack, worked off duty as well. He felt a shiver down his spine when he thought about her and it wasn't a good shiver of anticipation and excitement, rather a restless foreboding of peril. One afternoon about a week after the Ombardino's meeting, his phone rang at the SSU office.

"James Patrick."

"Hi, James, it's Julie Wiley."

"Hey, how are you, how's things going?" That chilly, prickly sensation nagged at the base of his skull.

"Very well thanks. James. Um, I called to tell you that Craig is out of the country for a week and the kids are spending the night tonight with my mom, giving me a break. I was wondering whether you maybe wanted to get a drink?"

James rolled his head to shake the chill, "Sure. Sounds good."

"You have any suggestions," she asked.

He thought for a couple seconds. "How about Café American? It's kind of mid way between your place and mine at the corner of Hampston and Belle Parkway. How about we meet there at 9?"

"Yes. I know the area. Can't say I've ever been there though."

"It's quiet, food is good. Kind of dark."

"Sounds perfect. I've been thinking about you James."

"Yea, me too. See you at 9," James said hoping the reluctance in his voice somehow wasn't transmitted.

They chose a table in the rear of the restaurant. A friendly peck on the cheek led to under the table groping. They had a few drinks. Julie left her car in the lot. James drove her to his place.

He drove down the alley behind his building and pulled into the underground garage. They walked hand in hand like prom dates.

As they rode up the elevator, Julie took the opportunity to reach inside James' pants. She whispered in his ear, "I don't know why I want this so bad, but I do."

Ninety seconds later they were struggling with buttons and zippers to get undressed in his bedroom. James went inside her, as they fell onto his bed. It was primal and raw, sexy and dangerous.

A ceiling fan in the bedroom threw a cool breeze that sifted over the two of them in waves. Julie wrapped her legs around James's waist. He interlocked his fingers between hers and raised her arms straight overhead. They thrusted into each other for several minutes, reaching a climax which left both lying on their backs, sweating and breathing like sprinters.

"Oh my God James. That was intense. Jesus, that was, like animalistic."

"Yea, maybe we should rest a few minutes and take it at half speed. I'll make us a drink and we'll decide what we should do for an encore."

James returned with two dirty Vodka martinis with 3 olives in each. He opened his dresser drawer and grabbed a bag of pot, rolling a joint.

"You smoke weed, you're a cop?" Julie asked, caught by surprise.

James handed her a martini, "There are cops and then there are cops," he said fishing an olive from his glass.

"There's a lot I do you might be surprised about. Who do you think gets the best pot anyway?

"Cops, huh?"

"The right kind of cops anyway. So, do you and Craig get high?"

"Occasionally," Julie said, lying. Craig did not do any drugs other than alcohol. She had not smoked any weed since before they had gotten married. In her mind, she hadn't done anything fun at all since the kids, until now.

While James rolled a joint, Julie thought maybe this is just what she needed to break her out of her doldrums, her depression, getting high and getting fucked. With Craig gone all the time and all the responsibilities of the kids and house on her shoulders, she felt trapped. Her choice for escape included prescription downers like Soma and Valium which her OB/Gyn prescribed for her chronic menstrual pain. She had been far removed from the recreational drug scene and had not given it much thought.

James lit the joint. The sweet pungent smell was the same as she remembered. They smoked the cigarette down. James was ready again.

Julie reached a plateau of comfort, she had not felt in quite a while. She was smiling and content. James told her she was stunningly beautiful and she believed him.

He reached under the bed and pulled out a small box that contained a fleshy 8" penis shaped vibrator, along with some leather straps and handcuffs. He and Vinny had produced dozens of movies that involved bondage and sex toys. He'd become a devotee years earlier.

"Let's have a little fun, huh babe", he said, waving the penis in front of her face.

"You don't need to use anything except what you have right here," Julie giggled, stroking James's attentive member.

"Let's just see what happens, how about that?"

"Oh, I don't care," Julie said as she laid back on the bed, stoned, eyes closed, smiling. "Just fuck me, come on."

James started off by fingering Julie, massaging inside her. He sucked on her hard nipples and she squirmed beside him. James could tell she was close to climaxing. He laid back on the bed and motioned for her. She eagerly sucked his fingers and then took his cock into her mouth.

A few minutes passed, James sat up and turned Julie on her stomach. He tied her ankles to the wooden posts of his headboard with slender brown suede straps. He handled Julie as if her legs were delicate flower stems. After tying her, he gently massaged her calves and feet with baby oil. Julie liked the tenderness but said, "James, this kind of feels weird, being tied up. I've never, I don't know what to do."

James whispered in her ear, kissing her lightly on the temple and cheek, "Go with it babe, if you want me to stop, just let me know."

He handcuffed her wrists together, locking the cuffs to assure that they wouldn't tighten up. He ran another suede strap from the chain links between the handcuffs to the footboard. He left enough slack in the straps and rope to bring her up on all fours, and gently lifted her midsection.

James took the vibrator, turned it on a slow pulsing setting, and slipped it inside her rhythmically moving it in small circles. She pushed against it and as she moved the strap to the handcuffs tightened.

Despite being locked, the cuffs still dug into her wrists. The pain intensified the sensations she was enjoying from the vibrator. Julie's moans got louder.

She grunted and pushed back against the vibrator until it was fully inside her. James could tell she was getting close.

He pulled the vibrator out and they fucked dog style. As their motion increased, the suede straps tightened, cutting off circulation to her feet. They started tingling and then hurt. The restriction and pain magnified the depth of Julie's orgasm tenfold. She quickly became a new fan of the bondage experience.

Over the course of next several months, Julie and James continued their affair. She enjoyed being controlled, skating on the periphery of sexual pain, enough discomfort to evoke a grimace, leaving no lasting evidence, should Craig ever look.

One evening after a particularly aggressive lovemaking session, she was rubbing her wrists, massaging the red handcuff marks away. James was applying some Aloe to the friction burn around his neck where, at his instruction, she nearly choked him to unconsciousness with his belt.

"You are one twisted man, James Patrick. Where do you come up with this shit?"

"Gotta keep up with the competition. Research baby. Research. All part of a day's work."

"What are you talking about?"

"I never told you about this, but I've got a little side business going in addition to my meager salary as a public servant."

"Like what?" Julie said, as she laid back on the bed and squirmed into her jeans.

"I'm in the movie business," James laughed, putting his thumb and fingers together in a box as if framing Julie for a shot.

"Me and a friend, we've been making porno flicks for several years now, and not just cheesy, bad quality B films. We're using state of the art video production and editing equipment."

"You're a cop. What do you know about making movies?"

"What we didn't know, we learned or hired someone who did know. Julie, I'm not kidding. We've consistently brought in good money selling these flicks all over. We've even got distribution in Europe."

Julie stood in front of the mirror, putting on lip gloss and eyeliner and spoke to James's reflection.

"So, we're doing things you've put in porn movies?" Her voice abrupt and aggravated. "I thought we were doing something special. This is bullshit James. Fuck you!" Julie flung her eyeliner pencil at James as if she were playing darts. He dodged and approached her.

"Hey, hey. It's not like that babe. I'm not an actor in the films Jules. I'm the producer, the director. Anyway, you and me would never do some of the things we've shot. We produce, well, let's say we've got the corner on quality freaky sex video. Some real weird and violent shit. Not what we do babe."

James stood behind her and looked at her in the mirror. She was looking straight back at him eyes still glowing.

He massaged the tops of her shoulders. The tightened muscles let go with his touch, "Don't get upset Julie. What you and me do is real, no movie bullshit."

She turned, they kissed. Her anger switched off, "Dammit James. Now I have to do my lips again."

They took advantage of Craig's growing canine business. His success required he travel at least a couple of days every other week and sometimes for longer periods.

Julie would occasionally prod James for information on the film making. She wanted to watch and meet the actors. It sounded so exciting compared to her housewife life. She wanted to be involved. James told her that his partner wouldn't allow outsiders around. He kept the identity of his partner secret. He didn't want her to know about the Bullpen, that he was tied to organized crime or how money was made and cleaned.

Julie kept her secrets from James as well. She never shared her maiden name. James had no idea who her father and grandfather were and how closely knit the spider web that they were weaving, actually was.

Both James and Julie were satisfied with the arrangement and each developed an attachment to the other, just south of love.

# Chapter Twenty Three

The work in a general assignment detective bureau with MQ was interesting. There were burglaries, robberies, an occasional murder, assault or rape. Lots of paperwork, crime scene processing, forensics and fairly normal hours. Hours of boredom, moments of mayhem.

I worked clinic hours around my detective bureau schedule. I put in three, 4 hour shifts a week at the Peoples Community Clinic of mind numbing, repetitive work. There was always a steady stream of diabetics, COPD'ers and seasoned citizens with the usual age related issues including cancer, heart disease and arthritis. The clinic was basically human factory work. Examine a patient; write a prescription; examine; write a prescription. The only redeeming value was that it paid well compared to my police salary. Thus, it allowed me to continue to be Detective Green and pay rent, child support and alimony. In so many words, I was working part time as a doctor in order to afford a career in law enforcement.

Sheila's anger and disappointment at my decision to return to police work lasted a long time. Other than the times I picked up the kids, or she dropped them off, we rarely spoke. After a couple of months, she started dating a chiropractor. She told me he did yoga, ate tofu and had gotten her into sharpening her Chakras. It must have worked. I certainly hadn't changed much, but we started getting along again.

I had a few relationships of my own. I dated a temp nurse who had been filling in during a staff shortage at the clinic. When her gig ended, so did we. Then I met a 24-year-old hard body phlebotomist from the hospital who wore me out with her incessant need for sex and conversation. I dated a lovely, divorced pharmacist from CVS whose only flaw was that she wanted me to come to her church, one of those new age cults with rock bands and trancelike ceremonies. My last girlfriend during that time was one of the city's 911 dispatchers. She had heard a little about me from the scuttlebutt after the shooting. Once the initial intrigue wore off of who this doctor and cop was, she was off too.

Jake and Olivia were busy with school and sports and didn't come over very often. With the case load in the detective bureau and my clinic hours, Sheila was right. I had become Jack Green incarnate.

I followed up with my shrink, Louise Brandeis, every so often, when I could fit her in. I continued to suffer chronic headaches, left shoulder and chest pain that occasionally brought on an anxiety attack in which I thought I was dying from a massive myocardial infarction. Consciously, I knew the chest pain had nothing to do with my heart, but my brain convinced me otherwise.

Louise and I explored my psychosomatic symptoms, the bizarre dreams and the MTBI/PTSD. We discussed the train and the depressive, damp darkness. Louise said it was a metaphor for my troubled journey through life. She said the unfocused, indistinguishable passengers were my relationships with my kids, Sheila and my father. She couldn't have been farther off base. Of course, I couldn't tell Dr. Brandeis that I was also carrying around the guilt of having murdered two men, despite receiving absolution from Harvey Keitel.

"Morris, you are the result of a number of events" she said at one of our last sessions. "The lack of loving parents, the physical and emotional abuse and that terrifying closet punishment took its toll. You missed out on normal, emotional development. You're in search of emotion and feelings. You're desperate to erase that protective numbness you have inside. You only come close to any emotion when you place yourself in extreme situations. And you require activities which foster a belief in your mind that you are a good person, thus the paramedic, police and medical careers, public service, saving lives, keeping the peace, solving emergent problems. They offer a fix, so to speak, to your needs. We just have to keep diving into what is going on inside of you. It takes time."

"Well, I'm tired of it all," I complained. "The nightmares, endless pain, the fucking headaches. It would have been easier had a chunk of that bathtub cut open my carotid."

"It would have been the easy way out, but, you know thoughts like that are all part of the PTSD. We'll work through this Morris. You are making progress, considerable progress. It just takes time and it would help if you made your sessions with a little more regularity."

I stood up and loomed over her, "Dammit Louise, you know my dance card is pretty full. I get in when I can."

"I'm not pushing Morris. I just want you to benefit from our work."

"I think I'd rather remain the unemotional, cold, distant, Howard Hughes bastard that I am, than delve into the minutiae of the past for one more second."

Louise stood and walked me towards the door as our time was nearing its end. "Morris, why don't you climb El Capitan, take up parachuting, or bungee jumping, white water rafting, something you can physically and safely perform that still carries some risk. You can decide when, where, and how you get your adrenalin rush. It's not quite the same as defibrillating someone back to life or the thrill of the hunt or being on the wrong end of a gun, but the chemical response in the brain is nearly the same. Risk activity may help you feel something in the now while we work through the past."

For that bullcrap advice, my health insurance company paid Dr. Brandeis $114.37 per hour. I would have told her to go fuck herself, but Dr. Brandeis was very liberal in her prescription of pain meds, and for a professorial type, she was easy on the eyes and a good listener. So, I sat on the couch in Louise's office and told her about my dreams, how and what, if anything, I was feeling and how my life was going. In any event, I was not interested in jumping out of a perfectly good plane or hanging upside down on a rubber band.

She had me on a combination of Duloxetine, Neurontin and Alprazolam which seemed to help my mood and limited the intensity of the headaches. I had gone through Vicodan and Oxycodone for pain and moved up to 80mg Oxycontin 4 per day along with whatever I could pilfer from the clinic narcotic cabinet without suspicion. The left shoulder and chest pain had become a gnawing ache, a prelude to what would become the tapping.

I found a crust of peace during my runs, especially on long, steep hills in the core of summer, in the ruthless heat of July and August. The long, gradual increase in pain and intensity climbing those hills was accompanied by an immediate release and relief as I passed over the summit and started downhill, seemingly without effort at twice the uphill speed. It evoked a feeling somewhere between flying and sex as the diminishing pain spilled just the right combination of neurotransmitters in my brain.

Despite my emotional and physical hurricane, my work product in the detective bureau was excellent. These were good times for the Oakview PD. Chief Montileone's FBI Uniform Crime Report statistics improved. MQ and I proved to be efficient crime solving machines. The department's drug team, even without

Tom and me, made several high profile drug arrests. The vice squad broke up a small prostitution and gambling ring. The city council gave the Chief a raise. Per capita, Oakview was listed as one of the safest communities in the nation.

For a little while, Chief Montileone stopped worrying about his decision to bring me back.

He had been warned it could pose problems, but it appeared everything was working out just fine.

# Chapter Twenty Four

I was putting away a case folder in the Closed Investigations cabinet when I noticed the Wiley Homicide file in the next drawer. The file was in one of those brown, accordion folders with the rubber band closure and was no more than 2" thick. I pulled it out of the drawer and took it into MQ's office.

"Kenneth, don't tell me this is the entire Wiley murder case. I've seen drive-by murders solved by confession with a thicker file than this. Hell, the report of my shooting with those Mexicans is easily 4 times thicker than this. If I recall, there were two dead kids and their father in this one weren't there?"

MQ cocked his head to the side, "Yes, well, that was not one of the more stellar pieces of sleuthing done around here. Fortunately, I was not involved in the investigatory process. I have a firm degree of plausible deniability for the fuck up that it was."

He lit a half-smoked Macanudo and leaned back in his chair. "As I recall, the cast of characters on the play bill included Detective Elwyn Bryson, and his ever so diligent and hard working partner, Detective Lawrence Johnson. They were the initial Sherlocks on the scene. They did the, if you dare to call it, processing and forensics. Will Newsham put his Waspy, well manicured hands on the case, and lest we forget, the all-knowing grand wizard, Herr Martin Weingart and his squad of Nazi youth were involved as well. Doc, they were all completely incompetent. The outcome never set quite right with me. However, it was officially closed by the prosecutor's office as a murder-suicide and Chief said, that was that."

"You mind if I take a look at it?"

"Sure, but it won't do you any good."

This turned out to be as prophetic and wise as any statement King Solomon ever made.

# Chapter Twenty Five

**W**e were working the day shift. I got in early, made some coffee and sat down at my desk, checking my inbox for overnight crime reports.

Like a marksman with a Remington 700 police sniper rifle at 2000 yards, the Wiley folder lay in wait. I felt a cold finger brush the back of my neck. A rumbling headache traveled over my scalp settling down to business in my right eye. A flash of burning pain that I had not had in quite some time, stabbed my left shoulder.

I mumbled to myself, "And just the other day Dr. Brandeis had said I was doing well, getting in balance with myself." I opened up my desk drawer and grabbed for the Oxy, taking another with hot coffee. Balance would be a few minutes away.

The original report recounting the events that led to the deaths of Craig, Robert and Taylor Wiley was an epoch masterpiece of seven pages, written by Officer Tom Pischoch, DSN 3271, dated the day following the murders. He described their response, search of the home, the location of the children and the discovery of their dead father. Pischoch's report listed Robert and Taylor as deceased victims. Their mother, Julie, was listed as an injured victim with contusions to the neck, wrist, ankles and forehead. Craig Wiley was listed as the deceased 'suspect' charged with 'Murder and Assault.' Officer Pischoch wrote that Detectives Johnson and Bryson arrived to process the crime scene, followed by Chief Montileone who took command.

My next clue that things were not what they should have been was when I could not find the crime scene log of who came and went. 'Locard's Phenomena' is a criminological tenet that states that no one can enter a crime scene without either adding something that was not there, or taking something away that belonged. No one was assigned to keep track of entry into the crime scene. The lack of a log to identify who may have contaminated the scene was indicative of how poorly the case was probably managed.

There were a dozen other supplemental reports of witness statements and evidence collection that had been written by Bryson, Johnson and a few other officers over the next six weeks. I opened up the folder containing crime scene and autopsy photographs. There were so few photographs, that I assumed there must be more somewhere else.

I walked into MQ's office and sat down across from his desk. "How did they know, within a day of the incident, that the father was the murderer? Did he leave a note, 'I killed my kids' and decided to let the wife go, signed Dad'? And how many murder-suicide cases have you worked where someone lived? The name implies the outcome. Someone gets murdered and someone commits suicide and no one survives."

I was firing questions off, demanding answers, but not allowing time for a response. "And the mother flees the house not knowing if her children are alive or dead? A mother wouldn't leave, would she MQ? Something is wrong here?"

MQ looked at me over dollar store bifocals, "Listen, do you really want something this bad cluttering up your already vitiated, cyclopic head? I told you, it won't do you any good."

"I tell you Kenneth, this is Watergate."

I went back to my office and read the supplemental reports. The story was as unbelievable as a rainbow on fire.

I read that Julie Wiley apparently was able to escape the murderous rampage of her husband and drive away-drive, not run. There was no sprinting down the street half naked, screaming for help while her children were being massacred like Indians at Wounded Knee. Our investigators did not seem to think a great escape by BMW was peculiar.

One of the patrol division officers, Herb Davidson wrote a lengthy supplemental report that was a flower amongst the weeds. He reported everything that Mrs. Wiley said to him while they were together in the ER. She told him that her husband had come home around lunchtime and had given her a handful of what he said, were blue vitamin pills. She told Davidson that she believed her husband had given her drugs to knock her out and that they were not vitamins.

She said that he picked the kids up at the bus stop and they came home about 3:45pm. He put them in their rooms. Mrs. Wiley said that her husband choked her, duct taped her mouth shut, tied her up with rope and handcuffs and forced her to have anal sex. When he was finished, he said they all had to die. Mrs. Wiley told Officer Davidson that she was able to convince her husband to untie her and let her go. She drove down to a neighbor's house, the Goldsteins.

I asked myself the obvious, "A psychopathic maniac has just bound, gagged and raped you. How do you convince him to do anything you want him to do?"

In his report, Officer Davidson indicated that he had also spoken with Mrs. Wiley's mother, who he identified as Mrs. Cindy Scalini. He reported that Mrs. Scalini arrived at St. Mark's and made the identification of the bodies. She said she could not believe her son-in-law would ever hurt his kids, that he was a good father and husband. I read the name 'Scalini' and the muscles along my left shoulder blade responded with a sudden vermicular cramp.

I stormed into MQ's office, "This case has ties to the fucking Scalini's? Cindy Scalini?"

Just saying the name again made my headache go nuclear, despite the meds. "Julie Wiley was her daughter, which makes her Anthony Scalini's daughter which makes her Francis's granddaughter. Tom is paralyzed and I am killed on the very same day that this family is massacred. So both of these cases orbit the Scalini family. I don't know how, or even if the two incidents are connected, but I will bet you that this is a triple murder MQ, not a murder suicide."

I rolled my shoulder, trying to relieve the cramp. "It's like September 11th Kenneth, and no one connected the dots. I've read all of maybe twenty pages of this piece of crap. There's something very wrong here." Gooseflesh painted my arms, "It's very wrong. I can feel it."

MQ blew out a fog of cigar smoke, "Do you want to know why I drink so much Bushmills, why I gobble Alka-Seltzers like Chiclets, why I'm fat as Santa? Do you want to know why my blood pressure rings bells every time they take it and my arteries are slowly clogging shut? Why I smoke a cigar on the way to work, one at lunch and one on the way home? It is because I work at this Goddamn fantasy department where we are all down the rabbit hole. Morris, I told you this would not do YOU any good, and it sure as hell won't do ME any good either. Opening this case up will create a Homeric journey that neither you or I, are up to at this stage in our lives. Let it go, Doc."

MQ pursed his lips, kicked back in his chair, littering his desk with cigar ash.

I stood, clenching my jaw. "We'll just see about that!" I returned to my office and finished reading the file.

No other theories of who may have committed the murders were developed. They wrote 12 supplemental reports in addition to Officer Pischoch's original. The whole file would fit in a manila envelope and could be mailed anywhere in the US for less than ten bucks.

# Chapter Twenty Six

The Wiley investigation was littered with obvious inconsistencies. The facts of the case were left standing alone like a bag of flaming dog crap on a Halloween porch. Apparently, I was to be the schmuck stomping on the bag and getting knee deep in shit.

Cindy Scalini was re-interviewed by Sgt. Will Newsham several days after the murders. In Newsham's report, Cindy's opinion of her son-in-law had undergone a complete overhaul. She said that Craig was abusive, especially when he drank. She claimed he was known to use marijuana, cocaine and had taken steroid injections. Mrs. Scalini related that she had seen suspicious bruises on her daughter and the kids in the past and was concerned that Craig was abusing them.

No one followed up on this drastic change in her opinion from what she had told Officer Davidson on the night of the murders. No one bothered to check whether the children or Julie Wiley had been seen in any ER's with injuries consistent with abuse. No one considered that any injury inflicted upon the granddaughter and great grandchildren of the don of an organized crime family would be an unhealthy activity for the abuser. If there really were some problems in the Wiley home, why wasn't Craig Wiley in a wheelchair or a shallow grave, long ago.

Cindy Scalini also mentioned that her daughter was suffering from anxiety and depression presumably due to the stress of her husband's abuse. Newsham included in his report that Cindy had given her daughter some Prozac, hoping it would help.

I guess it was too much for the detectives to take into account whether self-medicating with an SSRI anti-depressant medication could be problematic. Any moron could have Googled 'Prozac and Violence', irrespective of whether it was legally prescribed, and found a number of instances in which Prozac was associated with violent behavior.

A handful of friends that socialized with Craig and Julie came forward voluntarily and were interviewed. The friends did not believe Craig could harm his children. The interviews were conducted by Det. Johnson. They were very brief and telegraphed the need for a follow-up interview. There were no additional interviews.

I read the complete report twice over the next few days. I read every note, evidence sheet, laboratory analysis, autopsy record and written statement. There were Titanic tears everywhere in the investigation, black holes, vacuous spaces that apparently sucked out all common sense and police intuition.

I went into MQ's office with the intention of reporting my concerns in a controlled, unemotional, forensically objective fashion. I pushed a full ashtray and a half eaten Dolly Madison cinnamon roll from the corner of his desk and put the file down. I sat down and started in a monotone trying my best to control the agitation and anger. I didn't want to get stressed and trip the trigger on a migraine or the shoulder pain.

"This is one of the worst pieces of police work I have ever seen MQ. It would be of little consequence if it were the murder of a couple of crackheads, but these are two innocents, maybe three."

MQ didn't say a word. He waved his hand as if he were a traffic cop telling a driver to continue.

"The assumption made by the responding officers and detectives was that this was a planned murder-suicide, however, Mrs. Wiley survived. That fact alone, makes little sense."

My chubby partner nodded and spoke in a soft, even tone as if talking to a three year old. "Good. Very good. Now you understand. You're deductive processes have properly assimilated the data. We know it makes no sense doc. Nothing here makes sense. Therefore, it fits, does it not?"

"True enough. I still believe someone ratted out Tom and me. I'm convinced a Scalini was involved in the heroin trafficking, but our commander is such a pussy that," I stopped short.

The muscles in my left shoulder suddenly cramped up like a garlic press. I closed my eyes and paused, concentrating on control. I took several long, deep breaths, courtesy of the breathing techniques Sheila taught me during that brief stint in which I lived back in my own house.

"You alright doc?" MQ asked.

"Yea. It's the shoulder again," I said after a few breaths. The cramp released and I continued. "There's an interview with a neighbor. About an hour or so before the 911 call, this neighbor saw Mr. Wiley casually walking up the street, skipping actually. He was holding hands with his two kids and skipping, as they headed home from the bus stop. Nothing in there," I said pointing at the file, "explains what happened during that hour that made him go from happy dad to murderous dad, and any information we do have about what happened in that hour comes from Mrs. Wiley."

MQ sat at his desk impassively twisting a large paperclip.

I continued. "On the night of the murders, Detective Bryson interviewed her and videotaped the interview. He wrote that Mrs. Wiley was deceptive, that she was lying, and yet no one followed up on it, not even Bryson. For reasons unknown, Bryson does no additional work in this investigation after that first night. It's like the mothership came back for him, and he returned to Andromeda, never to be involved in this case again. What the fuck happened there?"

MQ threw the paperclip in a desk drawer and cracked his knuckles, "If I recall, Detective Bryson went on vacation and the Chief put Sgt. Newsham in charge of the case. Elwyn wouldn't have looked for extra work upon his return, especially if Will said the case was all but wrapped up. And with Newsham holding the reins, you now have your explanation as to why things were fucked up. That little twat couldn't find a 7-11 with a Garmin and an Atlas."

I persevered, "Elwyn's report said that he gave her Miranda Rights prior to the interview. He wanted to be sure that if she said something incriminating, he had it covered."

"One of the rare instances of adequate police work I suppose," MQ said.

"MQ, there is no copy of the Miranda form in the report. The form with her signature is gone."

MQ's lips pursed. I continued, "Elwyn wrote that the video of her interview displayed numerous inconsistencies and behavior consistent with deception. But, there's no evidence sheet for the DVD. And you know what else is missing? Ajay Rajeda, the medical examiner who did the autopsy on Mr. Wiley, swabbed the guy's hands for gunshot residue. The swab kit and the analysis is missing. Weren't you the evidence officer then?"

"Yes I was and whatever evidence they gave me was logged into the evidence book," MQ said, using that pre-school teacher voice again. "If proper police procedure was followed, the Miranda form, the DVD and swab kit would have been turned into me with a three part carbonless evidence sheet attached. I would have signed the top copy, pressing hard to make sure each sheet was authenticated. I would have assigned a shelf or cabinet location number, noting where the piece of evidence was stored. The pink carbonless copy of the evidence sheet with my signature and the location of the evidence in question should have been included in the report. If Bryson didn't turn in the Miranda form or the DVD to be placed into evidence, and whoever picked up the gunshot residue kit from the medical examiner's office didn't sign it over to me, I cannot fathom where they may be. Do you understand Detective Green?" MQ clipped defensively.

"Kenneth, I am not inferring you lost evidence. I am just letting you know that potentially critical pieces of evidence may be missing and that it didn't seem to matter to anyone whether the sole survivor and key witness was a liar."

So far, so good. The headache I was expecting stayed in the background like the dull sound of a distant surf.

"I don't quite see how the residue test is critical. The guy shot himself, so he would have tested positive irregardless," MQ said.

"I'll get to that in a minute," I said.

"Then proceed, by all means my good doctor. I promise I will keep my defensive surliness at bay."

I continued, "The murders occurred in Mr. Wiley's workshop. I looked at the crime scene photos. This guy had tool racks, and bins and shelves. It was more organized than a hardware store and yet the murders were totally disorganized. These were overkill murders. The girl was shot with a .22 caliber rifle and then her head was hatcheted with a machete until her brains spilled through the cracks. The boy was damn near gutted by the machete. These were weapons of opportunity in a rage. The killer used whatever weapons were handy at the moment of the killing. These murders were not arranged and planned. Hell, the guy had a 12 gauge shotgun if he planned to kill the wife and kids. This was spontaneous, out of control rage. And there's a lab analysis that I found misfiled. It had been stapled to the back of an interview of a neighbor. The lab report indicated there were absolutely no illegal drugs in Mr. Wiley's system. But, Mrs. Wiley had Prozac, Soma and Bendryl on board. My conspiratorial mind says the lab report was purposely misfiled." I handed him the lab reports.

"Jesus Christ Doc," MQ looked at me as if I just said we'd never landed on the moon.

"Murph, it's not like he snapped from being whacked out on PCP or something. So much for Cindy Scalini's allegations that her son-in-law was on pot and coke. This guy Wiley, he was organized and sober as a judge, but this murder was not. Despite what the report says MQ, this guy didn't plan these murders and my guess is, he didn't do them either."

MQ walked over to his coat closet. He pulled out the flask I had given him for his birthday, a nice ½ pint, leather-bound, stainless hip flask engraved with "MQ" in a thick Verdana font.

"We need some medicine to help us cogitate. Go get a couple Dixie cups from the water cooler. Put a little water in mine, it brings out the flavor," MQ said.

I got the cups, returned and closed MQ's office door. I felt a little better as a fresh coat of Bushmills painted my brain. I leaned forward on MQ's desk and flipped through the case file, pulling out a packet of 8x10 crime scene photos. I laid several of Craig Wiley in front of MQ.

"Jesus, Mother Mary, Joseph and the mules they rode in on Morris," MQ said with a look to the heavens.

"Can we discuss the crime scene without invoking religious drama?" I asked.

"There's nothing left of the guys head but squashed tomatoes doc." MQ's face took on the uncomfortable look of constipation.

"Pretty much decapitated in his recliner, but see how the Remington 870 is leaning neatly against his knee with the shell half ejected? Does it seem reasonable to you that the shotgun would stay in that exact position after firing? Evan after the dead guy's hands fall from it?"

"I don't suppose anybody at the lab checked that did they?" MQ asked, still grimacing.

"Not that I could find."

"Was there at least stippling on the guys face?" he asked.

"Yes, I will grant you that there was gunpowder soot around his mouth which would indicate that the barrel was very close to his mouth at the time it was fired. But that does not necessarily put his finger actively and intentionally on the trigger.

MQ interrupted, "A murder conspiracy? So there were other people involved? And someone put the barrel in his mouth and blew his head off?"

"I don't know where I am going exactly just yet MQ. But this is where the gunshot residue swab taken from Mr. Wiley's hands at autopsy is relevant. Two firearms were used in this offense, a shotgun and a .22 rifle right?"

"Affirmative. And I should have both firearms in evidence. For Chrissake, at least I hope I do."

"Murph, if I remember my forensics, most gunpowders have lead, barium and antimony. Some less common elements would be aluminum, sulphur, tin, copper, maybe a few others. The lab rats use a scanning electron microscope to ID the residue and X-ray spectrometry to identify the specific chemicals in each powder. They can determine what chemicals were in the .22 bullet and what chemicals were in the shotgun shell. If Mr. Wiley killed himself with the shotgun, and did indeed shoot the little girl, using the .22 caliber rifle, then he would have residue from both weapons on his hands. This would tend to implicate him in the murders, and my conspiratorial theories reside in upstate New York with Elvis's pregnant alien wife. But, what if he doesn't have the chemicals from the .22 caliber or the shotgun?"

"Doc, I hate to rain on that parade, but we don't often use gunshot residue testing in firearms cases. Most of the time, GSR analysis is only used as part of a bomb and arson investigation to identify powders used in devices. Seems to me, a few years ago the FBI stopped doing firearms GSR testing altogether. You know as well as I do, the FBI has had so many problems with their lab. There was that report that revealed cross contamination problems specifically with gunshot residue in their lab. I think they decided GSR was more trouble than it was worth in shooting cases."

"We need to see if the swab kits are in evidence. An analysis would clearly contradict the party line of a murder-suicide if he only fired one weapon," I said as I pulled another crime scene photo from the stack and laid it in front of MQ.

"Mrs. Wiley said she was bound, gagged and raped which puts this case squarely in the sexual crime ballpark. Look what our guys took pictures of, but didn't seize?"

The photo showed the contents of a white wicker sewing box with a wooden lid. The box included a collection of police gear including a city badge and ball cap, a SWAT shirt, a set of Smith and Wesson handcuffs, two penis shaped vibrators, a butt plug and studded leather ankle- restraints.

"Looks like a plethora of pleasure tools courtesy of a Larry Flynt store," MQ blinked his raised eyebrows a couple of times.

"A sex crime and murder and no one seized this box as evidence. And with a magnifier you can read the badge number. Yet, the report does not even indicate they tried to identify the cop whose badge was at a murder scene."

MQ yawned wide and loud. "Sorry doc, I didn't sleep all that well last night either. I'm concerned about my financial status. I found out that the wife has been spending most of her day and my paycheck on some home shopping club and eBay. The friggin UPS man is at my house more than I am. But I digress with my own tribulations, please Dr. Green please proceed."

"Well, if your next child is born in a brown uniform, you'll know why."

"At least she's giving it to someone."

"Moving on from your sex life and back to matters at hand, the evidence sheets indicated that they seized a men's, size large, plaid shirt from the bedroom. It was lying on the floor next to the bed in one of the crime scene photos. Mr. Wiley looks to be an easy XL size to me. But, there's no lab analysis for trace evidence from the plaid shirt in any report. I doubt if it ever made it to the lab."

"One has to wonder whose shirt it is and whether we still have it."

"Agreed. Let's return our attention to the dead guy MQ." I pointed at the headless picture. "Aside from the obvious trauma, what do you notice about Craig Wiley?"

MQ's eyes narrowed, furrowing a deep groove above his nose. He stared at the photo and squirmed in his chair. I didn't wait for him to speak.

"He has no blood on his arms, hands, feet or his pants legs. Where is the blood? The murder of those kids was hellaciously bloody. There was blood all over that crime scene. Why isn't he covered in his kid's blood? Did he take a shower after killing the kids? Why the hell would he take a shower? We're only talking an hour or so here. Not much time to rape your wife, kill your kids, shit, shower and shave. And look at his hair. It doesn't appear wet if indeed he did shower. Did he blow dry his hair before eating that 12-gauge?"

MQ continued to peer at the photo. His jaws were clenched, cheeks reddening. He took a pull from his flask and poured another shot in my cup.

"Where's the blood?" I asked.

MQ looked up with a deadpan face, nodding his head, "I remember asking Johnson and Bryson when they got back here after processing the scene, whether they had pulled the sink traps in the bathrooms and kitchen to check for blood or trace evidence. You know as well as I do that it's often just standard homicide procedure, so I figured they'd say 'Sure Sarge, nothing there', but, they said they hadn't bothered. They said it was irrelevant. No need because it was clearly a murder suicide. And if I recall, the crime scene, the house was turned back to the family within a day."

I shook my head in disgust and pulled out the picture of the machete. I laid it in front of MQ. Detective Bryson or Johnson, whoever manned the camera, took a nice close up as it lay on the workbench in the workshop after having been used to butcher the Wiley children. The flash from the camera had captured a glistening, red velvet sheen from the black plastic handle. A gelatinous mix of brain matter and dangling strands of blonde hair tinged red, hung limp from the quillon."

MQ winced and took another swig of whiskey.

"The entire length of the blade is streaked with fresh blood and clumps of tissue, the girl's brains, or maybe bowel from the boy," I said. "Look at the handle, it's soaked with blood. No one questioned why Craig Wiley didn't have any blood on his hands. They said he snapped and went crazy with the machete and rifle. I'm no psychiatrist, but I don't think crazed psychopathic murderers feel the need to wash up before committing suicide. He would have had to be bloody MQ. Craig Wiley was set up and murdered."

Suddenly, a cherry bomb went off behind my right eye and I puked Bushmills and some toast from breakfast, into MQ's trashcan. I wiped my mouth with my sleeve and gathered the file up. I shuffled out of MQ's office like an octogenarian going to dinner at 4pm.

MQ followed me. "Doc, you need me to do anything?"

"No. It's fine. I'll be fine." I stopped, turned and stood up, despite the dagger I felt in my eye socket. "I'm working this case Kenneth."

"I know," MQ said as he upended his flask once more. "It's likely to be a Sisyphean climb my friend.

So saith Sol.

# Chapter Twenty Seven

Criminal investigations largely depend on the proper collection of evidence, linking the perpetrator to the act. It's basic Crime Scene Investigation-CSI-101 that every police cadet is taught in the academy.

Criminal convictions require the skill sets of pale, underpaid, overworked personnel toiling away in a crime lab often using outdated equipment. It's pretty much the exact opposite from the current surplus of television shows in which the smoking hot forensic investigators with perfect cheek bones and 2% body fat, can get DNA from a fingernail scraping off a body found floating in a septic tank six weeks after the crime, and then, after being involved in a car chase and shootout, solve the case in 48 minutes. Nevertheless, real life and make-believe TV share one truth-physical evidence is the lynchpin.

To a good investigator, a new crime scene is virginal, and is accompanied by a sense of adventure. It's the old west with gold and silver just waiting to be plucked from the ground. The obscure miniscule story-tellers, the fibers, hairs and DNA are all there, tiny sparkles that when brought in front of a jury can become flaming Roman candles. Good evidence can be the railroad tracks to which your suspect is tied.

Police departments are businesses and just like any other, they have organizational structures and rules. They run on paper, memos, procedures, guidelines, budgets and politics.

To further the Wiley investigation would require additional department resources and forensics, some of which could be costly. We would need buy in from Chief Montileone, and that would not be a cake walk. His handling of my murder was at best inept, and in my mind, it was a conspiracy.

With the Wiley case, we were in essence telling the Chief, "Your initial team of investigators were incompetent. Their conclusions were wrong, and they were potentially corrupt, which means you, Chief Thomas Montileone, are probably corrupt and culpable." Somehow, we needed to say this in a nice way.

I surmised that providing the Chief with 'action steps' for what needed to be done to answer 'potential concerns', would be an easier pill to swallow than offering a treatise on how mismanaged and perhaps criminally negligent the investigation had been. Just before going home for the day, and without asking for input from MQ, I dropped a memo in the Chief's mail basket.

DATE: October 10
TO: Chief Thomas Montileone
FROM: Det. Morris Green
RE: WILEY MURDER INVESTIGATION EVIDENCE

Sir: Upon review of the Wiley murder case, I have discovered a number of potential concerns, some of which are related to evidentiary issues. While this case was officially closed by the prosecuting attorney's office, as you are aware, there is no statute of limitations for murder. Should further inquiry into this case occur at some point in the future, failing to have responded to these issues could be problematic and potentially embarrassing.

I recommend we conduct a cold case investigation beginning with the following evidentiary steps. I suggest all analysis be completed at the State Highway Patrol laboratory.

*TEST FIRING OF REMINGTON 870 SHOTGUN USING THE AMMUNITION SEIZED FROM THE SCENE FOR GUNPOWDER COMPOSITION ANALYSIS
*TEST FIRING OF REMINGTON 870 TO DETERMINE IF, HAVING BEEN FIRED, IT WOULD REMAIN IN THE POSITION IT WAS FOUND AS DEPICTED IN THE CRIME SCENE PHOTOGRAPH.
*TEST FIRING OF THE MARLIN .22 RIFLE USING AMMUNITION SEIZED FROM THE SCENE FOR GUNPOWDER COMPOSITION.
*FINGERPRINT ANALYSIS OF THE ROLL OF DUCT TAPE FOUND AT THE CRIME SCENE.
*BLOOD/FIBER/DNA ANALYSIS ON A MENS LARGE PLAID SHIRT FOUND AT THE SCENE
*LOCATE JULIE WILEY'S INTERVIEW, MIRANDA FORM AND VIDEO

*IDENTIFY THE CITY OFFICER, WHOSE POLICE BADGE, BALLCAP AND SWAT TEAM SHIRT WERE LOCATED AT THE WILEY HOME AS NOTED IN PHOTOGRAPHS.

Respectfully Submitted,
Det. M. Green, DSN 3261

# Chapter Twenty Eight

The following morning I arrived at the station about 8:00am and started to make a pot of coffee. As I went into the break room to get the water, I heard MQ.

"Morris, come on down to the evidence room."

I finished making coffee and walked down the hallway. The door to the evidence room was open and MQ was standing in front of one of the gun locker cabinets, his stubby fingers fumbling with a set of keys. MQ was particularly disheveled for so early in the morning. His suit coat was lying in a heap on a chair. His tie was haphazardly thrown on the floor 4 feet away. Sweat rings darkened the fabric of his maroon shirt. He was exhaling whiskey, adding an extra flavor to the chemical aroma of the evidence room.

"You look a little rough Kenneth. You feel OK today?"

"Doc, man, I feel great, let me tell you, I feel like Julie Andrews. The hills are alive with the sound of bullshit. It is so wonderful to flush our jobs down the toilet," he sang to the melody of the show tune.

MQ stopped singing and stuck a key into one of the locked evidence cabinets. His voice turned deep and ominous, "Watch closely Morris. I am opening up the cabinet which will mark the beginning of the end of my illustrious police career. I am starting down the dark path of unemployment, alcoholism and homelessness. I am hastening the arduous process of self destruction that I began many years ago. No, I don't feel OK doc, and you know why!"

"Perhaps we're right MQ. We prevail and obtain justice while keeping our job, our dignity our credit ratings and our personal lives," I offered, hoping humor would help.

"I can see why you are living in that bachelor pad Doc. Your old lady must have gotten tired of your continual optimism and pollyannic attitude. I don't know how anyone can be so full of shit so early in the morning."

I thought to myself, "A breakfast of Oxycontin, Valium, Duloxetine and Neurontin for starters." In addition to my usual morning breakfast of drug champions, I had taken a .75mg Xanax prophylactically before I left the house. I figured this encounter with the Chief or MQ was coming and I hoped the anxiolytics would help me maintain a professional distance from the case. I didn't want to zone out, get a debilitating headache or shoulder cramp. There was work to do and I hoped I wouldn't be puking into a trash can like a seasick tourist on his first Carnival Cruise.

"Listen, I wrote the memo to the Chief. I purposely did not put your name on it. Don't get involved. I will take the heat. I will push the issue with the Chief and powers to be. You just provide what evidence we do have when necessary."

He stood in front of the cabinet chewing his lip. "You know as well as I do that we are going to work this together, as a team. Fatman and Robin. You know that my conscience won't let me not work it. No, my allopathic friend, we will both go down in flames because of it. Except you can fall back on being a doctor, and I got nothing but this job."

"I'm sorry Kenneth. I should have given you a heads up."

MQ ignored me. "Lieutenant Hebert called me. This, after the Chief called him. The only good news so far, is that Hebert is on board. He said the Wiley case didn't sit well with him either. He'll run interference for us as long as it doesn't involve sticking his neck out far enough to get guillotined. I haven't heard anything from the Chief yet. Hebert recommended we find out what we actually still have in evidence and that is just what I've started to do."

MQ opened the cabinet and stale air rolled out. We put on latex gloves and started removing boxes and bags. We began the meticulous process of reconciling evidence sheets from the Wiley reports to the evidence sheets in MQ's logs and ledgers.

Fortunately, the detectives and patrolmen had followed proper evidence packaging guidelines. The children's clothing and any items exposed to body fluids were stored in brown paper grocery type evidence sacks. This allowed the evidence to dry naturally avoiding mold or bacterial contamination.

MQ opened the rectangular cardboard boxes containing each weapon. Each firearm was properly tagged and had a plastic safety loop through the breach. The barrel of the Remington 12 gauge shotgun was smattered with flakes of dried blood and crusty tissue.

The .22 caliber rifle had a turquoise bath towel duct taped to the end of it's barrel. "What the hell," I said, shaking my head.

"Hmm, don't see that every day. I guess someone thought a towel could function as a noise suppressor." MQ said.

"I read the entire report MQ. There was nothing in there about a homemade silencer on this rifle. Putting a silencer on a weapon used in a murder, says planning and premeditation to me. That would seem to back up their supposition that the husband planned the killings. Of all things, why isn't it in the report?"

MQ was quiet and stared at the rifle. The question was probably tumbling around in his head like bingo balls in a drum. The balls finally settled and he answered. "Because the arrogant, egotistical bastards didn't care what was in the report or in evidence. They never expected anyone to read it or ask questions, or ever open these boxes."

MQ picked the rifle up by it's checkered wood stock where prints would be unobtainable. As he placed it on the workbench, a bullet fell from the towel and clunked onto the table.

"What the hell? How did somebody at the lab miss that?" MQ said.

"MQ, have you noticed something about these weapons?"

"What?"

"There's no fingerprint dust on our gloves. I don't think anyone printed the weapons."

MQ looked at his gloved hands. "Well, that explains the bullet from the towel. No one at the county lab examined this rifle which means it was probably never test fired for ballistics. Now the level on my conspiratorial meter is rising."

"Well Murph, there's one good thing. There's a box of the .22 ammunition and five extra 12 gauge shotgun shells that the lab can use for residue testing. Bryson signed the evidence sheet on these, so he must have found them in the workshop or house."

"A ray of sunshine in an otherwise tornadic day," he said.

The professional distance I had hoped to maintain, rapidly diminished as MQ opened the thin, rectangular, edged evidence box commonly used for knives, swords and machetes. As the box opened, a hint of the distinctive smell of musty human decomposition marched out, the unmistakable smell of death. Even after all this time, it was as if the machete were proclaiming how well it had done it's part in the killings.

The entire 12" blade was covered in dried, crusted blood and dark, scablike tissue. Still glued to the blade were long, blonde, matted, strands of hair in a sanguineous brown honey-comb.

My ability to compartmentalize vanished. In an instant, I was no longer an objective observer, I had become a participant. I felt a cold whoosh down my back and smelled damp, stale basement air. It reminded me of the box, the enclosed stairwell my stepmother used for punishment. I reflexively shivered and I felt terrified. My heart started to pound, my chest hurt and I became nauseous. I knew the symptoms. Despite .75 mg of Xanax, I was having another heart/anxiety attack.

I started to pant trying to catch my breath. A muscle spasm struck my left shoulder blade with white hot fire. The pain was so intense, it temporarily overshadowed the anxiety. I left the evidence room, returned to my office and took two Flexerils and another Oxy.

I was unaware at the time that a train carrying two small children and their father had just passed by. They had reached out and tapped my shoulder. They were letting me know that they had waited long enough. It was time. The tapping had begun.

I closed the door to my office, turned off the light, and sat back in my chair. I did Sheila's breathing technique and concentrated on slowing my respiratory rate and pulse. After about 30 minutes, the mix of meds in my system lowered the level of pain and fear and I returned to work.

"Where the hell did you go?" MQ asked.

"Sorry, I had to take a phone call. Something at the clinic," I answered.

"Doc, after seeing all this, I need a break. I've got a few reports to go through. Then, let us go find sustenance." MQ shook out his coat, and locked the evidence room.

"Yea, a break would probably help."

Over an early lunch at a nearby Outback Steakhouse, we discussed options.

MQ pontificated, "This is going to be a defecating firestorm of biblical proportions. I mean the eruption of Mount Vesuvius will be considered a minor burp, compared to the tsunami we are going to produce. Opening a supposedly solved and closed murder/suicide case, with the implication that our department and the prosecutor's office fucked up, and that a murderer might have gotten away, is going to be as much of a political clusterfuck as a Monica Lewinsky blowjob or the Iraq War. Throw in the fact that there are Scalini's involved", he looked up to the heavens, "Blessed Mother of Calcutta, help us."

I had no appetite and picked at my chicken Caesar salad, "So, what are our best options going forward?"

"You opened Pandora's box, what would you like to do Morris?"

I thought for a moment. "I'd really like to go to the scene of the crime, the house, take a look around. Were you ever in there, at the scene?"

"No, no I was not, and I am damn glad that I don't have that first hand carnage cart-wheeling around in my head. The crime scene photos are quite enough. I see your point though. Going there now could be advantageous. We'd have a better perspective on where the key players were when whatever happened, happened. There are new owners. Mrs. Wiley never moved back in."

He stroked his dimpled chin as worry set in. "But, on the other hand, it may be a bit perilous to go to there. The new homeowners may not appreciate two detectives walking through their house. What if they complain to Montileone?"

"No harm in going by and trying to schmooze them into letting us take a look."

"You can be the primary schmoozer then. We'll embark on the Wiley debacle tomorrow."

"Have you given any thought to an overall investigative strategy?" I asked.

MQ mulled my words around as he sucked down the last of the dark beer foam from the glass, "I think our best bet will be to gather support from any of our peers who worked the case and may also have doubts." He waved to the waitress and pointed down at his empty glass.

"Let's face it, you're not Chief's golden boy anymore since your Mexican hat dance, and I have never been anything to him but a boil on his skinny ass. If we can garner a cohort of congruence amongst our fellow officers, guys who are not hemorrhoids to the Chief, we would increase the odds that Montileone will understand the implications this case holds. He's going to suffer through the usual paranoiac worries whether a cold case will reflect poorly on his ability as a Chief, but if we find enough sympathetic officers, especially members of the command staff like Lieutenant Hebert, we'll be in a better position. Let's do some recruiting for our cause."

"Yea, I agree with you MQ. Safety in numbers. In fact, I have a list of people, cops and otherwise, that I want to talk to."

"I'm sure you do Doc," MQ said, smiling at his fresh Guinness.

# Chapter Twenty Nine

The suburban home in which the Wiley children were brutally murdered, was a split level ranch at the crest of a cul-de-sac in a quiet part of town that rarely required the attention of law enforcement. A short time after the murders, Mrs. Wiley sold the house. I pulled up property records on the computer. The new owners are Pasha and Sofia Demitrov.

MQ parked our Crown Vic on the street. I took a minute, looking out my window at the residence. It hadn't changed much from it's appearance in the paltry set of crime scene photos.

The house was still sided with dark rough cedar, above a veneer of beige stucco and brick. The lawn was well kept, but simple, no elaborate landscaping, no stair step keystone walls or Chinese fountains. The garage doors were closed. In the rear of that garage, there was, or still is, a workshop where the lives of two children were taken.

On a cloudless and cool day, the air having the feel of fresh and clean satin bed sheets, I knocked on the Demitrov's front door.

Mr. Demitrov answered in a wife beater T-shirt, khaki cargo shorts and sandals. He was 50 something, 5'8", bald, probably tipped the scales over 200lbs with a barrel chest and a solid gut. His beefy forearms and thick digits said he was accustomed to working with his hands. He was sweating and out of breath, a hammer was dangling from his right hand.

"Good morning," We held up our badges. "I am Det. Morris Green with your police department. This is Sgt. Murphy-Quinn. Can we talk to you for a minute?"

Mr. Demitrov's bushy eyebrows arched, "Oh," is all he said and motioned for us to come in. The hammer clunked as he put it down on an entryway table.

"How can I help my police?" He spoke with a choppy, Eastern bloc accent.

Over the next few minutes we learned that the Demitrovs had emigrated to Israel during the breakup of the Soviet Union. They had come from Poland, the "old country." Their son, Ori, moved to the US for a 'goot job' in the late 1990's, taking the grandchildren. Mr. Demitrov sold his Israeli butcher shop and they moved here to be close to their son and grandkids. He looked like a man that would be comfortable in a white butcher's apron surgically wielding a meat cleaver over a Kosher calf.

MQ asked if he was aware that an "incident" had happened in his home. He was about to answer when Mrs. Demitrov entered the room.

"Ah, this my wife Sofia."

She was wearing white canvas bib overall shorts without a shirt underneath. Her face and chest were dotted with freckles. Well demarcated cleavage stared back at us. She used the back of her hand to wipe away a sheen of perspiration from her forehead.

Judging by the shallow etched smile lines and light crow's feet, she was probably a little younger than her husband, perhaps in her early forties, but she was still strikingly attractive with sharp cheekbones and deep emerald green, oval eyes. Sofia had long auburn hair that was loosely tied back with a red bandana. Large strands of bangs framed her angular face. She was a few inches taller than Pasha and possessed a hardbody that 30 year olds obsessively go to the gym to obtain.

The Demitrovs said that during the sale of the house, the realtor disclosed that there had been deaths in the house and garage. Sofia said, "We come from Israel, where death of innocents happens often. We were aware, but it did not stop us. Our son and grandchildren live nearby, so we move here. If children died here, their soul is with God. Not in this house."

I would soon find reason to challenge that assumption.

We explained that the original investigation of the murders had been completed. However, we were conducting what was called a "Cold Case" investigation.

"Sgt. Quinn and I have discovered some unanswered questions as to exactly how the murders occurred. Neither of us worked the initial investigation so we're looking at it with two sets of fresh eyes. The reason we are here is that we wanted to see the layout of the home to get a perspective on what happened where. If it's not too much trouble, could you walk us through the house? We understand that if this is not a good time we can come back."

Pasha motioned for us to follow him. "Please, do your job. We are building dry sauna in one of the rooms, so excuse mess," Pasha said. "You must see." He led us down the stairs to the lower level of the home to the master bedroom.

It was at the west end of the home. Pasha was quite proud of the sauna. "Sofia and me, we love heat. The "shvitz", very good for you, keep you clean, lungs open, young. You see how good Sofia looks," he pointed at his wife like he was showing us Door #3. "Schvitz."

He put his arm around her waist. A faint blush came over her face.

The sauna was built in the walk-in closet of the master bedroom on the lower level. This had been the Wiley's bedroom, the room where Julie Wiley was allegedly tied to the bed by her husband, choked and anally raped. The shotgun had been taken from the closet of this room, the closet that was now a sauna. Pasha opened the door of the sauna and dry heat spilled out.

"Desert heat, Israeli heat," I thought.

Pasha walked in, motioned for us and we followed. A small cedar bucket with water and Eucalyptus branches sat on a bench. Pasha grabbed the stems, reached around and struck his back, then his chest with the leaves.

MQ and I were splashed like the front row pew in a Catholic mass. Sofia and Pasha laughed.

"Eucalyptus, good for lungs and skin."

"It smells wonderful Mr. Demitrov. I bet this does clean out your sinuses," I said taking in a deep breath through my nose.

"You come, you both come, anytime. Take schvitz. Now, do what you need to."

We stepped out of the sauna and started our work. MQ videotaped the bedroom and hallway. I took measurements with a tape.

Sitting on the bed, I looked out the doorway of the master bedroom. All I could see was a long hallway. Midway down the hall, was a closed door which led to the furnace and laundry room. At the end of the hallway, was the den where Craig Wiley was found, seated in his recliner, a shotgun gracefully poised upright between his legs. I recalled the crime scene photos of this room. Craig Wiley's head and its contents were sprayed on the ceiling and walls. Blood covered the right side of the recliner as Craig Wiley's heart managed to pump out a good pint or so with it's last effort after his head was undocked.

Pasha and Sofia had no idea that their elegant, purple, satin couch was along the wall Craig's eyes, skull and brain had been stippled and sloshed.

The ceiling where the shotgun slug and wadding had penetrated after passing through Craig's head had been repaired. The Demitrov's had redone the ceiling with an ornate 2' square, white, drop tin ceiling. They had textured the walls with designs by sponges, and putty knives.

I took a few more measurements in the den. MQ finished videotaping and taking digital pictures of the entire downstairs. We went upstairs and walked along a wrought iron banister, towards the hallway leading to the bedrooms.

In the crime scene photos, Taylor Wiley's tennis shoes were in the middle of these steps, one lay on its side, the other overturned, laces still tied in a double bow. Her pink windbreaker was draped over the banister, a doll box lay empty.

We took more measurements, pictures and video, and went down the hallway to the children's bedrooms on the upper level. The Demitrovs had turned Robbie Wiley's room into a computer study.

Taylor's room was now their grandchildren's play and sleepover room. A TV, DVD/VCR player, Wii controllers and a PC were stacked on a wall unit and desk. Two twin beds along the walls were neatly made with quilt comforters.

MQ and I went to the garage. The last area to video was the workshop where the children were murdered. I recalled the crime scene photos. There were shelves on which golf clubs, pairs of rollerblades and ice skates were arranged in line by size next to some baseball equipment.

The Demitrov's shelving contained boxes with Hebrew lettering and a few odd and antiquated looking meat slicers and butcher block boards.

The next room, had been Craig Wiley's workshop.

I spoke softly to MQ, "This workshop is a long way from that downstairs master bedroom where Mrs. Wiley was tied up. She couldn't see it for sure, and at this distance how could she hear anything from the bedroom? How could she know those kids were in the workshop?"

"Isn't the old saying it's a mystery wrapped in an enigma?" MQ said, a sour look on his face.

As we spoke, my left shoulder twitched and a jolt of pain radiated up to the back of my neck. The rumble of a headache filtered through the morning's Oxycontin. I gulped some air and turned away from MQ and entered the workshop.

The L-shaped work bench that took up nearly the entire western wall and part of the north wall looked the same as it did in the crime scene photos. In Craig Wiley's workshop, his tools neatly hung on pegboard above the workbench and assorted hardware, paint, screws and nails were symmetrically placed on shelves. Two orange extension cords were neatly looped and hung on hooks.

The Demitrov's workshop was filled with woodworking tools, a power miter saw, a band saw, a sander, circle saws, a router and a drill press. A rake, a spade and a shovel stood in a far corner covered in a light coat of sawdust.

Peeking from behind the ignored lawn and garden tools, I recognized several dark, ladybug sized elliptical stains on the unpainted drywall. They were unmistakable, blood stain droplets. These were droplets that had flown off the machete as it was wielded by the killer. I looked overhead and noticed several more on the ceiling. My eye traced an arc, an arc of blood spatter with each successive chop into Taylor Wiley's skull. MQ took a number of digital pictures, videotaped the room and measured the blood spatter. I scraped the droplets off the wall and ceiling, taking a little of the paper backing of the drywall with it. I looked over at Pasha and apologized.

Mr. Demitrov smiled and said, "CSI, right?"

"Something like that, yes," I said, and put the evidence in an envelope.

MQ touched a friendly hand to Pasha's forearm, "Mr. Demitrov, this is a very sensitive matter. We would appreciate if you could keep our visit here something between the four of us."

Pasha looked at Sofia, "I was in Israeli Defense Force for many years. Sofia in army. We know how to keep secret. Don't worry."

I threw my notepad in the backseat of the Crown Vic and laid my head back on the headrest. "Blood spatter never photographed or retrieved, still on the wall and ceiling. Hell, I'm no spatter expert MQ, but I bet we can get an idea of the height of the perpetrator by the position and shape of the arched blood droplets."

"Precisely," MQ said.

My shoulder felt as if was being tapped with a steel icicle from a blacksmith's forge. MQ drove directly to Lucky's Bar and Grill just outside of town and we dove headfirst into Scotch and water. We finished our shift at the bar, thankful that the dispatcher did not call upon us to work any fresh crime scenes.

# Chapter Thirty

Hangovers notwithstanding, the plan for the following day included our search for allies in the quest for the truth in the Wiley case.

The first two officers on my list to interview and hopefully swing to our side were Sgt. Martin Weingart and Det. Elwyn Bryson. Weingart was an intolerant, loudmouth prick, but he was a decent cop. As luck would have it, Weingart was watch commander of his patrol squad that morning. MQ called him on the radio and asked him to come to the bureau office. A few minutes later, Herr Weingart appeared.

Sgt. Martin Bruno Weingart was tall, sinewy and foreboding with black and silver short cropped hair underneath his creased, 8-point police uniform hat. A serious man with a thin, well trimmed moustache cut to military specs at the corners of his mouth. His Clarino gun belt glistened, and his gold badge, belt keepers and service stars sparkled from the shining with Brasso he probably gave them every morning.

His shoes reflected the fluorescent light upwards toward crisp pant pleats, a straight gig line, and a starched uniform shirt. He looked like every command officer on a police academy recruiting poster.

Weingart stepped into MQ's doorway. "What do you two clowns want this morning? I haven't written the obligatory two moving traffic violations for Montileone, nor have I driven a circumference around Hooterville yet." He tucked his hat under his left arm and sat down in one of the chairs across from MQ's desk. The only thing he didn't do was click his heels together, salute and say Heil Hitler.

I leaned against the door frame next to Weingart's chair and spoke first. "Sarge, I was going through some old cases and came across the Wiley file."

Sgt. Weingart twisted in his chair and squared off with me, "For Chrissake Green! Haven't you raised enough hell around here? The last bullshit you started damn near got you killed and put Tom Reynolds in a chair. And he was a good man."

Weingart had struck below the belt. That was not how I had hoped the initial interviews would proceed.

"You know better, you asshole," I said. "It was a planned assassination during a drug deal. Don't hang anything on me when you have shit from the Wiley case all over you. You have two innocent, dead children and their innocent father dangling above your New World Order blockhead!"

Sgt. Weingart abruptly stood and poked a drill instructor's finger into my chest. "You don't know a fucking thing GreenBERG! Doctor, playing cop. Leave this job to the real police."

We were nose to nose. I could smell Weingart's Old Spice and anger. My right hand was flexing into a fist for a haymaker that was on its way in a nanosecond. For a short, stubby man, MQ was quick and agile. He was out of his chair, around his desk and in between us, pushing us apart as my arm was rearing back.

"Boys, we're all on the same side here. What do you say we all put our egos and big shwantzes away for ten minutes?" He put a hand on each of our shoulders edging us towards the chairs in front of his desk.

Weingart and I sat down slowly eyeballing each other. MQ cautiously went back behind his desk.

I defused more quickly, probably because of the 1mg Xanax I'd taken, "Yea. Well, you hit a sour chord Sarge."

"Well, you did too Green," he paused, settled back into his chair. He leaned back and crossed his legs, ankle over knee. "I don't know what the fuck you want to open that can of worms for. It's over and done. The prosecutor agreed that it was a murder and suicide. The dad went nuts and killed his kids, simple as that. And I'm glad the prick blew his Goddamn head off after what he did to those kids. I can still see it. It was as fucking bad as I had seen in a long time." He paused and looked deeply at the carpeting.

"Martin, you are probably the most experienced officer this department has," I said, stroking his ego, in preparation for what I wanted from him. "I am sure while you were in the city, you worked more violent offenses than most of the cops here in Hooterville ever will during their entire career. I read in the report that you and Elwyn interviewed Julie Wiley the night of the murders. You guys were sharp enough to give her Miranda rights in the event she made any incriminating statements. You must have felt that something was wrong. That maybe she was more than just an innocent victim. Your instincts told you she was being deceptive. Your gut told you that she was hiding something. That she was lying for some reason. Elwyn even wrote that she was deceptive in his report. What did she have to lie about Sarge? Her children had just been brutally murdered by their father. They screamed and cried. They were confused. Why is daddy hurting us? Where is mommy?"

I paused. Weingart was burning holes through the carpeting head slowly turning side to side. I was onto something and continued to drive the truck through the tunnel.

"Or did they ask, 'Why is mommy hurting us?' Martin, you sensed something didn't you? You knew she was hiding something. What was it?"

The room was still. Sgt. Weingart's head bobbed slightly up and down. He crossed his arms over his chest. After a moment, he looked up. His face was flushed and his eyes were moist.

The normally stoic and antiseptic Sgt. Martin Weingart was sniffling, his eyes tearing. His typically deep, demanding voice, now raspy coated with anger and a twang of despair, "That bitch left her house without knowing what happened to her kids. A mother does not leave her kids. She fights to the death for her kids. That bitch left," he paused for a few seconds, nostrils flaring as he gathered some air to continue what was obviously painful. "So, when we brought her in, Bryson and I suspected she was somehow involved. So, we Mirandized her. This was about, maybe 5 hours after her kids were murdered and her husband killed himself. She'd been to the hospital and we had her brought in. And this bitch was composed! She was overly helpful and polite. She wasn't hysterical or anything you would expect given the circumstances. It was bullshit! We asked her questions about what happened in the house. About what happened that day. About what ticked her old man off. About where she was when her husband was killing her kids."

"So, what did she tell you Martin?" MQ asked.

Weingart uncrossed his legs and leaned forward, "First she started off with some cockamamie story about being drugged and couldn't remember what happened. Then, she was all over the board, inconsistent, failing to make eye contact, looking down too often, squirming in her chair, crossing her arms and legs, twirling her hair. And she started a lot of her sentences with, "Honestly" or "As best I recall" or "As God is my witness", or "I swear." You guys have been to all the interview and interrogation courses. She did everything, every damn thing that nervous, guilty people do when they are caught."

I leaned forward towards Sgt. Weingart. "You suspected then and I bet to this very day, that she had something to do with those kid's murders. Why didn't you guys follow through?"

I wanted to add, "You looked the other way, just like you probably would have during the Holocaust."

Weingart snorted back some snot and then took out a handkerchief, blowing his nose and wiping his eyes. He spoke, voice still shaky. "I sure didn't expect to get emotional about that fucking case again."

He paused and straightened up, composing himself, "I have grandkids about that age and it really connects when I think about this case. I don't like to think about it. Anyway, I was off duty for several days after the murders. It was the bureau's problem. By the time I got back, Johnson and Newsham took it over. NMP, not my problem. Fucking Will Newsham, the brown-nosing twat, was running the investigation. Montileone's new pet. He became the golden boy after you Green."

"What the fuck are you talking about?" I asked.

"Come on Green. Montileone loved your ass. Athelete, college boy. You guys ran what, a dozen marathons together? And he lets you take leave, unpaid time off, to go to Mexico or whatever diploma mill medical school you went to. And lets you keep your fucking job! You were his golden boy. Of course that was until you capped those beaners and brought the kind of publicity he doesn't like. Since Montileone couldn't call on you that night because you got yourself and Tom shot up, it opened the door for Chatham Newsham's baby to become his new butt boy. No pun intended."

Weingart shook his head. "We didn't know it until the next day that the bitch was a Scalini. Once we found that out, everyone figured out PDQ why Montileone put Newsham in the middle of it. He probably got a call from the fucking Newsham Law Firm who said it would be good experience for his boy. The unsaid reason, she was a Scalini. So Chief put boy wonder in it to keep anything bad from happening to one of the family's own. Will Newsham stuck his fucking nose in the murders like he was some type of Columbo. He spent a lot of time with the bitch. Maybe he was fucking her, although I'm not sure she's his type, if you know what I mean. Anyway that prick couldn't solve a trespassing, much less a murder. He wouldn't make a pimple on the ass of a real policeman, the brown-nosing shit. No pun intended."

"Don't hold back now, tell us how you really feel Martin." MQ's sarcasm moderated Weingart's rant.

"Yea, right. I forgot. It's not politically correct to call it as you see it anymore. Fucking bullshit! Anyway, I was running a squad of patrol officers. My boys wrote the initial report of the murders. The detective bureau had the case, so I let it go."

"Doesn't look like you let it go to me Marty. Looks like you still have some issues with this case," MQ said. "Seriously, what do you think happened? What did she feel the need to lie about?"

Weingart tucked the handkerchief into his back pocket and clenched his jaw a couple of times. "I think she may have killed her husband and made up the story about him committing suicide. Maybe he didn't have the guts to pull the trigger. So she did it for him. And maybe that's why she was so squirrelly during our interview."

"That's one theory anyway. What part do you think she played in the murder of the children?" I asked.

Weingart took in a deep breath and paused for a few seconds. "I don't think she did the kids. You look at the crime scene photographs?"

MQ and I both nodded.

"I was there. I saw it firsthand. It was, well it was Goddamn horrifying. I just didn't see her as that much of a maniac. I could see her killing the old man. Hell, they all want to kill us at some point. But I didn't think she would kill her kids, her own flesh and blood."

"The more we look into this case, the more questions come up," MQ said. "We discovered that her Miranda form and the video of your interview never made it into evidence. Who had the DVR and the rights form the last time you saw them?"

"Bryson had it all. When she left the station with her mother, I remember he took the DVR and Miranda form into his office. That was the last I saw of any of it. Elwyn kept hold of everything. Ask him," Weingart said, his usual abrasive and clipped speech returning.

He stood and put his hat on.

"Are we done? I have to get back on the road."

"Yea. Thanks for taking the time to talk to us Marty," MQ said.

Before he left, he offered some words of wisdom, "If you open this case up, even if you're right about something, you'll find yourself in a world of shit, or worse." Three goosesteps and he was gone.

I closed the door to MQ's office. "Kenneth, now that was weird. Who would have ever thought Weingart would cry."

"No shit!" MQ agreed, "The dispassionate and normally brusque Colonel Klink showed an emotion that did not originate from testosterone. Very unexpected."

"This case keeps getting more interesting every day," I said.

"Yes, a labyrinth of telescopic hemorrhoids my good doctor detective."

"At least Martin is in agreement that there may be more to the mystery," I said. "Even if it is that she killed her husband."

MQ pulled up the work schedule on his computer screen. "Elwyn is off today. How about we talk to Newsham, apparently your replacement as butt boy for the Chief?"

"Butt boy bullshit."

"Hey doc, at least for a while you were in the center ring at the Oakview PD circus. I certainly never have been."

"Well, if I was, you can see where it got me?" I said pointing to my scarred right eye.

"Let's talk to Newsham as soon as we can," MQ said. "Weingart will undoubtedly mention our meeting at shift change. He'll call us incendiary provocateurs of the first degree. He'll tell his boys that we are way out of our league. It will get back to Newsham quickly, so we may as well strike first. I'll call him and get him to come in."

I refilled my coffee cup, checked voice and emails and waited for MQ to advise when our next step in the trials of Job would occur.

# Chapter Thirty One

Will Newsham was not in his office. MQ called his cell. Newsham said he was having a new hot water heater installed and wasn't coming in for a few hours. MQ asked him to stop by the bureau office on the way in. He was deliberately evasive, telling Newsham there were some evidence storage problems.

The Newsham family tree was crooked from a seedling. Granddaddy Augustus Newsham, founder of the Newsham Law Firm, was alleged to have been a loan shark and to have run illegal liquor and gambling operations in addition to his lawyering. His firm provided service to many organized crime figures in the early days. They had all made a fortune in real estate investments in Las Vegas.

Will Newsham's father, Chatham, and brother Spencer, are the principals in the Newsham and Newsham, LLC, law firm with offices in Chicago, St. Louis, Washington DC, New York and Las Vegas.

Over the past sixty plus years, the Newsham's have represented members of the Scalini family in various business and criminal matters. They are very good. Very few Scalinis have ever served significant time.

The Scalinis are suspects in the usual fare of organized crime activities, prostitution, gambling and, as Tom and I suspected, heroin trafficking and attempted murder.

Will is the baby of the Newsham clan with two older brothers and one older sister. The eldest boy, Spencer, graduated from Harvard Law and clerked for an Appellate Judge in Washington DC for two years, before becoming partner in the family business. The other brother, Mark, works for the State Department in Washington DC. Their sister is a stay at home mom in Ohio.

Will was an accident. His mother was 40, and his father had just turned 44 when he was born. As is often the case with the youngest, he was spoiled. He was accustomed to getting what he wanted, when he wanted it. And initially, Will wanted nothing to do with the family business.

Chatham had hoped that his youngest would join him in the firm and demanded that Will attend Harvard. Will had no intention of going east or working in the firm. He was different than his brothers. He had other interests and desires.

Will rebelled and a split developed between father and son. He moved to San Francisco. He attended San Francisco State University on student loans and earned a BA in criminal justice studies.

Will Newsham became a cop to further distance himself from the family and what he knew of his father's most important client. He took a job with the Carmel, California Police Department. It was a nice, easy going area with tall palm trees, coffee shops, and art galleries on nearly every street in the downtown area. However, he quickly realized that a law enforcement salary would not support the accoutrements to which he was accustomed. He joined the Army Reserves for an extra paycheck. He was acting in ways not expected of a Newsham.

Will struggled for a few years trying to remain independent. Out of desperation, when rent, car payments and student loan debt became overwhelming, he recontacted his father. Chatham came out to the coast a few times for extended weekends. They went on fishing trips, rafting and took in a few weekends of gambling in Vegas. Will liked the lifestyle his father's money brought, but still wanted the excitement and power that law enforcement and the military offered. Chatham offered his youngest a deal he could not refuse.

Chatham had a number of contacts in the law enforcement community and would find Will a position with a local police agency near home. Daddy would supplement his police and military reserve salaries for work Will would do 'on the side' for the firm, and daddy would pay off his student loan if Will came home.

Chatham Newsham knew that, as a member of the law enforcement community, Will could provide valuable inside information. Since the information would be coming directly from a family member, it could be trusted by his firm and his clients. This was something that could not be said with officers on the take or information from snitches. Trusted, valid intelligence was invaluable and Will would be paid accordingly. Will accepted the deal, moved home and took the job Chief Montileone was told to offer.

There is no denying that Will Newsham is intelligent. He probably has an IQ in the high 120s to low 130s. However, being smart does not necessarily translate into being a good police officer.

It typically takes several years for a police officer to acquire a sixth sense, the intuitive inkling that tells him to drive around to the rear of a warehouse, where, almost magically, he finds a broken window and catches a burglar. The instinct that will tell him that danger is close, that he should wear a bulletproof vest or carry a backup piece. The instinct that said don't let the Mexicans in the apartment until your team arrives. Just because you ignore that still small voice, does not make it any less valuable to a cop.

Newsham could be a cop for fifty years and he would never develop that police sense. Weingart was right. Will couldn't solve a grocery store robbery with video and five eyewitnesses. It's just not in his genetic makeup.

However, he made up for this lack of police ability with administrative proficiency. Will was able to advance his law enforcement career by playing politics and using his family's connections. Newsham became Chief Montileone's administrative aide. He excelled at filing the required state and federal law enforcement reports and at obtaining grants for equipment and resources. For a few years, Will took a load of clerical grief off the Chief's table.

Chief Montileone bypassed the usual promotional statistics such as number of arrests, convictions, and felony investigations required to test for advanced rank. He promoted his administrative aide to Sergeant. Chief explained that the lack of other suitable candidates forced an exception. That was a real morale booster to ten year patrolmen with great stats.

Around the same time that I was assigned to the Undercover Narcotics unit, a spot on the Metropolitan Vice Squad became available. As we later learned, Chief Montileone received a phone call from Daddy Chatham to facilitate Will's appointment to Vice. Montileone was not very happy to lose his aide and offered a mild protest. Chatham Newsham assured the Chief that the transfer of Will to the Vice Squad would be a "good thing" for him and the Oakview Police Department. With a wave of the magic Scalini-Newsham-Montileone wand, Will became a Vice Squad Detective. Their squad consisted of officers from the city, several counties and a number of municipalities. In that regard, it was similar to our drug task force.

Will spent his time monitoring complaints about prostitution at strip clubs or motels and reports of illegal gambling. The unit made some low level arrests but no large scale vice operations were uncovered while Newsham was assigned. Imagine that.

Vice Detective Sgt. Will Newsham was tasked by his father, with the responsibility of assuring that the Bullpen activities remained under the radar of law enforcement. To accomplish this mission, Will became associated with Vinny Scalini and James Patrick. During Will's assignment to the Vice Squad, the Scalini's Bullpen operation flourished.

In the interim between my death and the discovery of the Wiley file, the Chief promoted Will to Lieutenant after a skewed promotional process in which somehow all the other candidates, including MQ, scored poorly on tests. At the time of the cold case, we were dealing with Lt. Will Newsham.

# Chapter Thirty Two

The hot water heater was being installed in the house that Will shared with Oakview Detective Lawrence Johnson. Lawrence Johnson was at the other end of the IQ chart. Lawrence's bulb did not burn very brightly. He had developed a good policeman's knack, he just rarely wanted to use it. His personal life had been in the shitter for such a long time, that all he was interested in was bowling, fishing and beer.

Lawrence Johnson met his wife to be, Charlene, while they were both students at a local private college. Charlene had flaming red hair, silky skin and long legs. She was every bit of 5'10" with a lean, runway model figure that captured Lawrence's attention.

Lawrence had been a star high-school running back and was attending on an athletic scholarship, hoping to be drafted by the NFL. Charlene was studying accounting and tutoring struggling students, like Lawrence.

A knee injury ended Lawrence's professional football dreams. He defaulted to a career in law enforcement. He and Charlene dated, married, and promptly had two boys within their first five years of marriage. He was a decent father to his toddlers, but their marriage was bracketed with frustration and confusion. Charlene knew something wasn't right. She sensed the distance in their marriage and attributed it to the demands of the police work and the distraction of two young children.

Her momma and daddy told her it was her job to make her man happy. Charlene Johnson did her best Tammy Wynette, kept a clean home, raised the children and worked part time as a bookkeeper at a printing company. She tried to make Lawrence happy, but nothing worked. He found fault in everything she did and she became increasingly frustrated and confused.

One evening, she received an anonymous phone call. "I just want to let you know that your husband is screwing around with a nurse working the midnight shift at St. Marks Hospital."

"Who is this? What do you want?"

"We're both in the same boat honey. Our spouses have screwed us over."

"You don't know what you're talking about."

"Oh, I know enough Mrs. Johnson. I caught them in my bed, in my house and threw their asses out of my place."

"You don't even know me or my husband. Who is this?"

"I can tell you that your husband has a port wine stain the size of a softball on his left butt cheek. How about that?"

"That bastard," Charlene uttered as she threw the phone. Rather than confront her husband immediately, she called her brother Ronald.

Lawrence was working for the county police department at the time, on a permanent graveyard shift. Ronald followed him from place to place until Lawrence ended up in the driveway in front of St. Marks Hospital around 2am. A figure in a white uniform came out of the main entrance and got into Lawrence's car.

Ronald followed them to a condominium complex a short distance away. Lawrence pulled his police cruiser into the garage and the door closed behind it. The couple exited the garage through a side door. Glowing under the mercury vapor lamp, Ronald eyed his brother-in-law and another man in white, walking arm in arm to the front door of the condo.

Ronald called Charlene and gave his surveillance report. She didn't want to believe him. She woke her neighbor and asked her to watch the kids for an hour, feigning a family emergency. She drove to the condo and sat in Ronald's car.

Thirty minutes later, brother and sister watched two men walk out of the condo as the garage door opened. They paused, and under the yellow mist of the overhead light, the men kissed, after which Nurse John went back in the condo.

"That bastard. That cheating fag bastard!" Charlene screamed.

Lawrence started to back his patrol car out of the garage.

Ron pulled his car behind Lawrence's cruiser. Charlene stumbled as she hastily got out of the car.

"What the hell," Lawrence said as Charlene regained her footing and came towards him "Charlene?"

She slapped Lawrence across the face and screamed a flea market of obscenities at him. Charlene cried so hard she vomited on Lawrence's uniform.

Ronald stared at Lawrence and shook his head. He put his arm around his sister's shoulder and walked her back to the car.

Despite his pleas and supplications and his offer to go to counseling, Charlene would not have their children raised by a homosexual, and a cheating homo at that. Her strict Baptist upbringing would not allow any such arrangement.

A good lawyer and a conservative Judge resulted in Charlene's ownership of a good portion of Lawrence's salary and pension. Lawrence eventually left the county police, but the judgment followed him to the Oakview PD.

Over the years, Lawrence's once muscular frame had been jelly rolled, fried chickened and beaten by life, into its current state of disrepair. He had diabetes, high blood pressure and suffered from cardiac arrhythmias.

On a few occasions, when he stopped taking his meds, he passed out. One day in the detective office he slid to the floor like a sack of potatoes. He woke up as two paramedics struggled to put his bulk on a stretcher. A twenty-four hour Holter cardiac monitor discovered that Johnson's heart rate occasionally maxed out at over 220 beats per minute. He had developed a condition known as "SVT" Supraventricular Tachycardia. When his heart ran at that fast clip for any length of time, the pump failed to supply enough blood to the brain and it was lights out for Lawrence.

His doctor managed the condition with a prescription for Inderal, a medication that slows the electrical conduction of the heart. The medication enhanced Lawrence's predilection for inaction, but for the most part, it kept him upright.

Lt. Will Newsham arrived at the station in the early afternoon. He'd had a dedicated hot water heater installed to accommodate the new hot tub that he and Lawrence had recently purchased. Lt. Newsham strolled into MQ's empty office.

Finding no one there, Newsham yelled out, "Where are you guys?"

"Across the hall in evidence," MQ bellowed.

Will came into the evidence storage room. He picked up a glass ashtray lying on one of the evidence shelving units and held it up to the light as if he were examining the quality of Swarovski crystal.

MQ looked over at the chubby, rubor-cheeked, boy Lieutenant.

"Great work Will. That's from the burglary on Stafford Lane. I was going to superglue fume it for prints. We think the perp picked it up. Just like you did. Thanks a lot."

"Oh, man, sorry. I didn't know," he said, gingerly replacing the ash tray on the shelf.

An irritated MQ yelled out, "Morris, come on down will you? Lt. Newsham has made his grand entry."

I stepped into the room from the hallway. We had planned how to optimize our contact with Will. I began with basic interview dynamics. First, give your subject a command to follow which subliminally places the interviewer in a position of dominance and control.

"Lieutenant, come over to my office and we can sit in there while MQ finishes up in the vault."

I waited for Newsham to leave the evidence room and then followed him to my office. I pointed at a chair and said, "Have a seat."

Newsham obeyed and took one of the cheap, institutional, orange plastic chairs in front of my desk. I settled into the chair behind my desk. We chatted briefly about the new room addition. I listened to the freely flowing banal information about a glass walled shower, the gallons per minute and water jets per side of the hot tub.

I asked a few questions about the tub and took mental notes of his body language and voice tonality as he discussed these non-critical issues. After a few minutes, I had a pretty good baseline of his vocal quality and physical behavior while he discussed non-stressful issues. I was confident that there was going to be a change as soon as we inserted our concerns about the Wiley case into the conversation. I hoped he would get as jumpy as a poodle at a Mongolian BBQ.

MQ came into the office, sleeves rolled up, tie loosened three inches, wiping away a few beads of forehead sweat with a handkerchief. He sat in the other crappy chair, next to Newsham.

"What did you need MQ?" Will asked.

"I don't know if you've heard, but we are revisiting the Wiley case. The result of your investigation always seemed a bit ambiguous to me. Doc kind of stumbled on it the other day and read through it, and we found some things left undone."

"So I heard. Like what?" Will asked.

"The way I read it Lieutenant," I said, "Your premise was that Mr. Wiley bought the weapons he used, a machete and a .22 rifle, with the intention of killing his family-a premeditated murder. I'm not so sure about that. We looked at the photos you guys took. The crime scene speaks of spontaneous rage. When you were at the scene, did you look at Mr. Wiley's workshop? It was meticulously organized. Wiley was a neat freak. A place for everything, everything in its place. In my opinion, if this guy was planning to kill his family, it wouldn't have been the disorganized bloody, rage fueled massacre I saw in the crime scene pictures."

I noticed that Newsham dry swallowed several times before he spoke. He shifted positions in his chair and crossed his arms over his chest. "So, that's your opinion. So what if he was neat. The guy snapped."

I continued, "There are some unanswered questions especially dealing with motive. No one developed any definitive reasons why Mr. Wiley wanted his family dead, and this whole drugged and raped story of Mrs. Wiley's is questionable. I can't find labs that indicated whether anyone bothered to check if drug levels in her blood were consistent with being drugged. There are just a lot of things that could be done, that weren't. We're putting together a list," I said, leaning forward, putting both elbows on my desk, closing the distance between us.

Will leaned back and actually pushed his chair back a few inches producing an irritating screech on the tile floor. He looked down, frowned, took a large breath in, and exhaled before he began to speak.

He turned directly to MQ instead of me, his accuser. I guess he was indicating that I was incidental and the conversation was to be between them, Lieutenant to Sergeant.

"Sergeant Quinn, the case was formally closed by the PA's office as a murder-suicide. The guy snapped, killed his kids and himself. I interviewed the wife. She was traumatized and confused. Remember? Her family had just been murdered. There's no big mystery here. Why in God's name would you want to waste time on this one?"

"I think it's worth a cold case review," MQ said with nonchalance. "The Chief and Lieutenant Hebert are amenable. We can do it and still manage any new cases coming in, especially if no one screws up evidence that has not been processed on new burglary cases, Lieutenant Newsham."

"I think you are wasting your time. Mr. Wiley was a nutjob. It happens all the time. David Berkowitz, 'Son of Sam', sound familiar to you? How about that whack-job kid in Connecticut at the elementary school? There doesn't have to be a neat explanation or motive. People sometimes go crazy."

Newsham took a small clasp knife from his pocket and began scraping under his fingernails.

MQ and I made brief eye contact affirming our notice of the grooming behavior. Grooming, like stroking a moustache, scratching, biting or cleaning fingernails, picking lint, are all typical subconscious manifestations of response to stress. The poodle was nervous.

"We've been taking a look at the evidence and can't seem to find a few things Lieutenant," MQ indicated, watching Will as closely as the 9th inning of the 7th game.

I finished MQ's thought, "The video interview of Julie Wiley on the night of the murders conducted by Sgt. Weingart and Detective Bryson, is not in the bin where it should be. And her Miranda form is missing too."

Newsham stood up. He closed his knife and returned it to his pocket. He turned his back to us as if to leave, paused a few seconds and then turned back to face us. He spoke quietly.

"Yes, well, I don't know what may have happened to the evidence. Are you sure you didn't misplace them? What's going on in evidence MQ, what else are you missing? Do we need to audit the evidence?"

"No Will, they were not misplaced. Something is fucked up and it isn't my evidence procedures."

"Perhaps we should check everything just to be sure," Will said condescendingly.

MQ countered, standing as he spoke, squaring off with Newsham. "You can conduct a full 'blown' audit if you want. I'm sure you'll want to look into every 'crack'." MQ burst his way into a rant like a running back at full speed. "You shouldn't have been involved in the case anyway. Working a homicide, hah! You weren't a homicide detective or any kind of detective, then or now. Those were vicious murders that required investigation by real investigators. I'll get your fat ass roommate in here this afternoon. We'll get to the bottom of this!"

"Don't get in my face Murphy. Back the fuck off!" Will's face turned crimson, voice high pitched and cracking. "It is your problem if evidence is missing, not mine."

MQ stepped towards Newsham as Newsham started for the door.

"You little twit. You stepped on your dick somehow. I only hope the shit you pulled with this Wiley case is big enough to get you and whoever else fucked up this case into some real trouble, and that includes your fucking whirlpool partner."

"You better tread lightly Sergeant Quinn. Tread lightly," Newsham said, in between shallow breaths. "You don't know where you are going on this one." He stepped out of the office and walked briskly down the hallway.

I leaned back in my chair, interlaced fingers behind my neck, stretched out and said, "Well, that went rather well. At least you didn't call him a butt pirate. Your restraint was remarkable Kenneth."

"For your information doctor, I haven't a problem whatsoever with alternative lifestyles. My brother Gary has been in a committed relationship with Harold for 10 years. Just a lovely couple. And their house, to die for. In fact, some of my closest friends, when I was a younger man, lived unconventional lives. I consider myself rather cosmopolitan when it comes to gender issues. It's just a hot button issue for Will and Lawrence that I like to push. And it worked, don't you think?"

"Judging by his Magenta face and those swollen cables pulsing up his neck, you were successful."

# Chapter Thirty Three

As he pushed through the rear door of the police station, the neurons in Will Newsham's brain were firing like bottle rockets. He punched in Lawrence's cell phone number.

"Lawrence, it's me."

"Hey Will, what's up, what time is it?" Lawrence said with a dry throat, waking up from a nap.

"Lawrence! Get your ass up!"

"What the fuck, Will! What the fuck are you pissed off about now? What didn't I do this time?"

"Listen to me, Lawrence. MQ and Green are re-opening the Wiley case and they are going to double-team you about it later today!"

"Holy shit Will!" Lawrence squirmed to sit up in bed, pushing a pillow behind his back with his free hand. "You said we would never hear about that again. What the hell are we?" he stammered, tried to continue, but was interrupted by Will.

"They're making a big deal about the missing DVR of Julie's interview and the Miranda rights form. They'll ask about Mr. Wiley, like what his motive was, why did he do it, maybe some things about processing the scene. You'll just have to cover it like we discussed back then. Just say what we discussed back then and you'll be fine. Remember Larry?"

Will only called him Larry when they were either fighting, or making love. Lawrence did not feel passion in Will's voice.

"Dammit Will. Dammit. I knew this would come back. Dammit to hell."

"Just do what I say and we'll be fine Larry. Just do it. Just like last time. Now get up and get dressed for Christ sake. You have to be at work in about an hour."

"Yea, yea," he said, hanging the phone up. Lawrence laid back down and put the pillow over his face.

# Chapter Thirty Four

While we waited for Lawrence to come in, MQ pulled the schedules for that November and confirmed that Detective Elwyn Bryson had gone on vacation the day after the murders. I called Elwyn on the phone and put it on speaker.

"What's up Morris?"

"You hear we're taking another look at the Wiley case?"

"So I heard."

"We talked to Martin already, just talked to Newsham and we're waiting for Johnson. You processed the scene and interviewed Mrs. Wiley. Then what? What happened to the case?"

"What happened was I went on a two week cruise with the old lady. 25th anniversary trip. Did the Caribbean and Virgin Islands. We dropped some real coin on that one I tell you. But it was worth it. Anyway, by the time I got back, it was all but finished. Everyone said the guy did the kids and then himself. I was a little surprised at how quick they had come to that conclusion, but hey, it wasn't my case anymore. Newsham had it and he and Lawrence were sure that's how it went down."

"What did you think about the woman, Mrs. Wiley?" MQ asked.

"Oh yea. Martin and I were sure she was lying when we interviewed her. But I think it ended up that Will interviewed her at length and got a statement or something from her. They cleared her."

"You knew she was a Scalini, right?"

"I didn't when we interviewed her the night of the murders. I found out later after I got back. That's some shit isn't it? Added a whole new angle. But, I figured that if someone else was involved, I mean other than the father, we'd be hearing about bodies being found all over town. You know, with two bullets in the back of the head. Since there weren't any, it kind of added credence to the father being the perp. I mean, if somebody else killed Scalini offspring, heads would roll. I talked to Martin about it. We both figured it was just one of those things where a guy snapped."

"I see your point Elwyn," MQ said. "How about the evidence? We did an inventory and we're missing a few things. Martin said you had the Miranda form and the video of her interview."

"I did, but I left everything with Lawrence. As soon as Mrs. Wiley left the station, I was out the door too. I know my report was pretty sketchy. But I still had some packing to do. I handed all the evidence to Lawrence. He said he'd take care of it. Far as I knew, he did."

"Thanks Elwyn. I'm sure we'll talk about this again," MQ said.

"Sure thing Murph. I'll see you guys next week," Elwyn said.

"See ya Elwyn," I punched the speaker button off.

"Let's confront Lawrence with all of the evidence issues, I said. "He was last in possession. Let's see if he can answer why the labwork, DNA testing and fiber analysis wasn't done. Why the guns weren't even fingerprinted? Let's bring up the issues surrounding some of the stuff they seized at the house. Like why they didn't ID the cop whose badge, ball cap and shirt were found there. I could go on and on, but that's a starter."

"Sure, it can't hurt. At least we can watch him squirm and sweat. He'll say, 'Fuck you Green. Fuck you Murphy.' Lawrence is not known for his sophisticated oratorical abilities. As commander of this detective bureau, may I remind you that I review Detective Johnson's investigative reports. The guy's capacious Neanderthal skull is essentially a cavernous void. I'd replace him in a New York minute if I could, but he's under Newsham's and Montileone's umbrella. Fortunately, every now and then he'll clear up a bad check or stolen property case."

"I would imagine if it wasn't for Will's umbrella, Lawrence would end up homeless at some point." I said.

"Which in turn, my good doctor, is all the more inducement to cover for his sugar daddy."

Lawrence was a creature of habit. As soon as he walked in the bureau, he made fresh coffee and then hung around the upstairs city hall staff. There was always a birthday, someone who'd had a baby, someone retiring, someone who had found another job. A cause for celebration, cake, cookies, chips and dip.

Lawrence had a nose for finding the food. MQ heard Lawrence making coffee and stuck his head out of his office to catch him before he went upstairs.

"Hey Lawrence, come down to my office. Finish making coffee and bring me a cup, black. Thanks," MQ yelled, beginning the subliminal interview process as I had with Newsham. Lawrence grunted an acknowledgment.

Lawrence came into MQ's office and as directed, handed him a cup. MQ had a couple of uncomfortable, cheap maroon fabric chairs directly in front of his desk too, straight out of Office Depot discount. MQ pointed to the chair that was at the side of his desk. Lawrence squeezed his mesomorphic, apple-shaped mass into the chair. MQ took a seat to his side. I stood in the doorway.

"Thanks for the coffee Lawrence."

"Yea. What is it you want Murphy?" Lawrence asked.

"I am sure Will called you already so we can dispense with any bullshit," MQ said, apparently deciding against the friendly strategy to develop a baseline of behavior for this discussion.

"Yea, he called. So, you know he called. So what."

"It seems like you were the repository for evidence that never made it to me. Any idea on where the missing evidence is?"

Lawrence yawned, "I did what I always did Murphy. I would have put it in the evidence locker and locked it up like I do for all the shit we seize, and I did just that. I know I did. If it got lost, I don't have no idea. Evidence sometimes gets lost don't it, Murphy?" Lawrence shifted from one butt cheek to the other.

"No, it just 'don't get lost'. That's why we have evidence logs, lockers and shelves," MQ said.

"I know I did what I always do. I packaged it and locked it up in the locker."

Lawrence leaned back, stretched his trunk like legs straight out, crossing ankles and crossed his arms over his chest. His posturing was about as closed off to communication as you can get.

"All right, Lawrence," I said. "So, we're missing some evidence. We'll keep looking, but what the hell happened to investigating a murder case? As I understand it, Bryson goes on vacation and you and Will get the case."

"Yea so," Lawrence said with an open mouth yawn.

I thought to myself, "I know that yawn all too well. He probably took a double dose of his Beta Blockers and a Xanax to get through this meeting."

"I read the report Lawrence," I continued. "It's like it was investigated by long distance. No one did the basic things. No one asked the right questions. No one had the right forensics done. You're a better investigator than this, I know you are."

I glanced over at MQ who rolled his eyes around as if I had just said OJ was innocent.

"Morris, the PA's office said it was a murder-suicide. Simple as that," Lawrence said defensively.

"It's not as simple as that Lawrence," I countered and placed the folders containing the entire Wiley investigation on MQ's desk directly in front of Lawrence.

"This is the whole case. This paltry stack of paper. I know you've worked some Major Case Squad homicides. You know as well as I do that the lead and tip sheets for a single murder can be as thick as this whole report, and your case had three dead bodies. This report is full of holes and there's a hell of a lot of forensics that were left undone."

Lawrence uncrossed his arms and rubbed his chest with his right hand. I wondered if his heart were racing despite the meds. He was biting down, jaws clenching and unclenching, lips pursed. His hands were tightly wound fists.

"The initial search was inadequate, Lawrence," I said. "How come no one seized the family computer or obtained financial information? Mr. Wiley was running a business, a police canine business. You know there had to be some type of files. Maybe there were debts, life insurance policies, email lovers, jealousy. Did anyone even entertain the idea that Craig Wiley's job as a trainer of narcotics dogs for cops could have put him in someone's cross hairs? Maybe some crazed drug ring, bent on revenge. I can tell you there are dangers in working narcotics, if you catch my drift."

Lawrence cleared his throat and he began to pick invisible lint off his slacks.

Thirty seconds later, I began questioning again. "Lawrence, look at it this way. Craig Wiley was closely affiliated with law enforcement so he probably knew a lot of the things we know. He knew about narcotics, evidence, investigations. In any event, if a guy like that wanted to murder his family, planned to kill his family and himself, would he do it like he did it? Let me ask you. If you were going to kill your family, would you use a .22 and a machete, when you had a Remington 870?"

MQ added. "No sir Lawrence. It just does not add up. No one entertained even the remote possibility that this was not a premeditated murder. You and Will decided from day one, that this guy planned to kill his family, but as I peruse this stack of pulp, you sure didn't prove it. You sure didn't prove it."

A pregnant silence ensued as MQ and I shut up. Lawrence's head was subtly nodding. He was getting it.

MQ spoke in a subdued tone, "You would agree then, Lawrence, that facts supporting the premeditated angle are at best, tenuous?"

More head bobs and a muffled grunt. Lawrence's eyes briefly closed and his face contorted into something between a grimace and a scream. He opened his eyes. He uncrossed his legs and then crossed them again. He wiped the sweat from his flushed face with the palms of both hands. I could see the pulsations from his racing heart through his shirt. He sipped a little coffee. I couldn't hear the machinery in his jughead, but it appeared we had made a significant impact.

MQ rose from his chair, his voice once again abrasive, "And what about the police paraphernalia that you found in the house? Whose city badge was that? And wasn't it interesting that the box with all the cop apparel also had sex toys." He leaned down, his face at the same level as Lawrence's. "Mrs. Wiley said she and her husband had engaged in an act of sexual bondage and that he anally raped her Lawrence."

"It adds a rather bizarre sexual aspect to the murders, which makes the contents of the wicker box particularly relevant Lawrence. Yet, no one asked whether this bondage and rape, while the kids played upstairs, was usual behavior for this suburban couple. Seems a bit unusual to me. Doesn't it strike you as odd Lawrence? What went on in that house Lawrence? No one checked to see if perhaps they were swingers. Or, maybe someone was cheating on someone else with those pleasure toys which precipitated, not a preplanned murder, but a rage murder. It sure looks like a rage murder. There is clearly a sexual link to these murders and you and your boyfriend turned the other cheek."

Lawrence's knees were bouncing. A few of the beads of sweat met up and formed a large droplet that crawled slowly down his nose. He wiped it away with the back of his hand.

MQ paused for a good 30 seconds and let sweat and silence work. Silence is as good a tool for interviewers as a Leatherman would be for a MacGyver.

"You would think that the murder of two of old man Scalini's great grandchildren, would have required a more thorough investigation. How come there wasn't one? For Chrissake Lawrence, they were Scalinis, which means they were tied to the Newshams and yet the two of you didn't do a fucking thing. It certainly gives me cause to ponder Lawrence."

Lawrence's breathing increased to almost a pant. His red face started to lose color.

MQ followed up. "Perhaps we will uncover that the Wiley investigation was abandoned because of the Scalini connection, and since Will's daddy works for the Scalinis, maybe we'll find that there was pressure to close the case. Public corruption in a murder investigation. Hmm, it certainly gives one pause, does it not Det. Johnson? How do you think you and your roomie will manage in orange jumpsuits?"

I took the opportunity to hammer home a few points before Lawrence either pulled his gun or had a stroke. "And Martin and Elwyn said Mrs. Wiley was lying. Yet that evidence, the video of the interview, the statement by the only living witness at the house somehow disappeared."

MQ spoke up, "And you're immersed in the middle of this whirlpool of shit, big boy. And don't think you can rely on your pal to pull you out. This is family business, Lawrence, and you're definitely not family. If push comes to shove, he'll throw you under the proverbial bus. You really are a cretin if you think otherwise."

I had seen the look that was forming on Lawrence's face any number of times in the clinic. Patients passing kidney stones have it, especially if it was not their first time. They suffer with pain, current and anticipated, knowing the worst is yet to come.

An awkward, eternal silence of another 30 seconds crept by. Lawrence shifted in the chair, cleared his throat again, picked more imaginary lint off his pants, sipped coffee, rolled his head and then sat motionless.

MQ walked around his desk and thudded into his high back chair. "Chatham Newsham and the Scalinis stuck their crooked noses in to protect one of their own, and you knew it! You're part of the conspiracy to obstruct justice, Detective Johnson. What the fuck really happened? And where's my evidence?"

Lawrence closed his eyes. Except for the husky breaths, he was quiet.

MQ and I glanced at each other. We shared the same hope that perhaps Lawrence was going to give it up.

Lawrence opened his eyes and sat up straight. His fingers were curling and uncurling into fists. I wondered if this was about to be a confession or a brawl.

"I don't know nothing. What I know is in the report. As far as evidence, everything I had, I turned it in. That's all I can tell you."

MQ, stood up and leaned forward, knuckles on his desk, "No! That's not all you can tell me. That's all you will tell me. You know what Lawrence, that is just fine. Because when we do get to the bottom of this, and we will, I will relish the day you get indicted and fired. When, as the evidence and uniform property officer, I will take your badge, gun and ID from you. I want you to remember today as the day when you had the chance to do the right thing, but you didn't."

MQ was hell bent on ingraining a mental image on the Paleolithic brain of Lawrence Johnson, an image that Lawrence wouldn't forget for 10,000 years.

MQ continued using delicate brush strokes. "Remember this office, that uncomfortable purple chair you're sitting in, the shitty ink-colored coffee, the pitifully incomplete, manila folder lying there on the desk. That sorry excuse of an investigation you and Newsham did. Picture all of this in your memory will you Lawrence? Take a big whiff in, fill your senses. Do you smell it?" MQ asked inhaling a deep breath through his nose and using his hands to waft the odor towards his face. "I smell it Lawrence. Do you? I smell shit and it's all on you. You can smell it too, I know you can. Can't you Lawrence?"

Nearly imperceptible, but I noticed it. Lawrence pursed his lips and breathed in, his nostrils flaring. He smelled it.

"You can go now Det. Johnson. Go on. Go to work," MQ dismissed him as if shooing a cat off the porch.

Lawrence peeled himself out of the chair. As he stood, his face became gray. He shook his head and careened into the door frame.

"You alright, Lawrence? Wait a minute, sit," the physician in me said.

He ignored me and turned towards us. "Fuck you Murphy, Fuck you Morris."

Lawrence steadied himself and shuffled his bulk down the hall and out of view.

MQ sat down in his chair and reached for his cup of coffee, "Damn the luck doc, I thought just for a minute there, he was either going to kick the bucket or tell the truth."

"A little orthostatic hypotension from the stress. I thought he was going to pass out." I scratched my head. "I guess, in his mind, he cannot rat on Will. He's got to be asking himself, where would he go? Where would he live? Would the Scalinis come after him? He's tied to Will's hip," I said.

MQ displayed a huge overbite and said in his best Chinese. "Tied to his hip! You make gay joke Ha. Ha."

# Chapter Thirty Five

About an hour passed and Lieutenant Marshall Hebert stepped in the doorway. Lt. Hebert is 57-year-old weeble-shaped man, with delicate features and fair skin. Strands of his graying black hair, thin to a grid like combover on his shiny scalp. At the time of the Wiley cold case, he had been with the Oakview Police Department for 22 years.

Marshall had an MBA and retired at age 33 after a successful career as a stock broker with a large firm in Nashville. He had done well with real estate investments including part ownership of several shopping malls in Tennessee and Kentucky. He had built a formidable portfolio and was financially secure. Upon retiring, Marshall and Ellen Hebert moved from Nashville to the Oakview area to be closer to Ellen's aging parents.

Marshall was a Walter Mitty type character and had always wanted to be a police officer. At age 35 he'd attended the city's police academy and had been hired as a police officer with Oakview. The Chief hired me because I was a runner. He hired Marshall so he would have a personal financial adviser working under his command. In fact, Marshall served as the Chief's financial planner for two decades.

Officer Hebert did not have the look or strength of a warrior, but he was intuitive and street smart. He dealt fairly with his fellow officers, didn't make waves, and for obvious reasons, got along well with Chief Montileone. He easily moved up through the ranks. Lt. Hebert was Montileone's administrative aide before Newsham came along. He was none too happy to share the Oakview Police Department command staff with the likes of a Will Newsham.

"Well, boys. I just had a talk with the Chief about y'alls case." Despite having moved from Tennessee long ago, Marshall still maintained a hint of that southern drawl. "From the looks of Lawrence, you've had a nice chat with him too, huh? Good Lord! He looks like he needs oxygen. Anyway, I've been in Montileone's office the better part of an hour because of your memo Morris. Every dog has some fleas, but you sure made this one look like it has the mange," his tone painted with aggravation.

"So anyway boys," Hebert said, "I walked into Montileone's office and there he was, hunched over his desk. His old bald spot staring back at me. I reckon I'm getting thataway too." Marshall patted the top of his head. "But he looks rougher than usual. Not as bad as Lawrence, but y'all got the Chief rattled."

"We can only hope," MQ said.

"Well, now's your chance to shake and bake. Come on boys. He wants to talk, real quick."

My eyes narrowed. "He wants to talk right now?"

"Yep. You spilled the milk Morris. You're going to have to do some wiping up. No dawdling now."

The three of us stood in Montileone's door. Lt. Hebert was correct. The Chief did look rough.

Chief Thomas Montileone was in his late 60's. He was tall and thin, long nose, big ears, thin arms, spindly, gnarly fingers, sagebrush eyebrows and fuzz growing wildly out of each ear. A cross between Abe Lincoln and the former head of the Department of Homeland Security, that Skeletor, Michael Cherthoff.

The hair that rimmed his bald spot was a gray bird's nest that was tousled like his office, both of which needed cleaning and combing. He was wearing a wrinkled white shirt. His brown and red striped tie was flung back over his shoulder. A Styrofoam cup of coffee, apparently with a pinhole leak, sat atop a stack of reports in front of him. There were enough coffee ring stains on top of the report to form the Olympics icon. He was looking at a fingerprint card with a jeweler's eyepiece.

The Lieutenant started moving papers, unopened mail and magazines from chairs. He and MQ took seats in front of the Chief's desk. I stood off to the side, leaning against a filing cabinet topped with folders.

"Chief, you wanted to talk about the Wiley case. Here they are," Hebert said.

Chief Montileone put the eyepiece and fingerprint card down. "Yes, Yes. I did. So, what is it with this To-From memorandum and the Wiley case? That case is closed."

Lt. Hebert handed the ball off, "Morris, why don't you explain."

Before I could begin, MQ interrupted me with a phlegmatic throat clearing. He began diplomatically. "Chief, we are well aware that no homicide investigation is ever without problems. There are always loose ends that should have been tied up. There are always some evidence problems, witnesses that were never interviewed, statements that should have been taken. There are always issues, no matter how good your investigative team is. As the doctor has succinctly defined in his memo, we've found a number of issues in the Wiley case. A few things that we should do to assure permanent closure.

We need to complete some of the basic perfunctory forensics that were not done during the original investigation. For example, the weapons were not fingerprinted. I don't have an explanation as to why something so elementary as fingerprinting was neglected, but there is no report of a print analysis for the weapons. And, the shotgun that the male subject used to kill himself was not tested to see if it would remain static, in the position found next to his body. In addition, Morris and I found a .22 caliber bullet still wrapped in what looks like a homemade towel silencer that was duct taped to the barrel of the rifle used to shoot the little girl. We figure that if the county lab didn't find that, I guess they didn't do a very thorough job processing the weapons. And there's some residue testing we feel is important, as well as some lab and DNA work. And unfortunately, there's an interview video and Miranda form whose whereabouts are unknown."

"Hmm. Unusual that the lab would do such sloppy work," the Chief said biting his inner lip. He picked up his coffee cup and took a sip, and put it down on top of the fingerprint card. A new ring stain began expanding over the fingerprints.

MQ looked over at me and smirked. I knew what he was thinking. "Newsham and Montileone are two incompetent peas in a pod. Both dull witted and unable to keep from fucking things up."

MQ continued, "Perhaps the county lab was told that the case was a murder-suicide and not to waste much time on it. At this point, we don't know. But we want to make sure everything that needs to be evaluated is completed. It's only good CYA police work, Chief."

Chief Montileone focused his bushy eyebrows on my memo. He looked up at MQ, "How is it that you are missing evidence?"

"Well, that is a mystery chief. You and I are the only ones with keys to evidence room. I just don't have an answer for that one. We've asked the involved officers, Newsham, Weingart, Johnson and Bryson and no one knows."

"Maybe we should change the locks," Chief said.

"Good idea chief, I'll take care of that today and get you the new key this afternoon," MQ said.

MQ paused and I took that as a cue to enter in the conversation. "Chief, the primary stumbling block that resulted in the premature closure of the case was that everyone bought into the murder-suicide version. We recognize that it could have happened exactly how everyone thinks it did. And maybe, that's what we will find after we fully investigate this. In any event, we think Craig Wiley's family and those two dead children deserve no less than our best effort, don't you Chief?"

Montileone's eyes narrowed and his lips pursed, but he responded with the only sensible answer, "Yes, yes they do. Um, keep me advised as to your progress. And Sgt. Murphy, be sure to get a receipt for the new locks and keys." He picked up the jewelers eyepiece and returned his attention to the fingerprint card signaling us that the meeting was over.

"I'm surprised he didn't make more of a fuss," Lt. Hebert mentioned as soon as we were out of Chief's earshot.

"Yes. I am a bit dubious with his lack of resistance," MQ said. "One wonders if the old man has something up his sleeve."

"Proceed with your investigating. Soon as you can, get the evidence out of this zoo and off to the state lab. Do whatever interviews you have to do, and keep me in the loop on whatever it is you find. Try not to bite off more than you can chew and for Heaven's sake, don't bring Dateline down here."

# Chapter Thirty Six

etween our active investigative case load and going through every nook and cranny of the evidence storage facility to find anything related to the Wiley case, it was mid December before MQ and I loaded up the car with the Wiley evidence and took them to the highway patrol laboratory.

The three story buff -brick building was built in the '60s. With its rows of darkened windows and stark angular architecture, it bore a similar appearance to any number of the penal institutions of the same era. The lab's motto was emblazoned on a bronze plaque at the base of a large flagpole in front of the building. "Justice through Excellence in Forensic Science."

I struggled a little against the biting wind and 30-degree temperature carrying a legal-sized banker's cardboard box filled with the evidence for analysis across the parking lot and into the building. MQ managed well enough with the weapon cartons.

Security made a phone call from their desk and escorted us down two hallways. The guard pushed a ringer button next to a glazed window in a waiting area and left us. Ten minutes later, a bookish looking woman in a white lab coat with short cropped silver hair came out. She took off her glasses and hung them from the lanyard around her neck. The picture ID identified her as Sally Sunderman, Forensic Services.

"Hi. I'm Mrs. Sunderman. I spoke to one of you a few weeks ago, correct? A cold case for DNA and firearms if I remember."

"Yes. Hello. I'm Det. Green. We spoke. This is Sgt. Murphy Quinn."

We all shook hands.

"I see you've brought us a couple presents," Sally said with a friendly but tired smile.

I explained to Sally that we required a DNA profile on all four Wileys. We wanted a comparison of the trace evidence on all items.

"My dance card is pretty full, but your stuff will go in line," she said. "You do realize though, that since it's a cold case without urgency, we're probably looking at a minimum of a month."

Because we also required firearms analysis, Sally told us she would get any samples from the weapons and then send the long guns to Derrick Stone, the firearms examiner. "If you want to talk to him about what testing you want done, he's in the basement. Take the stairs at the end of the hallway. See you hopefully, sometime before Spring. Bye bye," Sally said with a parade queen wave.

We made our way to the Firearms section. Derrick was a country boy. Talking with him was a lot like talking with my old partner Tom, Lt. Hebert, or a cast member from Hee Haw.

Examiner Stone said he'd grown up with guns and had been hunting with his daddy and granddaddy since he was seven years old. He said he was 'one lucky sons a bitch' because he had transformed a hobby into a vocation.

We gave Derrick a brief synopsis of the case along with a copy of the crime scene photos. I pointed out the one depicting Craig Wiley seated in the recliner with the shotgun propped between his legs and the shell halfway out of the ejection port.

He immediately recognized the weapon at a glance. "Remington 870. I own three of them. A great shotgun, reliable and sturdy. Looks like it worked pretty damn good on that old boy there," he said pointing a thick index finger at the picture of Craig Wiley without a head.

"Damn fine mess you got there fellas."

"You got that right," I said. "Derrick, do you think the 870 would stay in place like it is shown in the picture? I am no firearms expert, but with the recoil of the shotgun, seems like the gun would bounce off the floor."

"Now, it might and it might not. Sometimes you're just surprised what a weapon will do. But, we'll test her and see just what she does. I notice that the shell didn't get ejected fully either. We'll test that function too. We'll put the shotgun in a similar position, see what happens. We'll do several test firings to see what is a reproducible event. As far as timewise, well, once I get the weapons from Sally, I'll try to get it done in two shakes of a lambby 's tail. It'll just depend on if anything high profile gets ahead of y'all."

"And we have a .22 rifle with a towel duct-taped to the end," MQ added, showing him the picture.

Derrick shook his head, "You know, I've seen a lot of this. Putting towels or wrapping some type of blanketing, foam pipe insulation, duct-tape, you name it, onto barrels. Some knuckleheads even think they can quiet down a revolver, can you imagine that? Dumb, just dumb. But, people want silencers, and they look it up on the internet and you get this kind of homemade junk. I'll bet you a hundred bucks that durn towel didn't make the report any less loud. This type of homemade crap never works."

"Well, whoever did this was probably not a gunsmith," MQ said.

"More like a gun nut if you ask me. I'll get a hold of y'all when I'm done testing the weapons," Derrick said.

We returned with hopes that sometime in the next few months, the lab results would prove to be a critical ally in proving our case. I hoped the lab motto was accurate.

# Chapter Thirty Seven

We were busy with crooks in present time. An auto theft ring composed of Bosnians were stealing cars from dealerships and parking lots all over town. There were three murders, two were of the misdemeanor variety, two crackheads stabbed each other. The third was a traditionally tragic death, a 74 year old man suffocated his wife with a pillow. She was suffering from Alzheimer's and Dr. Kevorkian was unavailable. We were also working case with the FBI involving internet child porn and a Catholic Priest. It was a busy time.

MQ and I checked in with the State Lab a few too many times and were told each time, in increasingly emphatic language, "Don't call us, we'll call you!" Our case was put on the back burner due to the volume of fresh investigations requiring analysis. Months passed without results.

The first of many steps towards my destiny with the Wiley case occurred on a particularly muggy, end of May day, temperatures were expected to reach 90 degrees. At 6am it was already 75. By the time I reached Verdell's, I was ready for water. I gulped down about 12 ounces, waved at Verdell and continued on.

I was rounding the path in the Blessed Sacrament cemetery when a stabbing cramp in my left shoulder stopped me dead. I hunched over, rolling my shoulders, pawing with my right hand at muscles, as they rapidly developed into a knot. I could not quite reach it and the pain was spreading up into my neck with the speed of a Colorado wildfire. I leaned up against a tree, pushing the knot hard against the bark. The pressure elicited a white hot burn and flashes of light in my peripheral field of vision. It was like being stabbed with daggers straight from the blacksmith's forge. I kept pushing and rolling my shoulder blade against the tree.

As the knot slowly melted, I retched up the water and fell to the ground. I rolled over onto my back, panting.

The sun crested over a bank of oak trees and the additional heat didn't do me any favors. I dry-heaved several more times. I felt as if I'd been beaten with a Louisville slugger and I still had a 5K run to get home, shower and go to work. I got to my hands and knees and did some deep breathing while performing a Cat and Camel stretch, courtesy of the Sheila Green yoga instruction. I stood slowly and leaned against a headstone. It had a large brown granite base with two heart shaped monuments on top. Each heart was elaborately carved with a floral outline and an epitaph:

> *"Children bring their own love with them when they come to us*
> *and we keep their love when they return to the Lord"*

> Robert Edward Scalini

> *"No jewel is as perfect as the innocence of childhood"*

> Taylor Ann Scalini

"What the fuck!" I sat down on the flat spot between their graves and talked to the headstone. "I've been running by your graves for what, over a year now? And here you both are, but you're Scalinis not Wileys. That's pretty interesting."

Straight ahead were two 6' Tuscan columns, in between stood a massive grey granite headstone ornately engraved with musical notes, roses and vines.

> *"Father, grandfather, great-grandfather, friend to many"*

> Francis Salvatore Scalini

"So this is the Scalini plot where all the scumbags are planted." I looked back at the children's graves. "Sorry you have to share your eternal rest with the likes of these fucks." I said. No one was around, so I pissed on Francis's grave for me and for Tom.

I could not find a marker for Craig Wiley. If the Scalinis can replace a father's name on a headstone, I guess they can decide who gets buried where.

I had to stop at Verdell's on the way back for more water and a short rest. He came out from behind the register and sidled up to me back by the water and soda machines.

"Yo Doc. You don't look so good. Too damn hot to be runnin' man. Too damn hot."

"That which does not kill us, makes us strong. Somebody said that Verdell." I rubbed ice on the back of my neck.

"Fuck that doc. Mad Dogs and Englishmen is what I think about when it's this hot."

"Well, I'm not English. Gotta go."

I made it home without any additional problems. I showered and took my breakfast of meds. When I finally got to the station, I pulled up the Wiley obituaries on the web. Sure enough, the Scalini grandchildren were buried in Blessed Sacrament Catholic Cemetery on November 27th. Blessed Sacrament was identified in the obituary as the Scalini family cemetery. There was no mention of the Wiley name in the obit. Craig Wiley was interred at Our Redeemer, a Lutheran facility, some 35 miles away.

It was finally a quiet day at the PD. There were no call-outs for a detective and I caught up with my reports on the auto thefts. I left the station at 3pm. I got home and noticed the red dot on my answering machine was blinking. Sheila had called to let me know that they had gone to her sister's lake house for the weekend. Like the hundred times when we were married, had she asked, I would have told her I couldn't make it. Her sister was nice, but my former brother-in-law was an egotistical asshole. In any event, something else in my life was always more important. This weekend, my excuse would have been that I was the on-call detective for the holiday weekend.

There was a Hallmark card with a picture of an American flag and a bald eagle taped to my refrigerator door. I opened it and it played *God Bless America*. At the bottom it read, "Have a good Memorial day!" and it was signed by Jake and Olivia. Sheila has always had a key to my place. They must have stopped by on their way out of town A scribbled note on the countertop from Sheila said they would be back Monday and that I should be sure to take my meds and not drink so much. There was nothing about, "Why don't you come out?" She knew better.

I took my Oxys, and made a double White Russian.

# Chapter Thirty Eight

The holiday weekend meant a skeleton patrol crew on the road. The station was empty when I got in the next day. I made coffee, and checked the overnight crime activity inbox. It was empty. MQ had taken a few days off to stretch his holiday out. I took the opportunity to do some work on the Wiley case.

According to the official police report, the first person Julie Wiley contacted after the murders was her neighbor, Bev Goldstein. Mrs. Wiley had escaped her husband's murderous rampage by driving down the street to the Goldstein's home. Bev Goldstein called 911 for her. I decided to see if the Goldsteins were home.

They lived about a hundred yards down the street. Their house layout was nearly identical to the Wiley's home, a brick ranch, split level, attached two car-garage.

The Goldsteins lawn was old Bermuda grass. It was well kept, bordered with black plastic edging and landscaped nicely with a few fruit trees. There were lilac and hyacinth bushes growing along dark stained wooden trellises. The garage door was open and both spaces were occupied by a vehicle.

I knocked, and like the night of the murders, Bev Goldstein answered the door. She was dressed in khaki Capri pants, a red, white and blue Women's Breast Cancer Half Marathon shirt, white anklets and New Balance running shoes. Mrs. Goldstein was a petite woman, at best a size 5, with convenient, short-cropped coal black hair.

"Hello, Mrs. Goldstein?" I said through the glass of the storm door.

"Yes, can I help you?"

"I'm Det. Green from your police department, Oakview," I produced my badge and ID case and held it up in her line of sight.

"Sorry to bother you on a holiday weekend, but do you have a couple of minutes? I have a few questions concerning an incident that happened in the neighborhood."

"Sure, I guess so. Um, my husband is here, do you need him as well?" Mrs. Goldstein asked, still looking a little unsure about a cop at her door, especially on a holiday weekend.

"Yes ma'am, that would be fine," I stood at the door, still holding my badge case up.

"Would you like to come in?" Mrs. Goldstein said, opening the door and calling for her husband.

"Yes, please."

I stepped in the house and pulled the exterior door closed behind me. The heat followed me in.

Philip Goldstein came into the hallway, drying his hands with a kitchen towel. Mr. Goldstein wasn't much larger than a size five either, his stature befitting a jockey. He was wearing a tan dress shirt and brown slacks, his tie tucked in between two upper shirt buttons. He had an apron around his waist. It looked like he had been cooking or washing dishes like a good husband.

"Phil, this is Detective Green from Oakview," Mrs. Goldstein said.

"Hello folks. Sorry to intrude on a holiday. Do you have a few minutes?" I asked, extending my hand.

I shook their hands. "Sure, how can we help," Phillip Goldstein said.

"We are taking another look at the Wiley murders. We're doing a cold case investigation of the murders."

Mrs. Goldstein's eyes widened. She glanced at her husband, "Really!"

"Please come down into the den detective," Mr. Goldstein said. "We'll be more comfortable."

I followed Mr. and Mrs. Goldstein down the stairs to the lower level where, in the Wiley's home, a Remington 870 had rested neatly between the knees of a decapitated body. Mr. Goldstein flipped a switch and a half dozen recessed ceiling lights came on.

I took a seat in a very soft and comfortable white leather couch, across from a wall of books, CDs, albums and an entertainment system organized and neat, like Craig Wiley's workshop. Mr. Goldstein took a seat at the other end. Mrs. Goldstein sat on a hassock in front of a matching rocker/recliner. Stainless steel picture frames containing photos of Mr. and Mrs. Goldstein and a young girl in front of Disney's Magic Castle sat on a dust free, glass end table.

"Your daughter?" I said, breaking the ice.

Mrs. Goldstein answered, "Sydney. We went to Florida over spring break a couple years ago. She's getting older. Who knows how much longer she'll want to do kid stuff."

"I know. Time goes by fast," I said, as if I were a family man.

"Sydney and Taylor, that was the little girl that was killed, they were the same age. They played together occasionally," Mrs. Goldstein offered.

I pointed at Mrs. Wiley's top, "I see you're wearing the half marathon shirt. You do the race?"

"Yea. I'm more comfortable at 10Ks, but my sister is a breast cancer survivor, so I ran it with her. You run?"

"Not as much as I used to or would like to. I've done, I guess, 15 marathons and a bunch of halfs, but I'm down to 10 miles or so as my longest run now. I try to put in about 25 miles a week. And my minute per mile is embarrassing. I might push it to do a half marathon this fall. Age, injuries, it takes a toll."

"Don't we know," Phillip said, pointing over to his wife.

"I tore a meniscus two years ago in my left knee," Mrs. Goldstein said. "I put up with the occasional locking and managed the pain with NSAIDS as long as I could. I had to have a meniscectomy this time last year. Beginning of the season too. Bummer. Surgeries and rehab put the kabosh on training. I'm just getting back into decent shape this year."

"You don't have to tell me. I've had my fair share of trouble," I agreed and shifted to matters at hand.

"The report indicated that you were the first folks to come in contact with Mrs. Wiley after the murders. That she came down here after it happened. I just want to get your recollection of the events of the day of the murders. How well do you remember that day?"

Mrs. Goldstein jumped into the conversation like a sprinting hurdler. "Oh yes. Remember it? Oh yes. I clearly remember it and so does Phillip. You don't forget things like that."

"What can you tell me about that day?" I asked.

"Why don't you go first Phillip? Mrs. Goldstein said. "You saw them first."

"Well, I work out of my house pretty often. My job is pretty flexible that way. I'm in pharmaceutical marketing and sales. I usually wait down at the bus stop for Syd around 3:30. On the day of the murders, I was doing just that, working at home. Like today."

Mr. Goldstein realized he was still wearing an apron and clumsily pulled it off. "I have a call to make later today. Go figure, a doctor in the office on a holiday weekend."

"Really, a hard working doctor?" I repeated with selfish irony.

"Yea weird, but their Iranian, so Memorial Day may not mean much to them. Anyway, on the day it happened, I think maybe Craig Wiley was pretty much doing the same thing, working at home. He raised and trained dogs, something like that, for the police I think. I was already down there, at the bus stop when he came down. He came down just before the bus got there. I said hello, he said hello. How are you. Like that, pretty much small talk. We gathered up our kids. I said see ya, or something like that, and we walked home."

"Tell him how they walked home Phil," Bev urged.

"I remember Craig was holding each of his kids' hands as they walked. Well, actually, they skipped up the sidewalk. They were ahead of us skipping, but when they got to our house, they slowed down, and waited for us. Syd and Taylor said something about calling each other later. We all said goodbye. They went on up the sidewalk toward their house. I mean, I was pretty much the last person to see them alive. It was quite chilling. I couldn't believe it when I heard he did what he did."

"Mr. Goldstein, I realize it was a while ago, but do you remember what he actually said."

"I mean, not specifically. A basic hi, hello, how ya doing? He said something like he'd been really busy, traveling. He said he was glad to be back. Something like that. I said I was busy too. We said see ya, take care. Something pretty abbreviated like that."

"We're trying to get some specific details of the day. How about clothing? What do you remember he was wearing?"

"Oh, I remember that. He had on blue jeans and um, black combat boots and a dark, navy blue, long sleeve shirt, like a pullover polo type shirt. It had an emblem or something embroidered on the chest. A gold or yellow crest or something official looking."

"Man, that is really good recall Mr. Goldstein. You sure?"

"Yea, well, he usually wore something like that. Like I said, he was some kind of dog trainer. He usually wore military type clothes. Usually he had on those pants, the ones with all the pockets. But I remember on that day he had on blue jeans. It was unusual, maybe that's why it stuck. But still the uniform looking shirt and the combat boots."

"What was his attitude, his demeanor like?"

"He seemed fine. Pretty normal I guess. The same as he was any other time we saw each other. Nice enough guy. I mean skipping up the street holding hands with your kids seemed pretty normal to me."

"Agreed," I said. "Anything else happen that you can recall?"

"Not really. I was just waiting for Bev to get home to watch Sydney. A little while later, she came home from work and I left for my meeting. I got back home about 7 and found the police blocking my street. They let me in after I showed them my driver's license with my address.

When I got to the house, I saw Julie's car parked kind of sideways in my driveway. When I came in, the Wiley's dogs were in my living room. I thought, what the hell is going on here? Bev brought me up to speed pretty quick. What a nightmare that was."

"Mr. Goldstein, had you ever met Mrs. Wiley?

"Sure. She met the kids at the bus stop occasionally."

"What was your impression of her?"

"She wasn't, um, very friendly. If we ever spoke, it was just a hi, how are you, fine. And she never walked down. She always drove and waited in the car. The kids would get in and she would drive back home. That was it."

"Mrs. Goldstein, you mentioned your kids played together? What did Mrs. Wiley seem like to you?"

"She seemed, well," Mrs. Goldstein paused, "She seemed, well, like Phil said. She just wasn't very friendly, or chatty. I think we probably shared more words the night it happened than we ever did the whole time we both lived in this neighborhood."

"She spent some time here, waiting for the police and ambulances," I said. "What can you tell me about what happened? What time she arrived, what she said, what she wore, how she acted. Those kinds of things would be helpful."

"Yes. Ok. It is, it was really terrible. I mean, it's horrible to even think about it, even to this day," Mrs. Goldstein said, hugging herself as if chilled. "As Phil said, he had gone on to his meeting. I was home cleaning the kitchen when the doorbell rang, it was about a quarter after 4. I answered the door and there was Julie on the front porch."

"What do you remember about what she had on? Anything, details can help."

"Detective, I can close my eyes and see her as if she were sitting next to you right now. She had on blue jeans, a long sleeve, gray sweatshirt that was turned inside out. You could see the inside seams and stitching of whatever logo or name was on it. She had brown clogs on, and she had a hair scrunchy on her wrist. I thought it was weird at the time, but her hair was wet. Her bangs were hanging down over her face. And she was wet, hands, face. Wet."

"Like she was sweating, or in shock?" I asked.

"No, wet wet. Not damp or shocky. I'm a nurse and I know shock. Her color was not shocky and her skin wasn't cool or clammy. If anything she was flushed.

And it was November, cold outside. I opened the door and there she was. She was wet, like from water, not shock. It was weird."

"What did she say when she came in?"

"I mean, she hadn't even gotten into the house and she started blurting, 'Help me, help me. He stabbed them, help me', things like that. She stumbled into the house and I had to grab her to keep her from falling. I led her to the couch and sat her down. Her sweatshirt was also very damp to the touch. Very odd. And what else was weird was that she drove to the house with her dogs in the car. She kept rambling about Craig stabbing the kids and trying to kill her. I called 911 and the police went to her house. One officer came here, then an ambulance. They took her to the hospital. I didn't sleep the rest of that night. It was so spooky with the police all around and the news crews. Awful, just awful. We had her dogs for a couple days until her sister picked them up."

"What else can you recall about what Mrs. Wiley did, or said while you were waiting for the police? What did she tell you happened?"

"She said quite a lot. That Craig had tried to strangle her and that he had stabbed the kids and was going to kill himself and that she was lucky to have escaped."

"I am so sorry you had to be witness to this. It clearly has left a mark on you both."

"Thank you detective. It really was surreal," Phillip said.

Bev continued, "I sat with her while she told the police officer what had happened. She held onto my hand, squeezing it. The story she told that officer was, I guess, I would call it bizarre."

"In what way?" I asked.

"First of all, I thought it was strange that she left the house without knowing, you know, what happened to her children. Detective, Green is it?"

"Yes, Morris, if you like, Morris Green."

"Morris, I sat there with her and listened to her tell the officer the entire story of what happened. Her story was so, well, I mean. I remember it because it was so farfetched."

"What about it was unbelievable?"

"Julie told the officer that she took the kids to school that morning. She said she was sick with the flu and went back to bed. She said that Craig had come home, and had given her some pills to make her feel better. The officer asked her what they were. Julie told him she didn't know, but that Craig had given her a whole handful of them and she took them. A whole handful of pills? Really?" She rolled her eyes. "You don't know what they are and you take them?"

"I wouldn't take a whole handful of anything without knowing what they were, especially if my wife gave them to me," I said. As if I were someone's husband.

Phillip chuckled.

Bev continued, "Julie went on to describe how Craig had come home with the kids, put them in their rooms and then came down to their bedroom. She said she was groggy, drugged from the pills. She said he tied her up, put duct tape over her mouth, put her in handcuffs and tried to strangle her. She told the officer that this was not the first time. That Craig had hit her before and tied her up. But she didn't think he would ever hurt the kids. I had no idea. I mean, she never mentioned anything like that to me. And then she started saying things like 'How could he stab my children, they were only babies. Why, why did he do it?'" Mrs. Goldstein shivered again and continued. "It's so creepy thinking about it again. The officer that was here asked her how she got away. Julie told him that she managed to get loose from her restraints and fought with Craig and was able to get away. I thought that was strange. That she was so drugged, but was able to get loose and fight off her husband?" Mrs. Goldstein shook her head and said, "Nope, I just couldn't believe it."

"And Craig was a strong guy. He was built," Phil said. "Big arms. A weightlifter my guess. It's hard to believe she could fight him off."

"Listen Detective Green," Bev said, "I worked ER for ten years. I've seen many a domestic abuse victim. Julie had a few red marks on her neck and wrists, I will grant you that. But they didn't look to me like fighting injuries. Just reddened skin. None of her nails were broken, her throat wasn't bruised, her face wasn't abraded from duct tape being pulled off her mouth. It sure didn't look to me like she had been attacked or fighting with anyone."

"And she told the officer at your house all this information?" I asked.

"Absolutely. I sat right there. He jotted down some notes so I know he was listening. And she made a few statements in a real matter of fact tone of voice, like, 'I hope he's dead. He killed those kids. He shouldn't be allowed to live.'"

"It was really, really creepy," Mr. Goldstein said, moving to the edge of the couch cushion. "And this whole dog thing. Pretty unusual in my opinion. She had presence of mind to bring the dogs, but not save the kids? I still don't understand that."

"Sounds like you both have some questions as to what happened."

"Detective, did you know Julie was on TV the day after the murders?" Mrs. Goldstein asked.

"I had heard that she was on the news."

Mrs. Goldstein continued. "I saw her and she looked so composed. I mean, she was probably medicated. I am sure she was sedated with Xanax or something. But, to go on TV the day after your children and husband are murdered is just, well it just was mind boggling. She told the reporter about how she should have left him after the first time he hurt her. At the end of the segment, she gave a warning to women who may be living with an abusive spouse to just get out before something worse happens. How on earth could anyone be on TV and do that the day after?"

"That behavior is peculiar to say the least," I affirmed.

"I want to give you something detective," Mrs. Goldstein said as she popped up from the couch like bread out of a toaster. She disappeared down the hallway.

"Oh, I bet she is digging out her notes," Mr. Goldstein mentioned.

"Notes?"

"Yes, detective, my notes," she said returning to the couch. "I thought this whole thing was way weird. The duct tape, drugging, the driving with her dogs, it smelled fishy to me. Like I said, I'm a nurse. I chart, I write details of patient care. The TV appearance was too much for me. So, after the news show, I was convinced that something was rotten in Denmark, so I took out a notepad and jotted these notes down. I figured the officer that was at my house would be having the same concerns and no one would ever need these."

Mrs. Goldstein handed me three pages of 5"x 8" handwritten notes. Her notes provided a detailed description of what happened at what time, when Julie arrived, when they called 911, when the officer arrived and how Julie was dressed. She described the sopping wet condition of Julie's hair, her clothing and her unbroken nails. Mrs. Goldstein used quotation marks for the statements Julie made.

Mrs. Goldstein also wrote a few additional comments she thought relative. She wrote that Taylor and Robbie missed a lot of school and that Sydney and a few of the other neighbor kids frequently brought their homework home for them. She wondered why they missed so much school. Mrs. Goldstein had dated the notes, November 23rd the day after the murders.

There were more pages. Nurse Goldstein wrote additional notes into her Wiley chart on June 12th, nearly 7 months after the murders. I read the notes.

"*Carrie Bergeron called me at 7:15pm today. Carrie is Courtney's mom, another child in Sydney and Taylor's class. Carrie said she had a run in with Julie that afternoon outside the Oakview Mall. Carrie said she noticed a car parked outside the Ann Taylor Shoe Boutique with two dogs locked inside. The temperature was in the 90s. Carrie said she waited a few minutes and the dogs looked like they were getting overheated. She said she was getting ready to call the police, but the owner came outside. It was Julie Wiley. Carrie said she asked*

*Julie how she was doing and she said that initially, Julie was pleasant. Carrie said she told Julie she should leave the windows in her car cracked open if she was going to leave the dogs inside. She said that all of a sudden, Julie "snapped" and called her a bitch and she should mind her own business. She said that Julie swung a shopping bag at her and hit her in the face. She said some tall guy with long sandy hair pushed Julie in the car and they drove away. Carrie said she had a scratch on her cheek. She went home, called the police. Carrie said an officer from Oakview came out to her house and took a report. We never heard whether Julie got in trouble over this or not."*

As I read, pulses of lancinating pain tapped my left shoulder blade. My face wrenched into a grimace as the pain increased. The muscles went into spasm, pulling my left shoulder up that it touched my ear.

"Son of a bitch!" I growled through riveted teeth, collapsing back to the left against the couch.

"Oh my God. What's wrong? Are you having chest pain?" Nurse Goldstein asked.

"No. No. No. No. Dammit. My shoulder. Muscle cramp, old injury, scar tissue. Happens for no reason. I'll be fine," I said through rapid shallow gasps. "Just give me a minute."

The tapping and grabbing of the muscles throbbed, shaking my upper torso.

Bev reached over and took my pulse. "A steady 55, yea you're a runner." She went over to a closet and returned with a stethoscope. "24 breaths per minute. No unusual gurgling or wet sounds. Try to slow your breathing down, take long deep breaths." She went behind the couch and palpated the back of my neck and shoulder blades. She found the knots and spasm causing the pain. "Oh my God. You are all cramped up detective. Your traps and rhomboids are a mess. I'll work it out for you. Is that OK? I was a massage therapist before nursing school. But that was a long time ago. Still, you never forget all of the techniques."

Nurse Goldstein rubbed and stretched my shoulder for a couple of minutes. The muscles did not totally release, but did relax enough to allow me to move my head away from my left shoulder.

I rolled my head around slowly and shook off the pain like a wet dog. "That really helped Mrs. Goldstein."

"It's Bev. And you're welcome. You need to see somebody about that. You've got a real irritated focal point in those traps. A sudden spasm like that can cause damage."

"Thanks. I will. I'm embarrassed. I'm really sorry folks," I said, my voice raspy as I struggled to breathe through the residual pain. I tucked the notes in my jacket pocket and stood.

Phillip stood up. "Hey that's ok. I've pulled my back a few times. I know how it is," he said, extending his hand. We shook again.

"Really, Detective Green, there is no need to apologize," Bev said. "But, you should see a doctor. There's something causing that spasm. You need to have that checked out. At the very least, you could get some medication."

I smiled slightly, "I will. Thank you so much."

"Would you please let us know what you find out about the Wileys? Tell us if you find anything other than what we heard. Other than that Craig killed the kids and killed himself," Phillip asked.

"I sure will. Thanks again, thanks so much. You both have provided much more information than I thought I would be getting today. I'll keep in touch. I promise. Here's one of my cards, the bottom number is a direct line to my desk. If you think of anything else, or have any questions, please call me. And Mrs. Goldstein, thanks again, you have a very nice touch."

"That's quite alright. Glad I could help. Maybe I'll see you at a 5K or something." Bev Goldstein extended her hand and we shook. It was still moist and warm from the massage. Our eyes met and she winked, then squeezed my hand softly twice.

"Yea. Maybe so. Thanks again. And you guys have a nice holiday."

Mrs. Goldstein smiled and shut the door behind me.

As soon as I returned to the Crown Vic, I rifled through my briefcase like a junkie burglar. I downed two Oxys with a couple swallows of the Stoli from my flask. I sat in the car for a few minutes trying to breathe deep as Mrs. Goldstein, and the former Mrs. Sheila Green frequently recommended. I wondered what that wink and squeeze was all about. Thoughts of a massage from Mrs. Goldstein and deep breathing would have to take a backseat to good old fashioned narcotics. I could not so much as look up into the rear view mirror without provoking more drum beats of that tapping pain that now radiated from my left shoulder to the top of my head. A vice like headache was deciding whether to totally ruin the rest of this day.

I took the notes back to the station, made copies and logged the originals into evidence. The drugs were working and another shot of Stoli kept the pain just below a scream. I called MQ at home and gave him an abridged version of what the Goldstein's had said.

"Well my good doctor, look what we've developed by posing a few questions, challenging the established hypothesis. Dammit, the outcome of this case would have been so different had anyone put forth just a modicum of investigative effort."

"Yep you're right about that Murph."

"You don't sound like your ebullient self, all agog with the potential for reigning hell fire on evil doers. What's going on doc?"

"Just a headache that's all."

"Me thinks it is more than that by the sound of your voice. Your Sergeant says for you to go home. Spend the day with your kids."

"They're out of town with Sheila. By myself this weekend."

"Well then, come over here. The ball and chain is making German potato salad with plenty of bacon and I'm putting on some pork steaks. A perfect holiday meal, huh Rabbi?"

"Thanks Murph. I think I will just wallow in my own self pity today."

"Why don't you find yourself a girlfriend Morris? Find some babe to keep carnal company with. I guarantee you that emptying your prostate will make you feel better. As a physician, you should know that."

"If I need company, I'll get a dog. I have a pretty awful track record with humans."

"Jesus Morris. Who do you think you are? Me? Those are my lines."

"Well Murph, you still have a family and a house and a BBQ on this Memorial day weekend."

"Doc, if you're not going to come over, go home and put your troubles and worries away in a Wild Turkey and 7-Up. We'll work on your people skills next week. How's that?"

"Sure thing MQ."

"Dammit Morris. This Homeric journey you've started with the Wiley case, it is righteous work, seeking biblical justice. And when justice is served, it will be because of your efforts. Feel proud you started this. This is all you my friend. I'm just along for the ride."

"Funny. That's how Sheila described her life with me, along for the ride. Maybe I am just here to be a bus driver."

"Driver or not, you are the best investigator I have ever known and my best friend."

"Thanks MQ. And your mine, except you're my only friend."

"Stop trying to emulate me. It takes years to become as proficient as I am on self immolation. Seriously Morris, we are going to persevere to the bitter end. And remember this good doctor, when competing hypotheses are considered, choose the simplest. Occam's Razor. In technical terms, the bitch did it. Now go rent a movie or a woman, get lost in a bottle, or do all three."

So saith Sol.

I hung up the phone. The tapping and cramping in my left shoulder charged forward like General Custer. This time, the spasm, or whatever it was, caused the muscles of my left ring finger and little finger to tetanize in flexion. The digits were pulled painfully into my palm. The pain of the sustained spasm was exquisite. I tried pulling my fingers straight, but they curled back like a party favor whistle. There was no stopping the cramp and the pain started to race up my forearm. My heart started to race. I knew the door was opening to an anxiety attack and I had no intention of spending the evening in the ER.

I drove to the clinic. It was closed for the holiday and I went in through the side staff door. Lenora, the front desk administrator kept the keys to the narcotics cabinet in her desk. I rifled through her drawers. Thank goodness security was lax at the People's clinic.

With considerable difficulty, using one hand, I cracked the top of a 5mg vial of Valium, drew it up into the barrel of a syringe and stared at the amber liquid.

"Well Morris," I said softly to myself, "You've reached a new low. Stealing injectable controlled substances and falsifying entries on the narcotics log. What's next? Smoking crack with your former junkie informants?"

I injected the Valium slowly into the vein in my left arm. My fingers relaxed and my body deflated. I laid down on the couch in my office. As the valium worked its way to my brain, a Grateful Dead song came to mind that pretty much summed everything up.

*"Drivin' that train, High on cocaine, Casey Jones you better, watch your speed.*
*Trouble ahead, Trouble behind, and you know that notion, just crossed my mind.*
*Trouble ahead, The Lady in Red, Take my advice, you be better off dead.*
*Switchman sleepin, Train hundred and two, is on the wrong track, and headed for you..."*

I remember humming the lyrics and then the blinds shut behind my eyes and everything went into a haze.

# Chapter Thirty Nine

found myself in complete blackness. I couldn't tell if I was supine or prone, in air or water. The darkness was shattered by an eye piercing bright light that bore down on me and illuminated my surroundings. I was standing on the train platform again, that ominous looking building behind me. The sound from the engine and brakes of the oncoming train was deafening. Gold and yellow sparks flying off the tracks struck my face, the pungent smell of burning flesh filled my senses. I caught a glimpse of translucent shapes peering at me from the passing train car window, and then I awoke. My face was contorted from the burns and I rubbed my skin to feel for blistering. My hair and the couch cushion were damp from dream sweat. I focused and looked around at unfamiliar surroundings. Finally, I recognized my office and I remembered. The syringe and vial lay on the floor. I sat up and noticed that I could turn my head, and my fingers worked properly, better living through chemistry. The clock showed that it was just after 3am.

I did some necessary housekeeping at the clinic to cover my tracks and drove home. I took a Xanax, flipped on the TV for background noise and light, and laid down in bed. My cell phone rang at 5am.

"Dammit. Shit," I said, hoping I didn't miss a call from the dispatcher while shooting up. The number told me it wasn't the dispatcher. It was Sheila's cell. I let it go to voice mail and drifted back to sleep. There were no dreams this time.

I woke up at noon. The weatherman on TV was assuring everyone that the warm weather was here to stay for the whole weekend and there was no rain in sight.

Surprisingly, I felt well enough for a run. The valium must have kicked the cramp to the curb. I downed half a Gatorade and slipped on my Nike's. Looking in the mirror on my way out the door, I thought, "It's true. That which does not kill us makes us stronger. Otherwise, I'd be long dead."

I cruised through the cemetery at a blistering 11 minute per mile pace, stopping briefly at the heart shaped stone to update the children. "It's looking more like your mother is suspect number one." I took another piss on Francis' grave and the rest of the run was uneventful.

I returned to the apartment to catch the ringing landline. I explained to Sheila that I'd been out all night processing a string of car break-ins and my cell phone had died. I figured, why tell the truth, when a perfectly good lie will do. I certainly wouldn't believe a word Morris Green uttered anyway, if I were Sheila. Given the status of our relationship, it really was irrelevant.

I asked how the kids were doing and how her family was and listened patiently, waiting until I could hang up. Her calling, her caring, was just another reminder of how fucked up I was and how much it had cost me.

I checked with the dispatcher to make sure I hadn't missed any calls. It had been a quiet night and day so far. I showered, made some ice tea and did laundry. As the afternoon waned, I picked up the Wiley file.

Continuing on in my chronological quest, I identified the other people who had contact with Julie Wiley on the night of the murders, the ambulance personnel and ER doctor. I pulled the ambulance run sheet out of the file and called the firehouse closest to the Wiley's neighborhood. One of the medics who transported Mrs. Wiley from the Goldstein's to the hospital, happened to be working the holiday.

Jim Purdo had been a paramedic for 17 years. We never worked together on a rig, but he knew my history as a para-medi-cop. We shared the "we've seen the same fucked up things" bond that only cops, medics, fireman and the military share. I explained the cold case investigation to him.

"It was nothing more than a transport doc," Jim said. "She had a few red marks on her wrists, but no other injuries were apparent. Nothing that required treatment. That's what I wrote in my physical assessment. Her emotional status, now that was different. That's for sure."

"How so?" I asked.

"We got the call to pick her up just after our other ambulance and a pumper had been sent out for the two children. Dispatch told us it was the mother of the kids and we heard the radio traffic about what was going on. We expected the mother to be whacked, freaking out. You know? But she wasn't. She was calm.

I charted her psych state as normal. Do you have a copy of the ambulance trip sheet with my assessment?"

"No. All I have is the run sheet. I don't have the report. I'm sure there's one in the system somewhere."

"I'll send you a copy if you need it," he offered.

"That'd be great. Thanks. Anything else you remember about the ride with her to the hospital?"

"Not really. She walked out to the ambulance and sat up on the bench in the back. She was quiet. One of your guys from Oakview rode with us to the ER. I can't remember who it was, but his name is in the report. We dumped and jumped. Margie Classa was the ER doc that night at St. Marks. She's still working ER if you need to talk to her. That's all there was to it doc. Just a really weird transport."

"Thanks Jim. Have a quiet day."

"Holiday weekend? Quiet? Yea. Too sure. We've run 7 calls so far."

"I remember. Stay safe."

"You too doc."

I had been to St. Marks a few times for a conference or a pharmaceutical rep presentation. However, I was not on staff there. Years ago, St. Marks had been the beautiful new hospital on the far edge of the suburbs, trendy and fresh, like a new shopping mall.

As a foreign medical school grad, they wanted me to spend additional time with a few of the internal medicine department staff members to prove I was capable of pushing patients through the doors. I thought that was a bunch of bullshit. Besides, I was busy fighting crime and had staff privileges at the university hospital near the clinic.

I wanted to find out what happened during Julie Wiley's ER visit but I foresaw some problems. This was not a fresh, urgent investigation. St. Marks might view their historical ER records as privileged medical information under HIPPA not to be released without subpoena or patient authorization, and we certainly didn't want to contact Mrs. Wiley for permission to obtain her medical records.

Neither did we want to bring the prosecutor's office into the mix at this stage by asking for a subpoena. There may come a time to take the case to the prosecuting attorney and remind him that his office is staffed by lazy and apathetic career government employees who let a triple murder slip by, but now was not the time.

I figured maybe I could obtain some information off the record. I called St. Marks. Jim was right. Just like me, Dr. Classa was working the weekend. I drove the 30 minutes into the burbs and stopped by St. Marks about 10pm.

I identified myself to the ER clerk as Dr. Green and asked for Dr. Classa. I was directed to the physician's lounge down the hall from the ER, just past the imaging department.

There was only one person in scrubs in the lounge. Dr. Classa was stretched out on a cheap, institutional green, vinyl couch, her head propped up on a pillow. Her tennis shoes were lying on the floor, and her bare feet were atop the cracked plastic bolster at the end of the couch.

She was tall and took the full length of the couch. Her long, dark hair flayed out over the pillow and arm rest. Margaret Classa was, politely-phrased, a full figured woman and her scrubs were probably a men's large. She looked to be in her late 30's. Her face was a bit weathered as if she had been quite intimate with the sun. She was reading this month's New England Journal of Medicine. Silver wire rimmed reading glasses were perched on the end of her ski slope nose. She looked over the top of the magazine as the door latch clattered shut behind me.

"Hi, can I help you?" she asked.

"Yes, I'm Morris Green. I'm one of the docs at the People's clinic. Do you have a couple minutes?

"Sure, what's up? We get a few of your people out here now and then. Most want to be transferred back to the university clinic."

"Yea. We are a bit more urban than St. Marks and our clientele generally likes to stay out of the suburbs." We made eye contact as we spoke. Her green eyes were speckled with what looked like gold dust. They were hypnotic.

"So, how can I help you?"

I pulled out my badge case and held it out for her to read. She scooted the specs back up her nose and stared at the ID card. A confused furrow appeared on her forehead.

I realized I was still staring at her face and those eyes, and blinked away the attention, "I'm not here in my capacity as a physician. I have another parallel life going on. I am also a detective with the Oakview PD. We have a case I'm working."

Dr. Classa rocked up from her supine position and sat up on the couch. The vinyl cushions whooshed and crackled. She put her journal down, "Oh, yea, you're that Dr. Green? I read a few of the articles in the paper, after you and your partner were shot. Right? You guys were narcs if I recall."

"It's been a while. I'm surprised you'd remember."

"My dad was a cop in Miami. It's where I'm from. He worked narcotics for quite some time and also got shot, so I'm attuned to that kind of thing. And I thought it was a bit odd that a physician was a narc, but what the hell, I worked as a paramedic while going through pre-med and even into the first year of med school. And 'they', you know, 'they'. Those people who do everything right, everything in order, according to their life script. 'They' said I was crazy. Kept asking me why I would want to work with all the studying?"

"Yea, I had, and still have, my fair share of those people," I said, thinking of Jim Farrar, my neurologist whose career path was perfectly planned and executed. "And there's more than just a few folks who think I am two bricks shy of a full load. I know all too well who 'they' are."

"Really, I was just bored with the bookwork," she said. "Memorization and mnemonics. I wanted some action and I got it as a medic. It's why I'm an ER doc."

"I hear you. Anyway, I am sorry to hear about your father."

"It was a long time ago, when I was in high school. Oh, yea, and he survived. Shot in the leg by some cokehead asshole. It's a long story. Anyway, so, how are you? I seem to recall you had a head injury or something. Are you good now?" She stood and stretched, rolling her shoulders. We shook hands. She had a strong, warm and confident grip. I grabbed another furtive glimpse of her eyes.

"I took a few unwanted metallic foreign bodies. I had some nerve and muscle damage, some ocular trauma, but the surgeons and plastics folks did a fine job. My partner wasn't so lucky. He's a paraplegic and retired on disability."

"Oh man. I'm sorry to hear that."

There was a momentary awkward pause.

"The reason I am here is we are taking a second look at a murder case. It actually happened the same night as my shooting. You saw the victims in the ER. Do you remember the Wiley children?"

"Ugh. Oh my God yes," she said sitting down on one end of the couch. "Yea, that's right. That was the same night. How weird, huh?"

I sat on the opposite end of the couch. "Definitely weird."

"Jesus, Dr. Green. The murder of those children was grotesquely gruesome, and that is something coming from me. I did my residency at the University of Maryland, the 'R. Adams Cowley Shock Trauma Center' in Baltimore. I'm sure you've read some of the studies coming out of there. Great traumaland. I mean some real bad ass, man's inhumanity to man. Killings and terrific industrial and vehicular fatalities. We saw it all. Since I'd been a medic and my dad was a career cop, I grew up with stories and pictures of blood and guts. But let me tell you, those Wiley kids are pretty high on the 'I remember that one' list. We just don't get that level of violence in this neighborhood very often."

"I'm glad you remember it. The case was closed as a murder-suicide. The father allegedly killed the kids, let the mother go and then committed suicide.

A few of us think it deserves a second look. Can you tell me a little about what you did and saw that night?"

"You don't think he did it?"

"Not sure at this point. We're taking a closer look at all the players. So, what can you tell me about the mom and the kids that showed up here?"

"Dr. Green, you know there are privacy rules and that I can't discuss patient information."

"I know Dr. Classa. HIPPA yada, yada, yada. How about we discuss the case off the record and if we need anything official, I will subpoena the hospital. I suspect you probably inherited your father's police intuition and any of your impressions of that night would be helpful."

"I really don't want to get placed in the position of..."

"I promise anything you tell me will be strictly off the record. Maybe you have some things you want to get off your chest about this case. I know I have some real concerns about it."

Dr. Classa chewed a bit on the inside of her lower lip. She stared at me with those kaleidoscope eyes.

"I get off at 7am. I usually go over to the Eat-Rite for breakfast because they still have a smoking section. It's about a mile from here, why don't you meet me there. We can chat a little more openly. Hopefully the monsters will be quiet tonight and I can get some rest. I'll try to collect my thoughts about that night."

"Sounds great to me. I'm a big fan of greasy spoons."

I handed her my police and my clinic business card with my cell phone number.

"Dr. Classa, if something comes up, a late code or you can't get away, just give me a call."

"I sure will. And, you can call me Margie."

"Ok, Margie it is. I'm Morris."

"See you at breakfast Morris."

# Chapter Forty

I was called out to process an apartment burglary at 4:30 in the morning. Unfortunately, the dispatcher's call did not startle me awake. I was already up. The 3am train dream again. This time the passengers stared at me through the fogged train window with freakishly large, round, black eyes, reminiscent of the 1960s Margaret Keane prints. Their eyes were magnetic, hollow pits that were both alluring and terrifying. It stirred up something in my brain and gut which kept me from going back to sleep.

I arrived at the Eat-Rite at about 6:30am and got a booth in the back smoking section overlooking the parking lot. I suspected that Margie Classa smoked, drank draft beer with a whiskey back, and possibly played Roller Derby.

Dr. Classa pulled in about a half hour later, behind the wheel of a silver Lincoln Navigator. The size 14 carbon footprint vehicle fit her nicely. She got out, flicked a cigarette across the lot and bought a newspaper from the stand. She was still in scrubs wearing a light beige London Fog overcoat. When she passed the cash register, I waved her back. She took her coat off and stuffed it and the paper in the corner of the booth seat. She settled in across from me, pulling a pack of Marlboro Lights from her scrub top pocket. She expertly tapped two out and offered one to me. I said no thanks and she lit up, turning obliquely to blow the smoke away from my direction.

"We were pretty slow last night. A car accident with a fractured femur, and a diabetic coma. Not too bad. I got a couple hours sleep."

"We had one B & E, fortunately a small apartment."

We spoke the same language of depersonalization in which people are not names, but conditions or events. At the department, I'll work a burglary, an assault, or a rape. In the clinic, I'll see a few pneumonias, some COPD'ers, and an occasional chest pain. It's easier to deal with conditions or events rather than people. People are messy and convoluted. They are needy, with any number of psychosocial issues in addition to organic ills or problems. Treat the symptom and condition, and the person will go away, making room for the next.

Dr. Classa continued, "I spent some time thinking about that night, putting what I remember in order. I checked the record room, but the physical chart is filed offsite and I didn't want to ask. If this is going to be official at some point, I didn't want to leave a paper trail with my name on it before then."

"Margie, I totally understand and thank you for even looking for the chart. What you do remember, will determine whether we need to subpoena the record. So, what do you recall?"

We ate our three egg, bacon, sausage and cheese omelets, our toast painted with thick butter and drank coffee for over an hour as she narrated her recollection. She recalled the female child with gunshot wounds to the face and hatcheting through the cranial vault, the male child, disemboweled from an abdominal stabbing and the woman with minor abrasions.

"The kids came in by helicopter," she said. "The boy had a subclavian IV and the little girl had an intraosseous infusion in her tibia. They'd put a bulky dressing on her head and the boy's belly. Not much else the medics could do but push fluids and hurry."

"What about the mother? What do you remember about her? Mental status, functional ability, clothing, anything.

"She was already here, having been brought in by ambulance several minutes before the kids came in. I was charting by the front desk when she and a police officer walked up to the registration clerk. I didn't know at first that she was part of the incoming drama. She had that thousand-yard stare. I thought maybe she was in for a psych evaluation or protective custody since she was accompanied by the police. I remember she had this sweatshirt on inside out. And her hair was wet, like stringy wet, as if she had been out in the rain, but it wasn't raining that night. She looked bewildered, like some of our homeless folks."

Margie closed her eyes momentarily, conjuring up a memory. She picked at a stuck piece of toast from one of her canines and said, "Anyway, I finished some charting and went back to the break room for a cup of coffee. Robbie, the triage nurse, came in and told me I had to check the woman the cops had brought in, and that she was the mother of the kids that were being coptered."

"So you evaluated Mrs. Wiley prior to the kids arriving?

"Yea. I initially spent about five minutes, one on one with her. I was working on another patient with chest pain, an MI I think. Anyway, I had to check on him too. So I was going between rooms making sure the cardiac guy stabilized. I talked to her, left, returned, examined her, returned. You know how it is."

I nodded, although my Caribbean ER experience wasn't quite so hectic.

"What was her cognitive status? Was she psychotic or in shock, or what?" I asked.

"Clearly she was traumatized in some fashion, but psychotic, no. She answered all my questions appropriately. She was by no means out of touch with reality. And then the kids came in and it got real busy. I returned to Mrs. Wiley's room later to tell her that despite our best efforts, that her children had died. It was strange, but when I told her, she didn't start wailing or anything like that, and she didn't want to say goodbye to them which I thought rather odd. By that time, her mother was there. Now that lady, the grandmother, she went bonkers, but she got it together enough to do the identification of her grandchildren since her daughter wouldn't. I wrote Mrs. Wiley a scrip for Alprazolam. Robbie filled out the discharge forms and the officer walked her and her mom out."

"Margie, was she at all sad, despondent, upset, angry? Anything that could be considered typical behavior considering the situation?"

"Hell, I don't know. Who knows what is normal under those conditions? She didn't break down or have any fits of hysteria, which would have certainly been understandable. Morris, you've probably had patients with blunted affects. She was in that neighborhood. She failed to display any emotional reactivity to the events. She said everything in a monotone with little expression. Her response was clearly what most of us would consider atypical given what happened. Shit, in Baltimore, we had a special room called the 'Wailing Room' for people who lost love ones in our ER, where all the screaming, hollering, praying and weeping went on. Trauma drama is noisy and disruptive and we usually had a lot of it going on. We put one of our LPNs down there with the grievers and wailers which kept them away from the ER so we could do our work. I can tell you that Mrs. Wiley was not a wailer."

"Funny, I worked in an ER as a paramedic, and we had the 'Grieving Room' for our wailers. Logistically it was all wrong. The Grieving Room was also where the coffee pot was. So if we had grievers, we had to go on a journey to the cafeteria for coffee. We thought the grievers were a real pain in the ass."

"Grievers and Wailers. I guess it's the same no matter where. You were a medic too? Medic, doctor, cop, renaissance man, huh?" she said, nodding her head, lighting up another smoke. We briefly locked eyes. I was captivated.

"Did you ask her what happened? What history did she give on how things happened?"

"Yea. I figured you were going to ask me that. I spent some time thinking about what she and I talked about. I did ask a few things." Dr. Classa took a long drag on her smoke, blew it out through her nose and sipped some coffee before continuing.

"Mrs. Wiley said she had been home all day. She said she had stomach troubles, her period or something like that. She said her husband had come home and had given her something, pills or something anyway, to make her feel better. She didn't know what they were but she said she got groggy. I thought maybe the guy drugged her. You know, gave her sedatives or something so he could kill the family uninterrupted. That's why I ordered blood and urine for a tox screen."

"Good thinking. Did she tell you what happened?"

"Yea. Kinda. She said her husband came home with the kids and then snapped. He went crazy. He tied her up on the bed, handcuffed her wrists, something like that, like bondage style. She said he choked her, it sounded like he raped her or at least there was some kind of sexual activity. Morris, it was weird though. She described all of this in like a Ben Stein monotone. Not an inflection, not a tremor in her voice. She may as well have been talking about curtains or carpeting. Blasé."

"Margie, did you guys do a rape kit exam?"

"I thought we should even though she was not really clear as to whether she was raped or not. I asked the officer if he wanted one. He called someone on his walkie talkie and a couple minutes later he told me a rape kit would not be necessary."

"Hmm, that is strange."

"I thought so too Morris. But, it was one less thing for me to deal with."

"Go on please. What else did she say? Did she say anything about what her husband did to the kids?"

Dr. Classa poured us both another cup of coffee from the carafe on the table.

"Nothing specific really. Just that he snapped and did it. She didn't go into how he did it, and I didn't ask. Their injuries pretty much told the story of how they were killed."

I finished off my toast. "How about her physical condition? Was it consistent with what she said happened to her?"

"Last night, I tried my best to picture any injuries in my mind. I don't recall that she had any marks or anything that matched her story of being tied up or choked. I do remember she had some superficial abrasions on her wrists, but I don't recall seeing ridged handcuff impressions. She had this frilly, pink and red elastic hair thingy on her left wrist. Damn, what do you call them? My brain is tired, shit. You tie your ponytail back with them?"

"A scrunchy?"

"Yea, a scrunchy. She had one on her left wrist and I had her take it off to examine her. No deep marks to speak of. You're a cop, you've put the cuffs on somebody too tight, the marks stay awhile. Maybe her husband was a gentle homicidal maniac and double-locked the cuffs, or perhaps they were fur lined."

"Dr. Classa, perhaps you want to expound on your experience with fur lined handcuffs."

Margie broke into an impish smile and laughed with a deep chortle. "Ha. You are a funny man, Dr. Green. As I was saying, no significant injuries to speak of. I don't think there were any abrasions on her ankles either. As I recall Morris, she looked pretty much ok. And aside from the scrip for the Alprazolam, we didn't provide any other care."

"You said you did lab?"

"Yea, yea. We took blood and urine samples."

"Did you probe for any details like what made the husband snap?

"Sorry Morris, I didn't. No reason to and I was pretty busy."

Margie stopped for a moment and lit another cigarette. She stretched her neck and shoulders, rolling them as she had in the doctor's lounge. "I gotta stop sleeping on that damn couch in the lounge. It screws up my neck."

"You need a good chiropractor? I hear my ex is dating one. I can get you his name," I said.

"I'll let you know."

"Margie, how detailed do you think your ER chart is?"

"It's the usual. I charted what she said, findings of my exam and I remember that I did make a note about her lack of emotional responsiveness," she snuffed her cigarette out in the ashtray.

"Oh, and I did write that the Officer, whatever his name was, declined the rape examination. If you are asking whether I wrote specifically that there were no marks anywhere else like on her face, wrist, ankles, I doubt it. I probably wrote, something like 'no other injuries noted on physical examination'. You know, unless a negative finding is pertinent to the management of the patient, we usually don't write it down. It's the ER, not primary care."

"I understand. Did she say anything about her being able to get away?"

Dr. Classa drained her glass of water. "No. Not about that either. But Morris, that's something I wanted to ask you about. So if I understand it correctly, she was able to save herself but unable to do anything to save her kids. Pretty fucked up if you ask me."

"Yea, big time fucked up. Welcome to my world."

"Sucks to be Dr. Detective Morris Green then, huh?"

"You don't know the half of it."

"So how far from kosher is this case?"

I leaned forward closer to her. "Between you and me Margie, it's a Southern Baptist Dixie pig roast. I can tell you that I will definitely need the ER record. I will be getting a subpoena for the chart."

She smoked a few more cigarettes. We shared several more cups of coffee and swapped paramedic and med school stories.

By the time most folks were logging on to their computers in their hamster cage cubicles, we were sweaty and tangled up under cool, 800 thread count sheets in Margaret Classa's loft. Our lovemaking was akin to our lives, fierce, frenetic and feverish, a turbulent Code Blue of focused tongues and piston fingers.

Once again, MQ, prophetic King Sol, was correct. As I drove home, surrounded by the sweet, wet smell of sex and the lavender lotion Margie used, I did feel better.

# Chapter Forty One

I was sore from the sex. It was the first physical pain I welcomed in a long time. I went for a long, slow run, a 10 miler, which took an hour and 45 minutes. It was LSD, a long, slow, distance which in my case was a long, slogging, distance. That which does not kill us makes us strong.

I had two days in a row, with nothing requiring my immediate attention in the detective in-box at the station. I spent a few hours with the Wiley file and thought about calling Margie. Maybe it was our similar backgrounds, but I felt we had connected at some level. When I left her place, she had given me a long, wet kiss goodbye, but didn't say anything about repeating, so I didn't call her.

I called Sheila when I got home and talked to the kids. They'd had a great time at the lake. They went for a ride in the pontoon boat went swimming and barbecued pork steaks. Sheila's dad let my son shoot a .22 rifle for the first time. Jake went on about how cool it was and that he had hit a bull's eye. It was another first for my boy, accomplished without his father. I put my cell on loud and vibrate and stuck it into my front shirt pocket in the event I got a call from the dispatcher. I proceeded to drink myself into unconsciousness and was out even before the weather and sports came on.

I was off work from the PD the next day, but had picked up a shift at the clinic. There was a steady flow of patients. I treated a work injury from the tool and die plant, a nasty laceration requiring a dozen stitches to the forearm to close a deep gash. It was definitely not my best cosmetic work, but the guy had tribal tattoos all over the forearm. New ink would cover any stitch marks.

Another worker came in bent over with back pain. I ordered some x-rays and prescribed some Flexeril. We had a couple of asthmatics wheeze in. It was just busy enough to filter the consistent Wiley noise in my head, nothing quite so dramatic as what pops into Margie Classa's ER.

When I had a break, I took the plunge and called her cell. It went to voice-mail. "Hey Margie. Morris here. I was, um, just thinking about the other day and it brought a smile to my face, something that I don't do often enough. Give me a call when you can. Bye."

I know it probably sounded lame, but it was true.

I was back at the detective bureau the next day. I made some coffee, and went into MQ's office. He was sitting at his desk, surrounded by a blue cloud of cigar smoke going through reports.

"Hey pal, how was the weekend?"

"Nothing really worth a shit around here. Pretty quiet. I filled him in on my encounter with Dr. Classa, leaving out the morning sex.

"Wet hair, no blood, no injuries. So she washes her hair and hurriedly changes clothes in the middle of a massacre? I think not," he said.

"She is suspect #1 in my book," I affirmed. "Whether she acted alone is still an unknown."

"Let's bring that bitch in. I want to sit across the table from her in the room," MQ said, but then added, "Scratch that. I think it would be premature to talk to her. What do you think doc?"

"We need more information on her and the Wiley family dynamic. We need to find out what Mrs. Wiley was up to at the time of the murders. Maybe the guy with her at the shoe store was her boyfriend then too. Maybe there's a love tri-angle. We'll probably only have one shot at talking to her. So, before we do, we need more intel on the Wiley family dynamic."

"I was at the station on the night of the murders. I had just sent her lawyer, you know, Will's Nordic brother away. The phone had rung and it was Craig Wiley's father. He called the station asking for information. I talked to him briefly. His name was…" MQ paused and scrunched his round face. "Victor, Victor Wiley, that's it. I told him to go to Sisters of Faith Hospital. That's where they trans-ported their son's body. He said he couldn't believe his son would ever harm those children. Understandably, he was in a hurry to get off the phone and to the hospital."

"There is no mention of anyone following up with Victor Wiley in the file," I said.

"Pretty par for the course," MQ added.

"I'll go on whitepages.com and find his phone number," I said.

"Why don't we just do it the old fashioned way," MQ said, pulling a phone book from behind his desk. "Technology is hastening the demise of our white matter. Pulp and pages my friend, will prove to serve us much faster than plastic and silicon. Perhaps a gentle colloquy with the grieving parents may very well offer additional clues."

From the phone book, we found that Craig Wiley's parents, Victor and Clarissa, were living in a relatively new condo development, not too far from the neighborhood where the murders took place.

An hour later, we found ourselves sitting on a red, green and blue floral print couch in Victor and Clarissa Wiley's great room. The condominium was open and bright with an attached sunroom and deck overlooking a wooded common ground. A stunning black baby grand held court in the living room with open sheet music resting on a brass holder.

Victor sat across from us in a rocker recliner that matched the couch. The chair was busy as Victor fidgeted. He was tall, easily 6'3, and slim, wearing a short sleeve white shirt and sharply creased and pleated tan Docker slacks. He was probably in his late 60s and had a full head of silver hair. He had managed to maintain a younger man's muscle tone, evidenced by a very firm handshake and the lack of any significant skin dangling below his triceps. He was deeply tanned. I figured he was probably a golfer. The only AARP regalia I noted were the white Velcro loafers.

Clarissa appeared fragile and wounded, petite at perhaps 5'2" and 100lbs. She had fine grey hair, cut in a short bob. She wore no makeup and had the classic early dowager's stance. Perhaps she was truly osteoporotic and her bent over posture was physiologic, or the world was simply crushing her. Her snow globe life had cracked on that November 22nd.

Clarissa sat still as a mannequin in a crimson red, Louis XIV style fauteuil. She was wearing a plain sleeveless summer dress that hung loose like drapery. Her legs were crossed neatly and her elbows rested on the armchair, with her fingers interlaced in her lap.

Between their two chairs stood a heavy, ornate mahogany table with bronze appliqués on each claw shaped foot. Atop the table was a collection of photographs. School pictures of their dead grandchildren and several pictures of Craig Wiley at various ages. One picture had him kneeling next to a sable German Shepard. He was dressed in navy blue, five pocket fatigue pants and a polo shirt with gold shoulder patches and some type of logo on the left chest. Craig Wiley's hand rested behind the dog's thick neck. Both were smiling. A prickly sensation wrinkled my left shoulder as I perused the photographs. I hoped this was not foretelling another episode like what had happened at the Goldsteins. I didn't think Clarissa could massage my neck.

"This is such a large place, very deceptive from the outside, you'd never guess there was room for a baby grand," MQ said to begin the interview.

"That's one of the reasons we moved here after we sold the house. We wanted large rooms, but no more grass to cut. And both Clarissa and I play piano. I enjoy the more recent virtuosos, like Vladimir Horowitz, Rachmaninoff, Stravinsky, Arthur Rubenstein. In fact the piece on the piano is Stravinsky's *Canticum Sacrum ad Honorem Sancti Marci Nominis.* Just wonderful, thrilling. Yet such a short piece. Are you familiar?"

"No sir," MQ answered.

I was thinking if he'd asked about Styx, Allman Brothers, the Dead or Bob Seger we could have had a conversation about music.

Victor continued, unimpeded by the musical void between us. "Clarissa can play show tunes like nobody's business. I can't tell you how many times we had the kids singing along to the tunes from *Oklahoma, Sound of Music* or *South Pacific.* That Taylor loved "I'm gonna wash that man right out of my hair, I'm gonna wash that man right out of my hair," his voice carried the tune.

Suddenly, the skin and muscles along my left shoulder blade paroxysmally twitched. It felt like there was a battalion of centipedes with needles for feet marching between my neck and shoulder. I flinched and closed my eyes hoping it would stop. Taylor Wiley's autopsy photo flashed before me; her matted nest of hair amidst the clotting blood and brain matter. Then, as if a film projector started up, I saw Julie Wiley, in the shower, in Hitchcockian style, the blood of her children, rinsing from her hair, arms and hands and swirling down the drain.

MQ noticed. "Morris. You OK?" He said, breaking the film show in my mind.

"I'm sorry," I said shaking my head. "I just had a wave of a migraine I think. It'll pass. Please go on," I reached into my pocket and dryly crunched on two viciously bitter Percocets barely tempered by a piece of Juicy Fruit.

MQ picked up the slack. "Mr. Wiley, I spoke to you on the phone the night it happened. You said you couldn't believe your son could have done it. Is there anything that you can think of that would have explained what happened?"

"No, absolutely no explanation. It was beyond making any sense. Craig cherished those kids, loved them deeply. He would be incapable of doing anything like that."

"How was their home life and marriage?" MQ asked.

"His job was going well, the dog training business. He had international clients. He travelled some. He was starting to make some good money. Oh, they still had some money problems, but what young couple doesn't these days?"

MQ nodded. Victor continued.

"They seemed to get along. Julie was cool to us for the most part. She had a very large and close knit family, and we were, just the two of us. Kind of outsiders to such a big bunch, but we all got along alright. No, detective, nothing can explain…" Victor's voice trailed off and his head bowed, the rocking chair pace increased.

"Mr. Wiley, we aren't convinced your son did this either. That's why we are taking a closer look at this case," MQ said.

The caustic taste of the pills brought me back into the now and I engaged, directing a question to Clarissa.

"Mrs. Wiley, how was your son feeling in the weeks before it happened? How was he acting?"

Mrs. Wiley remained a static, birdlike figurine. She looked at me, then past me, then over to her husband who was moving like a metronome in that chair of his. Her head, neck and hands remained still, only her eyes moved. Her gaze returned to me as she spoke.

"He seemed fine to me. I don't know how he was feeling that, that night."

"When you got together with Craig and Julie and the kids, like in the weeks prior to the incident, how did everything seem to you? Ordinary, normal?" I rephrased, hoping for a better response from Clarissa.

"Yes, they seemed fine to me. We talked about that didn't we, Victor?"

"Yes, yes detective we did," Victor said. "We had gotten together with them, oh, I would say about a week before. Well, with Craig anyway. Craig and the kids came over on their way to Wal-Mart. I asked him to get me some new batteries for the smoke detector. It had started chirping. Everything was normal with him and the kids. Her, on the other hand, I can't say."

He paused for a moment. The rocker produced a metallic click with each pass.

Victor shook his head, indicating 'No' to the same speed as the rocking, "One thing that bothered me detective, is when I saw her on the news the day after it happened. She looked like nothing happened. I mean I couldn't believe she was on TV. And she said in the interview that Craig hurt her and she went back to him. She forgave him. But I don't recall anything like that ever happening. I don't know what she meant by that. Julie never left him. She never left him to go back to him. You knew she was on TV didn't you?"

217

MQ answered, "Yes, I do recall she was on TV the next evening. I didn't see it, but my wife told me about it. She said nearly the same thing as you. About how incredible that this woman could be on TV so soon, and how composed she was."

"I don't know how she did it. We were devastated. We certainly didn't want to talk to reporters," Victor said.

I continued, "Did either of you ever see or hear Craig and Julie fight? Did they ever discuss breaking up or anything seriously wrong in the marriage?"

Mrs. Wiley didn't respond or move. Victor answered.

"I know they argued at times. In fact, I remember once talking on the phone with Craig and hearing Julie screaming in the background. Boy was she ever loud. Craig told me to hold on, and I heard him yell at her. Something about if she was ever home to take care of the kids, and what was so important that she had to go somewhere. I asked him what that was all about and he just said Julie was the B word sometimes. I guess they were like any young couple, they had their moments. And Craig, well, he did have a temper. I can recall patching more than one hole in the drywall at our house when he was a teen-ager and got mad over something and punched through the wall," Victor's head bobbed up and down half a dozen times, as he paused and appeared to be thinking.

"Oh, and there was this one time, only one that I know of. I hate to bring it up. It was oh, probably at least 6 months before. Before that night. I'd say it was about 11 in the evening. Julie came over with the kids and said that Craig was going crazy, smashing things and she was afraid. She said her mom and dad were out of town, so by default I suppose, she came here. She and the kids stayed here, Clarissa and I went over there. We didn't live too far from them at the time.

Craig was in the garage, this time he was the one fixing a hole in the wall. We went into the kitchen and there were busted dishes all over the floor. I asked him what was going on, what had happened. He said, 'Dad, she just gets on my nerves. She goes out with friends, comes home late. I'm busy with the dogs, the kennels, and she goes out leaving me with the kids. Look at this place, she doesn't clean up, she doesn't cook and half the time the laundry isn't done.'

"I asked him if he was worried she was, well, I didn't want to pry, but I asked him whether he thought she was sleeping around on him. He said he didn't know. He said she just liked to go out with her friends and have a good time. I think he felt like he and the kids were coming in second. Craig just wanted more of a traditional mother and wife than Julie was. And he got frustrated that night."

"Did anything come of their argument?" MQ asked.

"No. She went home and they got along I suppose. I know you may think that he probably snapped then, and maybe it is possible that he snapped again that night, but I am sure he didn't. Those kids were his life."

Victor lowered his head. A tan hand rubbed a few tears into sun baked, leathery cheeks.

Wise old Sol spoke up to offer solace, "Mr. Wiley, if it's any comfort, I can tell you I have a bucket of drywall patch at home. I have, on a few occasions, put my fist through a wall in anger and frustration. Yes, an irrational and destructive act, but it's cathartic in so many ways. It does not make me a violent man. My wife calls me a number of choice words I cannot repeat in mixed company when I do something so obtuse. And I know it's juvenile and irrational. You see, I have always struggled with anger management issues, but I would never physically harm anyone out of anger, especially my wife or kids. And I think perhaps the same was true of your son."

"Folks, I can attest to the fact that Sgt. Quinn has anger management issues and I promise that we will leave your lovely home without inflicting any property damage," I said. A hint of a smile darted across Clarissa's upper lip. Perhaps someone was inside that wispy scaffolding.

"Do you know any of their friends that maybe we could contact, people they hung out with?" I asked.

Mr. Wiley had composed himself and continued, "They had a few friends, but Craig and Julie really spent a lot of time with her family. I' sure you know who they are."

"Yes. We understand her maiden name was Scalini," MQ said.

"That's right. She was Anthony and Cindy Scalini's daughter."

"Did that give you pause, him marrying into their family," MQ asked.

"Craig said they were just like everyone else. He assured us that most of the hype about the Scalinis was just that, hype. We met the Scalinis over the years, at various things. Something at the kid's school, or a birthday party. Tony and Cindy were very gracious people, not at all hostile or gruff, or what one would expect, given the movies about the mob or mafia or whatever it is they are called nowadays. We met Francis and Ruth on occasion too, Julie's grandparents. Very nice people. So, no we weren't overly concerned about Julie's family. Whatever they did, you know, in the mob or whatever, didn't seem to be part of Julie and Craig's life."

"Did Craig have any close friends, buddies he hung out with?" I asked.

"Craig hunted with a friend of his, Mike, Mike Reznor. He couldn't believe Craig did it either."

Clarissa chirped in, "Mike calls now and then to check up on us. He's a nice young man," and then her head bowed down and she was quiet and still again.

Mr. Wiley continued, "Mike has had his own trouble too. His wife had a nervous breakdown or something. She had to go into the hospital. I remember it was a very hard time for him. I also got a phone call a few days after the funeral, from another one of Craig's friends. A friend he'd known since high school. He had been out of town when it happened and had just heard. He was another one that said Craig could not have done it. He said Craig was a great dad and he wanted me to know that there was no way he was ever going to believe that Craig did anything like that. He said that Julie was, uh, the B word, and that she made Craig's life miserable. But he said he couldn't believe Julie could have done such a thing either."

"Do you remember who that was that you talked to?" I asked.

"Sure, George Fennelman. They played sports together in school and I remember Craig saying he and George worked out together or something. George was in the auto business. I think Craig bought a car from him. I can get you his number."

"That would be great," I said.

Victor left the room and returned with a sticky note with George's phone number. "I couldn't find Mikes number, but I bet George has it."

"Mr. and Mrs. Wiley, did anyone from the police department ever contact you afterwards? Did a detective come over? Anyone talk to you?" MQ asked.

Unrelenting silence from Mrs. Wiley. Victor answered again, "No one ever came over or called."

"I'm sorry. Someone should have," MQ said.

Victor continued. "I stopped by the police station about a week after it happened and asked to talk to someone, just to see if there was any news. An officer came out and told me that they had discovered illegal drugs in Craig's blood. He said they had found out that Craig had recently purchased the rifle and knife that were used and that apparently, he had planned to do it," Victor paused and took in a choppy breath.

"We just couldn't believe it. That he was hyped up on drugs, that he planned it. But, but if they had the evidence, what more was there to say? We just learned to accept what we have to accept. What else could we do?"

MQ and I were well aware that the medical examiner's lab report said there were no drugs in Craig Wiley's blood. And in any event, the lab results wouldn't have been available within a week. So, whoever Victor talked to, was a lying piece of shit.

MQ perked up and asked, "Do you remember the name of the officer you spoke to?"

"No, I'm sorry I don't."

"Can you describe the officer?" MQ asked picking up the conspiracy scent.

"Well, let's see," Victor rocked, crossed his arms over his chest and looked up to the ceiling. "He, um, wasn't in uniform, but he wasn't dressed like you either. No coat and tie. He was in blue jeans and had his badge on a chain hanging around his neck. Probably about 30ish, brown hair, a bit pudgy, baby faced."

Victor looked at his watch. "Clarissa and I have an appointment this afternoon. Is there anything else?" Mr. Wiley stood. The rocker continued to undulate.

"No sir. Thank you both for talking with us," MQ said. "Perhaps we can get together again. Here is my card, and Det. Green will give you his. If you happen to remember anything, please call either of us. We are very sorry for your loss."

"Yes, here's my card, and I put my cell phone number on it."

Mrs. Wiley's hand reached out and took my card like a squirrel snatching an acorn.

"We're going to keep working on this and I promise I will keep you up to date on anything we find that may shed some light," MQ said.

We shook hands with Victor. Mrs. Wiley stood and silently shuffled off to another room like a hovercraft.

As soon as we got in the car, MQ unloaded.

"Holy fuck doc. What is the deal with those two? She's sitting like a statute with that impassive attitude about her own son, and her grandchildren. And he could generate wattage if that chair was hooked up to a coil. Friggin *Twilight Zone* in there."

He put the car in gear and we pulled away from the curb.

"Murph, if you were convinced your son was innocent, wouldn't you do everything you could to clear his name, your name? If you thought his wife was a bitch, other people thought she was a bitch and you even remotely suspected something was up, wouldn't you do something other than just accept it?"

"One would think. Perhaps they follow the serenity prayer by the letter. Accept what we cannot change. Or maybe someone put the head of a dead horse in their bed. Fuck if I know. And another thing. We know there were no drugs in Craig Wiley's blood. And the lab report is dated a month after the murders. Someone was lying. Our pudgy, round faced plain-clothes Will Newsham methinks."

"Very possible," I said. "Refresh my memory MQ. I don't recall seeing a tape or DVD of Julie Wiley's TV appearance in evidence, or a supplemental report about it in the case file."

"That's because there is no copy of her TV appearance in evidence. I suppose it was too arduous of a task for them to obtain a copy of the news report for review. What a bunch of sloths. Jesus, Mary and Joseph!" MQ's frustration requiring the biblical inferences and a slap to the steering wheel.

"We need to get it Murph. Maybe it has some close ups of her face. Something to document the presence or absence of any face and throat injuries. But, if we go asking a TV station for it, we may open ourselves up for questions we are not yet ready to answer. I don't think we want the media to know about any of this just yet."

"Absolutely no media at this point," MQ paused and beeped the horn twice, apparently signifying a solution. "But you know what we can do?" Two more beeps.

"What?"

"Vince Richards, the anchor for the 6pm news on Channel 8 is at the cigar shop every Wednesday afternoon for the Republican Kibbutz club. I'll have Vince check and, if the tape still exists, he can burn us a copy. I've seen his girlfriend waiting out in his car when he picks up cigars. He knows how to keep secrets, at least from his wife anyway. He'll do it for us and keep it on the quiet."

MQ continued, "Let's not ignore the fact we now know Craig Wiley had a temper and a violent streak. Who knows what he really thought of his non-domesticated, languid, bitch of a wife? Maybe she was going out on him. Maybe he had enough of her shit that night."

"Perhaps Sol. Maybe he did want to take her out. But, that doesn't explain why she's alive and the kids are dead. And, I might add, very nice touch on bringing out your own anger issues. It helped Mr. Wiley for the moment. Too bad it's true. You really do need to work on that MQ."

"Is that so? And you're the poster boy for emotional stability. I saw you dry crunching pain pills back there. Sometimes I fear you're turning into Elvis. Glass houses, my friend. Glass houses."

"Point well taken Murph."

MQ drove towards the station quietly and turned on a classic rock station. He started air drumming the dashboard to Boston's *More Than a Feeling*.

"We definitely need to interview that George Fennelman guy and Mike Reznor," I said.

"And probably a hundred other people before it's over." MQ said as he rolled down the window of our Crown Vic, fired up a Fuentes and sang along.

# Chapter Forty Two

Sgt. Murphy-Quinn called George Fennelman the following day. Mr. Fennelman was the sales manager at a Southside Nissan, Toyota and Honda dealership. He was anxious to talk, and asked that we come by his store as soon as possible.

Fennelman was holding a sales meeting when we arrived. His secretary, Eileen, escorted us to an office and brought us a carafe of coffee, Styrofoam cups and packets of cream and sugar.

Mr. Fennelman's glass walled office included an impressive array of wall plaques and trophies for annual best sales awards and manufacturer incentive ribbons. His desk also sported the requisite 5"x7" photo of the family. George had an attractive long legged spouse and four little kids. They had apparently been to France.

Eileen stood in the doorway as we waited for Mr. Fennelman.

"The last time we had detectives to see Mr. Fennelman was when that father killed those children. That was just terrible." Her voice had a shrill, nasal, from the Bronx, quality. Her clairvoyance caught us both by surprise, but perhaps George had mentioned the reason for the visit.

"Mr. Fennelman will be right with you gentlemen," she said and walked out of sight.

MQ looked at me and said, "Fran Drescher."

George Fennelman was a formidable looking character, easily 6'2", barrel chested with a narrow waist. He was wearing a black cashmere mock turtleneck, crisp, grey slacks, and a blue blazer. He sported straight blonde hair, just over the ears and collar. He had a ruddy, outdoors complexion and bright, blue eyes.

The fluorescent lights glinted off his gold name-tag as he entered his office. We showed him our equally shiny gold badges and introduced ourselves. We all shook hands.

I gave the 'cold case, fresh eyes' explanation concerning the Wiley case.

"You bet, glad to help," Fennelman said with a higher pitched voice than I expected from such a large man. He sounded more like a teenager whose voice was in transition.

"In fact, I think about it now and then," he said. "I still wonder. You know?"

"We wonder too and that's why we're here Mr. Fennelman. Did anyone from the police department ever interview you?" MQ asked.

"You bet. I remember talking to a detective from your department at the time. He like, came over here and asked a few questions. I told him Craig couldn't have done such a thing," Fennelman said as he plopped down in the chair behind his desk.

"Victor Wiley said you and his son were friends."

"You bet. Went to high school together. At the time it happened we were workout partners at the gym and like, did some power lifting together. We both had busy careers going on but we had time to get together. He was a good guy."

"It appears you're quite successful," MQ said pointing at the sales awards.

"Thanks. Lots of hours and aggravation, but it's a good company, 401K, health insurance, you know, the important stuff. That's my wife Candace and our 4 rugrats under the Arc de Triomphe picture. I won the trip. Anyway, she doesn't work anymore. So like, I gotta be on my game."

"Mr. Fennelman, what can you tell us about Craig and Julie?" I asked.

"First of all, he loved those kids. I told the first detective that they'd be better off looking at Julie as the more likely suspect between the two. She had a mean streak and a temper when she didn't get her way, but I wouldn't have thought she could do something like that. Anyway, I told him straight out that Craig didn't do it. But, like, like all the TV reports said he snapped, and everyone seemed to be sure about it."

"How long had you known them? I asked.

"Oh, man, it's weird. My wife actually went to grade school with Julie, but then Julie moved, going into middle school, and Candace didn't see her again. Then one night, we doubled and when they realized they knew each other, we like started socializing. You know, clubbing, float trips, going out to dinner, all depending on, like, once kids came along, the babysitter situation. Mike and Patty Reznor came out with us too. Craig, Julie, Mike, Patty, me and my wife. But

Julie was a real bitch, and really, it got on the wife's nerves, and we stopped going out as couples."

"Would you say Craig and Julie's marriage was rocky?" MQ asked.

"You bet. They had their ups and downs, mostly downs. Julie was like, she had champagne tastes and Craig was a beer guy. Julie came from a wealthy family and was spoiled. I guess you know who they are," he said rolling his eyes. "She was always like wanting more from Craig. For him to make more money, buy nicer cars, a bigger house. Like how could she not be? You know her dad was Anthony Scalini, right?"

"Yes, we are aware," MQ answered.

"She was the queen of like, all the expensive designer brands, kind of a show off. And Craig was just the opposite, Bud Light and blue jeans for him. He was like satisfied with his kids, dogs, and working out. He wasn't into having to show off like she was."

"So there was a considerable amount of friction in their relationship?" MQ asked.

"More often than not. Julie would like snap at him. She had a temper you know. I've been to their house when she was ragging at Craig, calling him, like a loser, and yelling at the kids too. Like, saying, 'Taylor, get your ass in here and pick up your jacket'. You know, saying stuff, like, you shouldn't say to kids."

"So you're saying she wasn't up for the greatest mother of the year?" MQ added.

"You bet. Like before he started traveling, you know who took Robbie to Cub Scouts and Taylor to dance classes? Craig. You know who cleaned the house most of the time? Craig. You know who went to like, the school meetings with the teachers? He did. She didn't. And when he was gone sometimes, he made up for it by going to their schools and finding out what he'd missed. Going out of town with work was a breather for him from her, and that made her mad. She bitched about being stuck at home all the time, but like she wasn't really. Her mom and grandma watched those kids a lot. I would see her out at a happy hour. She would say like, 'Craig's in Chile for a week. My mom's watching the kids'."

"Was she ever out with another guy?" I asked, exploring the fact that cheating hearts may be responsible for more deaths than the black plague. I was thinking maybe he would say a tall, sandy haired guy who likes shopping.

"Not that I ever saw. She was usually with a few of her girlfriends. It's not like I would have been surprised though. She would always be wearing like, low cut stuff when we went out, struttin' her stuff. If she did have a boyfriend, she kept it quiet. She never said anything to Candace about it. You know how women talk. Candace never mentioned anything like that."

"Did Craig ever say he was worried whether she was going out on him?" I asked.

"Worried? No, not really. I think he was past that point with her."

"Very cosmopolitan of Mr. Wiley," MQ said. "How about Craig, did he have a special friend?"

Fennelman's cheeks blushed. He ran his fingers over his hair, stood up and looked out the glass wall. Apparently he was satisfied the coast was clear and sat back down leaning forward and speaking in a lower volume.

"You know, like, uh, Craig was no angel. I'm not going to lie to you. He strayed a few times. Someone he picked up at a bar or something, a one-nighter. We had a girl that would come here and give salesmen a blowjob during a 'test drive' for twenty five bucks, a real Lot Lizard. He would come by now and then and take a test drive with her."

"Did Julie ever find out?"

"No. I don't think so."

"So, as far as you know he wasn't seeing anyone regularly?" I asked.

"Well," he paused, pinched and scratched an imaginary Goatee. "Like in the month or two before he died. He like, he was different. He was calmer. He hardly ever complained about Julie. Like for instance, in the past, he'd come back from being out of town and usually he would be pissed off about what she did or didn't do. But he wasn't anymore. He was happier, easier going. I'd ask him if he needed a test drive when the lizard came by and he would say no."

"And, you attributed this change in attitude to what, Mr. Fennelman? Drugs? A girlfriend? What do you think?" MQ asked.

"Drugs, never," Fennelman paused, stared down at his desk and rearranged a stack of papers. "He like, he told me he met someone. Someone that was special. He said she was kind and sweet and cared about him. She cooked, kept a nice house. Not at all like Julie. In the months before he died, at least Craig was happy."

"Did you know who she was?" I asked.

"No, he wouldn't tell me."

"More importantly, did Mrs. Wiley know?" MQ asked.

"I don't think so. I never heard of any drama about it. But, like after it happened, I thought it was something important. If Julie told her dad that Craig was cheating on her, who knows what could happen. And I told the detective that come out here just that."

"What did the detective say?" MQ asked.

"He said they were exploring all possibilities".

"Do you recall who the detective was?" I asked.

"No. Sorry. I didn't get his name. I guess I should have."

"Can you describe him?" MQ asked.

"Oh, like, about 6 feet, chunky, dark hair. Kind of a baby face."

MQ and I nodded to each other.

"Could it have been Sgt. Will Newsham?" MQ asked through angry tight lips.

"Yea, that sounds right. Sergeant Newsham."

"So, if I understand the dynamic correctly," I recapped, "Mr. and Mrs. Wiley were both miserable with their home life. Mrs. Wiley is spoiled and temperamental. Mr. Wiley finds someone who makes him happy. And then something happened. Something happened that night to bring it all down."

MQ added, "Mr. Fennelman, if you don't think Craig did it, what do you think happened that night?

"I don't know. I wish I did. But I would bet like my last dollar, that Craig didn't kill his kids."

The flush had left George's face. He looked tired. Discussing the murders grounded the spark from the salesman of the year. "Have you guys talked to Mike Reznor yet?"

"No, not yet," I said, "Craig's dad said Mike was a hunting buddy."

"You bet," he said. "Mike is a car guy like me too. But he's also a big hunter type. He and Craig hit it off with hunting and stuff like that. They were both like, way into guns and knives, gun shows, military stuff. Did you guys know that Patty, Mike's wife, was the last one of our friends to see Craig alive? Craig was over at their house, like an hour or two before all of it happened."

"No. we didn't know that. Our report indicated that Mr. Wiley was at the Reznor's the night before the murders, but not the day of. Are you sure?" I asked, glancing a surprised eye at MQ.

"You bet I'm sure. Mike told me Craig borrowed a movie the night before and brought it back that afternoon. Mike wasn't home so Craig left it with Patty, and that was like just an hour or two before, well, before it happened."

I took out a pad of paper and scribbled a few notes. Any information concerning Craig Wiley's activities just prior to the murders was valuable.

"Do you stay in touch with Mike? MQ asked.

"You bet. He works at the Dodge dealership over in Oakview, not far from your station. I see Mike probably like once every couple weeks at an auction or like some supplier conference, some car thing. You know, we're like, car guys, we do a lot of the same type things. He's had a tough way to go though. His wife, Patty," Fennelman shook his head, "she was always like, edgy, emotional, kind of depressed, always sad about something. When her folks died it really got her down. But man, after Craig and the kids, she like nosedived big time. She was taken to the hospital, got like shock treatments, a real mess. Ended up in like a home. I felt bad for Mike. His hunting buddy ends up dead and his wife has a nervous breakdown. He had it pretty rough. You want me to give him a call?"

"Please. If you can get Mike on the phone that would be great." MQ said.

Fennelman called the Dodge dealership and was able to reach Mike Reznor. He handed the phone to MQ. MQ arranged to meet Mr. Reznor that evening at 6pm at the Reznor home.

"Mr. Fennelman, thanks for all your help. If you happen to think of anything else, please give a call. We may want to talk to Mrs. Fennelman at some point too," I said.

Fennelman was willing to help in any way to clear his friend's name. He said he would mention our visit to his wife to see if she remembered anything else. He said he would call if she did.

We walked through the showroom of $30,000 cars to our $5000 detective unit.

MQ opened up as we got in the cruiser. "Well, for one thing, if that guy said 'like' or 'you bet' one more time, I was gonna shoot him. I'm no Strunk and White, but for Chrissake. If I had a dollar for every time he said like, we'd be on our way to the casino."

"Makes you wonder, how the hell can a guy like that be successful at sales," I agreed. "You'd think people would go, 'Like I'm outta here' or 'get me someone that doesn't talk like a Valley girl.'"

"You're right Doc, the guy is no Demosthenes. However, I suppose being a master orator with command over the Kings English is barely a requirement for selling cars."

"You bet," I said.

"Ok. I'm just a little ferklempt here," MQ said as he started the car and pulled out of the lot. "What a labyrinth of possibilities this is becoming. She's a princess bitch. He's a cocksman with a temper. What do you think Anthony Scalini's response would be if he found out that his son-in-law was getting $25 blow jobs in the front seat of a Honda? Or that he'd found a nice girl and was going to divorce the princess. Do you think that maybe, just maybe, he would be a bit miffed if his little girl complained? Would he be pissed off enough to teach Craig a lesson?"

"And you're going with the theory that maybe some Scalini goons went over there to fuck Craig up and something went terribly wrong during the lesson? If so, where's the dead goons that killed Francis Scalini's grandchildren."

"Just a postulation my good doctor, something to consider. We have murder, sex, organized crime. All we need is gambling, and we'd be 1950s Vegas. I am beginning to feel better about this congeries of facts we're amassing. If we are to believe what we've heard so far, our intrepid, baby faced Lieutenant purposely withheld information in a murder investigation, which in my book is obstruction of justice. I can't wait to watch him and Montileone squirm when we take this to fruition. Let's get a bite to eat and collect our thoughts. We have a couple hours to kill before going over to the Reznors." He turned directly into the parking lot of a TGIFridays.

# Chapter Forty Three

MQ found our way to the Reznor's home. They lived in a modest red brick ranch. We noticed an expansive attached, three-car-garage finished with a fresher looking red brick that appeared to be a more recent addition.

We pulled in the driveway. "Murph, like it looks like, car guys, like need space for their, like, their cars." I said.

MQ belched Friday's rib tips. "I swear I will throttle this guy if he even says the word like more than once."

MQ rang the bell.

A woman opened the front door and looked at us through the glass of the storm door. We flashed the tin and identified ourselves. She did not look well. She was short, painfully gaunt, with bony angular facial features and a sallow complexion. Dark circles rimmed expressionless eyes. She reminded me of our clinic patients undergoing fruitless chemo or radiation. She was shoeless, in worn blue jeans and a loose fitting, pale yellow, knit sweater with several specks of what looked to be grape jelly, just below the neckline.

She pushed the door open and stepped back, motioning with a slow hand wave to come in.

She led us to a fashionably furnished living room where two 6' black leather couches and two red leather recliners formed a semi-circle facing a large flat screen.

"I'll get Mike. Come, sit down." Her words came out dry and measured. She disappeared into a hallway.

"Whoa. An automaton. What's up with her doc?" MQ whispered.

"Hard telling," I answered softly.

She returned a moment later with her husband who was not the picture of health either. He didn't appear in need of immediate IV therapy, but he was no cover boy for Men's Health magazine. Reznor was circus tall and lean. His short-sleeve tan dress shirt fit him like a sail. He had dark, bushy, curly, black hair, a little longer than the usual businessman's style. He was clean-shaven with a pebbled, pock marked face. We shook hands.

"Hi, I'm Mike, this is my wife Patty," Mr. Reznor said.

Mrs. Reznor nodded at us, but did not accept our extended hands for a shake.

"You can stay with us, or go back to your room," Reznor said to his wife. She didn't move.

"She's just having one of her days today, they come and go. Please sit down guys," Mr. Reznor said.

MQ and I sat on one of the couches. Each of the Reznors took a recliner.

"George said you guys are looking into the Wiley case?"

This time, MQ went over the spiel regarding the cold case investigation, our fresh eyes, and asked the Reznors for their recollections of the event.

Reznor's lanky frame leaned forward towards us, elbows on his thighs.

"I can tell you right now that Craig Wiley did not kill those kids. They were his reason for living. The pecking order for Craig was kids, dogs, hunting.

"Where did Mrs. Wiley fit in? MQ asked.

"Julie? Probably last. She was a real hag to him. He tried his best to please her, but she always found fault with everything he did. She was one whacked-out bitch, excuse my French."

"That's quite alright. Please expound on that," MQ said.

"Aside from just being a spoiled, self-centered rag, one thing you should know is that Julie was taking Prozac at the time it happened. Craig told me that. She had been having mood swings and her mom gave her some Prozac. I guess her mom's nuts too. But with all you hear about Prozac and suicide, I just figured that taking that type of medicine without a doctor's prescription was wrong and could be, well dangerous."

"Did you mention that to anyone?" MQ asked.

"Oh yea. It was on my mind big time. I can tell you one thing, Craig wouldn't ever hurt his kids and he would have died protecting them from anyone who tried. I'm damn glad you're looking into this, damn glad. It's about time. I told that detective that, too. I told him the same damn thing."

"Do you remember the name of the detective?" MQ asked almost sounding bored of the question.

"Hell, it's been a while. There was two of them showed up. I remember one was big and fat and he sweated a lot even though it wasn't even that hot. The other was chubby, too, not as much as the other. He was young looking, dark hair, thirtyish. That one was a Sergeant. I remember he made a point of telling me he was running the case. Don't remember their names though, sorry."

MQ and I exchanged glances knowing full well who the two detective weight-watcher candidates were.

"We understand that Craig Wiley was over just before the murders. How was he? What can you tell us about his attitude?" I asked.

"He absolutely was here, and he was his usual self. Him and Julie had gone to some dog conference or something like that at a resort over the weekend. I think Julie's mom watched the kids. He said they had a good time and hoped Julie would be less of a bitch that week. You know, after getting away and all." Mike Reznor shook his head. "You see, she just wasn't the right person for him. Or for those kids. She would have been better off single. Anyhow, Craig brought over a new .22 rifle that Sunday that he had been plinking cans with in his backyard. The damn fool wrapped a towel on the end of the barrel with duct tape and said it was like a silencer. I told him I doubted if it worked. He wanted to shoot in my backyard, but I said 'Hell no dude', I don't want the cops showing up. Silenced or not, shooting in your backyard is something you can get a ticket for. But I dry fired it and it seemed like a decent little .22."

"Was that unusual? Craig bringing weapons over to show you," MQ asked.

"No, not at all. Not at all. Earlier in the summer he bought some throwing knives at a gun show, and brought those over here. We were getting pretty good too. My tree in the backyard is witness to that. Lots of strikes in the same area from 7 yards. So, in answer to your question, no, not at all. I told the detectives that this stuff with the weapons and all, and just in general, that was all normal for Craig."

"So he liked to collect weapons?" I asked.

"I don't know about collecting. Just that Craig liked weapons of all kinds, pistols, rifles, knives. I do too."

"So was he his usual self on that Sunday, the day before the murders?" I asked.

"Yea, nothing unusual at all. I can tell you, he was not having a nervous break-down or anything like that. I know about those things, let me tell you. Just normal Craig."

"Can you go over what you did on that Sunday?" MQ asked.

"Sure. So, after messing with the rifle, I had rented a movie and he stayed and watched it with Patty and me. And then he went home. Oh, and he borrowed the movie because Julie might like it. He was like that. He was always trying his damndest to please her. And speaking of her, I guess you know that Julie's dad is Anthony Scalini."

We nodded and Reznor continued, "I've never met him, but Craig said he was a pretty nice guy. Craig said his father-in law was into deer hunting too. They got a place near here, and a place in Iowa somewhere. Craig went with him a few times. I mean, you see so much stuff about gangsters in the movies. Goodfellas, Godfather. Craig said it didn't seem like that with him. He said Anthony never messed with him, and was always nice to him and Julie. Julie's family was real close, and that they even helped him and her financially when they were going through a rough period, when his dog business was just starting up."

"How was their marriage? Were they both happy or were there problems, infidelities, things that could cause tension in the house?" I asked.

Reznor stood up. He addressed his wife in short, concise sentences, "Patty, we're going outside. I need a smoke. We'll be right back in."

We stepped out on the front porch. Once Mike closed the door behind him, he lit a Winston. "I wanted you guys to know something. I don't know if it matters, but I didn't say nothing to the other detectives at the time. And I always thought it might mean something in the scheme of things with who Julie's dad was and all. You see, occasionally, Craig, uh, would, uh. Well, I told him that was a lot of risk for a little tail, but on occasion, he would,"

MQ cut him off, "We understand that Craig may have gotten a test drive blow job or had a one nighter during his marriage."

"Yea, right," he said, blowing smoke out the side of his mouth. "And he may have been involved with someone at the time it happened."

"Someone more than just a head job?" I asked.

"I sure think so," Reznor said.

MQ asked, "Did he tell you who he was seeing?"

"No, he never did. Just that he really liked whoever it was, but he said it was complicated and he didn't talk much about it. And after it happened, I thought, well, did Julie find out and have him killed? But why the kids? I know it sounds like some cheesy Johnny and Frankie movie bullcrap, but I've always wondered. In the back of my mind, I figured it couldn't be, because they would never hurt the kids. If Julie wanted Craig whacked, well, that wouldn't be too much of a stretch, the bitch that she was. Well, I could see that. I wouldn't have put it past her to make up something bad enough about Craig that her daddy wouldn't have any other choice, but not the kids too. Nope, not the kids too. It just made no sense to me. I've pretty well talked myself out of thinking that Anthony had anything to do with it," Mike threw his cigarette butt into the yard.

"Thanks for giving us your thoughts on that," MQ said. "We're not going to eliminate anything as a possibility. But, I agree that murdering your own grandchildren doesn't quite fit."

Mike tucked his pack of smokes in his shirt pocket, "I'm glad you think so. And I'm glad to have finally told someone, just in the event."

"We'd like to ask Mrs. Reznor a few questions too. We understand that Craig came over a few hours before the murders and spoke with her," I said.

"Yea he did. In fact I called home then, when he had come by, and dropped off the movie."

"About what time was it that you called?" MQ asked.

"I was on my way back from delivering a car. I was going to be home about 6 and I was about 3 hours away, so around 3 or so."

"Do you mind if we talk with your wife about that day?" I asked.

"We can give it a shot. Hopefully she'll talk some about it. It's a tough one for her. When Julie's mom or grandma couldn't watch the kids and she wanted to go out, Patty watched Taylor and Robbie. She was pretty close to them. She wants kids in the worst way and we've just not been able to have one. And so she kind of, well since Julie didn't give a shit about them, Patty was really close to them. So when it all went down, she really took it hard."

We returned to the living room and found Mrs. Reznor sitting quietly in the recliner.

Mike knelt next to her and lifted her hand, putting it in between his. "Do you think you could answer a couple questions about the Wileys? These detectives are looking into the case."

Mrs. Reznor looked at us and slightly nodded her head in the affirmative. She pulled her hand back and folded both neatly in her lap.

Patty Reznor was sitting Indian style on the recliner. The recliner made a barely perceptible squeak every second as Patty started to rock. I thought maybe she was going to be a combination of Victor Wiley's rocker movement, and Clarissa's heavy desolation.

"Mrs. Reznor, our report said that you saw Craig the day that it happened. How do you think he was acting?" I asked.

Her bony chin raised up as she processed the question.

It was difficult for me to turn off the physician completely when functioning as a detective. At times the dual perspective is distracting, other times it can be helpful. Patty Reznor had had a breakdown. The treatment regimen can include everything from counseling to side-effect laden pharmaceuticals to electrocon-vulsive therapy, another example of the old adage, if the disease doesn't kill you, the cure will. Patty Reznor looked to be semi-living proof of that. I wasn't optimis-tic that she would provide anything of assistance.

A few seconds later she spoke, slow and methodical. As she began, she inserted the tip of her left index finger in the corner of her mouth. Between words, she nibbled on her fingernail. The rocking continued.

"Mike was not home when Craig brought the movie back."

"Ok, thank you," I responded. "Craig came over and brought the movie back. Mrs. Reznor, was Craig happy that day or angry about something?"

Simple choices for easier responses.

"Happy."

"What time was Craig here?"

"Hmm, three."

"Craig was here at three 'o'clock? Are you sure about the time?"

Pause, processing. She closed her eyes, "Yea. Before the bus stop."

Mr. Reznor offered explanation. "The Wiley kids got off their bus, oh, about 3:30, near their house. Craig came over and dropped the movie off on his way home to get them at the bus. So he would have been here around 3 to make it to his house by 3:30. That's right. Because I figured I must have called just around 3, since Patty told me I just missed him."

As he spoke, Patty crossed her arms over her chest and her head bent down. She bent slightly forward at the waist as you would if you were having abdominal pain. The rocker leaned forward with her.

Mr. Reznor reached across his wife and gently sat her up, although her chin was still planted on her chest. "You OK honey?"

"I don't like to talk about these things Mike."

"Honey, could you get us some ice tea. I made a pitcher, it's in the fridge."

Patty peeled open slowly, stood and shuffled off to the kitchen.

Mike let out a breath of exasperation and resolution. "Her brother and one of her sisters have been in and out of mental hospitals for the past ten years or better. Her parents were fine, but I think there's some kind of depression gene the kids got. Before, when we were first married, she was terrific. Man, she was funny, she loved to cook and…" Mr. Reznor paused, his eyes closed. We waited as he drifted from whatever past he had found, back to the now. My guess is that he probably traveled that path often.

"Patty's parents, especially with her dad, man they were really close. Her folks were very important to her. And her dad died suddenly, a heart attack. And then her mom shortly thereafter. Broken heart we think. This all happened about a year, a year before Craig and the kids. And then we found out we couldn't have a baby. Patty took it real hard. She changed. She got a depression, a bad one, a real son of a bitch. The doctors put her on anti-depressants and anti-anxiety type medications. We went through the Prozacs and the Wellbutrins, Haldols all of them. She got pretty squirrely when she was on a few of those. That's why I thought the whole thing with Julie taking Prozac without seeing a doctor was important."

Mr. Reznor looked over at the kitchen. "I don't want her to hear me talking about this. Sometimes it sets her back, if she starts to dwell on those bad times."

He continued, "It took a while, but finally, she started to come around. She started to come back to someone like her old self. She was happier. She started cooking again and keeping the house up. I don't know if it was the medication, or just time, but whatever it was, I started to get my Patty back. And then, Craig and the kids," Mr. Reznor glanced at the kitchen again.

"When that happened, she took a nosedive. She had to be taken to the hospital. The doctors said it was a severe depression. They figured that the death of Craig and the kids tripped something, maybe bringing back all the bad times from her folks dying, and it was all too much for her to handle. And it put her over the edge. She's had about everything you can get. Counseling, medication, even shock treatment, the whole works. She's on a shitload of medication now. But she does have good days where she is almost normal. Hopefully with some time, she'll come out of this. You want to ask her a few more questions? I'll go get her."

"Not right now Mr. Reznor," I said. "If it's ok, we may want to come back another time."

"Sure, just give me a call."

"We're sorry for what you've both been through," I said.

Mike Reznor leaned back on the couch, rubbed his face with both hands, drawing them down slowly and crossing his arms over his chest as he said, "Sometimes I wish she just had cancer or something that they could cut out or radiate or something. But this psychiatric shit is a real motherfucker."

We left the Reznor's having more fingers to point in the direction of Julie Wiley.

# Chapter Forty Four

Over the next few days, MQ and I wrote additional reports reflecting the information obtained from our recent interviews. Our suspicions of an intentional cover up, led by Will Newsham had become more solid with each contact.

We rolled into my favorite running time of the year, summer, and still no word from the state lab. Sally Sunderman had gone from 'Don't call us. We'll call you.' to having her secretary tell us to check back in four weeks, every time we called.

Despite nagging left shoulder pain, I had not had another episode requiring IV medication. I ran a half marathon in June and during my training runs, I made it a point to stop by Blessed Sacrament cemetery a couple of times each week.

Stepping into the shade, I'd lean against the silver maple on the side of Taylor and Robbie's headstone. While stretching my calves and quads I would bring them up to speed on the progress of the case. My usual message went something like, "Just want to let you know we are held up by the bureaucratic inefficiencies of our state lab, but it isn't looking so good for your mama."

When a welcome breeze blew during our chats, I imagined they were listening. I had no idea they were, and at this point of my dysfunctional life, I saw nothing unusual about having cemetery conversations with murder victims. It was certainly ironic. I had long given up on any particular faith and hadn't gone to the "Shalom Israel" cemetery to visit the graves of my parents in years. Yet, there I was, again and again, graveside in a Catholic cemetery talking to the dead.

I had missed any number of my weekends with Jake and Olivia this summer. If it wasn't the bureau on call schedule, clinic shifts, or races, I was busy with

Margie Classa. It turned out Margie felt something too and we repeated and repeated. My addictive personality was no less pathologic when it came to sex, and Margie and I found something intense together. We were spending at least three nights a week together. Being with her was like an infusion of life. In some ways, she reminded me of who I was, before I became who I am. Whatever it was, I chose it, over spending a weekend with Jake and Olivia. It was another toll to pay at a later date.

While we waited on the state lab, there were some forensics that could be done discretely by trusted friends at our county lab. I dialed Ajay Rajeda's office. Dr. Rajeda was the pathologist who performed the Wiley autopsies. He was also the resident expert in blood spatter analysis. Dr. Rajeda and I had worked a case some twenty years ago when I was just a fresh policeman. Well before trace evidence, DNA and forensics were part of everyday police lingo and on every prime time TV show.

In that case, it was Ajay's analysis of the blood droplets and blood pooling in the victims bedroom that bolstered a family's claims that their teenage daughter did not commit suicide. Ajay indicated that the blood spatter was too far away from the victim and the droplets were shaped in the wrong direction to support the fact that 16 year old Nancy "Gumdrop" Washington shot herself in the right temple.

Gumdrop expected her boyfriend Lorenzo to kill himself in some sort of murder/suicide love pact. Once Lorenzo shot Gumdrop, he chickened out. He tore up their suicide note and called the police. He said that he had come by to visit and found that the love of his life had shot herself in the head. Until Ajay's analysis, his story was the official version. It was a lot like the Wiley case, one survivor, one story.

The case never went to trial. Once confronted with the blood pattern analysis and the only possible scenario that fit the scene, Lorenzo confessed. He did sixteen years and the Washington family obtained closure. Because of Ajay's work, Gumdrop was not forced to find someone to tap and haunt to obtain justice.

Dr. Rajeda answered on the third ring with an accent still heavily tinged from his Indian homeland.

"Pathology, Dr. Rajeda."

"Ajay. Hi. Morris Green here."

"Hello Morris Green. It has been a long time. How are you? The eye?"

"It's good Ajay. I'm up to 175 readers though. Old age, irrespective of the injury."

"Don't I know. No line progressives and a new prescription every year for me. Once we cross that 40 line, I am afraid it is a steady decline no matter what. So, how can I help you today?"

"We're doing a cold case on a triple murder. The Wileys, a father Craig and two kids Robbie and Taylor. You recall it?"

"No, not really. Let me see. Hold on I'll pull up their names." A keyboard clattered.

"The Wiley case," I repeated.

"Oh yes, here it is. Oh yes. The two children and their father. I see here that I did do the post mortems. Let me see here. One child, disemboweled, the other, yes, I do remember. Yes. Yes. Overkill. The other one, little girl, shot and some edged instrument slicing brain matter."

"We have your autopsy reports, but don't have a blood spatter analysis. Did you look at crime scene photos?"

"Let me see here. No. No. It does not look like I did any spatter work on this one. Must not have been any question."

"Do you know who from Oakview attended the posts?"

"Oh, well now, there have been so many since then. Let's see here. Yes, here it is. Sgt. W. Newsham was there for the post mortems. And, let me see here. No. No. There were no follow up calls from him after the post. Nothing about spatter concerns. Nothing here but the autopsy."

"That make sense," I said more to myself than Ajay.

"Oh, yes now, Will Newsham. Yes. I remember now. Yes I do. In all of my years Morris, I've rarely had an officer trying to tell me how to do my job. He was quite irritating. He wanted me to just do an external. Can you believe that? He said it was a murder-suicide and we needn't waste time on it. I told him we do thorough work here. We don't jump to conclusions. We look at the evidence. He was annoyingly persistent. We did not listen to him Morris."

"Ajay, I need some help on this one. I'm going to bring over copies of the crime scene and autopsy photos along with a synopsis of what the original investigation concluded as well as our focus of a cold case we're doing on this one. I'll include some questions I'd like you to answer if you can. There's no urgency if you're slammed. We're still waiting for DNA analysis at the state lab anyway."

"Good luck with the state. With their budget cuts, and case load, their lab may take quite a while."

"No kidding. It's been there for months."

"Unacceptable Morris. Simply unacceptable. Yet the state builds the most obnoxious sculpture park with statutes of governors near the capital, and they don't have the money to fulfill the equipment and staffing of their laboratory. I'm just hoping that our county budget remains intact. I cannot lose any more people Morris. In this office, I'm down to two other pathologists and only three assistants in the morgue. But, yes, certainly, bring the jacket over and I will be happy to look at it."

"Thanks Ajay. This one is kind of touchy, so if you could keep the results confidential. This is being handled by MQ and me. Only us, no one else from Oakview should know. Is that ok?"

"Very fascinating Morris. Now I am most interested. Of course I will prepare a report for you only."

The building which housed the Medical Examiner's department was a good 45 minute drive from Oakview. Like many of our county buildings, it had been built during the post WWII construction boom in what had been the suburbs, but had now become mid town as the middle-class white flight took place in the '70s and '80s. It had been remodeled, wings had been torn down, others were added on. It had become a hodgepodge of different color brick and steel over the last 20 years. A new complex way out in the new suburbs was in the planning stages, years away from breaking ground.

I parked in one of the 'police only' spaces outside the morgue and made my way through the maze of offices. I took the elevator to the basement. Ajay was out to lunch. I left the sealed folder with his secretary and headed for the Toxicology department. Typical governmental beaurocratic nonsense had placed Toxicology at the other end of the building.

The misfiled lab report indicated that at the time of his death, Craig Wiley was not under the influence of anything. He hadn't just jacked some crystal into a vein, snorted a gram of coke or fired up a crack rock. No recreational drugs of any kind were detected. There were no prescription medications floating in his bloodstream either. He didn't even register a blood alcohol content. At the time of his death, Craig Wiley was sober as a judge.

On the other hand, Julie Wiley was not. Her blood revealed the presence of Fluoxetine (Prozac), which supported Mike Reznor's information. She also had Carisoprodol (Soma Compound) and Diphenhydramine (Benadryl) in her system. The lab reported the levels of each drug in her system in terms of mcg/ml, micrograms per milliliter of blood. Because the toxicology report never saw the light of day, no further quantification of the analysis was performed. Crucially important questions remained unanswered.

Such as, how did those levels of drugs affect Julie Wiley's physical and mental abilities? Could she have fought off the alleged attack by her husband? Would her memory be affected? Could she even drive? These were good questions that had not been asked.

Tim Hendershot, MD, FACMT is the head of Toxicology for the County Medical Examiner's Office. We had worked together more than just a few times over the years. Tim was instrumental when we were called to work a drug overdose death.

Investigating the death of an otherwise healthy doper, left one to ponder whether the death was a result of some new chemical experience? Perhaps an unexpectedly potent heroin had made it on the street. Was it some new cocktail mix of drugs, or were the drug and the amounts indicative of a suicide?

Dr. Hendershot was the go to guy, and unlike most lab rats, he enjoyed discussing the crime scene with case investigators and would occasionally even come out to the scene. He said the scene would talk to him. Dr. Hendershot was a good medical detective. His reports were concise. His courtroom testimony was clear and convincing.

And, underneath his crisp white lab coat, Dr. Hendershot dressed impeccably. Pineider sterling silver cufflinks and a three piece, Savile Row suit were the norm. He almost always looked as if he was on his way to a five-star restaurant for a four-course meal.

Dr. Hendershot sported a headful of thick, dark, brown hair with a shock of white at the temples. In his early sixties, he could be a GQ model for the boomer generation. The detectives who worked with Dr. Hendershot gave him the moniker, 'TipTopTim' or 'Triple T'.

In addition to dashing, Triple T was a brilliant scientist and clinician. He had earned a PhD in pharmacy from the University of Southern California and had done a brief stint doing research in molecular pharmacology, followed by med school at UCLA and an ER residency.

Tim said he moved here, taking a position with the county after he'd had enough of the earthquakes, sun and surf in California.

Triple T and I shared similar interests in medicine, forensics, and rock. Tim was a drummer, and had a Slingerland set of drums and a Ludwig kit in his basement. Every now and then, I took a practice amp, my Gibson SG and a 12 pack over to Tim's house. For a few hours, we turned into teenagers.

I flashed my badge at the Toxicology department secretary through the glass partition. She leaned towards the porthole. "Detective, he's on the phone. Have a seat. You know Dr. Hendershot, it could be a while." A few minutes later she buzzed me in and I made my way down the hallway to the lab and Dr. Hendershot's office.

"Hey TipTop, how are things?"

"Morris, how are you my friend? Long time," he said coming around his desk and giving me a hug. "Must not be a social call, unless you bought a new axe and want to jam. I was at Guitar Center last week and they had this exquisite 1971 Gold Les Paul, to die for. I immediately thought of you when I saw it. Oh, yes, and how's the eye? Sit down Morris, please."

"Vision is fine. It's good enough that I saw that Les Paul too. But $4200 is a little steep for an extra guitar that I won't have enough time to play. I pick up my SG or Strat once a week if I'm lucky."

"I know, I know all too well. I haven't hit the skins in two weeks. I understand completely. So, what mayhem have you for me?"

"Tim, we're doing a cold case from a while back. Your office was tangentially involved in the original case. The victims were Craig Wiley, the father, and his two children Robbie 10, and Taylor 7. A survivor was Julie Wiley, the mother."

"Yes, yes, I do vaguely remember. The two kids killed by their father and he killed himself. Damn well one of the more tragic ones. You're correct. I don't recall doing much on it. I know I never testified on it."

"Here's what I need Tim," I handed him a folder. "Here's the lab report you guys did back then containing values for Soma, Prozac and Benadryl in the mother's blood. I need to know what the effects of the levels of these drugs would be for this 125 lb. woman. At the time, she reported memory lapses of what happened during the murders. However she was able to escape the attack from her spouse and flee the scene by driving a car to a neighbor's house. I just want to know how fucked up she would be under those drugs at those levels, and what she would, or would not be able to do. The initial investigation did not clarify her expected functional ability."

"Right. Hmm," he said paging through the folder. "Looks like Gwen did the original analysis. And that's, well that's all we did. Hmm, 55-56 kilogram woman you say. Given the circumstances, adaptation and response to stress would be a given if one's husband is trying to kill you. Interesting that she could function so well. Amnesic, but an escape by driving?," he peered over his glasses. "Hmm, interesting."

"Tim, that is just one of the many unusual circumstances we have in this case. I hope you can help out on this one."

"Not to worry, my friend. Now, you know as well as I do, the Diphenhydramine and Soma are depressants and depending on levels, could affect recall and functional ability. Prozac, that's a wild card."

"Oh, yea, I forgot to mention. We believe the Prozac wasn't hers. That her mother gave it to her. She was self medicating."

"My goodness, the plot thickens. If mom gave her offspring some of her very own Prozac, perhaps she recognized in her daughter some untoward personality changes prior to the murders. That's what we call a clue in the business, right Morris?"

"And there are other clues that give one cause to question the original investigation. In any event, keep this on the down low will you, Triple T? Give me a call when your analysis is finished? No one else at the station is to know."

"Certainly Morris. Cold case, on the down low you say. How tempestuous. It will be my pleasure. I'll handle it personally, just for you Dr. Detective."

# Chapter Forty Five

A week later I got a call from Triple T. It was just before 5pm. MQ and I had been in federal court all day testifying in a case involving a ring of identity thieves who had stolen tax records from a H&R Block office in Oakview and used them to open bogus bank accounts all over the country. We were heading back to the station when I got the call on my cell phone. "Morris, I've completed the analysis. Do you want to come by and get the report or shall I put it in the mail?"

"MQ and I are 30 minutes away from your office. We'll come by now if you'll still be there?"

"Oh, I'll certainly be here. In fact we're all working a little overtime. We've got a nasty little cluster of heroin overdoses. There's some exquisitely clean brown powder, 90% purity, out on the street right now. Our citizens are just dying to get hold of it."

"Nice Dr. Death humor Triple T. See you in drive time," I said, wondering whether it was heroin coming from the Estrilla family in Mexico to the Scalinis.

With traffic, it was nearly 6pm when we arrived at the Medical Examiner's office. Because it was after business hours security had to buzz us in at the back door where the bodies are delivered and picked up. One of the autopsy techs let us in. We found Tim's staff assiduously working around a complex of mass spec, gas chromatography and spectroscopy machinery.

Triple T was at his desk. He had taken his lab coat and suit coat off and was sporting a white collared, Catalina blue dress shirt and pin-striped black slacks with maroon leather suspenders. He glanced up from a report momentarily to acknowledge us, while he continued to read.

"Give me just one sec Morris." He shouted over to one of the techs. "Mary, you're right. Damn this place. Recalibrate both of the damn machines Mary."

Tim put the folder down and asked us to sit down. He shuffled through a plastic hanging file holder behind his desk.

"Oh, hello Sgt. Murphy-Quinn. So nice that you've come along. Sorry about my outburst. We're trudging through a little mechanical difficulty. For our volume, we need an additional, oh never mind. My budgetary problems are not yours."

"We understand completely Triple T. We just appreciate the help," MQ said.

"Well, detectives, let's see here, I'll read you the highlights and you ask questions if you need to, fine?"

He looked up over the wire rims on the tip of his nose.

"Please proceed Tip Top," MQ said.

"OK. Julie Wiley, 56kg female. Compounds identified included Carisoprodol, the Soma compound, at a level of less than 2mcg/ml. As a muscle relaxant Carisoprodol is usually taken in a therapeutic dosage range of 200-350mg doses, four times per day. A single dose of 350mg would result in a peak blood concentration of somewhere about 2mcg/ml at one hour, and decline thereafter. So, the concentration of Carisoprodol in Mrs. Wiley is consistent with a single pill taken an hour or better, earlier. This amount would not significantly affect her sensorium or functional capabilities. It would not cause memory loss or impair her ability to drive."

"So she took one Soma pill and she would functional. Not at all surprising Triple T," MQ said.

"Now, onto the Fluoxetine, the Prozac. This drug has a long half-life, about one to three days and will be detectable for that period of time based on concentration. Patients receiving 20 to 60mg daily, usually will average around 0.1mcg/ml, with a range that I've read to be between 0.025 to 0.475mcg/ml. That is approximately what we found here. Mrs. Wiley had a Fluoxetine concentration of 0.04mcg/mL. Certainly not an excessive or unusual finding here. She was taking some Prozac, probably at the dosage recommended to her, by the mother, yes?"

"Right. The Prozac was from the mom," I said.

"How self-medicating with an SSRI, the Fluoxetine, affected this woman's capacities is, unfortunately, unknown," Tim said. "But, I would not expect amnesia or a significant functional impairment with an SSRI. It's just a wild card in this instance. Fine?"

MQ and I both nodded.

"She had a concentration of 0.4mcg/ml of Diphenhydramine, the Benadryl. You both know that Benadryl is an OTC drug and is usually considered non-toxic. Fatal adult overdose concentrations have been seen in 8-31mcg/ml. So, she was nowhere near overdosing herself.

I used a volume of distribution calculation to determine what her blood concentration of the Diphenhydramine would be. The results tell us that her .4 mics would have been as a result of ingestion of about 100mg, and with a half-life of approximately 8.5 hours, the amount of Diphenhydramine in her system could have been taken over the last 2-3 days. The longer time would have required her to ingest additional amounts." Triple T stopped and pursed his lips. "I'm losing you here, yes? Too technical?"

"I don't know about Morris," MQ said, "But I can tell you I was not the class valedictorian in Organic chemistry. Yes, you are taxing my rather austere mind."

"Sorry. Right. I'll get to the point. Each Benadryl tablet, capsule or caplet is typically 25mg. The recommended dose is 1-2 tablets every 4-6 hours as needed, up to 50mg, four times a day. Fine?" We nodded again.

"The maximum recommended dose is 12 caps or 300mg per day. Even four tablets, 100mg, for a woman her size, would not produce a significant sensory deficit, perhaps a tired feeling, fatigue, much like I feel now, perhaps sleepiness, requiring a nap, which I certainly could use now. I would not expect memory lapses or cognitive impairment at those levels. Fine?"

"How about the synergism between the Soma and Benadryl? I asked.

"Morris, at her levels, I still would not expect significant deficits. She could recall events, she could drive. I guess that is really all that you needed to hear."

MQ stood, reached across Tim's desk and extended his hand for a shake. "Tip Top, your celestial wisdom has once again made my fucking day."

We all shook hands.

"Oh, by the way detectives. I spoke to Ajay a short time ago. He mentioned that he was finished with the file you sent. You may as well check in on him while you're here."

"Thanks Tim," I said. "I'll give you a call and bring my gear over to jam some time."

"That would be delightful Morris. Please make it soon. Ta-ta gentlemen."

We stood in the doorway of the pathology office. Ajay's secretary was gone for the day. We found Dr. Rajeda hunched over a large microscope, mumbling to himself. The Mumbai native was very dark skinned with jet black hair which he kept in a crew cut. He was short and stocky and wore a lab coat, splotched with purple and pink from Gram stains and remnants of a few lunches. Sartorially, he was the opposite of Triple T. Under the smock, Ajay wore wrinkly, canvas or white hemp clothing. Even in bitterly cold weather it was not unusual to see Dr. Rajeda in shorts and sandals. He said he carried the heat from India in his blood.

We entered his office as Ajay continued to mumble and move the small dials on the microscope.

MQ cleared his throat.

I spoke up, "Hey, Ajay. Have a minute?"

Dr. Rajeda jostled upright, apparently surprised by visitors after 5pm. "Oh, I didn't hear you come in. You startled me."

"Stealth and silence are our ninja trademarks doc," MQ said taking a karate chop stance.

"Hello MQ," Ajay said with a warm smile. "Good to see you without a body bag."

"We were just picking up results from Triple T on the Wiley case and he said you were finished too."

"Oh yes. I have looked at the Wiley file very closely. I think you will like what I've prepared for you."

He pushed away from the microscope and rolled his chair over to another work table covered with files, magnifiers, x-ray view boxes and two laptops. Dr. Rajeda inserted a disc in a laptop that was hooked to a powerpoint projector. The disc opened up.

"I have placed the photo images from the crime scene and post mortems on disc. I made powerpoint slides for you. I assume you will need something for court."

"We hope so anyway," I said.

Dr. Rajeda clicked on a few icons on the laptop. The wall in front of his work-table lit up with a four foot by four foot image of Craig Wiley lying on the stainless autopsy table. He stepped around the table and pulled a film screen down.

"Turn the light switch off please Morris," Ajay asked.

Dr. Rajeda looked at his watch. "I have an appointment in a few minutes. Do you mind if I just go over the important points? You can take the disc and my report with you and we can go into detail when I have more time."

"Sure. That would be great Ajay," MQ said.

"As you can see, Mr. Wiley is in a blue polo, wearing blue jeans and is shoeless. There is significant blood on his upper torso from his head trauma. There is no blood on his hands, pants or his feet and ankles. Do you see?"

"Yes we definitely see. No blood," MQ said.

Dr. Rajeda flipped through images, and described several other close-up slides he'd made of Craig Wiley's hands and feet. He circled the hands and feet with his red laser pointer and said, "See, No blood."

Dr. Rajeda advanced to other slides he'd made from the crime scene photos. "There, on the dog crate is the machete used to chop the girl's skull. The handle is wet with blood. The killer's hands had to be bloody. Do you see the pools of blood from each child? A significant volume of fluid," he shook his head. "There are not an adequate number of photos taken of the crime scene. It would be better had they taken more, but we do see here that the scene was largely a room of blood."

He circled the blood, the laser pointer dot disappearing in the crimson.

My shoulder cramped as I nodded in agreement that the detectives were incompetent fucks.

"Very bloody," Ajay emphasized. "The perpetrator or perpetrators would have had blood on their hands, shoes, pants and feet. It is not possible otherwise. You can see how the first responders tracked complete footprints of blood out from the scene." The laser pointer outlined the combat boot prints of the cops and/or ambulance personnel.

"The only way the man on the table committed the murders is if he cleaned up, washed his hands thoroughly and changed clothes prior to committing suicide."

"You are so fucking right Ajay. I just wanna kiss you," MQ said stepping toward Dr. Rajeda.

"That is not necessary Sgt. Quinn. Perhaps a simple lunch would be sufficient."

"You got it doc, a smorgasbord buffet of international culinary delight," MQ said.

Ajay continued flipping through slides, "There were very few photographs inside the workshop where the bodies of the children were found. Very few pictures that included the wall and ceiling of the workshop." He stopped on one slide of the wall and ceiling where I had removed blood droplets from the Demitrov's.

Ajay continued, "I compared the few pictures from the night of the murders with the one's you took, last year I think it was. It is quite interesting that the scene was not cleaned thoroughly and that the spatter was still present. I am quite glad you took so many pictures from different angles. I was able to trace two distinct arcs and make a few calculations concerning the hatcheting of the little girl. According to the post mortem, the child was struck seven times. There was a spatter pattern for the swings. But I could identify two arcs."

My left ring and little finger started to cramp into flexion. I massaged them furtively and pulled them straight. I reached into my pocket, and grabbed a 10 mg valium I had pilfered from the clinic and quickly swallowed it.

"Look at the pattern of the individual droplets." Ajay said as he clicked on close-ups of each droplet. "You can see the various elongating ellipses changing to near circles. We can trace a complete arc. Based on the blood droplet shape, the best estimate I can give is that your perpetrator is less than 5'10'. If the perpetrator were taller the droplets would be different shapes."

"And our dead guy, Craig Wiley is an easy 6'2", I said. "You are Quincy, Ajay, friggin' Quincy, M.E."

"Simple physics Sam," Ajay winked. He ejected the CD and handed it to me. "Call me next week. We can go over everything in detail if you so desire."

# Chapter Forty Six

ally Sunderman called the week before Thanksgiving. Sally apologized and said that, unfortunately for us, cold cases always got pushed to the back of the line. Sally said the analyses and firearms testing were completed. She would be very happy if I would pick up the evidence and get it out of her way.

The next day, MQ and I went to the lab to pick up the evidence and talk directly to the forensics personnel.

We showed our badges and IDs and made our way to the lab, asking for Ms. Sunderman. Sally came out a few moments later.

"Well, we got it done in record time, just under a year since your submission. Your tax dollars efficiently at work," Sally said with a conciliatory smile. She stuck her hand out. We shook hands but neither of us grinned. "Seriously detectives, I am really sorry it took so long. It's been crazy. A busy caseload, equipment break-downs," she paused. "And you don't want to hear about my problems. I must say, your quick response to pick up your evidence is refreshing. Most of the time I have to call our troopers a couple times before anyone shows up. But, seeing as how you guys called more often than my daughter's boyfriend texts her, I guess this is important to the two of you, huh? I am really sorry guys."

"We understand it's not your fault," I said.

"We need something scientifically objective to shift the ballast to our side. We're hoping you have some provocative minutiae that will break our case wide open. And if you do, it will have been worth the wait," MQ said.

Sally raised her eyebrows at MQ. "Well, I don't know about provocative minu-tiae, but I can give you a synopsis of what I found. How about that for starters?"

"That will be perfect," I answered.

Sally picked up a folder and opened it. She took her glasses from her lab coat pocket and perched them on the tip of her nose.

"Let's see here. We used the blood standards you supplied of Craig, Julie, Taylor and Robbie Wiley for DNA comparisons to other submitted evidence. We examined a white T-shirt, a blue woman's nightshirt. Craig Wiley's DNA was on the white shirt. Julie Wiley's on the nightshirt. But, let's see, yes. Here it is. The police ball cap and T-shirt and the green plaid shirt you brought in were found to have trace evidence, and it was not consistent with any of the Wiley DNA. It is from a male. Well, at least that might be a clue huh detective?"

"It certainly has possibilities, if we knew for sure who wore it. Did you run the DNA from the shirt in a database for comparison to knowns?" MQ asked.

"Yea. We do that automatically. It did not match anything in CODIS," Sally said.

"How about blood on the plaid shirt, any blood?" I asked.

"Nope, no blood on the shirt," Sally said turning another page as MQ muttered something about our luck.

"The hair and blood on the machete and children's clothing were indeed Taylor and Robbie Wiley's. We did not find any unsub blood," Sally paused.

She took her glasses off and stuck them through her hair on top of her head.

"I can tell you, this was not a particularly pleasant analysis. This one goes down as one of the more gruesome cases we've had in a while. The kids' clothing was shredded and starched stiff with dried blood. Long strands of the little girl's blonde hair were matted to the handle and blade of that machete. Brain and what I identified as bowel matter covered the length of the blade. It's disturbing to even think about it."

"Sorry Sally," I said, hoping the 2mg Xanax I took an hour ago would keep muscle cramps at bay.

"Hey, I'm no Pollyanna," she said. "I love a good murder just as much as the next forensic freak, but not children. Gets in my craw. I don't even want to think about this one or see your crime scene photos, that's for sure."

Sally returned her glasses to her nose and her attention to the file. "On the droplets of blood, there are a couple that are listed here as collected last year. What were these?"

"We went back to the scene last year, to take a look. Neither of us had been there before. The new home owners had not changed anything in there. We were lucky," I said.

"I should say so," Sally smirked. "You guys were lucky because the DNA in those droplets was consistent with Taylor Wiley."

"Not unexpected," MQ said.

Sally flipped another page. "We also found DNA consistent with Craig Wiley on the barrel and stock of the 12 gauge shotgun. There was no trace evidence or body fluids that were useful for DNA analysis on the .22 rifle, and no discernible prints on any of the weapons, not even a partial print."

"Which always causes one to wonder if a weapon was wiped down," MQ said.

Sally closed the file. "And that's pretty much it for the lab forensics you asked for. Allen Derrickson has the weapons and reports if you want to go get them now. Let me call him real quick and make sure he's in." She picked up her phone.

Sally nodded her head indicating Allen was in the firearms lab.

"I remember the way to the firearms section from last time. Ok if we just head that way?" I asked.

"He's expecting you."

"Thanks again Sally," I said.

Sally gave us a copy of our lab analyses and walked us out of the office. "Stop by on your way out and I'll have your evidence boxed for you."

"Hey, fellas. Welcome back," Allen Derrickson said, sticking out a hand, blackened with grease and gunpowder. "Oh shit, hold on," he said as he quickly retracted his hand and wiped it off with a shop towel. We all shook hands. Allen grabbed the Wiley case folder and opened it, "Here's what I got for you."

We walked over to a work table. Both of the guns used in the Wiley case lay on cardboard.

"Like I figured, the towel didn't do jack for noise suppression on this here .22 rifle. What's with these darn fools? Knuckleheads, that what I would call these types, I swear. There was a 3.9 decibel reduction in sound, not worth wasting a good towel for. And the .22 fired just fine with, and without the towel."

Now, this 12 gauge," he said picking up the shotgun and holding it vertical, the butt on top of the table. "It's a dandy. And, oh yea, that copy of the picture showing the victim in the recliner with the shotgun standing up in between his legs was really helpful. We set up a domain test. That's where we try to recreate the scene and see what happens, comparing it to what is in the picture. Anywho, I leaned the 870 on a chair, actually got an old recliner that my sister-in-law was going to sell for five bucks at a garage sale. I suspended a gel block just touching the end of the barrel to simulate a human head. We pulled the trigger with a dowel rod. That gun bounced like a damn superball, and ended up lying three feet away. Needless to say, the shell didn't hang up in the ejection port like it showed in the picture. Strike 1.

So, I figured I better put more structure around the weapon. I got a mannequin this time, put it in the chair, replaced the head with a gel block, then I took a couple 2x4s, and extended them from the chair on either side of the shotgun. I put a sandbag on each 2x4, lightly touching the receiver, simulating if the victim had his hands on the trigger or held it with his knees, something like that anyway. Once again, the gun just jumped away. Strike 2.

I tried a third time, sandbagging it tightly. I was thinking maybe the guy was squeezing it with his knees before he pulled the trigger. This time, it bounced, leaned over to the side against one of the 2x4s, and slid to the floor. Now, in this setup the ejection port stayed shut. The shell didn't partially eject. I repeated this two more times with the same result, jumps up, ends up on the floor, and no partial ejection. Strike 3, 4 and 5.

Anywho, I think it's pretty unlikely that Mr. Remington 870 is going to stay upright and in place without additional support. I ain't no ME, but I'm thinking once the weapon discharged and removed your victim's head, that his legs would have gone limp and the gun would have either bounced out of place or just fell over. Either way, I'm ready to say that it ain't gonna be standing straight up like your picture showed. I'd have to be asking some questions about whether that ole boy killed himself or what. The picture showed he was sitting back in the recliner after the impact. I don't see how he could have been any help in stabilizing that weapon between his legs once his head is gone and he's laying back."

"We don't either Allen. You really put some effort in this one. We owe you man," I said shaking his hand again, excited and thankful for the results.

"Naw you don't. Me and Sally talked about this one. Y'all just go find out what happened that's all I'd like to know. Here's your report and I'll box up your guns."

# Chapter Forty Seven

We drove back from the state lab and headed for a local tavern, the Fire and Ice. Not that we needed one, but there was cause for a drink.

We got a table in the back, got a pitcher and a basket of buffalo wings. I started the conversation, "We're certainly quashing the assumption that Craig Wiley murdered his children and killed himself. Mrs. Wiley lied about everything from the bondage to the drugging. If we had her in the room, we'd get it out of her MQ. I know we would."

MQ took a cigar out from a Macanudo tube. He bit off the end and spit the tip on the floor. He was quiet while he fished all of his pockets for a lighter. "She'd never come back to the station. We might be able to show up at her door unannounced and ask a few questions. If she is as much of a narcissist as Newsham, she might say something we can use, but more likely, she'd be indignant and lawyer up."

MQ put the lighter to the Macanudo and filled the space between us with grey smoke. "And you know the Newshams will protect her as well as the Catholic Church has covered for card carrying NAMBLA priests. You want a cigar?"

"Fucking Newshams," I said, and ignored the offer of a good smoke.

"Doc, we've got circumstantial evidence, strong hypothetical details, but no smoking gun to tie her down, no pun intended. We're nowhere near having an indictable case against her. The same languid, incompetent sloths at the prosecutor's office that failed to recognize this case for what it was then, are still there, suckling on the County teat for their paychecks."

I took a long pull from my beer, "Kenneth, how about we send the case to the FBI? The BAU folks, the Behavioral Analysis Unit at the National Center for the Analysis of Violent Crime. You know, the profilers. We could ask them to do behavioral and victimological studies on the Wiley family. Give us their objective opinion on who was at risk for becoming a murder victim and who was a more likely perpetrator. They could review the case in light of the new forensics we've gotten from Triple T, Ajay and the State lab."

MQ spoke as another large cloud of cigar smoke circled us. "We include what we learned in our interviews with the Goldsteins, especially her notes. What your Dr. Classa said about Mrs. Wiley's behavior, her physical appearance and demeanor the night of the murders. We provide the historical Wiley family dynamic from Victor and Clarissa, Mike Reznor and George Fennelman."

I continued MQ's thoughts, "Once they did an analysis, we could ask them to develop an interview strategy for Julie Wiley, should we get the opportunity. If we can get the NCAVC to support our position, we'd be in a stronger position with the Chief and the PA's office."

"It sounds good over wings and brew," MQ said. "Just remember rabbi, anytime you bring in the feds, you bring in tsuris.

So saith Sol.

# Chapter Forty Eight

MQ and I proposed our FBI-BAU submission to Lt. Hebert. We laid all the cards on the table from the Demitrov's to Ajay Rajeda.

It was desperately quiet for several minutes as he flipped through the lab reports and crime scene photos, old and new.

Lt. Hebert did not have a dog in the hunt in this case. He did not approve reports or handle evidence at the time. Whether this case led to allegations of mismanagement or worse, his day would remain the same. In fact, if the shit hit the fan, the Chief could end up indicted, fired or retired, leaving a career path opening.

"I don't think we have a choice but to stir the mash at this point," Lt. Hebert said. "Having the FBI review this case would be the best course. It'll definitely help when and if we take this to the PA's office. Plus, you all will only have one chance at interviewing Mrs. Wiley. That is if she doesn't immediately lawyer up. And if she does agree to a sit down, we want to optimize our chance for success."

"What do you think the Chief will say?" I asked.

"We're just gonna keep this between the three of us for now. He closed his file folder and patted the top of it. "I foresee a firestorm boys, with the Scalinis, the Newsham Law Firm, subpoenas, the media. I want you both to know that, while I would not have traveled this path to the river, I will support your efforts." He smiled and winked.

"Thanks Lieutenant," I said.

"That is," he said waving a finger at the two of us, "So long as the fallout doesn't dust me. That boy, Will Newsham has stepped on my toes a few times and I would not be upset if his applecart crashed. We'll keep this FBI referral confidential, although around this place, with all the wash women, gossiping hens we call police officers, I'm not all that sure it will stay a secret for long. Let me know once the case is in the hands of the profiling unit." He gathered up the folder and stood up. "Once they have it and there's no going back, maybe then I'll broach the subject with the Chief. He'll be madder than a bunch of mosquitoes in a mannequin factory, for sure."

"Hopefully, it will be too late for him to do anything about it," MQ said.

"He'll just be left to stew in his own pot. Do either of you have a contact at the FBI office to handle the submission?"

"Yes Lieutenant," I said. "Sasha Lenhart. I've worked with her before on some organized crime drug cases. She'll like the Scalini angle."

"All right then boys. We're off to the races. Prepare your submission request quick as you can and let me review it before you send it. Continue working your regular bureau cases. Do whatever it is you need to further the Wiley case. Remember now," more finger waving, "No 20/20 or 60 Minutes anytime soon, OK?"

# Chapter Forty Nine

FBI Special Agent Sasha Lenhart was 47 years old and had been at the FBI for 22 years. She was nearing retirement. Sasha had spent the past 14 years working overt and covert organized crime and narcotics investigations in the Midwest. She spoke Spanish, Farsi, French, and Russian and had earned her MBA along the way. She was tangentially involved in the Estrada-Estrilla case, providing background intelligence information on the Mexicans as we prepared for the buy bust that ended in my death. She had identified the two men I subsequently murdered. We'd gotten drunk one night after a meeting and ended up locking lips and groping each other in a parking lot for a few minutes before she remembered she was married.

Despite having a good thing going with Margie, I wondered whether Sasha was still married.

I called her, filled in the details of the case and let her know what we needed from the bureau.

"It will probably take a few weeks to get the paperwork through the system in order to send the file to Quantico," she said. "In the meantime, make copies of the complete initial investigation and the information you've obtained in the cold case review. Include all crime scene photos. And they will need a crime scene sketch to scale. Include all lab reports, and anything else you want the BAU to know. I'll give you a call when I need you to bring everything in."

The government wheels ground slowly and it was the end of July when the BAU submission was finally authorized and ready to go. The temperature was particularly brutal hovering at 100 degrees for several days in a row. The night time temps never dropped below 80 for another five. The heat and humidity had taken six lives in the area. I had hospitalized a handful of clinic patients. It was the same story nearly every summer. Some patients not taking their insulin and not eating, others drinking too much alcohol and not enough water, or there was no air conditioning on the second floor of their building.

The upside was that it was great running weather for more passes through Blessed Sacrament and my secret conversations with the Wiley children.

The FBI office was a good hour drive from the police station. We loaded the car with the Wiley case and left the station at 8:30 for the 10am meeting. About halfway, the AC on my Crown Vic quit. We finished the drive with windows down and volumes of profanity. MQ had broken into a deep sweat. Droplets beaded his forehead and dripped off the tip of his nose. The collar of his yellow shirt was soaked. My white shirt stuck to my arms and back.

I pulled into the parking lot and we unloaded the Wiley case. MQ carried a 36" cardboard tube containing scale drawings of the Wiley residence and a thick accordion folder. I struggled with two bulky cardboard file boxes that contained everything else."

We walked into the lobby of the FBI office, greeted by a wintergreen gush of sweet, processed chilly air. We stood in the vestibule flagging our arms like birds. Security had us run the box and tube through the screener. We locked up our weapons. We were issued temporary ID badges, and waited. Sasha signed us in. She was exactly as I remembered, still a pixie, 5'5" at most, with short, curly blonde hair, high cheekbones and thick lips. She hadn't aged much since last I saw her, and was still strikingly attractive.

"Come on guys, this way," she said with a wave.

We followed Sasha through the maze of agents working out of 8'x10' grey, fabric walled cubicles. Each rectangular rabbit hutch, identical with computer, desk, phone and filing drawer. Sasha was a supervisory special agent, an SSA, and had a small aquarium style office with a large smoked glass wall overlooking the rear parking lot of the FBI complex.

"Agent Lenhart, this is my partner Sgt. Murphy-Quinn, and this is the Wiley case," I said, placing the boxes on her floor while MQ and Sasha shook hands.

"Great to meet you Sergeant. It's Sasha."

"It's very nice to meet you Sasha. Detective Green has said some very flattering things concerning your work."

"Well thank you very much. From what Morris has told me, your case has a lot of areas for concern. Of course, I'm interested in the Scalini connection. Aside from an occasional extortion or gambling debt issue, we've not seen much activity from them."

Sasha knelt down and opened the box. Oh, boy, looks like you've brought the works. And how are you Morris? Still a doctor as well as a detective?"

"Yep, the candle still burns from both ends."

"My hats off to you. I have enough with just one job."

"And you? I figured you would be pulling the pin soon. You're getting close I imagine. I thought I might see you on MSNBC or one of the reality shows as an FBI consultant."

"Not yet. Close though. One more kid in college, then maybe I can get outta here. Don't look for me on TV. They want the flash for their talking heads, not the tired old soldiers. Everyone expects Jodie Foster or Angelina Jolie."

"Don't sell yourself short. You have what they want," I said.

"Thank you Morris. That's very kind. Do you have Botox at that clinic of yours? Maybe a quart of that and some lipo for my muffin top," she said pointing two fingers at her waistline. She laughed and it was contagious.

"If it's any consolation, I have no plans for retirement, not even close," I said. "At least the government has a decent pension. I have a 401K at the PD and at the clinic. It's tanked a couple times with 911 and the economic bullshit. I have enough in both to buy a really nice car. With two kids and an ex-wife, they'll probably end up taking me out of the PD or clinic on a stretcher."

"Sorry, Morris," Sasha said.

"Shit happens."

An uncomfortable silence ensued. Finally Sasha broke it, "Sit. Sit down guys. You look beat already. It's the heat. Dammit it's hot out there."

MQ took out his handkerchief and circled his face. "The ninth ring of Dante's Inferno."

"And my AC went out on the way over."

Sasha turned and opened a small fridge behind her desk and handed each of us a cold bottle of water.

We were profusely appreciative. I spoke after a long swallow. "Anyway, the original investigation is in manila folders and the cold case in blue ones. Everything is labeled to make it straightforward for your BAU people."

MQ tucked his handkerchief in his pocket. "We were able to acquire a copy of the TV interview Julie Wiley gave the day after the murders. We thought it may help your people get a visual of her, and our concerns. She looks fantastic for a grieving, abused widow. It is pretty bizarre."

"I remember watching that too. It was a WTF moment. I was thinking that woman must really be off the reservation to be on TV after her two kids were killed. And from what you've told me so far, it sure sounds like the mother is concealing something."

"Yes. She's most likely a murderous witch. What do you think a response time will be?" MQ asked.

"I would say you're looking at a bit of a wait. They've got an impressive case load and are short staffed right now. Since 911, the financial meltdown and every-thing else that has happened in Europe, Africa and the Middle East, everyone is either on terrorism or fraud. I'm guessing a couple months, maybe longer per-haps. Who the hell knows anymore?"

"It's been a long journey just to get here," I said. "A little longer isn't a big issue."

"Thanks for understanding. Once they get to it, they do great work. I'll review what you have here and get it out to them as soon as I can. If I need anything else, I'll give you a call."

We walked out of the FBI into hair dryer heat with a sense of apprehension and excitement.

"It's like leaving your baby with a new babysitter," I said, turning back to look at the federal building. "You know everything will be ok, but you still worry."

"Well Doc, your Special Agent Lenhart seems confident, but I've never had much faith in federal bureaucracies."

So saith Sol.

# Chapter Fifty

T hree weeks later, with the Wiley Cold Case sitting on a conference room table in Quantico, Lawrence Johnson attended a birthday party for one of the police clerks. As he shoveled chocolate swirl ice cream atop fudge cake into his bloated face, he overheard Lt. Hebert's secretary talking about the Wiley case being sent to the FBI profiling unit.

So much for the confidential nature of police work.

Johnson left the party, cake plate in hand and returned to his desk. He called his roommate.

"Will, the Wiley case has been sent to the FBI. We are so fucked. What're we gonna do? They're gonna find out."

Will cut him short, "Shut up Lawrence. Calm down and shut the fuck up on the phone. Don't say another word. Get in your car and meet me on the Target store lot in fifteen minutes."

Lawrence pulled up next to Will, drivers window to drivers window as cops often do in parking lots. Will's left arm was hanging out the window. His fingers were tapping the car door.

"Will, the Chief sent the Wiley case to the FBI profiling unit. You know, the guys like John Douglass, Roy Hazelwood, those guys. They're really smart and can figure out that something isn't right. Fuck Murphy and Green. What are we gonna do if the feds come down here and start asking questions? There could be some real trouble. You know what I mean. This could be bad for us."

Will pinched the skin between his eyebrows. "So, those two humps actually did something with it. Shit. I didn't think they could get anyone interested." He thumped the steering wheel with clenched fists. "God damn them anyway."

He closed his eyes for a few seconds to think. He hadn't even told his father that Green and Murphy-Quinn had been revisiting the Wiley case, much less the possibility of any involvement by the FBI.

"Lawrence, just keep your fucking mouth shut. Don't say anything to anybody. If there is talk about the Wiley case going to the feds, just say something like, 'The FBI. Wow, we sure are getting big time aren't we?' Something, stupid like that. It shouldn't be too hard for you. I'll take care of it."

"Will, I just worry. That whole deal was bad. That woman Julie Wiley, that bitch!"

"Jesus Lawrence, are you listening? I will take care of it. Don't I always? Go back to work, act normal. Work your cases. Be your usual charming self. Go tell Green to fuck himself and MQ that he's a midget. Act normal. I'll take care of it."

"Alright, alright. I will. What are you gonna do?"

"I'll get hold of dad. We'll use our connections. You know, my dad, my brothers. We can handle this. We've certainly disposed of more difficult problems than just a profiling case."

"Yea, yea, I know, but I'm the worrier," Lawrence reached out his window and squeezed Will's hand. Will pulled back.

"Cut the shit Lawrence. It will be fine."

"You're right Will. See ya tonight."

"Yea. Now go back to work."

The two unmarked police cars went their separate ways. Will called his dad at the law firm. Chatham answered the call just as Will's police radio blared out information on a shoplifter in custody at the Home Depot.

Chatham heard the dispatcher's nasally tone. "Will, Will. When are you going to get out of police work. Good Lord son, isn't the Army Reserve duty enough of a thrill for you? Can't you get your jollies by shooting fully automatic weapons one weekend a month?"

"Isn't it helpful at times to have me in the business?" Will asked.

"Yes, it has been helpful to have you there for certain purposes, but I'm beginning to think that we would be better served with you working here at the firm."

Will interrupted, "Dad, listen."

"No Will, you listen first. You've done well as a conduit of reliable information, but I think it is about time for you to move on. I want you to work on your police exit strategy. We have other sources that are providing what we need. Can you do that son?"

Lt. Will Newsham was not ready to give up his law enforcement career, but in an attempt to placate his father he said, "Ok. I'm thinking about that as well, but, for the immediate time frame, I need to discuss something with you."

"Promise me you will work on your exit strategy Will."

"I promise dad. I'll talk to Vinny and meet with James. There's something we need to talk about,"

His father interrupted, "And I will speak with Tony and Francis and Frank Jr." Chatham said. "And within a month, I want a date at by which you will announce your departure from Oakview to take a position as Director of Security for the firm. Sound fair to you?"

"Yes, I promise," Will paused and took a breath. "Now, about what's going on dad," he paused. "It's the Wiley case."

"The Wiley case? What? I prayed to God we would never hear about that ever again," Chatham said.

"It wasn't on my agenda either dad."

Chatham exhaled deeply and ran his fingers through his hair, "What has happened? What now Will?"

For the next few minutes, Will narrated everything that had happened since Det. Green stumbled over the Wiley case. His father uttered an occasional, 'Jesus' and 'My God.'

"Dammit Will. Why didn't you tell me? Now we're way behind on this and that is a dangerous place to be."

Chatham Newsham kneaded the space between his tired eyes. "We would never allow Julie Wiley to be interviewed without counsel, but who knows what she'll do on her own. But, Will, son, the overriding issue is the additional scrutiny as this FBI profiling unit looks over your investigation. I wish to God you would have let me know from the beginning." The phone was quiet for a few seconds.

"I'm sorry dad. I didn't think they would get any traction. I didn't think anyone would pay attention to them. I thought Montileone would have stopped it."

"Well, he is a man of inaction, so no surprise there. But I have no idea why your Chief didn't call me or Anthony and at least notify us. The Chief will be in jeopardy, too, if this thing explodes. So much could have been done a year ago had we known."

"Chief screwed the pooch on this one dad."

"Perhaps," Chatham said, his mind calculating his next move and several more, as if playing chess. "I'm going to call Mark. Your brother may be able to help with this."

"Dad, great minds think alike. I was planning on calling him. I am sure he has connections in Quantico."

"Yes, I know he does. And that's why it would have been helpful had you notified me earlier. I'll call Mark. You work on getting out of the damn police department, and see if you can find out exactly what they sent to the FBI."

"I will, dad."

"Love you son."

"Love you, too, dad."

# Chapter Fifty One

Mark Newsham, the middle son, had worked in the intelligence community of the State Department for nearly 16 years.

The fact that he was Chatham Newsham's son was an issue during his hiring process. However, he passed several polygraphs and a thorough background investigation. None of the background investigators found evidence that Mark was involved in his father's or his father's client's businesses. Mark had a law degree, spoke fluent Russian, Spanish, Mandarin and Farsi. He was exactly what the State Department needed.

Over the years, Mark had provided assistance in any number of high level investigations involving CIA, FBI, DEA, ICE and the NSA. He was well respected in the intelligence community.

Chatham Newsham had called Mark on occasion for information.

Mark was a good son and provided what he could without jeopardizing his career. Using covert and surreptitious skill sets and contacts he'd made over the years, Mark was able to assist by giving information concerning certain drug trafficking routes that Chatham's clients found helpful. And he had been able to use a few connections to obtain a quick immigration pass for some of his father's associates.

Chatham Newsham took a deep breath as he settled into his chair behind the expanse of his teak desk. He hit the speed dial button for Mark's cell phone. "Mark, it's dad. Do you have a minute?"

"Oh, um, hi dad. Oh yes. I'm here in DC for another week. Then I'm going to Turkey for a couple of weeks. What's going on with you?"

"Staying busy. It's hot as hell here. How is it there?"

"Warm and humid, just like home. So, what's going on, dad?"

"Mark, I have a little problem. I should say your brother Will has a problem and thus it is my problem. I hope you can help us."

"Sure. What has he gotten into now dad? I assume he is still playing soldier and cop, flexing his manhood for all to see. And last time I spoke with him, he was, um, still living with Lawrence. Why doesn't he just come out of the closet. It's not the '60s. No one cares anymore, except those homophobes in places like the law enforcement community and the military. Exactly where my baby brother has chosen to reside."

"I know, I know. I've given him the word to get out."

"He certainly can't get out of being gay dad. I guess you mean what, police work or soldiering."

"Yes, well, I want him to retire his badge. He can still be a weekend warrior. I have no problem with service to our country. Mark, I assume your cell phone is clean?"

"Of course, cleanest the government can offer. Encryption, non-traceable, all the works. The, um works, you know," Mark Newsham said, assuring his father what he already knew.

"Will's department botched a murder investigation a while ago. One of the people involved could come under closer scrutiny by the federal government. This person knows some things about the activities of one of my most important clients. And the word 'Omerta', holds no significance to this person."

"Maybe I'm not interpreting you correctly dad. Sounds to me like this person has the potential to be a liability, and even a hostile witness? If I remember my history, those persons, um, weren't usually much of a problem for your client."

"Yes, well. This person is a first degree relative in our client's family."

"Oh, um, I see. But if it's Will's agency, an Oakview case, why are the feds involved?"

"A couple of detectives who work at your brother's department, conducted a second investigation. According to your brother, they have come up with a considerable amount of evidence that questions the original investigation's findings. The case has been sent to the profiling unit at Quantico."

"They must have turned up some really interesting new evidence, otherwise, the local FBI field office would not have accepted the referral for the BAU."

"Well, I am now officially more concerned. Do you know someone who could help us with this?"

"By help, what would you want to happen? As soon as the case was submitted a paper trail was initiated. Um, it won't just disappear. They will have to look at it."

"So I assumed."

An aggravated Chatham Newsham leaned back in his chair, stretched his legs out and rubbed his aching right knee and silently mouthed, '*Damn knee, damn Julie Wiley, damn police department, damn FBI.* "

"Well, um, if we would have known sooner, there's a strong chance that we could have had the submission denied, and that would likely have been the end of it, dad."

Chatham crooked the phone with his right shoulder and tapped the top of his head with his left hand. He hoped a solution were swirling in the air that would somehow osmotically pass into his mind with the taps. No magical solutions appeared. "I thought there was no harm in asking you."

"Hmmm," Mark muttered over his cell, "No harm in asking dad, no harm. I'll look into it. Maybe I can find something. I'll let you know before I leave the country."

Chatham stood up, fiddled with a few folders and walked to the side of the desk. "Thanks. We'll figure something out Mark."

"Hey, dad, why don't you plan on coming out next month. I'm taking the last week off. Painting bedrooms. Oh joy, huh?"

"I may come up, but I don't think I'll be much help painting with my arthritis."

"Just come. Um, I'll paint. You can fish. Deal?"

"Deal. Talk to you in a few days. Love you son."

"Love you too dad, Bye bye."

# Chapter Fifty Two

Two weeks later, Chatham Newsham sat at the head of the table in his firm's largest conference room. Dark mahogany paneling, thick, multilevel crown molding, heavy drapes, and floor to ceiling bookshelves lined with law volumes and a rolling ladder lined the room, which smelled of lemon oil furniture polish, and the quiet musk of old books. Several brown, orange and green tasseled Persian rugs covered the hardwood floor. A five tier Crystal chandelier hung above the table, it's 35 bulbs easing away the dark stuffiness.

Chatham sat in a high back, brown leather chair with brass tacked arm rests and leather buttoned upholstery. To his right, police/soldier/son Will. The phone next to Chatham buzzed. The seat springs squeaked wearily as he sat up. He picked up, "Thank you Louise. Please, bring them in."

Louise opened the door to the conference room. Louise Fletcher had been working for the firm for nearly 20 years and had been Chatham's personal assistant for most of those years. She was trim and tall, and wore a brown tweed suit with a matching scarf around her neck, the ends of which bumped her thighs with each step. Louise always wore a pants suit and a silver necklace with a cross. She wore her salt and pepper hair short in a manly style and used makeup sparingly. She was one of those women whose age was difficult to tell. She could be in her late forties or early sixties.

Vinny Scalini entered the room, chest strutting like a rooster in the henhouse. He sported a dark blue, pin striped suit. Vinny was 5'8" and all of 180lbs. The handmade Italian tailoring did what a $3,500.00 suit is supposed to, maximize the best traits of its owner. In Vinny's case, it showed off his broad shoulders. All his weight, the gut from beer and pasta, was forward, hanging over his belt. His thick, dark, wavy hair was combed back. Vinny had gone for, and nearly accomplished, a Mini-Me, fireplug version of Steven Segal.

Vinny was followed in by James Paul Patrick. Casually dressed, James wore a black suede sport-coat, a black silk mock turtle neck and black jeans. He carried a leather satchel and walked with a slight limp.

Chatham partially stood, and pointed a hand at two chairs across from Will. "Good morning Vincent, James. Please have a seat. Thank you, Louise. We won't need anything else."

Louise nodded and slid shut the large pocket doors.

Chatham began, "I know we have all had various individual discussions on this issue over the past couple of weeks, but I wanted to do this one time together so we can finally close this out and move on to things less distasteful. Anthony is at Lake Tahoe, but they have been advised that we've been able to mitigate the FBI problem."

With a grin, Vinny said, "Yep, me and James were able to save the day." Vinny Scalini stood. "Yea, well, first off, Mr. Newsham, my father wanted to attend, but he is having a, he is having something done at the hospital. A test. He sends his regards."

"Vincent, I hope it's nothing serious," Chatham inquired.

"No, Mr. Newsham, just routine follow up after his colon surgery last year."

"Give him our best," Chatham said respectfully.

"I will. Thank you," Vinny said.

"Please, Vinny, you don't have to stand," Chatham motioned for him to sit down.

"OK. Yea, yea yea," Vinny scooted his chair towards the table, put both elbows on top and leaned forward. "Anyway, as you know, we have had an interest in some of the players in this fucking thing. For some time now, we've had problems. Detective Green caused us that, uh, inconvenience with our friends south of the border. And now, again, fucking Green. You would think he would have learned a lesson the first time. But with cops, who knows?" Vinny looked over at Will, "Sorry Will, I didn't mean cops like you. I meant…"

"It's fine, Vinny, I know what you meant," Will said.

Chatham spoke to the men assembled around the table, "We're all familiar with the Estrilla incident, the Wiley mess, and Detective Green. Go ahead and bring everyone current Vinny."

Vinny continued, "Mr. Newsham, it was good thinking to have Mark get the names of all the guys at the FBI who was gonna work on the Wiley case. We ran the names in our computer at the Bullpen and voila. As luck would have it, Supervisory Special Agent Daniel Oromando of the Behavioral Analysis Unit happened to dine at the BullPen a couple of times in the past several years. He partook in some of our tasty deserts at the club with some barely, legal young girls. And I must say his method of enjoying his desert was unusual, and involved what I would call," Vinny paused and smirked, "well, there's no beating around the bush here. Friggin' torture! He really hurt those girls. It cost him extra which he had no problem in paying. And, it's all on video."

James removed a folder from his satchel and handed it to Vinny. Vinny opened a manila envelope and passed out several 8"x10" photos of Agent Oromando and a girl maybe all of seventeen. She was naked, handcuffed, her wrists over a doorway chin-up bar, toes barely touching the floor. Her bare back and the back of her thighs were bleeding from multiple linear welts. Oromando stood next to her, naked and shiny with sweat as if he had just exited a wet steam bath, a cat o' nine tails was in one hand, his erect pecker in the other. The final picture depicted the girl, lying on her back on the floor. Oromando was straddling her torso. The lens captured a strong urine stream splashing the girls face.

"Isn't life grand?" Vinny said.

Chatham briefly looked at the pictures. His eyes momentarily closed and his head shook with disgust.

James took over for Vinny, "I placed a call to Agent Oromando and explained the situation and the solution of squashing the Wiley profile. As you would expect, he denied everything and was pretty arrogant. It took a second call in which I played some of the audio over the phone. He got the big picture. I gave him our assurance that we would do nothing with the photos or video if he would only do what we ask. My guess is that this was not his first whip and pee. To make a long story short, we have a gentlemen's agreement now, and he may be a resource we can call on in the future."

The phone on the conference room table rang. Chatham answered and hit the speaker button. Mark Newsham was on the phone for this conference call, dialing in from his gate at Dulles.

"Sorry I'm late, everyone," he said.

"Mark, we're all here. You missed James's and Vinny's narration. In any event, the problem is solved to our satisfaction."

"Oh, great. I'm glad you were able to work it out."

"Mark, thank you for your help. It made all the difference," Chatham said. "If you have to go, go ahead. I can give you the details later."

"Thanks. I've got to go. Talk to you in a week or so."

Will spoke up, "Hey, Mark, it's Will. I'm here at dad's office. Were you going to invite me up to fish instead of paint?"

"Well, ya know, Will, I thought you were pretty busy with all of this, and didn't think you could get away. Of course you are welcome. Bring Lawrence too."

"We'll check our calendars and let you know. Take care, bro," Will said.

"Travel safe, son," Chatham said as he punched the speaker phone off.

James took a two page letter from his briefcase. He handed a copy to Chatham.

"Mr. Newsham, this is a copy of the letter that Supervisory Special Agent Oromando will be sending to Chief Montileone and the local FBI office."

He handed another copy to Will.

"I like this part," James said and narrated. "*After consideration by the members of the FBI's BAU, it would be inappropriate for the bureau to give any further consideration in this matter. While the additional circumstantial information offers additional theories, it is the opinion of the BAU that Craig Wiley murdered his children and then took his own life.*"

"Very diplomatic and exactly what was required," Chatham said. "Thank you, James and Vinny. Given the unpleasant circumstances, very nice work."

Vinny nodded his head slowly, affirmatively.

"Vinny, I'm sure your family is pleased this is finally closed," Chatham said.

"We certainly are," Vinny said.

James added, "Once again, the video from the Bullpen saves the day."

"No one can argue with that," Chatham said. "Will, I hope this extinguishes the interest in the Wiley case at your department."

"It does dad," Will said. "Without support from the FBI, Murphy and Green will be unable to get any interest at the county prosecutor's office, even if they were to take it there. No one is going to buck an NCAVC determination. The case is closed for good."

"Excellent, Will. Now, I have some ideas for the Oakview PD that will limit any additional headache."

Chatham explained his plan as everyone at the table listened and nodded in agreement.

"I'll have a talk with the Chief as soon as he gets the letter," Will said. "I'll see to it that Green and Murphy are instructed to move on."

# Chapter Fifty Three

MQ and I sat down with the analysis from the BAU. Sasha faxed them over with profuse apologies and no answers.

*"The following assessment was prepared by SSA Daniel Oromando of the National Center for the Analysis of Violent Crime, Behavioral Analysis Unit (BAU), Quantico, VA. The case review is based upon materials provided by the Oakview Police Department. The conclusions in this report are based on the knowledge, experience and research conducted by the members of the BAU team."*

The report was 22 pages in length. The analytical team included a retired forensic psychiatrist from Walter Reed, an FBI laboratory supervisor, three FBI profilers, an ATF agent and a former commander of the LAPD Robbery-Homicide squad.

Per our request, a victimological analysis was conducted. Robbie and Taylor Wiley were found to have a low victimological risk. Aside from turmoil in the Wiley's marriage and Mrs. Wiley's poor parenting and temper, the team found nothing in the cold case investigation that indicated the Wiley children were at immediate peril of death or serious physical injury.

The report commented that Craig was not under the influence of drugs or alcohol at the time of his death. However, in the next paragraph they reported that he was known to have a history of marijuana, cocaine and steroid use, and was known to have had a violent temper. The report indicated that these factors increased his victim risk and potential for involvement in violent acts.

MQ read three pages and threw his report on his desk, "What a bunch of crap! How can they say the children were not at risk? Jesus, Mary, and Joseph. Julie Wiley was abusive to her kids, and she had a violent streak. We documented that in the cold case. She smacked a woman with a shopping bag. And the only person who said the guy was using drugs and was violent was Mrs. Wiley. What? They didn't believe our interviews? They didn't believe the lab analysis? Didn't these federal fucks read our report?"

"Let's read the whole thing before we take anyone hostage," I said. We both continued reading.

The NCAVC analysis reviewed the crime scene photos and the ME's report. They indicated that Craig Wiley's position in his chair and the autopsy findings were consistent with a self inflicted gunshot wound. No comment was given on the position of the shotgun neatly between his legs, or the results of Alan Derrickson's extensive testing.

The report indicated that Craig Wiley had no defensive wounds, such as those he would have sustained from an attacker or from anyone he had attacked. They said the lack of any 'combatant' wounds, supported the suicide.

The children's injuries were described as grossly exaggerated in comparison to Craig's solitary GSW. They said the children's injuries were consistent with a rage attack. They postulated that the rage could have been projected directly at the children or they may have been the recipient of the anger intended for other person(s). The report further indicated that the use of multiple weapons suggested overkill, commonly associated with interpersonal relationships.

MQ had gotten to that part as well and said, "Noticeably absent is the correlation that rage and overkill conflict with the initial hypothesis of cold blooded pre-meditation, and that multiple weapons were used because they were handy, not because they were planned to be used. How hard is it to kill a child if you planned to?"

He was right. I could only shake my head and continue to read.

The section describing the home life of the Wiley's indicated that Craig and Julie were both party to the poor marriage. Apparently ignoring the Fennelman and Reznor interviews, the analysts concluded that Craig had been a violent and abusive spouse.

In a review of the crime scene photographs and description of the workshop, they reported that the lifesaving attempts by paramedics disturbed the crime scene making any analysis speculative. They reported that the scene was very bloody and transfer of evidence of the crime to the perpetrator would likely have occurred. The analysts did not respond to the information provided by blood spatter expert Dr. Rajeda.

The report included comment on Julie Wiley's condition. That Mrs. Wiley had been drugged by her husband and had depressant medication levels in her system that would have made her lethargic. They ignored Tip Tops quantification that she would not be significantly, functionally or cognitively impaired.

The report related that the very aggressive manner and the physical effort required to commit the three murders, made it unlikely that Mrs. Wiley was involved. They conveniently ignored Sally Sunderman's analysis of the plaid shirt with unknown subject DNA. The report said with no physical evidence or other linkage to suggest a suspect other than Craig Wiley, the possibility of a third party in the home at the time of the murders could not be entertained.

The team acknowledged that Mrs. Wiley's appearance on the videotaped TV interview the day after the murders did not reveal any apparent injuries. They indicated that there was no way of knowing if makeup was used to cover the injuries. The psychiatrist opined that she appeared to be responding in a manner consistent with a victim of trauma who may have been sedated.

MQ broke the uneasy silence of our reading. "What kind of bullshit is this? They say that Julie Wiley had been completely cooperative with investigators, but fail to mention that Bryson and Weingart found her to be deceptive. And there's no reference to the concerns we expressed over the missing evidence. Perhaps public corruption leading to obstruction of justice in a murder investigation is not within the purview, of the mission, of the elite NCAVC fuckheads!"

I could only shake my head as another of those vermicular muscle cramps started its way from my shoulder to my neck.

The report concluded with, "*Physical evidence always supersedes behavioral indicators and circumstantial factors. We find no physical evidence and no additional information that would alter the original findings of the investigation. Should new evidence be uncovered and provided which would suggest that other persons were involved, then the NCAVC may be of further assistance. Thank you for allowing the NCAVC to be a part of this investigative process.*"

# Chapter Fifty Four

Behind his cluttered desk, the Chief opened the letter from the Behavioral Analysis Unit. He'd already had a brief talk with Chatham Newsham, and had expected to be admonished by Anthony Scalini, but fortunately, Scalini never called. He read the report through relieved eyes. "You dodged the bullet on that one Tom," he said to himself.

The Chief's secretary buzzed him, "Call on Line 1, sir."

The Chief pushed the blinking light, "Chief Montileone."

"Chief. Chatham Newsham here."

"Oh, hello, Mr. Newsham. I was just reading the FBI letter you said I would be getting. I'm just glad that it is finally over."

"Yes, the Wiley business. It brought up some bad memories. That was a difficult time. We are just lucky that things turned out the way they did. Something like this can never happen again."

"Of course. Of course. I am sorry about that," his voice becoming raspy from the stress. "I, should, I should have kept on top of these things. Please tell Anthony I'm sorry. I just never imagined they would come up with anything and no one notified me in a timely fashion about the submission to,"

Chatham interrupted, "I just wanted to let you know that sometimes one has to make changes for order to be restored. You may want to consider something along those lines. I am sure Will can help you get things straightened out. Once things are rearranged, I'm sure you will find that your department functions more efficiently, and efficiency always leads to high profile, newsworthy arrests or drug seizures."

Chief Montileone clearly heard the inference by the lead counsel for the Scalini organized crime family. Over the past two decades, he had received episodic calls from Chatham Newsham. Chatham had provided information that resulted in the Oakview PD making a substantial arrest of some sort, or recovering large quantities of drugs or stolen goods, or breaking up low level prostitution rings. The Chief was well aware that the arrests or seizures were choreographed to strengthen the Scalini's position in the city, but dealing with the devil was all part of remaining Chief for nearly 30 years in an area where many municipalities changed commanders every 5-10 years.

Whatever Chatham meant this time, it would mean good press for a change, at a time when he needed it badly. He'd spent too much of his budget on new cars. A sexual harassment complaint against one of his sergeants was going to trial, and a recent allegation of excessive force meant headaches and misery in front of the city council. Good publicity and a pleased city council would take the edge off those problems.

The Chief coughed loudly, clearing the nervousness from his throat. "Excuse me. Sorry. Yes, well, Mr. Newsham, I was considering making some changes in assignments. Rest assured that we will make the necessary changes to assure that those problems won't happen again."

"I knew you would understand. I've spoken to Will. He can help with the details. Thank you, Tom."

"Thank you Mr. Newsham. And please express my apologies to Tony. I wanted to…" Click. Chatham Newsham hung up.

The Chief took a sip of cold coffee. He sat back in his chair, massaged his temples and called Lt. Newsham's extension.

Will came in several minutes later. "What do you think about this, Will?" the Chief asked, waving Oromando's letter in the air.

"Chief, I told you these guys were on a witch hunt. Now we have the BAU and the General Counsel in Washington DC advocating the results of our initial investigation. I don't know if Green and MQ will believe it. They think everything is a conspiracy. Maybe it would be a good idea if you made it crystal clear to them that the Wiley case is officially closed and that no further investigation will be done."

"I will. The Wiley case is officially closed," he said banging his fist on the desktop like a gavel.

"Chief, maybe it wouldn't be a bad idea, given all the problems we seem to be having with some detectives, perhaps we should make some changes there and with evidence control."

"Yes. Well, yes. Good idea. Perhaps that is something you would like to handle? I'll put out a memo that you are taking over the Detective Bureau and as Evidence Officer and that should be that."

"Chief, I don't think I am the best candidate for evidence. Probably someone like Sgt. Finney. He is very detail oriented. I think he has his CPA."

"David Finney, a CPA? Did I know that? Hmm, very well then. We'll do that."

"And rather than moving me into the Detective Bureau, I think we should consider some other personnel rotations."

"What do you have in mind?"

The following day, MQ and I received a memo from the Chief.

*"Attached to this memo you will find a letter from Supervisory S/A Daniel Oromando. Agent Oromando has indicated that it remains the opinion of the BAU that Craig Wiley murdered his children and then took his own life. There is no evidence to suggest that Mrs. Wiley or anyone else was involved in either the death of her children or her spouse. This department considers this case officially closed. There will be no further investigation or forensics conducted on this case. There will be no further attempts to contact any victims or witnesses. Should any new leads develop, any additional investigation will be coordinated through the Chief's office.*

*As of the first of next month, Sgt. David Finney - commander of Squad C will be transferred to the Detective Bureau and will take over the duty of Detective Bureau Sergeant and Evidence Officer. Sgt. Murphy-Quinn is transferred to the patrol division to command Squad C. Det. Green will be transferred to the patrol division under the command of Sgt. Weingart."*

# Chapter Fifty Five

MQ made his way to Lt. Hebert's office as gracefully as a tornado has its way with a trailer park. I followed at a safe distance akin to the speed in which the Governor of Louisiana acted to evacuate New Orleans as Katrina headed into the Gulf.

MQ threw the memo on Lt. Hebert's desk, the memo landing atop Hebert's pen in hand. Hebert looked up into the eye of the storm.

"Lieutenant, what is this bullshit? The Wiley case is shit canned and I get dumped on? Will Newsham and his little band of miscreants are behind this. And I bet Newsham's old man put the squeeze on the Chief's testicles too. This reeks of just another Oakview cover up, a conspiracy every bit as clear as Lee Harvey Oswald as the lone gunman."

Once again, Sol was incredibly intuitive.

MQ plopped down in a chair in front of Hebert. I stood in the doorway.

"Ah, Dr. Green, good to have you here as a witness as Sgt. Murphy-Quinn works on destroying what is left of his career. Come in, close the door."

MQ began another rant, but was stopped short by the Lieutenant.

"Confound it, Kenneth. Darn it. Give it a break. Yes, the Wiley case is officially closed. If you do anything else, without notifying Montileone first, you do so at your own risk. Let it go for now. You can't bring those little ones back to life."

MQ stood, forehead red, fingers loosening up his tie, his face beginning to shine with sweat and Scotch. He was not in the accepting mood. "Let it go and transfer me to the patrol division? Fuck that!"

Hebert said, "Just shut your trap and listen for a minute Murphy. Good Lord, let me speak."

"Go ahead, make my lugubrious day even better, LT," MQ challenged as he sat back down, squirming in his chair every five seconds as if his hemorrhoids were ablaze, perhaps they were.

"Finney doesn't want to be in the bureau and he doesn't want to handle evidence. You know as well as I do that without the two of you in the bureau, the case closure stats will nosedive. If ya'll will give this a few months, I will work on getting you both back in plainclothes."

"No fucking way we'll ever be back in the bureau," MQ said. The frown lines and creases on MQ's head looked like windshield cracks. "Montileone and the Newshams are burying us and you know it!"

"Kenneth, will you just trust me on this. At my age, I don't want to be the only rooster in the henhouse. I need you fellas."

MQ sat back muttering words of frustration and anger under his breath.

It was my turn to vent. "I guess I just turn in my detective shield and drive around in circles while Adolph Eichmann makes my life a living hell? Lieutenant, I have to go with MQ on this one. We got fucked."

"I can't argue with either of you on that point Morris. But we have to make lemonade out of lemons, or so the saying goes."

"How about the saying no good deed goes unpunished Lieutenant?" MQ spouted, "I'm just gonna pull the pin and get the hell out of this fuck me fantasy. I'll be in a damn van down by the river!"

"Good grief, MQ, I don't want you to quit. Give it a few months. Let me at least try."

MQ turned in his chair and looked up at me. "Doc, you can see the writing on the wall can't you? You'll work under Weingart for about ten minutes and quit. You'll go work at the clinic full time and live happily ever after making some exorbitant physician salary. Since all I have is this job, old Sol will be writing traffic tickets on the midnight watch until they find him stroked out on the Costco parking lot. Come on doc, let's take leave from the delusions of our Lieutenant."

We shook our dejected heads in unison and shuffled out of Lt. Hebert's office. "They beat us doc, they won," MQ said.

So Saith Sol.

# Chapter Fifty Six

We took our whipping and put on uniforms. MQ had to be refitted due to the 30 lbs. he'd put on since going into the bureau.

For me, working for a bigoted, Holocaust denying asshole, was nearly as painful as burn unit skin grafting. To make matters worse, Weingart's shift had recently gone from rotating shifts to permanent nights. 11pm to 7am, the assassin of the body's normal biological clock. It interfered with my sleep and my clinic work schedule.

Then there was the actual duty of a patrol officer, DWI's, traffic accidents, burglaries, domestic disturbances. We were the poor schmucks responding to what MQ said amounted to putting 'Bactine and band-aids' on our citizens' problems.

A typical day began at 11pm. Work 8 hours, then a couple drinks at Grady's tavern on the way home to wind down. I'd get home, take an Ambien or a couple of Oxy's, pull the black curtains closed and doze until one to get to the clinic on time. I developed fleshy canoes under my eyes and went through each day in a fog.

I stopped running by Blessed Sacrament and chose a short route that took me through a maze of strip malls and condo developments. I didn't have the energy for distance running, nor did I feel the need to discuss my failure with the dead children.

Obviously, they felt otherwise. With no further attention given to the Wiley case, my headaches returned with a vengeance, and even worse than the migraines, muscle spasms reverberated like thumping bass drums tapping my left shoulder. At times, it felt like something were alive and moving under my skin. I couldn't have been more wrong.

Margie sent me for an orthopedic and neurological consult with a couple of specialists at her hospital. Neither found anything new to explain the symptoms. I was told to continue the pain meds, just as Jim Farrar had said years ago.

Then the whispers started, unintelligible gusts of high pitched murmurs. At first, I thought it was just a change in my chronic 'rock and roll' tinnitus, but I soon recognized these sounds were different. I heard something, a purr of garbled, hushed voices.

To drown out the hush and keep the world safe from yet another psychopath, I followed the doctor's advice. I took my drugs and more. I phoned in pain medicine scrips for a few of my terminal cancer patients who would never use them. I took samples of narcotics and the expired pain meds home.

I was combining Xanax bars with Valium, Soma with Robaxin, Naproxen with Oxycodone, and double or triple doses of Oxycontin when nothing else worked. All of the pills swilled down with Vodka in a variety of cocktails, tonics, White Russians and Greyhounds. I didn't care whether I overdosed or not.

Despite the attempts to self-anesthetize, the whispers would not stop and I wondered if I had taken the exit ramp to schizophrenia lane. If so, I would travel it alone. Just as I had not mentioned my cemetery discussions with anyone, I would not mention the voices to Margie or anyone else.

The only redeeming value to the assignment change was that Margie understood. Her father, the Florida cop, had been in uniform for part of his career. She said that she liked the crisp look of a man in uniform. I appreciated that, and fortunately, Margie worked nights too and we could have sex in the morning when we both got off work, and then sleep together during the day.

She patiently listened to my tirades about how the corruption within my department extended to the FBI. How my detective career had been derailed because all I wanted to do was solve the Wiley case. I could tell she had difficulty in believing that organized crime could influence the FBI, but she didn't have a better explanation for the result. I told her that I was living, or dying proof of the reach they had. She withheld whatever comments concerning paranoid persecution complexes she may have been postulating.

This time of my life was difficult, but it wasn't all a continuum of the rings of hell. Margie accompanied Jake, Olivia and I to an occasional dinner, movie or museum on those few weekends when we were both off work and my kids had nothing else going on with their friends. They liked her. They said she was a lot like me, but normal.

I guess due to the nature of our work, Dr. Classa and I didn't discuss long term relationships. We both knew how fragile life was, how easily it vaporized right in front of you. We chose to live in the now, unfortunately, my now wasn't all that great, and was soon to get worse.

Along with the tapping and headaches, the dreams increased in frequency. I was waking up 3-4 times a week from the nightmares about trains.

We were at my place one morning.

"Morris, wake up," Margie complained through a husky, sleep interrupted voice. She rocked my shoulder. My eyes slowly peeled open.

"Jesus, Morris. You were yelling and rhyming like a rapper or something. "I tried, I tried, I really tried. Bad people should just fucking die," she said with a face full of pillow wrinkles. "You usually mumble, but this time you were as clear as day. What the hell?"

"I'm sorry, Marg. I saw them this time. In the train, the passengers were the Wiley kids and their father, clear as fucking day. They were just two kids and their father looking at me from a window. Then it changed, and it was Harvey Keitel yelling at me. What the fuck?" I propped up on my pillow and sat up in bed. I leaned over and turned on the lamp on my nightstand.

"Dammit, Morris. Could you give me notice if you're going to turn on the Hollywood spotlights"

Suddenly, it felt as if an ice pick from hell ripped into my shoulder blades, sending waves of agony through me. I let out a shriek and curled up in the fetal position.

"What is it, Morris, what's going on? What is it?"

"My shoulders, my neck, they feel like they're in a vice inside a blast furnace."

Margie lifted up the back of my T-shirt. "Jesus, Morris. Your traps are in spasm, they are hard as plywood. What the fuck.?" She kneaded my shoulders continuously for a good 10 minutes and the muscles relaxed a little. I unfolded and sat up. Margie grabbed her stethoscope, listened to my heart and lungs. "Other than the spasm, you're fine. Now, get out of that soaked shirt. Ghost children or not, you'll get the chills if you stay in it."

I pulled off the shirt and went into the bathroom, threw some warm water on my face and took a Valium. I crawled back into bed.

"You feel better?"

"Yea. Thanks for the rub a dub. That was the most realistic dream I have ever had. Those kids, they know I let them down. They're doing this to me."

"Morris, this isn't Rosemary's Baby or some zombie, stigmata thing. No messages in blood oozing out of your shoulder blades. Dead children are not tying your muscles in knots. You're exhausted, Morris, stressed out to the max. Red-lined. When you're in your 50s, you can't keep burning the candle at both ends and obsessing over things you can't change. You guys busted your asses and did your best. Let it go, honey."

"There's something else," I chewed my bottom lip for a moment and turned off the light. Darkness would make it easier to tell her about the voices. "Margie, I need to tell you something. I've been…" She interrupted as I was about to tell her I was afraid I was losing my mind.

"Can it wait, Morris? I need my beauty sleep."

She yawned again and stretched her arms overhead. I brushed a strand of her long hair from her cheek and cupped one of her breasts, "Have I told you, that you are beautiful whether you're sleep deprived or not and that I am one lucky son of a bitch to have you in my life."

"Save it, Romeo. It's only 11am. Turn off the light. No toying with my girl parts until I've had another couple hours." She kissed my cheek and turned over.

I laid back, staring up at the ceiling waiting for the valium sleep.

# Chapter Fifty Seven

I met Myra Sutherland on a bitter cold November day just before Thanksgiving, November 22nd, the anniversary of my brief death and the Wiley murders.

I was off from the PD for a couple of days. It would have been a great morning to sleep in, but I was working the day shift at the clinic. The windows in my office were taking a beating from pea sized hail. It sounded like a Geiger counter at the Fukushima plant as I sat at my desk going through patient charts.

Myra Sutherland was in her mid forties although she looked as if she was eligible for Medicare. She was painfully thin with dishwater blonde hair and a ruddy, Okie, dustbowl, complexion. Her hair was tied back in a ponytail, emphasizing the strict and knifelike lines of her face.

Myra's green khaki housekeeping uniform fell loosely around her. The pants were too long and buckled over dingy, white, tennis shoes. She ran a rainbow colored feather duster over the blinds in my office. Her back was to me. "What a nasty morning out there. I hope this isn't a taste of the winter that we're coming into," she said in a thick Irish brogue.

I answered absentmindedly, "Me neither."

"You hear them don't you?" she said. "Children's voices, don't you know. They're talking to you."

"Excuse me. What did you say?" I said as a shiver traversed the length of my spine.

"The pretty little girl with the blonde hair and the handsome young lad. They're talking to you."

She looked up at the brass name plate on my desk. "To you, Dr. Green, they're talking to you. They say you can hear, but are you listenin'?"

"Who, uh, what are you talking about?"

"Oh, you're hearing them, yes ya are. Yes. They're right here. Right here," Myra said pointing her duster at my file cabinet.

I swirled in a mixture of confusion and grimaced as my left shoulder cramped. I grabbed it with my right hand and massaged the muscle. "Who, what do you see?"

"I see them," Myra pointed again at the cabinet.

"Who? What are you talking about? No one is there."

"Ah, you can't see them. Hmm," Myra said nodding her head. "You can't see them. But you can hear them. Maybe you should consider yourself lucky about that Dr. Green."

"Excuse me, but what are you…" Myra interrupted.

"Hearing them is quite enough I suppose. I've been witness since a child. My mother, my grandmother, two of my own children. We can hear them, and see them. The spirits, the ones that haven't crossed over. For some reason or the other, they're stuck here. Stuck at a train station, waiting to board. To go on to the next stop."

My mouth gaped, I sat spellbound, cold and confused. I thought, "The blonde girl, the boy. Train station. How does she know?"

Myra returned to her window shade dusting, her back to me again. She continued working and talking in a soft, undulating Irish tone that was disquieting and comforting at the same time.

"Unfinished business for many. Sudden deaths, violent, unexpected. A soul with its divine purpose denied. Oh, there are any number of reasons why they linger doctor. But they're here. And they're made of nothing but energy. Electric energy is how you feel them."

"This is fucking unbelievable," I said.

"Oh yes. You're one of them. One of them they've attached to. They probably visit you in your dreams. The early morning dream, the same one. Early mornin', it's them."

"Yes. Absolutely. I mean, when I can sleep at night, at night, like normal people, the dreams are usually at 3," I was stammering, "Yes, at 3 in the morning."

Myra continued to dust the file cabinets. "And the time, it's nothing so dramatic as this whole business about the hour of the dead. This whole foolishness with 3:33 being half of the mark of the beast. Crap. A bunch of crap I tell you. And it being opposite of 3pm when Jesus was supposedly killed. Foolishness. The dead, aren't bound by our time, they don't wear a Rolex now, do they?"

I watched the stick figure busily working. "What is it you know? How, what do you, what do you know?" I asked.

"Early morning hours, it's your deep sleep. They call it REM I think, although I can't for the life of me remember what that stands for. It'll come to me later, probably when I'm on the next floor. But the deep sleep, the dreams. It allows them to get into your spirit, your unconscious and that usually happens between two and four in morning. They can visit in your dreams at any hour. Deep sleep dreams is what they are all about. And what you have, are visitors that are in-between worlds. In between the physical world, our world, and the other world, the netherworld. Spiritual beings. Whatever name you may wish to use. We are more open to them during that time. As I'm sure you're quite aware."

"Uh, yea, I dream… what do you mean, I…" I was stammering again.

"What do you dream Dr. Green? You have the same one or two dreams all the time do ya?"

"Yea, yea I do."

"What is it about? Will you tell me?"

I told Myra about the train station dream, the train, the children, the passengers, Harvey Keitel.

"I wouldn't be knowing about this Harvey, but you're another one with the train station. Buses, trains, planes, all the same idea really. They're goin somewhere. Pretty common with these ghosts. Always indicates a movement between the worlds. Either waiting on the platform and unable to board, or eternally riding the damn thing which tells of a spiritual blockage to the passing from one world to the next. Not that hard to figure out that one, the train."

I remained silent.

"You know doctor, they often find a vulnerability, a weakness. They aggravate a physical or emotional condition to get your attention. Like a splinter in your finger they are. In some cases, they'll send someone to the looney bin, make em mad as a hatter. In your case, by the way you're holding yourself, I expect your visitors are causing you some problems with your neck or what is it? They're trying to make you listen to them, do their bidding, so to speak. Does that sound familiar to ya?"

"My shoulder," I said. "So, you actually can see? What? What, is right there?" I asked pointing at the file cabinet. "What is it you see?" I looked up at the oval name patch on her shirt, "Myra, what do you see?"

Myra put her feather duster on her housekeeping cart. She leaned over my desk and reached out a gristled hand with the texture of a glazed doughnut, "Myra Sutherland. Nice to meet you, Dr. Morris Green." We shook.

"Them. I see them. Those that are talking to ya," Myra leaned towards me and softly said, "The whisperers, Dr. Green. Those that are whisperin' to ya."

She stood in front of my desk and turned obliquely to face the file cabinet. "There is a little girl there, cute as a button. And the boy, he's there too, older, not in his teens yet, though. Dark hair, a handsome young man."

"You see them?" I asked, staring at nothing but a grey metal file cabinet.

"Oh yes. I see them as if they were really here. Just like that."

"Just like that, Myra?" I asked.

"Just like that, Dr. Green. So, why are they here? What is it that they want from you? You can answer that. I am sure you know," she asked.

"It's a long story. And, it's complicated."

"I've got time," Myra said glancing at her watch. "I'm ahead of schedule," she said, sitting down in the chair in front of my desk. She crossed her bony legs, her scuffed tennis shoe rhythmically bobbed up and down, waiting.

I wavered, "I don't know. This is so bizarre."

"Maybe talkin' will help. I'm a good listener."

My gut told me it was alright to tell this complete stranger one of my closest secrets. "Well, I was a police detective for many years. Those kids are from an old homicide case. The story line was that they were killed by their father and then he committed suicide. However, the facts indicated that the mother was involved somehow, and quite possibly, the father was murdered. We worked it, but we were unable to make the case."

"And that's a good enough reason for them, isn't it now? You took an interest, they noticed," Myra said.

"It was a disaster. There were outside influences, political machinations, a cover up and the case was closed. I can't do anything else with it."

"Those kids they're stuck and they want to move on. They want you to make it right. To keep going, keep at it. I can tell you one thing, they won't stop until you fix it. I sense their deaths were terribly violent and sudden. They are stuck, trapped here, Until whatever it is, until it is made right."

"So, you're saying I'm being haunted. This tapping sensation causing my shoulder to seize up, the headaches, the nightmares waking me up? All that from ghosts? Children ghosts?"

"Apparently so," she said with a nonchalant wave of one hand.

"All because they want me to bring them truth, justice and the American way. Let me tell you, I'm no Superman, far from it. I'm wore thin. Nothing personal, Myra, but I don't know if I can buy into this whole supernatural, righteous justice concept."

"Now, Dr. Green. You know it's true," she wagged that bony finger in my direction. "You've known for a long time. You just haven't accepted it yet."

I kept my skepticism afloat. "Accept that I am being haunted until such time as I solve their murders and get justice for them?"

"That's about it in a nutshell."

"That's a tough pill to swallow."

"You have any better explanations for your dreams and your pain?"

"How about the fact that I was shot and still have a bullet in my back. And that I died too, but they brought me back. And that I have nerve damage and scar tissue that can cause pain, and a head injury and PTSD."

Myra nodded her head in the direction of the filing cabinets and appeared to be listening to the little specters over there. "And you were shot on the same day of the children's murders were ya?"

"How did you know that?"

"They told me."

I felt a trickle of cold sweat drip down my back and I dry gulped, "Yea, both of our incidents happened on the same day."

"Coincidence you think, do you now doctor?" Myra asked. "Well, well, Dr. Green. Not only are you tied to the case in the name of justice, but they have a taste of your soul. A part of your soul is moored to them. They must have attached it as you all were passing, except you returned. You're bound to these children, Dr. Green. It's a very strong bond."

"A bond?"

"A bond of your souls, very powerful."

"So how do I unbound?"

"You help them and you help yourself."

"We worked the case hard and got screwed at every turn. I can't do any more. I just want them to go on to someone else. Find someone else. Let my soul go. Maybe someone else will have better luck. I don't suppose you can just do a quick exorcism?" I asked only half joking.

"Dr. Green, you're not possessed by a spirit requiring exorcism, no, nothing like that at all. It's pretty simple. You bring justice, you free them. You free them from the in-between. And they leave you. Your pain goes with them. Your soul goes free. There's no one else that can do it for them."

"Alright, I'll go along for the time being. So, can they just tell me who their killer was so we can all go about our business? Tell me where the smoking gun, the evidence to get the killer is? Can they identify their mother, or whoever? Can you speak to them, get some answers?"

Myra paused. Her foot stopped bobbing. She looked at the file cabinet. Her nostrils flared as she took in several deep breaths. She was nodding her head, her lips pursed, her eyes narrowed and closed to slits.

She continued, "They want it known that their father was not involved. I can see him now, but he is in the background. He's a powerful looking man, tall and thick. I'm sensing from him that he says, 'I'm one of the good guys. I'm a good guy I would never hurt them'. He keeps saying that. "I'm a good guy'. I see him in a dark uniform, with a badge. No, or perhaps patches, yellow or gold patches on his shirt. Was the father a police officer too, is that what this is about? He was one of yours?"

I thought back to the visit with Victor and Clarissa Wiley and recalled the pictures I had seen of Craig in his canine trainer's uniform. Long sleeve polo shirt with his company emblem on the chest and embroidered gold patches on each shoulder.

"Holy shit! He wasn't a cop, but he did wear a uniform," I paused, trying to put together rational thoughts. "Ask the father what the hell happened? Get the kids to tell you what happened. They know. Tell them we're sure their mother was involved, and that there was another person in the house at the time that may have participated in the murders? Who did what and how do I prove it? If they want their freedom to pass on to the pearly gates, it's about fucking time they helped."

"This communication we have, it's not like what we are having. I understand them in a telepathic sense. And I can tell you that the father was not involved at all. Not at all. He..." Myra paused again, and took in a few more nasal breaths. She was eerily still. Her eyes were completely closed now and the only part of her body that moved were her lips. Her face turned the color of old concrete.

"There was another man there at the time. Not the father, another man. A man with close ties to the mother. This one is not like the father. Almost opposite, wiry in build, light hair. The children, they knew it was all wrong. He didn't belong."

It was Myra's turn to shiver. She shook like a wet dog.

"And, the mother, she didn't love those kids. Oh no. They were in her way. She didn't love them. She can't. She's incapable of loving. That is, anyone but herself."

Myra leaned back, her breathing increased to nearly a pant. "A terrible, frantic, red rage enveloped the mother that day. A horrific rage, Dr. Green."

Myra stopped. She leaned forward, doubling over. She took another deep breath in and let it out slowly, gradually unfolding, opening her eyes. She planted her elbows on her knees, steepled her hands and rested her chin atop her fingertips.

My eyes were tearing up. I pulled a tissue from the box and rubbed the wetness away.

I spoke in whispers, "I tried, I really tried. Every step of the way, someone or something kept the truth at a distance. Every time we tried, something else happened, blocked us again and again. I don't know what else to do for them."

Myra took hold of my hands. Her touch was surprisingly gentle as she massaged my wrists, palms and fingers. "I know this is a lot to take in, Dr. Green, but they need you. They need your help. They know you are the one person who will help. There's no one else."

"Ok. I'll try. I'll go over it again. I will, I promise. Tell them. I'll look for an angle, something new. But I don't need any more prompting. I can do without the friggin' dreams and the knife in the shoulder blade. Tell them to stop that shit, stop the friggin' dreams and the pain," I demanded. "Do you understand what I mean? Can you tell them?"

"Oh yes, I hear you quite loud and quite clear. You don't want them to visit."

Myra stood and took a bottle of water from her cart. She took a long pull. "I understand Dr. Green. Really, I do, but we cannot control them. We can only watch and listen. I was three when I saw my first spirit. If you wish to think of terror. Think of that. Three years of age, and visited by spirits, some not very pleasant. My mother helped, but still it was…" she paused, "Let's just say I'd trade you for your back pain and dreams."

Myra continued. "There are so many out there, Dr. Green, so many beings in between, and many are malignant ones. Full of evil, negative energy, angry souls, trapped in between because of what they've done during their time in the physical plane. And they seek out people like us, my mum, my children, the ones they know can see them. They don't like to be seen. It frightens them, they feel vulnerable and they don't like that. They just don't like people like me."

"I am sorry you are saddled with such a burden."

"We make our way around the bad souls, the best we can. But, your little ones are innocents, they mean you no harm. The dreams, your shoulder. Think of them as Post-it notes from the other side, a reminder."

"Post-it notes that I could do without. I suppose relative to your situation, my problem is minimal. I cannot even imagine what it must be like for you."

"It's a dog eat dog world out there Dr. Green and I'm wearing Milk Bone Underwear."

We both chuckled and hugged each other.

The leathery color had returned to her face. She winked one of her spider webbed eyes. "And by the way, there's one other soul along for the ride. Another one. Way in the background Dr. Green. Do you know? Another lost one, looking for you, Dr. Green."

"Oh for Chrissake! Really? I don't have any other unsolved, lost-in-transition cases. Give me a break here."

"I'm like that news station you have on in break room here, Dr. Green. I report, you decide," a faint smile crossed her face. "Nevertheless, it's there."

I just shook my head. "I'll worry about that one later. So what do I do with the dead that I do know about. I'm at my wits end here. The rage around Mrs. Wiley. Does that mean she did it?"

"A circle of fury indicates out of control violence. It could be her, or someone else with her. Either way, she was right there in the middle of it. If she didn't do it, she knows. She was there with them when it happened. Dr. Green, you'll figure something out. Something will happen that will lead you. It always does. It's how these things work. Have faith."

"I haven't had faith in such a long time Myra."

"I know. I can sense you're lost. Have faith, Dr. Morris Green. Something will happen. It always does. You just have a little faith, Dr. Green, something most certainly will happen."

Myra turned away, stopped at the doorway and nodded her head a couple of times toward the filing cabinet. I guess she was acknowledging something my ghosts said. The wheels of her cart squeaked down the hallway.

The moment she was out of sight, I took a quick pull of Stoli from the bottle in my desk, savoring the bitterness followed by the warmth. I leaned back as the rumblings of what would soon become a full blown migraine waged battle with the Vodka. With closed eyes, I reflected upon the revelations from housekeeper Myra Sutherland- spirit medium-communicator with the dead.

"So, Myra confirms that Julie Wiley was in the middle of the murders," I thought. "You certainly don't have to be Jeanne Dixon to figure that out. And she says justice must be served and the guilty must be punished so the little rugrats and their old man can cross over to the Elysian Fields, Nirvana, Heaven, or wherever the fuck good people go when they die.

But what if I don't find them justice? Do the little specters continue to drive 16 penny nails into my head and back until I eat my gun? This bullshit will only stop if we put a needle in the vein of the killer or killers at midnight in the state prison. Fuck that and fuck those kids." I took another pull from the flask.

It was troublesome that Myra Sutherland knew some things about the Wiley investigation that she could not possibly know, and I could not explain that. A physician, even a drug and alcohol addled one like me, leans towards evidence based sciences, the proving or disproving of hypotheses and theories by scientific analysis, reasoning and experimentation.

The ephemeral intertwining of my soul with the Wiley children at the time of our deaths, and the demands by spirits in transition for justice was a lot for me to accept.

Nevertheless, my gut told me Myra was 100% correct, and my gut had always served me well. I kneaded the ropy nest of muscles at the base of my skull, hoping the headache would be short-lived.

Lenora stepped into the door frame with a patient chart tucked under her arm. "Dr. Green! You have Harold Westerhold in room 3. Nasty abscess on his left buttock. If you ask me, the thing needs to be drained doc, probably staph. Lucky you."

"Yea. Lucky me."

My feet hit the floor. I popped two pieces of Juicy Fruit in my mouth to mask the vodka.

"Something will happen. Have faith, something will happen," that's what my ghost whisperer said. I hope to hell she's right.

# Chapter Fifty Eight

Just as Myra predicted, something happened. In fact, two 'something will happen' events, occurred. One concerned a traditional murder-suicide. Traditional in the sense that someone was murdered, and the killer then committed suicide. The second occurred when Will Newsham made the acquaintance of a handsome civil engineer from Marietta, Ga.

Dan Wolfe was 37, had a BFA in literature, an MBA from Emory and razor-cut, wavy, black hair. 6'4" with a sculpted physique and a fashion sense that required annual visits to New York's William Fioravanti. Dan was in town, staying at the Hyatt for the annual conference of City Managers and Planners being held in the downtown district.

He asked the concierge and learned that a local establishment called Compartments was the best alternative lifestyle club. The concierge told Dan in a thick Chicago accent, "Compartments is very nice and very clean, with a very nice clientele. My daughter, she's an L, he said putting finger quotes around the 'L.' "She says it has a 'crisp and fresh' atmosphere. Whatever the hell that means."

Dan thought of iceberg lettuce, but nice and clean sounded absolutely fine. He had long ago stopped going to the loud, smoky, techno, dance clubs. He just wanted to relax, have a drink and enjoy the sights. He'd recently broken off a three month mistake with a married commodities trader and thought that he wouldn't mind meeting someone, if just to talk. Compartments was a short taxi ride from the hotel.

Will had been at the club for a few hours before Dan arrived. He figured someone he knew would show up, or he would relax, get a good buzz and just people watch. No one would be at home anyway. Lawrence was on the evening shift and would probably have to work overtime. He'd heard that Lawrence was the recipient of another one of Lt. Hebert's tirades earlier in the day about the department crime stats.

The transition, without MQ and me in the bureau, was not going too well for Lawrence. As Lt. Hebert had prognosticated, crime solve rates were plummeting and the Chief and the Mayor were none too happy about that. To no one's surprise, Lawrence was just not able to carry the work load and clear crimes.

The bar at Compartments was a wide stainless and chrome playground slide looking beast that had been heated, welded and hammered in the shape of oscilloscope type waves that flowed for thirty feet down the center of the room. Shimmering rope lights flickered along the edge of the bar and from a parallel chrome overhang long stem wine glasses hung. The lighting was controlled by computer to enhance the appearance of wavy motion.

Off-white, ceramic, bar stools in the shape of goblets were evenly spaced. The supporting stems cast a shadowy glow onto patron's legs and feet from a series of oval light inserts. Bartenders in sparkling black and silver tuxes were mixing drinks, some with flair, some basic.

On the walls of either side of the room were small compartments, hence, the moniker. The compartments were best described as stacks of cubicles much like those in the game show Hollywood Squares, except instead of being in the shape of a square, the compartments were stair stepped. First one, then two high, then three, then two, then one, repeated twice along each wall. Each compartment was roughly eight feet by eight feet. Twinkling pink, purple, amber, blue and clear rope lights outlined each cubicle. The interior walls of each cubicle were flat black.

A single, hanging, chrome light was centered over a circular, three foot, ceramic, grey table in each cube. The edge of the table was trimmed with delicate, soft, gold, rope lighting.

Four stainless goblet stools circled the table. A black or red leather loveseat sat along the back wall of each compartment. The walls were decorated with stainless steel and chrome abstract shaped cutouts and a few had prints by Pollock, deKooning or Rothko.

Compartment patrons understood the club rules that allowed a modicum of romance in the compartments, but no nudity. There was to be no bodily fluid exchange within the confines, thus maintaining that crisp, fresh and clean reputation.

Dan ordered a gin and tonic at the bar and stood next to Will, who was seated on one of the goblet barstools. Dan scoped out both sides of the room from his vantage point, noting the groups of patrons in the cubicles. Waiters and waitresses disappeared behind the compartments with trays of drinks, going up stairs, appearing as a framed figurine within the square and then returning with empty drinks on their platters. Dan estimated that the bar was at least one hundred feet in length, and was probably three stories tall. "There must be a rather robust gay community here," he thought.

Will spoke, "First time at Compartments?"

"I hope it didn't look like I was gawking. It's just an interesting blend of architecture, the wave of the long bar and the stark geometry of the cubes. I like it. It's crisp and fresh," Dan said, making eye contact followed by a downward sweep of the man next to him.

"Hi, I'm Will."

"Hello. I'm Dan," Dan said as he extended his hand. They shook firmly.

"I can't say I've ever seen a bar like this," Dan said.

"Every time I come here, I think that Paul Lynde is laughing somewhere," Will said.

Dan chuckled.

"Are you new to the area or just in for business?"

"I'm here for a conference, City Managers and Planners. I'm the planner for Marietta, Ga. Very boring conference, and it is a week long, my God. I hope tomorrow will be better. Three more days of this, ugh," Dan said with a smiling scowl. "And you Will? You are, local to the Compartment?"

"Yes. I'm from here. How funny though, I guess you could say we have a little something in common. I am a police Lieutenant with a municipality about twenty miles from downtown. I'm involved in a number of projects with our city planner and administrator. Maybe you met him, George Light? We're doing several improvements this year, public works, parks, road infrastructure," Will said, standing up to close a little of the ground between he and Dan, testing the waters.

"I haven't met him yet, but there are a lot of us at this conference. I would bet parks and road projects are not nearly as exciting as police work," Dan remarked. He didn't back up as Will moved a little closer.

"Oh yes, we're always engaged in high speed pursuits and running gun battles with evil doers. Some days I just cannot contain myself," Will said smiling.

Dan chuckled again and Will liked the perfect teeth and attractive, wrinkled tan lines Dan exhibited when he laughed.

"Would you like to grab a compartment and chat a bit Dan? How about that one over there. I think that is where Goldie Hawn would have been."

"I don't know Will, are you sure it wasn't where Wally Cox sat?" he said, winking and brushing his hand against Will's.

Will left Dan's hotel at about 2am and slept on the couch to avoid waking Lawrence and having to explain his whereabouts.

# Chapter Fifty Nine

Will met Dan the next night and they repeated the previous evening of cocktails and a carousel of pleasure at Compartments. Will felt as if he had met an emotional, social and intellectual match. He didn't want to think in terms of kismet, but he felt delightfully new and content.

It was 1am and they sat side by side in a back table at an all night diner down the street from the hotel. Over coffee and toast, Will and Dan engaged in discussions of what they were reading, from John Grisham to Nicholas Sparks. They shared opinions on the budgetary considerations and political machinations that push a municipality forward. Dan occasionally slipped a hand under the table and kneaded Will's thigh.

In conversation, Dan Wolfe mentioned he was from a fairly prominent Atlanta family, and that his father was a partner in a large criminal defense law firm.

Will asked Dan if he had ever heard of the Newsham Law Firm.

"Are you kidding Will?" Dan laughed and clapped his hands. "How bizarre. You're that Newsham?"

Will's eyes narrowed a bit with wonder. "Guilty as charged. Youngest male of Chatham and Anna Marie. And you know the Newsham name how?"

"Let me tell you this story. What a blast. My God. It really is a small world. That six degrees of separation and all that." Dan spread some apple butter on wheat toast, handing Will a toast point.

Will smiled, munched and listened, staring with both envy and satisfaction at Dan's GQ face.

"There was this mob case, years ago. Jimmy "Sweet Roll" Bustamanti and some of his compatriots had freed about a half million bucks from some pension fund. Someone from the fund caught on and threatened to call for an audit, or the cops, something like that. As you would expect, the pension guy's car blew up, with him inside. Jimmy was charged with the theft and murder. Wolfe, Tuttle and White represented Jimmy in the financial case. The Newsham firm handled the murder case. Your daddy got "Sweet Roll" off. Lack of physical evidence, and of course by time of trial, there were no witnesses to testify against "Sweet Roll."

"Dad is good at that," Will said. "Were you working for Wolfe, Tuttle and White?"

"I was just out of college and my father had me running errands, picking up papers at the courthouse," Dan said. "I was deciding whether to get my MFA or MBA. Pop put me to work in hopes that somehow I would decide on a JD. Well, as you see, I didn't pursue a legal career."

"I know what you mean, only so well. One of my brothers drank the Kool Aid and is a partner at the Newsham Law Firm. When he joined the firm, I half expected dad to put a sign on his Jaguar like Fred Sanford. 'Newsham and Son, Attorneys at Law'"

"Fathers," Dan chuckled, "What can you do with them?"

"Don't I know," Will said, "Dad has been bitching at me to quit the police department and work for the firm in some capacity, security. I don't know Dan, I like my job. I like the occasional thrill. You know?"

"Oh yes, I understand totally. Excitement and risky business is addictive. You'd miss the episodic thrill of those running gun battles, but even more than that, Will, we both wanted to show our fathers that we could make it on our own, and we have, have we not?"

Will glanced towards the front of the restaurant. The waitress was taking an order from two obviously drunk, college kids. No one was looking their way. He leaned in and gave Dan a long kiss.

Will walked Dan back to the hotel and stayed until 4 in the morning. He drove home slowly to savor the evening. He decided to sleep on the couch in his office, rather than deal with Lawrence.

It had been a long time since Will had strayed. The last time had been long ago, when he was still in Vice. He and Lawrence had become homebodies and rarely stayed out late. This was a first in quite some time.

At 9am, Lawrence punched Will's office extension.

"Lt. Newsham."

"Where have you been the last two nights?"

"What do you want, Lawrence. I'm busy."

"Where were you?"

"Just out with some people," Will answered.

"Yea. Like who, Will?"

"Some clients, some clients of, my dad's. It's a case they are bringing to trial soon. Some uh, surveillance. I'll be out tonight as well. I'm really busy right now, Lawrence. I'll tell you all about it, tomorrow. We'll talk tomorrow. Gotta go." Will hung up.

"Busy my ass!" Lawrence threw the phone across the kitchen. It splattered into pieces against the refrigerator door. He paced back and forth along the butcher block island. He felt like water on a hot griddle, and not just because of Will. He was unaccustomed to the longer bureau hours, the heavier caseload, the bitching from Lt. Hebert. His in-box was filled with shit and more shit. He'd complained to Will about it. Will told him he would help, but he never did.

"And now he's staying out all night and he's too busy. Fuck him," Lawrence said, picking up the phone battery and back plate putting them back together.

A little over 12 hours later at 9:30pm Lawrence followed Will's jeep. "I'm a detective. I can do this," he said. "Traffic's pretty heavy, he shouldn't be able to spot me."

Lawrence followed 2 car lengths behind. Will pulled into the parking lot of Compartments. Lawrence parked across the street with an eye on the Jeep. "That lying ass. He's not surveilling anybody for his dad at this place."

Will went into the club. After an hour or so, the lot was full and there was a line forming to get in Compartments. Lawrence figured that with the crowd, he might be able to go inside without Will seeing him. His imagination was busy creating worst case scenarios. As he was getting out of his car, one of those scenario's strolled out of the club with Will. Ever the gentleman, Will held the door for Dan Wolfe.

"God dammit! Tom Selleck look alike!" Lawrence muttered getting back in his car.

Lawrence's surveillance continued to the downtown Hyatt. Will valet parked. The two men walked into the lobby of the hotel. It had not dawned on Lawrence that he had played a part in a similar drama with his ex-wife, Charlene, many years earlier.

Lawrence's life was just like his detective bureau inbox, full of shit.

# Chapter Sixty

As a Lieutenant, Will Newsham had his own office. It was nothing extravagant, just a 10'x 12' box, at the end of the hallway next to the staircase. The front wall was composed of four large glass panels with vertical blinds that clacked every time the A/C or furnace kicked on. His workspace was secured with a solid wood door upon which a burnished, brass, name plate hung.

The three remaining walls were a warm burnt orange which Will painted himself, not satisfied with the standard, municipal beige. Will had decorated the room with a 4' palm plant in the right rear corner behind his desk and an American Flag stand to the left. He'd hung a print of the *The Runaway* by Norman Rockwell on one wall and scattered his college diploma and a dozen or so certificates of training he had completed on the others. There were no plaques containing awards for valor or recognition of duty above and beyond. Will had never received a commendation.

Lawrence took the back stairs up to Will's office. He'd thought it best if he had the element of surprise and anonymity. Nosy secretaries and clerks did not need to know what was about to transpire.

Will Newsham was plodding through crime statistic reports from the previous day when Lawrence blew through the doorway like an Indonesian tsunami. He slammed the door shut as he entered. The glass panels and blinds shook. The Chief's secretary peered down the hallway. The hallway was unoccupied. She put her earbuds back in and continued her transcription.

Lawrence stood directly in front of Will's desk, knuckles dragging. He was panting, out of breath from the steps, his face blushed and his tie undone. He had not slept and had the same clothes on he'd worn the day before. He looked more like a Shar-Pei than a detective.

As soon as the door closed he spewed a plethora of indictments. He told Will he had followed him to Compartments and the Hyatt, describing Dan to make sure Will knew he had been caught.

Will leaned back in his chair as Lawrence showered him with a fusillade of accusations. His tone oscillated between anger, jealousy, hurt and dejection. It did nothing but aggravate Will.

As Lawrence continued his tirade, Will listened, shook his head and thought of their time together. He had been a good friend and lover to Larry. He'd bent over backwards to keep him solvent. They'd had a good time together. Whether he continued to see Dan was irrelevant. Will had made the decision over the last two days that he and Lawrence needed to split up, move on.

Lawrence, on the other hand, had nowhere to move on to. He couldn't ask his grown kids for help. They had their own lives and anyway, he didn't want to become a burden to them. Charlene still held a grudge against him for what she said he had done to their family. He doubted if he could even stay a weekend at one of their children's homes without her going ballistic, and Lawrence had no other family or close friends to call upon.

Over the past few hours, Lawrence had been reviewing his options and had developed very few. In this moment of desperation standing in front of Will, he played his only ace card.

"I know a lot of shit about you Will Newsham," Lawrence said as he glared down at Will. You can either stop fucking around, quit this fucking bullshit, or I'm going to tell the powers to be about what is going on around here. About how you, your daddy, the Chief, the Scalinis, how all of you are a bunch of crooks. About the protection scams you ran for the gangbangers, the tit for tat on the drug arrests the Chief got, the fucked up Estrilla and Green shooting too! About how you all fucked up the Wiley case, and what we did. Someone would be interested to know that we destroyed evidence, lied about nearly everything!" Lawrence was breathing faster. He wobbled a little on his feet, a bit lightheaded, but anger and desperation kept him on task,

"I thought I was pissed off at you then when the Wiley case went down, you shit. You screwed her didn't you? You screwed that Wiley bitch, just because you could. You did it because that is what manly detectives would have done and you're still trying to show everyone that you are all man. You're a real piece of work, Will, you know that?" Lawrence's face was beet red, his voice strident and he spoke through anxious and difficult breaths, "I may take a fall too, but you were the one who told me what to do and what to say. You, and fucking James, and that fucking little midget Vincent! What do you say to that, Will?"

Lawrence had thrown the Hail Mary, there was no going back now.

Will steepled his fingers as he sat up and rested his chin on his fingertips. His voice was soft and steady. "What are you planning to do, Lawrence? Call the feds? Call the prosecutor's office? Lawrence, we've already closed the Wiley case on all fronts, including the FBI. Any support you could possibly gain from doing something as asinine as that would be from MQ or Green, and they've become irrelevant. No one else gives a shit. If that was a serious threat, I suggest you alter your tactics." Will's eyes narrowed and his voice deepened to a scratchy growl, "Don't even mention the Scalinis. You have no idea where that could lead."

Will leaned back in his chair and exhaled deeply. "Why don't you calm down now? Take a seat, take a breath for Chrissake." Will pointed at the chair in front of his desk, "You look like an overripe tomato. Did you take your blood pressure pill today? I sure hope so. Anyway Larry, we can work this out. We always do, don't we?" He said with a taut, closed mouth smile.

Lawrence sat down and took a deep breath. His anger ratcheted down as he reached for that elusive glimmer of hope.

Will apologized, "You know how I get if I drink too much, Larry. I had too many cocktails and I was just not thinking. I'm sorry, I really am. It was a mistake. I didn't mean anything. I didn't mean to hurt you. I'm sorry."

"Fuck you, Will. Fuck you!" Lawrence said with little energy or intention. He'd run out of gas.

Will told Lawrence to go home, take a shower, get some sleep and that they would talk tonight.

Lawrence left the office, ambled down the stairs and drove home. He hoped desperately that Will was being honest.

After having fumbled with the information about the cold case and the profiling unit, Will knew he should bring Lawrence's actions to the attention of his father right away. A threat to the Scalinis was nothing to be taken lightly. He knew the most appropriate and less complicated route would be to call dad and let him handle it. However, his gravitas would not allow it. He and his boys could handle this, one way or the other.

Will called a meeting with James and Vinny at Ruth Chris's. He was purposely sketchy about the reason for the meeting, but assured them that it was important, and that he was buying. They met a little after the lunch crowd thinned.

Will had taken off his uniform shirt replacing it with a powder blue, Polo, golf shirt. He arrived first, got a table in the back and ordered a Chardonnay.

Vinny showed up shortly after him. He was dressed in a black suit, with a bright, white, pinpoint collared dress shirt, a solid red tie, and turquoise cufflinks. A heavy gold chain dangled from his right wrist.

"You look nice Vinny, who died?" Will asked.

"Nobody I know of, yet, you prick. Just another day at the Bullpen. We have some, special folks coming through later. I'm just making a good impression as host."

A few minutes later, James sauntered in. He was in desert camo pants, an orange American Eagle T-shirt and black, high-top, Converse, felony flyers.

Will's eyes roved up and down James's garb. "I guess you're not making the meeting at the Bullpen." He took a sip of his wine.

"No, not tonight," James said. "Tonight is Scalini, immediate family business." He looked over at Vinny and said, "And we all know, I'm not blood."

"You can fuck off too, Jimmy boy," Vinny said, and then turned his attention to Will. "So, what's the big deal we got to talk about today, Will?"

They ordered drinks. Will was direct and frank. He told his long time associates about his fait accompli with Dan Wolfe which resulted in Lawrence's detonation. Both men were well aware that Will and Lawrence were lovers and the fact that Will strayed was not all that surprising. He had before. However, Lawrence's response this time was surprising and dangerous.

As he spoke, James and Vinny exchanged "Holy fuck!" glances.

"Hell hath no fury like a scorned man," James said trying to ease the tension radiating from Vinny like heat from summer asphalt. "He's your guy, Will. Do you think he's bullshitting? Is this just spurned lover talk or should we take this seriously?"

Vinny interrupted, "Yea, deadly fucking serious, you fuck. My old man and Uncle Tony, Chatham, they definitely don't need this headache after what we just went through with the fucking FBI." Vinny glanced over at James, and then back to Will, "It looks really bad on you, Will, like you can't control your fucking house again and again."

"Hey, no argument from me. I agree. It is fucked up. But Lawrence jumped in the deep end of the pool by himself. It's up to him to make it to the side. I don't know what the hell is with him. He knows better than to threaten me, threaten us. He's just lashing out because he's hurt. I really don't think he would ever bring heat on us. He would lose a lot too."

"You got that right man," James said. "Lawrence has everything to lose by threatening you. You're his meal ticket. He's got nothing without you, the house, the boat, fuckin' nothing, but, if he's mad as hell, and desperate, that makes him very dangerous."

The waiter came to the table, Vinny waved him off.

An awkward silence followed. Will took a gulp of his wine. James sipped at his Jim Beam. Vinny took a pull from his Heineken. No one spoke for a couple of minutes. The waiter returned and hovered like a hummingbird.

Vinny had enough of the waiter, waved him away, "Hey, man, get the fuck outta here, will ya. We're trying to talk, a little privacy for Chrissake. I'll call you over when we're ready to order."

The waiter shoved his order pad in his apron and scuttled away.

Will spoke first. "I'll do damage control. Let me talk to him tonight. I'm sure I can soothe his hurt feelings. We'll work something out. I'll let you both know tomorrow whether we still have a problem on our hands."

Vinny drained his beer with one long swallow. It clacked loudly as he set it on the table. "Fucking right, you'll handle it. I expect you to handle it." Vinny stood, brushed the wrinkles from his coat. "Or I will." He turned and walked out without another word.

James waited for the door to close behind Vinny before he spoke. "You know he means it Will. You better get control of this. Otherwise, he will. You know he will."

"Yes, I am quite aware of what Vinny could do," Will said. He waved for the waiter. "You hungry James? I am famished."

# Chapter Sixty One

After the lunch, Will returned to the PD and finished up some paperwork. He arrived home to find Lawrence in their great room, watching a DVD of Bill Dance Bass Fishing. A half eaten 16" Meat Lovers pizza was on the coffee table, next to 7 empty Busch bottles.

"Ah, a gourmet delight, beer, pizza and bass fishing I see," Will said as he walked through the den to their bedroom. He called out to Lawrence. "Man, what more is there to life, huh Larry?"

Will changed out of his uniform pants into a pair of jeans and the blue Polo. He was shoeless and returned to the great room and sat down next to Lawrence, grabbing a slice of Pizza.

"Are you thinking normally now Larry?" Will asked.

Lawrence had the remote for the big screen TV in his right hand. With a smooth and wide arc that would have made Venus Williams proud, he slapped the remote onto the crown of Will's head. The thwacking noise was louder than the yelp Will made, as the remote disintegrated into several unusable pieces of plastic. Will was dazed. A quick stream of warm blood rolled down his forehead, stinging his wide-open, star seeing, disbelieving eyes.

"Dammit. Larry, you shithead! What the hell do you think you're doing?" Will grabbed pizza napkins to stop the bleeding.

"Payback you fucker, that's what. Payback for screwing around, for making me work my ass off in the bureau. For putting me in the position of having nothing of my own and having everything in your name. How do you like being hurt, bitch?" Lawrence said as he stood up, and calmly twisted off the cap of a beer bottle and threw it in Will's lap. He ejected the Bill Dance DVD and returned it to its case.

Will went to the bathroom to inspect the damage. The collar on his shirt was stained with blood. He took it off and threw it in the bathtub. He washed his scalp with Dial soap and held pressure with a washrag on the expanding goose egg to stop the bleeding. He went into the kitchen and wrapped a few ice cubes in a paper towel. .

Will backed into the sink as Lawrence came into the kitchen, unsure if Larry was going to hit him with a beer bottle.

Lawrence stood on the opposite side of the butcher-block island. This time, he spoke in a soft and controlled tone. "You may have some bad-ass friends, and your family is tied in with Vinny's family, but you're still Will Newsham. You ain't no tough guy. You ain't no James or Vinny. You're a white bread, rich boy hanging on the other side of the tracks for the thrill of it. You've never had to do without anything, never had things go south on you. And you've always been that person, and Will, that was fine with me. We got along great, didn't we? But I just can't live like this anymore. I need to get my life together, too."

He walked to the doorway of the kitchen and turned to face Will. His anger returned and he balked with the beer bottle. Will flinched, dropped the ice cubes and cowered next to the refrigerator.

"You put me in a bad position with the Wiley case. You put me in a trickbag with all the fucking illegal stuff we did. But, I guess it took your whoring around the past few days to make me realize that it ain't me that's the bad one. And it's payback time. No matter what happens, you're gonna get yours. Fuck you, Will."

Will heard Larry's truck start up and the engine noise drifted down the street. He picked up the phone and called Vinny, but it went to voicemail.

James was munching on tortilla chips at a Chevy's when his cell rang.

"Hey, it's Will. Larry is off the reservation man. We're gonna have to do something definitive." He told James what had happened.

"Oh man, that is fucked up. I hate to hear that," James paused. He plucked his chin with his thumb and forefinger and looked up at the ceiling. "Where is he now? You don't think he's on the way to the prosecutor's office or FBI or something do you?"

"I don't think he's en route to anyplace but a bar. He was already drunk when I got home. God damn him, I think I need stitches. What an asshole! If I know Larry, he is on the way to the Bluffs Bowling Alley. He'll sit there and chain smoke and drink beer until he's totally goggle- eyed, bitching and moaning about how fucked up his life is. Damn him anyway. How the hell did this get so out of control? You think I should go out and find him, reel him in?"

The line was quiet. Will lightly touched the mushy spot on the crown of his scalp, praying for an answer in the negative. He didn't want to have to deal with Lawrence.

James complied. "No. I think it best if you stay put. I'll take care of it tonight. I'll call you later."

James hung up before Will could say anything else. He dialed, got Vinny's voicemail. Rather than leave a message, he called the Bullpen and had one of the girls take the phone to wherever Vinny was. Vinny listened and grunted, "Fuck those two fanooks," several times. He went to his office and conferenced a call with his dad and Uncle Tony. He received instructions.

Vinny apologized to his guests, two Scalini cousins from San Francisco who had brought in a couple of executives from an internet search company. Vinny left the four men on plush leather couches in the capable hands of the girls. The internet execs would have a good time, all documented digitally for the Scalinis to use at some opportune moment.

# Chapter Sixty Two

James drove by the bowling alley. Will was right on, Lawrence's truck was there. He met Vinny in the parking lot of a McDonalds about two miles away.

James got into the passenger seat of Vinny's red Mini Cooper. "Dammit Vinny. I wish you drove a big fucking car like all the other gangsters. Didn't you ever see *Goodfellas* or *Analyze This*? You need a big black Lincoln man. Getting in this can of tuna is a pain in the ass, literally, Vinny."

"Yea, well maybe that's exactly why I don't drive a friggin' boat. It's what everybody expects a guy like me to drive. This one is like what you'd figure a stockbroker to drive, and it's hell on corners. Pretty smart, sneaky, huh? Like undercover cops driving pieces of shit like that old Toyota Corolla you drove."

"I suppose that it makes sense for narcs, but what would be the harm in driving a BMW or a Saab? This matchbox is straight from a B European movie," James said. The stiff black and red leather of the passenger seat made a crisp, crinkling sound as James attempted to stretch out his stiff right leg.

"Enough about the car already. I got a plan," Vinny said. "Here's what we do. I brought some roofies from the club." Vinny reached into the pocket of his jacket and pulled out four blue caplets. "I figure one of us goes in the bowling alley, buys a round, spikes his drink, next thing you know Larry is out. We put him in his car, put it in drive and send him off the side of the road. Kaboom," Vinny said, speaking with his hands as if directing one of their porn movies.

"Yea, well, uh, that's one way, but I don't know, Vinny. The chances of witnesses seeing us with Larry could be a problem I'd like to avoid. I was thinking of something else. Will says Lawrence is probably already drunk and still drinking at the bowling alley. He'll be buzzed when he leaves. Let's intercept him as he goes home."

Vinny's face drooped as he realized his plan had evaporated. He nodded and put the roofies back in his pocket.

"These roads are pretty quiet at this hour," James continued. "There won't be much traffic, no witnesses. We box him in with our cars. You slow down ahead of him while I pull in behind. We'll lead him to the shoulder on Bluff road."

"I like this, James. Smart, real smart," Vinny said.

"Lawrence has got to be worried after what he said to Will, so we can't play this cheap, Vinny. So be ready. But he'll probably be shitfaced, and that works to our tactical advantage. We have to do the takedown quickly."

"Like a SWAT team. Like lightning," Vinny's eyes sharpened with excitement as he tucked a stainless .45 pistol in his waistband.

"Right, Vinny, SWAT," James shook his head and rolled his eyes. "Anyway, so he stops. He'll get out of his truck and do his usual "Fuck You" bullshit to whoever he thinks is fucking with him. This is where you come in. You get out of your car. He'll see it's you, but you say shit like, 'Lawrence, we got to talk. We got to work this out.' Something non threatening, Vinny. Look friendly, if that's possible."

"Hey, hey backoff, jackoff. I'm a God damned actor in case you forgot. I can be Florence Nightingale nice, you prick."

"Great, Vinny, just keep him busy, his eyes on you. As you're talking to him, I'll come up from behind and taser him in the ass. When he is out, we do what you just said. We put him back in his truck, take him to a curve, put his fat fucking foot on the accelerator pedal, and he busts through the guard rail. He goes off the edge. It's a good eighty foot drop up there. Then you get your kaboom. He'll be dead before he wakes up."

"Why so much work, James. Why don't we just run his drunk ass off the road? We can use your bigger car to do that," Vinny said, "Yea, your big friggin car, and I'll fix any dents you get at my guy's place."

"Thanks so much for your offer of body work, Vin. Forcing him off the road would be a lot simpler, but it comes with forensic problems. That scenario would probably lead to a vehicular homicide investigation. They would look for paint transfer from the car, my car, to his truck. They could identify the make and year of the car by the paint. They would find witnesses at the bowling alley. They would interview anybody Larry spoke with in the hours or even days before his death. The cops would go through his old cases, looking for anyone holding a grudge against him. When a cop is killed, it gets serious," James explained. Vinny nodded.

"Vinny, listen, the real beauty of my plan is that it'll look like he passed out at the wheel after he left the bowling alley. Shit, he'll probably have a blood alcohol of at least a .20 anyway. They'll do an autopsy and find nothing except injuries from the crash. If the taser leaves any red marks, they'll never see them with whatever injuries he sustains in the crash. Either way, no questions, just an accident. And if for some reason, there are a lot of cars going by, when we are on the road, we just follow him home and take him when he gets to Will's. Then we'll drive him back up here for the kaboom. Either way it'll work."

"Jimmy, you are one devious mother fucker. Good thing you're on our side," Vinny said, grinning with a pumpkin head smile.

"Yea, well years of tactical police planning, paid for by your tax dollars."

James peeled himself out of the tin can and winced as he put weight on his right leg. He limped over to his car. He looked back at Vinny. "Fuck you and your hot wheels piece of shit!"

Vinny flipped him off. The two men drove to the bowling alley and waited in the back of the lot.

Lawrence left the bowling alley a few minutes after midnight. He threw his bowling bag into the bed of the truck. The heavy bag caused a loud metallic rattle of whatever years of rust and inattention to maintenance had loosened. Lawrence bobbed and weaved like a boxer as he found his key, and worked to open his driver's door.

Vinny and James watched from their respective cars as Lawrence opened the driver's door. He stopped momentarily and lit a cigarette while leaning on the door frame. He smoked about half of it.

"The fat fuck is probably thinking about what the fuck he's gonna do now that he's blown his sugar daddy deal. No pun intended," Vinny said to James on his cell phone.

Lawrence flicked his cigarette into the lot and got in the truck. The tired motor reluctantly cranked a few times before several puffs of grey smoke blanketed the ground beneath the rear bumper. As soon as Lawrence started the truck, Vinny left the lot to be in place ahead of him.

Lawrence sped out of the lot and threw a little gravel in the process.

James kept his window open as he followed the truck keeping a comfortable distance. The air was damp and cool in the bluffs. A thin bank of fog slithered across the valley towards the burbs. James glanced up. It was overcast, neither the moon nor a star made an appearance on the night Lawrence Johnson was to die.

Lawrence's truck coughed a few times and belched a couple more puffs of grey smoke as it climbed Bluff Road. Lawrence crossed the center line several times and weaved onto the shoulder twice.

"Maybe the fuck will go over the edge by himself," Vinny said to James.

The sharp curve James wanted to use to end this problem was coming up. He told Vinny that it was time to slow down and stop Lawrence.

Vinny slowed his car until it was directly in front of Lawrence's truck. He slowed down to about 20mph, then 15, then 10 and turned on his emergency flashers. Lawrence honked and slowed, skidding a few feet to avoid rear-ending the crazy fucker in his way. James turned his headlights off to avoid notice. As planned, all three cars pulled onto the shoulder.

Vinny slid out of the Mini before Lawrence was able to pour his bulk from the truck. The porn director began improvising like a seasoned member of the Screen Actors Guild.

"Holy shit! I thought that was your piece of shit truck, Lawrence. You damn near ran into me back at the bowling alley, you drunk fucking jackoff," Vinny yelled as Lawrence's feet unsteadily touched ground.

"Vinny?" Lawrence asked quizzically, squinting to bring Vinny into focus.

"Yea, it's me, you dumb bastard. You damn near hit me back there," Vinny said quickly closing the distance between them. He was animated, talking loudly with his hands, tapping his chest Tarzan-like, pointing at Lawrence, bobbing his head up and down to make sure Lawrence's attention stayed on him instead of James.

James softly approached from behind and jammed the probes of the taser into Lawrence's butt. He pulled the trigger, sending 50,000 volts into Lawrence's gluteals. Lawrence felt the sting and immediately slumped to the ground as his large muscle groups seized and he lost motor control. His eyes rolled back. Vinny and James grabbed him.

Manhandling Lawrence's limp mass back into the truck was like herding cats. They were finally able to fold and bend him into the middle of the truck cab. James squeezed into the driver's seat. He drove the short distance to the hairpin curve ahead. Vinny followed in the tin can.

James stopped the truck on the right shoulder. Lawrence moaned and his head raised up. His eyes began to open. James tased him in the ass again and Lawrence slumped over.

"Gimme some fucking help here Vinny!" James hollered from the open driver's door.

Vinny got in the passenger side of Lawrence's truck. They propped their victim up in the driver's seat. "I don't want him to fall out of the damn truck that's for sure," James said, as he snugged the seat belt over Lawrence's thick belly.

James put the transmission in neutral. "Vinny, turn the steering wheel as far to the left as you can." Vinny turned the steering wheel towards the bluff and wrapped Lawrence's flaccid arms over the wheel and onto the dash. He got out of the truck and came around to the driver's side.

James placed Lawrence's right foot on the accelerator pedal. He put Lawrence's left foot on top of his right foot and jammed the left knee under the steering column to hold the pedal down. The motor revved, the tach showed 3800rpms. Smoke poured out of the exhaust as the engine raced.

The two men leaned into the truck holding their prey in position. The exhaust was choking. Vinny coughed and spit on the road.

James closed the driver's door and yelled, "Vinny, I'm gonna put it in drive. You move out of the way now. I'm gonna make sure he goes towards the bluff."

Vinny stepped back, continuing to cough. "Fucking bullshit!"

James put the truck into drive and held onto the wheel, skipping alongside. The truck jerked forward picking up speed. With his bad leg, he was unable to keep up. He held himself on the door frame, his feet dragging while they headed towards the sharp curve. As they crossed the center line, James let go of the doorpost. He felt a sharp pain as he landed on the pavement.

James lay on the shoulder of the road trying to catch his breath.

Vinny watched as the truck broke through the guardrail and took a header.

Vinny caught up to him and offered a hand up. "Man that was fucking beautiful."

James winced as he stood. He bent over at the waist trying to catch his breath.

"Son of a bitch Vinny! I cracked some ribs. Shit! How many bones do I have to break because of that bitch!"

"Yea, well you were the one who fucked her. This bullshit is on you."

"Fuck you. How the fuck was I supposed to know she was your cousin."

"You shoulda," Vinny started to say but James interrupted him.

"Fuck it man. It's old news and over now."

The two men walked to the edge of the road and looked down at the smoking truck, upside down in a dry ravine 80 feet below.

Will's phone rang at 5:20am. It was the dispatcher advising that Det. Johnson's truck had gone off the Bluff Road and that he had died at the scene. His vehicle had been towed to the police impound lot and his body had been taken to the ME's office. The dispatcher said it looked like he had been drinking.

As if he was a card carrying member of the Screen Actors Guild too, Will answered with shock and disbelief.

In the days that followed, a traffic accident investigation was undertaken by the State Highway Patrol. A traffic reconstruction expert was called in. The standard accident crime scene photography and measurements were taken. A study in physics would be conducted to determine speed, direction of travel and braking effect. Lawrence's vehicle was thoroughly examined for defect or contributing factors. Witnesses at the bowling alley and the bartender were interviewed.

The accident investigation revealed that Lawrence broke through the guard rail at 22 MPH. Lack of braking and subsequent skid marks or brake pad wear indicated that Lawrence may have passed out prior to leaving the road. His BAC was .23, almost three times the legal limit for intoxication. The bowling alley patrons indicated that Lawrence had been bowling and drinking long neck bottles of beer steadily for a couple of hours. The bartender could not estimate how many he had, and said that he had no idea Lawrence had driven to the place.

He also said that Lawrence had a few shots of Jaegermeister with Mick Wachter, another bowler, about a half an hour before Lawrence left the bar. Mick confirmed that Lawrence was shitfaced.

The State Patrol investigation concluded that Lawrence Johnson drove his truck off the bluff as a result of his intoxicated state. The State Highway Department replaced the damaged guard rail.

Pathologist Ajay Rajeda conducted a post mortem examination. It revealed severe coronary artery disease, a fatty liver and an enlarged heart. Given his physical condition and medical history at the time of death, the cause of death was listed as natural and the manner of death as accidental. The body was released to the funeral home.

Someone put a wooden cross along the road next to the shiny new guard rail. "Lawrence Johnson" was stenciled on the horizontal arm. A bouquet of artificial flowers lay next to the stick.

# Chapter Sixty Three

When Lawrence was killed, I was off work from the PD for three days. I'd gotten up early to get my run in before clinic duty. Early December, it was cold, my breath fogged, and my shoulder and legs ached during the first 15 minutes or so of the run. As I approached the steep hill passing under the highway at about the 3 mile mark, I finally warmed up and cruised into a comfortable pace. This route had become my favorite irregardless of temperature or weather as it included long hills that dipped deep and crested tall. Despite the cold, I felt the sweat trickling down my back under the Gore-Tex suit.

I showered, dressed, and drove to the clinic listening to a CD of the Beatles' Rubber Soul. I hadn't turned on the radio to learn of Lawrence's untimely demise, and no one from the department had bothered to notify me. As I weaved through traffic, my mind wandered to my upcoming trip to California.

LA, LAX, traffic. Headache. My sister Carol, a 3-time relationship loser, was getting divorced, again. Dysfunctional lives, the legacy from Elaine and Jack Green that their offspring shared. Carol had asked if I would come out and help her move, again. The Beatles had just broken into Norwegian Wood when my cell phone buzzed.

"Hey Doc. I thought I'd call you in case you heard it on the news," MQ said.

"Heard what?"

MQ filled in the details concerning the tragic course of events leading to Lawrence Johnson's death.

"I tell you, Morris," MQ paused.

"Yea, I kind of feel bad for the poor guy, too, Kenneth," I offered.

"Hell no. Fuck him," MQ said. "Lawrence bore little resemblance to a professional law enforcement officer. He was a lazy, lying, fat fuck. A lackluster example of what promise the human race offers. The world is a better place now that his drunk ass tumbled off the highway."

"Try not to hide your feelings, Kenneth. It can cause stress."

"Not to mention the barrier he was to justice in the Wiley case. He could have helped. He chose not to, and look where we are today. Perhaps this was a constellation of karmic payback for the shithead."

"True enough, he was of no help at all, but he was a lost soul, MQ," I said, thinking this may be a good time to tell MQ about my encounter with the skinny medium. Speaking of karma and souls could be a good segue.

"How about, I feel bad for his boys. How about that for a little compassion?" MQ asked.

"Yea. I do too. The way I hear it, I doubt if his ex-wife cares whether he's dead," I said. "But his boys, they're grown now, grown men I imagine. Listen, MQ, I want to," I started to tell MQ about Myra Sutherland when he interrupted.

"I don't think he saw his boys that often, doc. At least he didn't talk about them. Of course he hated me. So he wouldn't talk to me anyway, about anything."

"I remember his boys, Larry Jr. and um," I paused, unable to recall the younger boy's name. "I remember years ago, Lawrence and his wife brought Larry Jr. into the clinic once to see me for something, flu or bronchitis something like that, but that was way back when his kids were little. That was a long time ago. Sheila and I were still in that glow of lust and love, and I was pretty new to practicing medicine at the time."

"The younger one was Carl," MQ said. "Those boys are out of high school now I imagine. Maybe, just maybe, if they have a larger intellectual capacity than their faygala old man, they're in college."

"His wife was Charlene, right?" I asked. "A thin, tall redhead if I recall correctly. I remember her saying something that I wasn't supposed to hear. The same thing everyone said back then. 'If he's a good doctor, why is he still a policeman?' You know, the usual, 'What the fuck is wrong with Green?' The bullshit that everyone said back then.'"

"Yes my friend," MQ agreed. "A valid concern posited by many of us who wondered what the hell was wrong with Dr. Morris Green that he stayed at the Oakview circus once a graduate from medical school."

"In any event MQ, they were both worried about their boy. At least that was something redeeming about Lawrence, huh?"

"Yea, a real Ward Cleaver, that Lawrence," MQ said.

I heard MQ's chair groan and his boots hit the top of his desk. He was leaning back, probably feeling victorious that he had at least outlived Lawrence.

MQ said the highway patrol was doing the investigation and the allegations were that Lawrence was drunk as a skunk. He said he would keep me up to speed on the progress of the investigation and the arrangements.

MQ's parting words were, "And it's too damn bad his boyfriend wasn't in the front seat with him as he took the plunge!"

I decided against opening a discussion concerning supernatural spirits over the phone.

"Give me a call when you know the arrangements," I said.

# Chapter Sixty Four

MQ called the following day. "The Chief put out a memo about the arrangements. I have it right here. There's a wake at McCauley's Funeral Home today from 3pm to 9pm, and tomorrow from 11am to 2pm, followed by a procession to Holy Trinity. Officers attending are expected to wear their dress blues except I didn't get a new dress uniform in which to display my rotundness with such sartorial splendor, so I will be in my usual work attire."

"Yea, I don't even know where my dress blues are. Probably in a box in Sheila's basement somewhere. I guess I'll be in uniform too. They're putting him in the ground pretty damn quick aren't they?"

"Yea. I thought only members of the tribe were boxed and buried so quickly. I'm pretty confident that Lawrence was never a Bar Mitzvah boy," MQ said.

"Probably no sense in delaying the inevitable I suppose. Will's probably paying for the funeral expenses. Maybe he's grieving and wants it over and done with."

"Doc, my conspiratorial mind still has to wonder. It sure looks like the drunk fucker just ran out of luck., but given the circle of evil in this crowd, who knows for sure?"

So saith Sol.

"Yea. Who knows," I agreed.

"In any event, we're doing the usual police funeral routine," MQ said. "I have been ordered to drive a car in the parade. I don't suppose you'd want to go along with me for company?"

"Sure. I'll go by the wake tonight after I get off work and meet you at the station tomorrow morning. Surely we'll go for a drink after the procession."

"Just because he was a liar and scoundrel, doesn't mean we can't drink to his memory," MQ said.

I left the clinic a little after 3pm and headed over to McCauley's.

I waded through the crowd beginning with the smokers standing outside. I shook hands and exchanged stories with cops and friends. A few flasks of whiskey were passed around. Funerals were always a great place to catch up with guys on other squads or from other departments. The usual banter was circulating. Somebody was demoted, someone quit to take a high paying job with a private contractor in Iraq or Afghanistan. Someone was screwing one of the dispatchers. Someone's wife was fucking someone who was not a cop as she searched for a normal mate.

A color guard of two young officers from Oakview PD stood on each side of the casket. I took my place in the line leading to the casket to give my respects.

Lawrence was in full dress uniform in an ornate, mahogany casket. His fingers were interlaced, holding a cross. He must have suffered a significant head and facial injury as the make-up job was extensive. As I filtered by, I said a brief prayer for his indolent soul and moved on to express my condolences to the widow Johnson and Lawrence's boys.

As I made it through the line, I saw Lawrence's ex-wife, about twenty people away. The only time Lawrence said anything about Charlene was when he was complaining about money problems and the financial ruin she had caused. He rarely spoke about his boys. He'd apparently had limited contact with them over the years. The divorce was messy with an undertow of Lawrence's sexual preferences as the causative factor, but it was never openly discussed.

Charlene was still tall and skinny. The red hair I had remembered, was dyed coal black and pulled back in a ponytail. The years, and perhaps a difficult life raising two boys by herself had worn her down. Her face reminded me of an old Indian squaw.

Charlene had slipped her small frame under a black, one piece, knit dress that was cut just above her bony knees. A silver necklace with a large, oval shaped jade pendant hung loosely from her neck. It was just above where cleavage would have been, had Charlene had more than four percent body fat. With the heels, she was probably close to 6' but could not have weighed more than 120lbs. She was mechanistic and sticklike in her movements. She had that same exhausted appearance as Myra Sutherland.

Larry Jr. was easily 6'2" and heavy, but not fat. He had short, cropped, light red hair and a ruddy complexion. He wore a black suit, Clarino shoes, and stood erect, shaking hands firmly and brusquely with folks as they passed by. His face exhibited little expression as he greeted the line of condolence wishers.

Carl was a bit shorter, leaner, and had tousled brown hair that hung over his ears and shirt collar. He had a fair complexion, with youthful flushed cheeks and deep dimples. Carl was animated and smiled broadly as he met former friends, relatives and associates of his father. He was dressed casually for a funeral in khaki Dockers, a white dress shirt and boat shoes.

I shook Charlene's hand, and made eye contact. Despite her beef jerky appearance, her green eyes were surprisingly clear and sparkly. There were no tears, no puffiness, no evidence of grief. Neither hand held a Kleenex.

"We only met once. I'm Morris Green, I work at Oakview. I'm sorry for your loss," I said shaking her hand, covering it with my other hand like a preacher. Her hand was dry and scratchy like tumbleweed.

"I remember you. You're Dr. Green. You saw Larry Jr. when he was just a youngster, a little boy, a long time ago. Late night, like 11 at night. He had a terrible, just awful, chest cough. You met Lawrence and me at that clinic. That was right nice of you," she said as she pulled her hand back.

"Yes, I do recall the visit. I guess that big guy there is Larry Jr.?" I said pointing over to the meat next to her in line.

"Yes, that's him. He's my big boy. He's a strong one, not like his dad, who was…" Charlene stopped, took a breath and continued, "Well, he was what he was and, well, thank you for coming." Charlene turned to the next visitor behind me. Apparently, my time with her was up.

I shook hands with Larry Jr. and Carl. We talked briefly about the late night office visit to the clinic, and some police chit-chat about their dad.

"Dr. Green, sir, I, uh, I have to talk to you in private about something," Larry Jr. said. "Can we go outside for a minute?" Larry Jr. got out of line and headed towards the door.

"Mom, I'm going out for some air for a few minutes. Be right back," he said over his shoulder, getting out of her line of sight before she could answer.

We walked in silence through the crowd. Once outside the building, Larry Jr. asked me to follow him to his car. Larry drove a dark green, late model, Ford F-250 4x4, diesel. He popped the locks open with his key fob and motioned for me to get in. I stepped up on the runner and hopped up on the passenger seat.

"Nice truck, Larry. What have you been up to?"

"Well, sir, I did four years in the army. I went in right after high school. Figured I'd be one less responsibility for mom. I did two tours in Iraq and about a year in Alaska, of all places. I was hot and sweaty in one place and froze my bejingles off in the other. Iraq was pretty bad for a lot of the guys, but I didn't think it was that bad. Then again, I didn't get hurt either."

"What did you do in the service?"

"I was trained in fleet maintenance, so I was working on trucks, Hummers, generators and the like. I didn't go out on a lot of patrols. I had it pretty good but didn't want a career in the military. So, when I got out, I got hired by American Cargo Lines as a logistical coordinator. I do mechanical maintenance for the local ACL shop. It's a good job and we get a deal with Ford for vehicle purchases. I got like 20% off on this truck."

"Good for you, Larry. Thank you for your service. I'm sure your father was proud."

"Yea, I guess so."

"You weren't interested in police work?"

"I thought about it, Dr. Green, but my dad was a miserable person for as long as I can remember. I don't know if it was the job, or because he and my mom were always at it, but, I figured I would keep away from all of it, including being a cop."

"I understand. Neither of my kids show any real interest in police work or medicine, which I think is just fine. Anyway, Larry, I wish you well. You sound like you have your act together."

"Thank you, sir," Larry said as he reached in front of me and pulled out a tan business envelope from his glove box.

"Sir, this will seem pretty strange to you. Dad gave me this a few days before he crashed. He told me to keep it hidden and secret. He said that if something happened to him before he retired from the police department, or if he died under some kind of unusual circumstances, that I should get hold of you and give this to you. He said if I couldn't get hold of you, as a last resort, I should give it to Sgt. Murphy-Quinn. He didn't care much for Sgt. Quinn, so he said it was best if I find you."

I thought back to that day in MQ's office when we had interviewed Lawrence about the Wiley case. When he had lied and told us to fuck off. MQ huffed, puffed and glowered over him. He told him he would celebrate the day Lawrence was fired and indicted over the case. MQ had painted a visual image for Lawrence to recall. Apparently, he had remembered.

"My dad made me promise to never open it and never tell anyone about it. He wouldn't give me a clue what was in it and said I was the only person in his life he could trust. And that I had to give it to you if something happened. He said you were a good detective and didn't know why you stayed at Oakview, especially after you got shot."

Larry turned the envelope over and over several times while he spoke before handing it to me. It was a standard, tan, business 8"x11" envelope. The envelope had been securely taped shut with yellow police evidence tape. Handwritten on the front of the envelope was:

> To: Dr. Morris Green-For Your Eyes Only
> In the event of my death
> From: Det. Lawrence Johnson

I held the envelope gently, read and re-read the inscription. I could feel something inside. It felt thick, like folded over sheets of papers. I also felt something flat and hard, like a coin. I turned the envelope over, held it up to the window as if the sun could penetrate through.

I asked myself, "What kind of dilemma was going on in Lawrence Johnson's life, that he felt the need to write a letter to me? I could not be characterized as an ally. He knew that I was solidly in MQ's corner and would have been more than happy to see him fired and indicted. If he was going to reach out to me, why didn't he just call me. What secrets are in this envelope?"

"Sir, sir?" Larry Jr. asked rather loudly, bringing me back from that part of my brain that was searching for answers. "Are you going to open it?"

"Yes, um, yes I will. But not, not just right now, Larry. This could be something very personal about work, or something of evidentiary value from an investigation. I don't know, but I think it best if I open it someplace other than here," I tucked the envelope inside my sport coat.

"Larry, I am sure your father was very proud of you, proud of your service in the military, and that you turned out to be such a fine young man. He would have appreciated that you kept your promise by delivering the letter without looking inside."

"Well sir, curiosity killed the cat. I knew there had to be something special in there and he made it crystal clear that you get it. I'm glad I'm done with it," Larry said as he opened his door and stepped out onto the lot.

I came around the truck. "Larry, let me have your phone number. Once I've had a look, if it is something that involves your family or something personal that you or your mom need to know, I'll call you. OK?"

"Yes sir, I would appreciate that. Thank you."

Larry handed me one of his business cards and wrote his cell phone number on the back. I handed him one of my clinic cards.

"Larry, I think it best if we keep this our secret, at least until I know what is in there. If anyone asks, your dad didn't leave any letters or notes about anything. Can you do that?"

"That's fine with me sir. Just let me know what you need me to do."

We shook hands. Larry went back inside to finish his part in the wake. I got in my car and took the envelope out from my pocket. I fondled it again. I wanted to rip it open and spill out the mystery.

A confession, truth, lies, facts, rationalizations, anguish, hate, guilt, evidence, a smoking gun, it could have been any of those.

I laid it on the passenger seat and closed my eyes. Muddled, high pitched whispers swirled around my head like a swarm of bees. As usual, I couldn't make out any words.

A familiar electrical current sprinted down my neck and landed with a thump in my chest and shoulder blades like hitting a pothole at 60 miles per hour. I spent the next several minutes talking myself out of a panic attack and doing diaphragmatic breathing befitting a Sheila Green yoga session.

# Chapter Sixty Five

I drove directly from the funeral home to the clinic. At the time of our transfers out of the detective bureau, MQ and I were confident that everything related to the Wiley case would be destroyed or conveniently disappear. In the unlikely event that the tide would turn in our favor at some point in the future, we copied the entire Wiley case file. We made copies of every one of the pitifully few glossy crime scene photos. We took digital pictures of all the physical evidence, close-ups of the clothing, the shoes, the restraints, cop paraphernalia and weapons. If Newsham and Montileone destroyed everything, we could at least tell the prosecutor that the pictures were accurate depictions of the evidence. I kept the Wiley file in a locked closet in my office.

It was late afternoon and the clinic was closed. Donnell, one of Myra Sutherland's co-workers from the maintenance crew, was vacuuming the lobby using one of those backpack units. I waved and spoke, anticipating the question as he powered off the vacuum.

"Too much paperwork."

"It's always something, ain't it Doc? I already done your office and the patient rooms. I'm just finishing up in here and I be gone."

"You're right. It's always something. Thanks Donnell. Have a good evening."

Donnell nodded and went back to the carpets.

I wondered, 'Is Lawrence's death and this letter the 'something' that Myra Sutherland said would happen?'

I unlocked my room and laid the envelope on a work table, flipping on the overhead fluorescents. I put on a pair of exam gloves.

Lawrence had written his initials over the evidence tape in several places. Initialing tape was common police procedure when sealing evidence in a package to assure the seal remains intact. Pulling the tape disrupts the initials, which indicates that someone opened the evidence.

Lawrence fastidiously taped all four edges with evidence tape and had written "LJ" on every edge. No one was going to be able to open the letter without damaging the tape. At least that was the message he meant to give to Larry Jr.

I photographed the exterior of the envelope, making sure the initials and all markings were documented. I picked it up. A vibrating hum traveled from my hands to my chest and neck. I waited for the spasm and pain. It didn't come. The sensation that followed felt like I was sitting chest deep in a warm whirlpool, not at all uncomfortable. Clearly this was unlike most of the physical sensations brought on by my specters. Maybe, they were satisfied with the most recent turn of events.

I used a razor knife and slit the taped edge opposite the metal clasp. I opened the envelope optimistically apprehensive. I half-ass expected a cloud of smoke and a genie to appear. The genie would solve the murders with a wave of her magic wand, sending the dead children to wherever they were supposed to go.

No genie. Inside, there was a standard white #10 business envelope. It was addressed in much the same manner as the larger one, except the handwritten black letters were smudged. It had obviously been handled a few times. The top edge was ragged, torn open. Lawrence had not bothered to reseal it.

December 25
In the event of my death
From: Det. Lawrence Johnson, Oakview PD

The envelope was dated Christmas day, five weeks after the Wiley murders. It contained several more sheets of paper. I could make out the edges of the hard object inside the folded sheets. It felt like it could be a key of some kind.

I unfolded several sheets of blank typing paper that Lawrence apparently had used to wrap the hard object. I dumped the key, a small, circular, chrome one, like the keys used to open soda machines, certainly not a safe deposit box key, but nonetheless it had the potential for unlocking something.

I removed a three page, handwritten letter on wide-lined notebook paper, signed by Det. Lawrence Johnson.

My hands trembled. The warm, comfortable hum morphed into a steady buzz that oscillated up and down my spine like an expensive massage chair. I read Lawrence's rambling note.

"Green, if you're reading this I am dead. Dead! And I was probably murdered. I don't know for sure if Will set me up. But I bet he knew THEY were going to go after me. I'm not surprised if it was Will. He was a real selfish prick sometimes. THEY, is the fucking Scalini's. Fuck them and fuck Will too. I want you to go after them all. Kill them all if you can.

"The first time I wrote this stuff down was on Christmas day, about a month after those Wiley kids were murdered. I was in a bad way at the time with the holidays and all. I was afraid that what we done was gonna come back on us. I thought they were gonna try to kill me, but after a while nothing happened so I threw the first letter away. I don't know why I saved the old envelope. Maybe to remind me of what I wrote back then and what I should of done.

"Don't you worry Green, I saved what you need. This is a new note I just now wrote figuring there's a good chance I'm gonna end up dead this time for sure.

"Will had put me in a tough position over the years. I mean, he was nice for taking me in where I could kind of hide out from Charlene's lawyers. But, it wasn't all peaches and cream living at Wills. I am sure all of you suspected, but Will and I were more than roommates. Big shock huh? Hey it ain't like I didn't try. I tried being straight and married Charlene and look what happened. I sure wish I could go back for a do-over on a lot of things. In the beginning me and Will got along great. Instead of paying rent, we worked out a deal where anything I bought would be titled as Will's so Char couldn't get at them. I bought the two boats we had, and the trailers, and the four wheelers. That way I had some things and money. On paper, I didn't have nothing. So without Will, I was fucked. I didn't like that, but I didn't have no choice.

"When the Wiley murders happened, I didn't want to go along with what Will and his daddy said. I really didn't want to. I was at the scene. It was bad. But I had to go along. If I told MQ, or the prosecutor, Will would get fired or indicted, or worse and I would be screwed too. Either way, if I said no to them, I would be out on the street or dead. So I didn't do nothing. I just kept my mouth shut and went along. I knew what we did was wrong and so I'm owning up to it now. I'm dead anyway so it don't matter for me, but for you, I put a lot of the stuff you guys were looking for in locker 327 out at the Bluffs Bowling Alley. I've kept it in the locker all this time. You got the key now Doc.

"When all this first happened, you'd been shot and were off work. But when you guys started working the case and you and MQ busted your asses on it, I was getting worried. Will just told me to shut the fuck up about it. But after that day in MQ's office where you guys basically said you had it figured out, I was really worried.

"MQ was such a prick that day, threatening me, and saying he was going to take my badge. You were there, you heard him yelling and screaming like he does. I decided to cut him out of this, fuck him anyway. No glory for the fat leprechaun. You were usually fair to me. And you were nice enough to meet me and Char at your office that time Larry was sick. And it seemed like you cared more about the Wiley case than MQ. The little midget fucker was along for the ride, far as I could tell. So I'm dumping it all on you Doc. Sorry about that.

"I hope my boys are not taking my death too hard. I think since I wasn't really all that much in their life after Charlene and I split up, that it will be a little easier. Lawrence Jr. is one tough SOB and I am very proud of him for serving his country. He has always been the more serious one, and that's why I gave him the duty of handling this letter.

"Carl is a great kid too but not as responsible as Larry. He is so much fun to be around, maybe he'll end up a comedian or something. He always made me laugh.

"The evidence tape on this letter better not have been torn because I made Larry Jr. promise. You better not be reading this Larry or I'll come back from the grave and kick your butt.

"Tell my boys that I'm sorry I'm dead, and won't be around for them. And say I'm sorry to their mom for giving her so much grief, but she had her own problems.

"Doc, you and MQ were right about a lot of things with the Wiley case. First off, Julie Wiley had something to do with it. She sure did twirl Will around her fingers, making out like such a poor innocent victim and he was her hero. He'd pick her up at her mom's house, that's where she was staying after the murders. And they'd be gone for hours. He said he wasn't screwing her, but I wouldn't of been surprised, the lying whore that he is.

"And you know, Will never worked a murder before and didn't know what the fuck he was doing. He never was on the Major Homicide Squad like we were or nothing like that. His daddy made Montileone put him on the case. His daddy told Will to do certain things and Will even fucked that up. Daddy Chatham was pissed off I can tell you.

"Mr. Wiley didn't kill his kids. The bitch did it, or so I think. And maybe she had some help. Will would never tell me for sure, but I'm pretty sure this guy James was there when it happened. You know James, he was a city cop. And he's been working with the Scalinis for a long time, if that tells you something. We found a city PD shirt and one of James' old city badges in the Wiley's bedroom in a box of stuff. He was friends with the Wiley's. Will said they were having an affair. I don't know if it was James and her, or a threesome. With that bitch, could have been anything, maybe a foursome with Will in the mix of it too. He'd never say.

"Will said he talked to James. He said that James didn't know nothing about the murders. That's bullshit I think. But I am pretty sure if he had a hand in killing the kids, he would of ended up like Jimmy Hoffa. But Will pushed anything about James under the rug. I was thinking Mrs. Wiley killed the kids and James killed the husband and helped her with the cover up. There was never nothing written in a report about James, or that he was at the house. So James skated on ever being involved.

"Julie Wiley was a lying piece of shit. You'll know what I mean when you watch Elwyn's interview. She is nervous as a whore in church and she can't answer a one of his questions right. Elwyn should've said something when he came back from vacation. I bet Weingart told him to forget it. Weingart bullied everyone, probably Elwyn too. I don't know how you can work on his squad. Weingart knew Will was fucking up the case, but he wanted Will to fuck up the case and look bad. Weingart hated Will and me. He called us fags when no one was around. We wrote him up to Montileone and you know how far that got. Weingart is such a big headed, full of himself asshole, Nazi prick and the Chief is just a pussy bitch.

"Since no one knew about James. Weingart was sure a woman couldn't do what was done to those kids, so it had to be the husband and he convinced Elwyn to think that way too. Plus once Will stuck his big head in the case and started running the investigation, the two of them just backed off and let the case go.

"Read her statement and it is so full of shit it ain't even funny. It's nothing like what she told Elwyn on that tape. You compare the two and that was why the tape and Miranda had to disappear.

"I was supposed to get rid of all this stuff, but I kept it, figuring I may need it someday which turned out to be the other day. Which brings us to why I'm writing this new letter and why I'm dead.

"What happened was, I found out that Will had found someone else. I watched him and caught him with this guy. Will told me it didn't mean nothing, but I could tell our days were coming to an end. I blew up, and told him I was going to spill my guts about the Wiley case. Pretty stupid huh? Like a damn woman caught her husband cheating.

"I wasn't thinking straight. I didn't know who I was gonna tell for sure. But one thing is for sure, someone would've listened what with all the shit I got in the locker. Will don't know I saved this stuff. So he said no one would believe me anyway. He said the Wiley case was closed by the FBI and the Chief. He said I should think about what I'm doing because there could be some serious consequences. He said because if I did anything, I wouldn't have a place to live, no boat, no nothing. He wanted his cake and to eat it too as he always had gotten, spoiled rich kid. But this time, for some reason, I had enough of his shit. Place to live or no, I was pissed off.

"So probably what happened was Will called daddy for advice. Daddy would have called the fucking Scalinis and told them they had a problem because of me and then I got whacked. Go to the bowling alley, open up locker 327 with the key. You got enough now to put them all in prison. Go get those fuckers for me."

Lawrence Johnson

"Yeah! Yeah," I yelled out in a Howard Dean victory shriek. I wanted to spew confirmation and vindication to someone. We were right. Years of physical and emotional pain were coming to an end. My spiritual hitchhikers were soon going to punch their tickets for their final train ride to Heaven's Gate. I peeked out my door, expecting the excitement and agitation to have leaked out and drawn attention. The hallway was empty and silent. Even Donnell was gone.

I wanted to run up the stairs at the Philadelphia Museum of Art like Rocky Balboa with my arms raised in victory. Instead, I did fifty jumping jacks and three sets of 12 pushups to force the buzzing electrical energy into kinetic motion. I stood in front of the letter, sweating and panting.

Some of the nervous energy did dissolve with the exertion. My breathing and heart rate returned towards normal. I grabbed a Corona from the small fridge in the corner and slugged away half. I made copies of the letter and both sides of each envelope. I packaged Lawrence's envelopes inside a larger one and taped it shut, initializing the seal with my initials 'MG' as I had done thousands of times as a detective. I locked the originals in my safe and hooked the bowling locker key to my key ring.

I picked up the phone and called the station desk in the event MQ was working.

"Oakview Police, Sgt. Murphy-Quinn. How can I help you?

"MQ, it's doc."

"Hey, I heard you were at the funeral home. Where did you go?"

"When do you get off duty?" I asked, trying to keep my voice steady. The department's phone lines were taped and I didn't want to telegraph any news.

"6 tomorrow morning, I'm king of the Oakview graveyard shift tonight."

"How about some coffee when you get off?"

"Sure?" MQ said with a hesitation. "What is it, what's going on, doc?" Long time partners can read the nuances in vocal inflections.

"I'll meet you at that place Therese works," I said cryptically.

"Jesus, Mary and Joseph, Doc," MQ said.

I could imagine his eyes rolling and head shaking.,

"Just meet me for coffee, will ya?" I implored.

"Oh hell, why not. I'm game. 6:15. I know where," he paused. "I was going to go home and try to catch a nap before the funeral procession, but there's a certain vicissitude in your voice. Some exigency. What happened, doc?"

"I will see you there at 6:15," I said, and hung up the phone.

# Chapter Sixty Six

Our days off night shift duty didn't coincide so Margie was working. I stayed at
my apartment and slept straight through, waking at 4:30am. It was refreshing
to sleep past 3 without pesky visitors or vivid dreams. Perhaps my ghosts knew
that we were on the right course.

I was energized with a good night's sleep and went for a quick run. I turned
left out of my complex, heading north, still avoiding the cemetery. I did the
3 miles in 28 minutes, a respectable jogging pace for my old clunker of a body
with worn knees, a bad back, and a liver the size of a basketball.

The coffee I started before heading out was waiting. I stretched, did a few
minutes of breathing exercises, took a shower and dressed. I put on black jeans
and a bulky pullover knit shirt to hide my pistol. Lawrence's letter instilled a
healthy dose of paranoia in me. If 'they' did kill him, who else is on the list. I
tucked my stainless 9mm in my waist band and grabbed an extra twelve round
clip. Better to have and not need, than need and not have. I left a message on
Lenora's voice mail at the clinic that I was attending a funeral and taking a personal day off.

MQ was seated at the back of Bob's Golden Oldie's Diner, affectionately
known in the area as Bob's G-o-d. As long as we'd been going there, we never met
Bob or God. The walls were covered with thousands of album covers from the
50s and 60s. A cup of coffee was waiting for me, having just been poured by one
of our favorite waitresses.

"Hey, hey there Doc. How you been darlin'?" Therese said with her southern
Georgia drawl. "I haven't seen you in a while. What's shakin' bacon?"

"Just living the dream T. You look fantastic, new boobs?" Therese pulled me into her and hugged me. She pinched one of my ass cheeks, cocked her head to the side and winked a heavy, Tammy Faye style eye.

"You are so full of it, Morris. You know these girls are all me," she said pushing them up from under. "New bra though. An expensive one. Glad you noticed. You still eatin' grits with honey baby?"

"Yea, that sounds good. How about you Kenneth, have you ordered?" I asked as I slid across the booth seat opposite him.

"No, I haven't and I didn't get hugged either. I'm feeling a little disconsolate and isolated," he said, looking down, his lower lip protruding.

"For goodness sake, MQ, can't you just say 'I need a little lovin' too?'"

Therese leaned over and put an arm over MQ's pudgy shoulders and gave him a hug, pushing his face in between her girls, and giving a little shake which splashed over to his face, now smiling broadly.

"Now that we've made my best detectives happy, what do you want MQ, the usual?"

"Yes please, but I'd like onion rings instead of fries today, I need some vegetables in my diet. Is an onion a vegetable?"

"Nothing is a vegetable if it comes out of a deep fryer," I said as I sipped coffee that was strong and hot.

Therese tucked the order pad in her apron. She turned away and walked towards the kitchen with her pelvis swaying like the stripper she was a decade, two kids and three trailerhomes ago. As if on cue, the jukebox started playing Roy Orbison's *Pretty Woman*.

"So, Dr. Strangelove, did you get a message from the grave from Lawrence?" MQ asked with surprising clairvoyance.

"Well, actually MQ, I did hear from Det. Johnson," I handed copies of Lawrence's letter across the table.

MQ read the letter and muttered a few, 'Jesus, Mary and Joseph's. "He called me a leprechaun? My big, fat, white, Irish ass." He read on. A smirk accompanied his declaration, "Major revelation here, whoa, stop the presses, they were lovers." He finished reading as Therese brought our food.

We sat in silence for a few moments until she sauntered away.

"What do you think Sol?

"I think Officer Patrick has some explaining to do, don't you think?"

"He's definitely on the list."

"Have you gone to the bowling alley?" he asked.

"Not yet. I thought it best if we both go," I said, pouring honey on my grits.

MQ pointed his stubby finger across the table and said, "You are still the primary on this case whether we're in the bureau or not. Lawrence was right. This case held much more meaning for you than me. You pushed it through the grinder and, as a result, it is your soul that is scarred, more so than mine."

So saith Sol.

He crunched into a large onion ring, and looked down at his plate quietly munching. He finally said, "Mother of God, Morris. The Miranda warning, the interview? How serendipitous. Could it be that for the first time in this debacle, we'll get a break."

MQ left his car at Bobs and I drove. 45 minutes later, we were standing in front of locker #327.

"Whatever is behind this locker door, will surely alter the future of quite a few people," I paused.

"Yes Morris. Hopefully it will put some folks on death row. Open the damn locker already."

"Not to mention maybe it will end my haunting," I thought.

"Hold on, Doc," MQ said, pointing his digital camera at the locker exterior. "We'll document this with some pictures."

I turned the key, opened the door. We peered inside.

"Hmm, another big surprise, a bowling bag," MQ said, and took another photo of the bag inside the locker.

I pulled the bag out and peered into the locker, sticking my head inside. I shined a penlight up and around the interior to make sure nothing else was mysteriously taped to the top, or stuffed in a corner bend of sheet metal. Satisfied, I closed and re-locked the locker door.

"Let's get out of here before anyone notices us," MQ said.

I pulled out of the lot and we headed back. MQ unzipped the bag, looking inside and taking inventory.

"A DVD. Some pages of paper, a CD and a small evidence box. Surely, a propitious turn of events, doc!" MQ pulled the box out of the bag. "Ajay's gunshot residue kit."

"Some days you're the bug, some days you're the windshield. Today, maybe just maybe, we're the windshield," I said. MQ rezipped the bag shut. "Let's get somewhere to go through this. Not on damn Bluff Road."

We drove past a shiny, new piece of guardrail on the way back down Bluff Road. MQ rolled down his window, waved his middle finger at it and yelled, "Fuck you and thank you Lawrence! I hope you are enjoying your time in whatever level of hell you're burning!"

"That was civil of you, MQ. Now, where do you want to go?

"I can tell you, the last place would be Oakview. I don't want to telegraph anything about this case. If Montileone finds out we have new evidence, he'll take it from us and probably incinerate it."

"Or maybe hand it over to the Scalinis," I said. "I'd rather not give them another reason to kill us just yet. We can go to the clinic."

MQ looked out the window for a minute, before turning back to me. "You do realize that whatever we find may ultimately answer our questions, but it will most likely bring misfortune and calamity to you and me. You may consider us dinosaurs. This treasure, my good doctor, may ultimately be our ice age and subsequent extinction."

So saith Sol.

# Chapter Sixty Seven

aving called in for a personal day, my appearance at the clinic was met with a few puzzled glances by the staff.

Lenora glanced up from her keyboard, phone cradled between her shoulder and ear. I nodded at her. She watched us, Dr. Stan Laurel and Oliver Hardy, carrying a bowling bag, as we waltzed through the waiting room. Fortunately she was engaged in conversation and couldn't break away to give me the third degree.

I unlocked my room, and we pulled chairs up to the table along the back wall and sat down. I handed MQ a box of gloves. We each put on a pair.

MQ pulled out the gunshot residue test kit, CD, DVD and several sheets of paper from the bag. He unfolded the pages.

As promised, it was Julie Wiley's original, signed Miranda form. The Miranda was witnessed by Det. Elwyn Bryson and Sgt. Martin Weingart, dated November 22nd at 22:35 hours.

There were six pages of lined Oakview Police Department Witness Statement forms. Julie Wiley had written a statement. A statement that never made it to the official report.

The statement was written on November 23rd. Julie Wiley's large, feminine, cursive letters filled line after line. I held the six page statement in my hands. "Why would she write a statement if this whole thing was going to disappear anyway? Where would she have done this? At home, at her lawyers?"

MQ shook his head, "Like the Voynich manuscript, a mystery to be sure. We can be confident that the statement is nothing but deceit and fabrication."

I was going to ask him what the hell the Voynich manuscript was, but was sidetracked as I read the opening lines. I read the first paragraph out loud to MQ.

"I, Julie Wiley, being a witness or person with information in a matter currently under investigation by the Oakview Police Department do voluntarily provide the following written statement. Pertaining to the events occurring on Monday, November 22nd, this is what I remember to the best of my recollection and knowledge concerning the deaths of the children and their father. Thank you to the wonderful policemen who have helped me during my time of need. It gives me hope that there are such nice people in the world."

MQ scowled. "What a collection of rationalizing legal verbiage. Clearly from her solicitor to obfuscate and further the calumny. Hope for the future. Bullshit! Legalese under the management of the Newsham Law Firm, LLC, no doubt. She was being coached as well as Vince Lombardi did the Green Bay Packers. I have to agree with you though. Why even allow her to write a statement?"

"Remember Murph, Lawrence wrote that Will fucked up and pissed off his daddy. A written statement makes no sense whatsoever. Maybe this was one of Will's fuck ups by trying to act like a detective and a lawyer."

MQ picked up the DVD. "This is the interview, no doubt. And Lawrence sat there in my office and lied, straight to my face. He told us he put all the evidence in the temporary evidence locker." He held the DVD up, shaking it as if it were a tambourine. "And then he said that it must have just gotten lost, or that I, as the Evidence Officer, must have lost them. Driving off a cliff was a fitting end for the dullard!" MQ harrumphed.

"As it turns out, his temporary evidence locker just happened to be at the bowling alley," I said.

I turned on the DVD player and popped it in. Static and snow faded to the familiar landscape of our interview room. The rectangular room is eighteen by twelve feet. A five foot table is in the middle. There are two chairs on each side, one on each end. There are no windows, no pictures on the walls and no magazines. There is nothing to cause a distraction from the business at hand, which is getting a confession. There are stack trays containing blank Miranda forms, witness statement forms, and forms for the guilty to write their admission or confession. The interview room is equipped with two covert cameras that were running as Julie Wiley was led into the interview room by Det. Bryson. The tape is split screen showing the frontal and side views at the same time.

Mrs. Wiley was wearing a gray sweatshirt, turned inside out. Embroidered green lettering could be seen across the chest. It was a "Notre Dame" sweatshirt. She had on blue jeans. Her hair was pulled back in a pony tail.

"Please have a seat over there, Mrs. Wiley," Bryson said.

She complied. So far so good.

Sgt. Weingart followed and sat at the end of the table furthest from the door and nearly out of view.

Det. Bryson sat across from Julie. He said he was sorry that they had to talk now and gave his condolences. He said he realized that she had been through a lot and that, if she would rather, they could talk later. He said he was sure she was tired from all that happened and then having to spend a few hours in the ER. He gave her another opportunity to delay talking at that time.

In a breathy, almost sexy voice, Mrs. Wiley said, "Your Officer Hebert has been so helpful, so kind, so nice. He was with me the whole time at the hospital. He explained the police procedure and that I may need to talk to you detectives. I would just like to do it now and get it over with. I mean if that's ok with you."

Elwyn took a Miranda form from one of the trays. He explained that they didn't have any reason to think she was involved in any way, but this was just procedure. Julie stated she completely understood.

"You have the right to remain silent. Anything you say can and will be used against you in a court of law."

"You have the right to have an attorney present during questioning."

"If you cannot afford an attorney, one will be appointed for you."

"Do you understand these rights?"

"Knowing these rights, do you want to talk to me now?"

After each of the sentences, Mrs. Wiley verbally affirmed. She initialed and wrote *'Yes'* after each line. She signed the bottom of the page and dated it. Det. Bryson and Sgt. Weingart signed as witnesses.

Elwyn Bryson had been a cop for 30 years and a detective for a decade. Despite being burnt out, he was steady and dependable. His work product resulted in about a 70% crime solve rate. He'd worked any number of murder cases and had good interview and interrogation skills.

Sgt. Weingart was in charge of a patrol squad and hadn't been involved in investigations for at least ten years. His interview skills could be generously described as rusty. He had a note pad on the edge of the table. He was probably going to take notes while Elwyn conducted the interview.

Fortunately, Bryson ran the interview. He started off with a series of open-ended questions that had easy answers. These were non-critical questions designed to reveal a normal baseline of the suspect's behavior, voice, body language and general demeanor, when discussing things not relevant to the crime. Things like address, date of birth, employment, how long had they lived in Oakview.

Mrs. Wiley sat with her forearms and hands on top of the table, fingers interlaced. She sat upright with a good posture, leaning forward somewhat toward Elwyn. She stayed in that position while answering the easy questions, occasionally brushing a loose strand of hair behind her ear. She faced Elwyn and made good eye contact. She spoke evenly with a tired, but pleasant look.

Elwyn asked her how her day had begun that day. He was leading her gradually towards the murders.

Julie Wiley said she was sick in the morning with her period and stayed in bed all day. She talked for a full five minutes about how her menstrual cycles had been terribly painful since she was a teenager. She spoke of doctors she had seen and how her mother was the same way, that it must be some type of family curse in their genes, and how lucky men were not to have to have periods or the pain of childbirth.

Elwyn steered her back to the issue at hand, asking her to begin with what happened in the morning.

She said that, despite being sick, she got up, got the kids dressed for school and made their lunches. She complained that they were late because Craig forgot to set the alarm clock. They had missed the bus, so she drove them to school. Elwyn asked her where Mr. Wiley was in the morning. She said he had already left for an appointment to see a client by the time she and the kids awoke.

She went off on a tangent about how the school district was not as good as she had hoped. She figured when they moved into this area, the schools would be so much better, but as far as she was concerned, they weren't.

Elwyn let her ramble for several minutes, watching and listening.

I spoke over the tape. "So far, she hasn't exhibited anything I would have deemed particularly deceptive."

"I agree, doc. She's making herself out as mother of the year. What a bitch. Tell me something, does this look like a woman whose children were brutally murdered and whose husband just killed himself less than six hours earlier?" MQ asked.

"This is bizarre, Kenneth. No doubt about that."

Elwyn asked her if Mr. Wiley was troubled or if there were problems at home or with finances, something that may have contributed to what happened.

She said that they had been having some financial troubles but they were working their way out of a bind.

"My husband's dog business was picking up, but he never made anywhere near the money we needed." she said sounding aggravated. She pulled the pony from her hair and shook her head. Her hair was matted and she combed it with her fingers.

Elwyn returned her to the task at hand. "Your husband left the house in the morning. When did you see him again, about what time? Mrs. Wiley, I'd like you to narrow the time down to when it was that he came home. What time did he come home?"

The question tripped a kinesic switch and she leaned back in her chair and folded her arms across her chest, clearing her throat. "He, uh he stopped by once in the morning to check on me."

"And what time was that Mrs. Wiley?"

"That was, before lunch. He…" She cleared her throat again. "He only stayed a few minutes and then left to go meet with another client or something like that. I was feeling worse so I took a couple Advils. I slept on and off all day."

"So he was there before lunch. What time was that?"

"I don't know. I didn't look at the clock."

MQ spoke, "You notice her avoidance, the change in her attitude and body language when Elwyn asked her what time her husband came back. Something is going on there, doc."

I nodded and we watched as she continued to spin her yarn.

Elwyn moved on and asked, "So, your kids went to school. What time did they get home?"

She fidgeted in her chair. "The bus drops them off at the end of the street about 3:40, 3:45. I usually go down and wait for them."

"What time did you get down there today?" Elwyn asked.

"I didn't. I, I, I was still sick in bed and I, I didn't go. Craig stopped by later and said he would pick them up so I could sleep in."

"So that was a second time he came home? He stopped by in the morning before lunch at a time you can't remember and you took some Advil's. And now this time he stopped by to tell you he would pick up the kids. What time was this?"

Elwyn glanced over at Weingart, whose head was down, probably jotting down a few notes. Julie Wiley was silent.

"About what time was it that he stopped by the second time to tell you he would get the kids?" Elwyn prodded.

She momentarily looked up at the ceiling. She stared at her fingers and started pushing back her cuticles as she spoke. "Honestly, detective, I wish I could tell you for sure. I don't know. It had to have been some time in the afternoon, I can't tell you for sure. I had gotten up to go to the bathroom, and I could hear him in the kitchen. He brought me in a couple of what he said were vitamins to make me feel better. I took the pills, but I think they just made me sleepy."

"And this was noontime, 1 or 2? What time was this, Mrs. Wiley?"

"Oh God, I just don't remember. My cramps were bad and I think the pills he gave me made me groggy. I don't recall looking at the clock or my watch or anything."

"But it was before the children would have been at the bus stop?" Elwyn asked.

"Oh, yes. For sure. It was probably lunchtime or a little after."

"So he brought you some vitamins and then what happened?"

"He warmed me up a slice of pizza from last night. Yea, so it had to be lunch-time. I ate it and felt a little better. I told him I would stay up to get the kids. He said that I should just rest. He told me to go back to sleep and that he would be back in time to get them at the bus stop." She paused, looked directly up at the ceiling again and then said, "He rubbed my shoulders and it felt good. I must have fallen asleep when he left."

MQ reached over and hit the pause button. "Surely Elwyn saw and heard all of this bullshit. The speech qualifiers, invoking God and saying honestly. Picking her fingernails, and shifting positions. She is making this shit up as she goes."

"And that is exactly what he wrote in his report Kenneth. That she was decep-tive and inconsistent. Shut up and let's watch." I hit the play button. MQ grunted.

"So, you went back to sleep. What do you remember next, when you woke up?" Elwyn asked.

"Craig had come home. He woke me up and asked how I was feeling. I told him that uh, the pills he gave me helped." She picked fuzz balls of lint from her inside out sweatshirt.

"When was this? Where were the kids at this time?" Elwyn asked.

"Um, I think Craig said they were upstairs in their rooms watching TV. He said he told them to be quiet since I wasn't feeling well."

"Did you see them, or did you hear them in the house?" Elwyn asked.

A long, fifteen second pause as she pulled her sleeves down over her fingers and used them to rub her eyes. "I never saw them," she said as she sniffled a few times.

Sgt. Weingart left the room and returned with a box of Kleenex. Mrs. Wiley took them and said thanks with a tight lipped smile. Elwyn continued his line of questioning.

"Are you able to continue, Mrs. Wiley? Do you want to take a break, do this tomorrow?"

"No, I can do this," she said, abruptly sitting up with Emily Post posture. "I need to do this. I need to help you. You all have been so kind to me. I need to repay the kindness."

"What a crock of shit!" MQ muttered.

Elwyn continued, "Ok. The kids are upstairs in their rooms. You and Craig are in your room. What happened next?"

Mrs. Wiley took a couple of tissues from the box, one in each hand. She rubbed her eyes in a circular motion. She slumped in the chair and crossed her legs, knee over knee.

"He got into bed with me and asked me if I wanted my back rubbed again. I get awful back pains with my period. And I said yes, that would be wonderful. He got in bed and had me lay on my stomach."

Then she stopped talking.

When suspects stop talking, they are usually thinking about what to say next or wondering what the detective is going to ask next. The silence increases stress on the subject. The suspect feels that if they don't keep talking, explaining and cooperating, they will seem more guilty. Silence is golden. Elwyn let the silence work, he let the silence prompt her, rather than asking a question. It was silent and still for half a minute.

Mrs. Wiley crumpled the tissues, interlaced her fingers and placed her hands in her lap. She abruptly sat up straight in her chair, as if she had just been scolded for her for poor and unladylike posture. She was as far back in the chair as she could be, as far away from the table and Elwyn as was possible without moving the chair. She bent her head down, and continued her story.

"He, he had me lay with my head at the end of the bed, so I could watch TV while he rubbed me. He went into the bathroom and got some baby oil and put it on my back and massaged me," she sobbed a couple of choppy breaths and stopped again.

There was another pause of 15 seconds.

Elwyn prompted her this time. "So, you're getting a massage, the kids are watching TV, everything is fine. What happened next Mrs. Wiley?"

"This is so embarrassing, detective."

"It's all right, Mrs. Wiley. We will keep things confidential, just between us. We just need to know the truth about what happened. Please go ahead if you can." Elwyn lied like any good detective. Nothing in a murder investigation is confidential.

"Well, he, he said he wanted to, have sex with me. That he was horny. I told him, 'gross', I was on my period. Really, this is so embarrassing." She crossed her arms over her chest.

"Mrs. Wiley, we understand," Elwyn said. "But anything you can tell us will help figure out what and why this terrible tragedy happened."

Mrs. Wiley cleared her throat, looked up briefly and then back down at the table. "Ok, thank you, detective, thank you for being so nice. Craig, he said he would just rub himself, and that he wouldn't you know, go inside me," she paused for a few seconds again. "You see, we had a, um, a kind of a game we played. I would let him, let him tie me up and it made it better for him. So, we did that."

Sgt. Weingart probably didn't mean to mutter anything out loud, but his, "What the fuck lady?" came out clearly on the tape. Mrs. Wiley looked over at him. Her lips pursed, eyes narrowed. There was a glare of fury, no blushing or embarrassment.

Elwyn glanced disapprovingly at Weingart and returned his attention to Julie.

"Mrs. Wiley, we're not here to judge what two married adults do in the privacy of their own home. I know this is difficult, and very personal, but having a chronology, a step by step description, helps us understand what happened. And I want to thank you for being so helpful and strong."

"I just want to figure out what happened, too," she whined looking down at her feet.

"Ok then," Elwyn said. "So, you were going to play a game, which is perfectly fine and normal for many married couples. Please go on, help us understand what happened." Another 15 second silence.

"Craig, he has, you know, he is a dog trainer, sometimes for the police. Well, he, he has a lot of police stuff. He has some handcuffs and we use them in our game. So, he put me in them."

Elwyn's face was bland, non judgmental. "And then what?"

Mrs. Wiley continued. "He would put me in the cuffs and then he would tie the cuffs with a little clothesline to the footboard so I couldn't move. I know it sounds weird, but it helped him if I was like you know, weak, and he was strong. He had man problems. He had to take pills and sometimes he snorted some coke in order, to you know, be able to do it. He's my husband so I wanted to help him so I went along. And so, and then he, used the other clothesline to tie my ankles to the headboard.

And so, I was, tied up, and he went into the other room to get some baby oil. And he was gone, a few minutes or so. I must have dozed off because I couldn't see the clock to tell the time. I didn't know how long he was gone or when he came back."

In the corner of the screen, Weingart was scribbling. He'd probably picked up on her inconsistency about the baby oil. A few minutes ago, she had mentioned that Mr. Wiley had gotten the baby oil before the bondage.

Mrs. Wiley started to breathe more rapidly. Her head bent down, chin to chest. She rocked back and forth slightly.

"You're doing fine, Mrs. Wiley," Elwyn leaned forward, coming closer to her. He spoke softly. "So, you are in a defenseless position, he has control over you and you can't do a thing. You are powerless. What happened next?" Elwyn asked.

"He…" Mrs. Wiley continued to rock back and forth in her chair. She blurted out, "He lied!"

Her chin was still to her chest.

"How did he lie, Mrs. Wiley. What did he do to you?"

"He got between my legs behind me and, and, he put his hands around my neck and tried to, he tried to choke me. He was choking me and I couldn't breathe. And I kept asking him, what are you doing? What are you doing? You're hurting me. You're hurting me. And, he forced himself into me, into my rear. And, I said, you're hurting me. You're hurting me. But he wouldn't listen, he wouldn't stop."

She glanced up at Elwyn and then back down at the table. There was another pause. She continued to stare down at the table.

Elwyn and Weingart exchanged glances during the pause.

MQ noticed the glance. "I bet Bryson is silently screaming at Weingart to keep his big Hessen mouth shut."

Elwyn broke the quiet spell. "So, what you are saying is that your husband tried to choke you and then forced you to have anal sex with him."

Mrs. Wiley looked up and a token of a smile passed over her face. I rewound the tape to watch in slow motion to make sure I had seen what I thought was a smile. "She's happy that Elwyn seems to be buying her story."

"Yes. Yes that's right," she said. "And when he was done, he sat at the end of the bed and he said real loud and mean, 'Now, now, we all have to die!' And I've heard that tone of voice before. Oh yes, I've heard that before and he meant it."

She bent her head down and wiped her eyes with the crumpled tissues in her hands. Her hair fell loosely down, bracketing and hiding her face. All that was visible was the top of her head. Her words came out of the shadows. "Now we have to die too."

Mrs. Wiley stopped rocking in her chair. She sat up partially, shoulders rounded, leaning toward the table. Her eyes were closed. She blew her nose. While her head was up and the Kleenex was over her nose and mouth, she glanced briefly at Elwyn and then closed her eyes shut.

"Look at that bitch," MQ said. "She peaked up at Elwyn to see if he was still buying her story,"

"That's what it looks like to me too," I said.

Elwyn asked, "What did he mean by that we have to die too? Did he say he did something to your children already?"

"Yes, I mean, he said that he, that he couldn't provide for his family like we deserved. And I told him we could work this out. And that we could talk about it and that it would all work out."

More scribbling by Weingart.

"What did you think he meant by we have to die too? What about your kids?"

"He had that look on his face, and that tone in his voice that meant he had done something bad to them. I knew I needed to get help." Mrs. Wiley resumed her back and forth rocking. The chair made a shrill, grating sound. The microphone picked up every irritating squeak.

Elwyn was catching the scent of the fox. He continued, charging forward. "What do you think he had done? How did you know for sure that he had done something? What did he say that you knew he had done something?"

Mrs. Wiley ignored his question. "I begged him to untie me. I was pleading and crying, and, and begging. And telling him it would be alright. And he said "No, it wouldn't!" And then, then he got up and went to our closet and got out the shotgun and said he was going to kill me and then himself. He sat on the end of the bed and put the bullets in it while I was laying there."

"Mrs. Wiley, I want to know what happened to the kids? What did he say he did?"

She disregarded Elwyn's persistence. "I was laying there, crying and he was loading the gun. He was loading the gun. It was awful, horrible. I was scared to death. I was, I was really scared."

"So, you're still tied up on the bed and he is loading the shotgun. You're scared to death," Elwyn paraphrased her, hoping to advance the story, keep her talking.

"I kept begging him to untie me. To untie me so we could work this out. And finally, finally, he untied me. And he took the handcuffs off me. But, he had hold of the shotgun. And he said I could either stay and die with him or get out. So, I pulled on a sweatshirt, and some jeans. He pointed the shotgun at me and told me to get out of the house. So, I walked like, backwards out of the room."

"So, you ran from the house trying to get help?" Elwyn asked.

I was confident that Elwyn knew she had escaped by four wheels rather than two legs. He was probably just checking to see whether she would correct him.

"Yes, well, I mean no. I mean, my car was there, so I got in my car and drove down to a friend's house. She called 911 for me."

"I understand your dogs were in the car. What was that all about?" Elwyn asked.

"I really need to use the little girl's room," Mrs. Wiley said with an exaggerated expression of urgency on her face.

"I'll take her," Weingart said. Sgt. Weingart escorted her out of the room.

Elwyn looked up at the camera. "She is all over the place. Her story is all wrong. Something else is going on, other than just what she's saying. That's for sure."

# Chapter Sixty Eight

While Mrs. Wiley was using the restroom, Elwyn left the interview room. He returned with a can of Pepsi and put it on the table in front of her chair. Weingart brought Mrs. Wiley back into the room. She took her seat.

"For me?" she asked with southern belle innocence.

"I thought you might need something with some sugar. You've had a long day," Elwyn nodded.

She took a long draft. "Thank you. You both are such kind gentlemen. Thank you. All of you have been so nice."

Weingart grunted.

Elwyn leaned over and whispered something in Weingart's ear. Weingart nodded and Elwyn left the room. He was gone for a good five minutes. During the break from questioning, Julie Wiley sipped the soda and ran her fingers through her hair over and over. She pushed more cuticle back on each finger. She continued to undulate in the chair and her knees bounced. Weingart sat quietly. He looked as if he was going over the notes he'd written.

"Elwyn is giving her time to think, time to worry. Good strategy," I said.

"We'd have done the same thing, doc. And she is worrying. Look at her. The proverbial whore in church," MQ responded.

Elwyn reentered the room and spent the next ten minutes going back over what Mrs. Wiley had initially said. He had her go over the day's events again. He prefaced this review with, "I just want to make sure I have everything exactly correct."

Her story changed.

In the second version, the alarm clock woke her up on time, but the kids were slow to get dressed and she had to drive them to school. Of course, this was in contradiction to the original version where the alarm clock did not go off.

In this updated version, Mr. Wiley came home only once, after picking up the kids at the bus stop. This version didn't mention the fact that he gave her vitamins or made her a slice of pizza.

The sex scene was similar, but Mr. Wiley never left the room. He tied her up, choked her, anally raped her, and this time, he also put some duct tape over her mouth.

For the next 10 minutes, Elwyn worked on offense, whittling away at each inconsistency, trying to find out what happened to the children. Her pat answer was a whiny, "I don't know, I'm confused." Finally, he quizzed her on why on earth her dogs were in her car.

Mrs. Wiley started crying. "I don't know. Maybe they just jumped in there when I got in. I don't know. I don't know. Why does it matter?"

Elwyn leaned over the table and closed the distance between them. He locked eyes with her. "Because you and your dogs survived and two little children were slaughtered. That's why I want to know!" Elwyn was hoping the inferred accusation would provoke something out of her, anger or more fury and that she would blurt something out. It was a gamble.

"I'll tell you, you," Mrs. Wiley's coiled and jerked forward toward Elwyn rising out of the chair. But, she caught herself. She slowly leaned back and sat down. She grabbed more Kleenex from the box. "I'm tired, I'm not thinking straight. They gave me some medicine at the hospital. It's making me fuzzy. I'm confused. I don't understand."

Elwyn's tone returned to empathic, "Mrs. Wiley, I just want to understand. I want to understand what happened. And your account of what happened keeps changing. This was a very traumatic event I know. It is the worst thing that can happen to a parent. But we both know, there is something else going on. There is something that is confusing. It's confusing even you. Whatever that is, it is keeping you from telling me what really happened. What is it that is confusing?" Elwyn looked directly into her face to gain eye contact.

Mrs. Wiley looked away. "I just want to go home. I don't want to talk to you anymore."

"I really think there is something, something that you're having a hard time talking about. We can work through this. The worst is over. We can get through this," Elwyn said evenly.

Julie folded her arms over her chest again. She looked up at Elwyn. "I can tell you one thing that didn't happen. And that is that he didn't do it. If that is what you're trying to think happened. Like I had something to do with it? No! He did it!" her voice boomed loudly in the room, strong and crisp. "He did it, he killed those kids and the bastard killed himself!"

Elwyn responded calmly, in a matter of fact tone. "No one has alleged that you did anything. Except your story has changed, and that usually happens when someone is not sure of what they are saying. Did your husband come home once or twice? Did he make you a slice of pizza or not? Did he give you some vitamins that made you sleepy? Did he duct tape your mouth or not? Mrs. Wiley, please, help me understand."

"I don't care if you understand or not. I don't give a shit. I want to go home, I want to call my mom. I want, I want to call my lawyer."

"Mrs. Wiley, please. Do you think you need a lawyer at this point? We're just talking, trying to piece things together. Let's give it a little time. Maybe you'll remember something. Maybe you'll remember more clearly what happened. I bet a little bit from each of the stories you said, is what really happened. Let's talk some more. We'll get it straight."

"No, I want my mom. I want to call my mom, my mom and my lawyer. I want my mom and I want my lawyer!" she demanded like a spoiled 6 year old, arms folded over her chest.

"Perhaps we can talk tomorrow. I'm sorry if we upset you," Elwyn said as he stood. A moment later the screen went to snow. Apparently Elwyn stopped the recording.

MQ spoke first. "She is unable to repeat her story of wild canard. It is nothing but improvisation and concoction."

"My guess is Elwyn sensed that continuing the interrogation would be controversial at best. Any prosecutor, judge or juror would be influenced by the fact that this poor woman who had lost her children and husband earlier in the day, and as we know, one who had been given tranquilizers in the ER, couldn't have concise recall. A person under those circumstances couldn't be expected to have clear recollection of the day's events. Anything that Elwyn would have gotten from that point on, after she lawyered up, would have been questioned as to whether she had given it voluntarily. Not only because of Miranda, but a confession, even if it wasn't forced, would evoke some weird sense of pity by a jury. Obviously our detective took a more prudent approach, perhaps more conservative than you or I would have. Elwyn was probably thinking they'd have another crack at her. That tomorrow's another day."

MQ disagreed. "Spare me the Scarlet O'Hara crap doc. Elwyn knew she was lying. He should have snatched the Pepsi and those tissues from her hand and gave her a Tom Cruise, 'I want the truth!' He could have gotten a confession from that bitch if he wanted to spend another couple hours working on her. But Elwyn didn't pursue the prey. You know why? Because, he's a fainéant slacker who was leaving for vacation the following day. He didn't want to get involved in anything that would interfere with his cruise, or whatever he was going to do. And what's more, if I remember correctly, his report of the interview was barely one page. Nothing specific."

"Right you are Kenneth. His report did not define the inconsistencies, he merely referenced them. I have it here. I think he could have written it in 5 minutes." I pulled a folder from a file cabinet and started reading from Elwyn's report. "Mrs. Wiley was deceptive and inconsistent in her reporting of the events leading to the deaths of her children and husband. She provided two different stories. These inconsistencies are readily apparent on the video tape of her interview. At this time, the reason for Mrs. Wiley's deception remains unknown. Further investigation, including re-interview, should be conducted as soon as possible."

"The lazy fucker was going on vacation and had to pack," MQ repeated.

MQ pulled out a couple of Hemingway Short Story cigars from his coat pocket. He unwrapped them both, clipped the ends and handed me one. "These were on sale at cigar shop. I know you like them."

"Thanks, Kenneth. I like them because they're shorter and you can finish them without getting overloaded on nicotine." We lit up.

"In any event doc, it's pretty telling is it not? Finally, confirmation of the known." We both sat back in our chairs and puffed away.

"It's weird, seeing Mrs. Wiley so up close and personal," I said. "All this time during the cold case, how she was that night has been kind of nebulous. I am sure you noticed, in those close-up videos of her face, there were no red marks on her neck, no scratches. Nothing to indicate she was choked or that duct tape had been on her skin. Exactly what Margie said."

"Margie. That's Dr. Classa the ER doc right? You still enjoying each other's company?"

"Yea. She's a fun girl. It's a good thing I have a good aerobic capacity from running. Otherwise, I'd probably be dead. She's checking to see if she can get off work to go with me to Cali. I gotta move my sister again."

"Damn, doc. Your sister goes through husbands quicker than Zsa Zsa. What is this, number four or five?"

"What can I say? The Jack and Elaine Green curse. Dysfunction follows their offspring like the Peabody Ducks. And it's only her third ex-husband," I said as I switched on an exhaust fan. .

I handed MQ the first page of Mrs. Wiley's six page statement. "Check this out. Look at the witness initials at the bottom of each page," I pointed. "Look at the bottom Kenneth. WN, Will Newsham had her write this."

"We know now that Chatham had an organized plan," MQ said. "He had Mrs. Wiley on the evening news the next night portraying her as the poor, pitiful victim of spousal abuse. This written statement, clearly does not fall into the Newsham Law Firm defense strategy. You're right, it's Will's fuck up."

The statement was a flowing river of turd. It was a detailed account of the minutiae that happened at the Wiley household that day. Everything, from what color socks Taylor wore, to the Transformers lunchbox with two packs of Ho-Ho's that Robbie carried to school.

Julie Wiley wrote as if she were a combination of Harriet Nelson and Maria Von Trapp. She quoted the lyrics from some Sesame Street song she sang every morning when she woke the children for school, and how she brushed Taylor's hair with 50 strokes each morning and evening.

She wrote that she took the kids to school and returned home to lay down. She recalled a phone call from a girlfriend just before noon in which they discussed going out on Wednesday for happy hour.

She wrote that her husband returned home around lunchtime. He brought a movie from Mike Reznor's and they watched it. He warmed her up a slice of pizza, got her a Coke and gave her a whole handful of blue pills to take. The pills were supposed to help her cramps and back pain. She said Craig smoked some pot and did a couple lines of cocaine while they watched the movie. He was always smoking pot and using cocaine. She wished he didn't use drugs in the house.

She wrote that Craig gave her a few more pills to take before the movie was over. He left the house saying he was going to return it to Mike Reznor.

She woke up when she heard Craig in their room. She saw on the clock that it was 3pm. She tried to get out of bed to get to the bus stop, but she was very woozy from the pills. Craig said he would go get the kids and she should just rest.

She dozed and woke up when he came into their bedroom and slammed the door. She asked where the kids were, and he said they were watching TV in their rooms. He brought her another handful of pills which, again she wrote that she took.

She described the bondage activity that Craig made her play. Once bound, he started choking her and forced himself into her rear. There was no mention of duct tape in this written story. When he was done, he left the room. She was so groggy from the pills that she didn't know how long he was gone from their bedroom.

When he returned, he got the shotgun out of the closet and said that they had to die. She asked him if he had hurt the children or stabbed them, and that he just said they had to die too. She knew he had done something bad to them.

"My big, fat, white Irish ass!" MQ threw the papers to the floor as if they were covered with maggots. "She has clear and precise recollection of everything that happened before the murders. She can recall specifics of phone conversations, but she is so groggy she can't recall how long he was gone from the room? And never once did she describe the children as 'my kids', or 'our kids'. It was always 'those' or 'the' kids. The bitch killed her own children. She did it or was there when someone did."

"Is it any wonder this never made it to the light of day," I said, picking up MQ's copy and handing it back. "We've already disproved her claims of being drugged with Triple T's report. Her statement is even more damning with these claims of taking pills on multiple occasions throughout the day."

"And if you recall, Craig Wiley's blood did not reveal any controlled substances," MQ added. "Obviously he didn't smoke some weed and do a couple lines of cocaine."

Perhaps this was really a turning point, the something that Myra Sutherland mentioned. We sat in silence and finished reading the statement in which Mrs. Wiley recounted her daring vehicular escape with her dogs in tow.

She wrote that the dogs must have known something bad had happened and just jumped in the car as soon as she opened the door. She wrote about going to the Goldstein's, the call to 911 and her trip to the ER with the kind policeman. She closed with a sweet and sickening statement:

*"I will always remember the kind and thoughtful gentlemen that handle these difficult situations with such sensitivity. The kindness with which I was treated by the members of the Oakview Police Department gives me hope for the future."*

MQ threw the statement onto the table. He was flushed, and looked in pain. I had seen this look on my old partner's face before. It was usually due to his reflux. This time it had nothing to do with bodily functions. He shook his head in disgust. "Where are my boots to wade through the crap spilling out of this bowling bag. Put in the CD doc. I am sure there is something akin to a Grimm's Fairy Tale on it."

I inserted the disc in the computer. We craned our heads at the screen. The disk contained information taken from the Wiley home computer. Officer Telling was the self ordained, home schooled, Oakview computer guru who fancied himself as a forensic computer geek. Telling had made copies of what he felt was pertinent to the investigation on a single disc. Contrary to standard computer forensic protocol, they did not seize the computer as evidence, take it back to the station, or burn a mirror image of the entire hard drive as any rookie forensic expert would have.

Telling copied data and computer activity surrounding the time of the murders, from 1pm to 5pm. The disc contained multiple images of hard core porn, BDSM and lesbian sites which were visited during those hours preceding the murders.

We finished flipping through the images. I popped the disc out. "Someone had been playing with the computer during the time frame in which Mrs. Wiley was allegedly dazed and drugged into confusion and amnesia, and Mr. Wiley wasn't home during much of that time. If it wasn't her, who was surfing porn sites?"

MQ leaned forward in his chair, gnawing on the end of his cigar like a rawhide bone. He abruptly stood up and paced back and forth, hunched over like Lieutenant Columbo did when he had that one last question to ask the perp. He looked up, his face crimson. "It doesn't matter doc. They will still win. No one will care whether her face and nails were perfect. No one will care whether she lied by written or recorded word. No one will care what is on this disc. It doesn't matter whether someone else was in the house porn surfing while two children were being butchered. This is corroboration, but only for you and I. Like I said, 'Confirmation of the Known'."

I interrupted the bad juju spewing from my old partner, "We'll take the residue kit to Sally Sunderman and Alan Derrickson for the gunpowder analysis and have them retest the weapons."

MQ continued the diatribe, "Montileone wouldn't allow the referral or pay for it, that's definite. Hell, Doc, we don't even know if the weapons are even still in evidence. They may have already destroyed them. The case is shut down. Really all we have proven with our bowling bag contents is that Lawrence Johnson obstructed justice by hiding evidence. And of course, he's dead. Any allegation that Newsham was behind a grand conspiracy to protect Julie Scalini Wiley would be successfully attacked as Lawrence's 'sour grapes' for Will's unfaithful behavior. Hell hath no fury like a man's scorn."

MQ plopped down in his chair and searched his pockets. His Hemingway had gone out.

The brief optimism and hope I had felt from Lawrence's bowling locker dissipated like steam.

I stood and paced as MQ had just done. We resembled opposing trial lawyers. "We can have the analysis done at a private lab. I'll pay for it. We could use the porn surfing in a time line to further refute Mrs. Wiley's inconsistent statements."

"Jesus Morris, don't be so pollyannish. Son of a bitch, where's my friggin' lighter?" he asked continuing to pat pockets. "The obvious conclusion by the Chief, the prosecutor's office, the FBI's Violent Crime Unit, etcetera, would be that Craig Wiley was a pervert, and Mrs. Wiley just thought he left the house to go to work. He was in the other room, playing with his wanker while she slept, or some such prevarication as that. Hell, if push comes to shove, Mrs. Wiley could admit to being a computer porn addict, and claim she was too embarrassed to talk about it before. And even if the gunshot residue was analyzed and it came back that Mr. Wiley did not shoot both weapons, it does not put a firearm in the hands of Mrs. Wiley or anyone else."

I opened a desk drawer, shuffled through post-it note pads and paper clips and tossed a red Bic lighter to MQ. "Kenneth, I know what happened."

"Right," he said through a haze of smoke.

"I know what happened in that hour in which the Wiley kids were slaughtered and I know this evidence supports it."

"What the fuck are you talking about?" MQ said, waving to clear the air.

"I need to tell you something Murph. I didn't know when I was going to find a good time to bring this up, but I guess this is as good a time as any."

MQ leaned back in the cheap chair, the plastic and aluminum creaking. "What now, my friend?"

"I met this woman. A woman with an incredible gift of sorts," I said.

MQ sat up straight. With an Irish accent every bit as strong as Myra Sutherland's he said, "A woman you say. So, my son, you've come to confess that you've been unfaithful to the good Dr. Classa. By the size of her, you could be in danger. How long has it been since your last confession? Now, do tell Father Murphy all about it, and don't leave out any of the scurrilous or wicked details."

# Chapter Sixty Nine

shook my head and chuckled. "I am sorry to disappoint you. My experience with this other woman isn't of a sexual nature. She works here at the clinic, janitorial, housekeeping department."

"And this is relative, how?" MQ asked leaving the brogue behind.

"She's a, she has a rather remarkable talent. She has a gift," I paused, searching for a word other than psychic.

"So maybe she's a redhead with double Ds looking for a short, chubby, fair skinned boyfriend?"

I smiled. "Well, yes. She is Irish. But I'm sorry, Kenneth. No double Ds or red hair. She's flat chested and skinny, but she has this gift, or as it turns out, more of what she described as a curse. For lack of a better description, she can see dead people. You know the movie *The Sixth Sense,* that type of thing."

I pulled my chair in front of MQ's and sat down. He leaned forward and rested his elbows on his knees. He shook his head from side to side, "So, my son," the brogue making a momentary comeback. "What date shall we designate as the day when you finally had your breakdown? Shall we use today?"

I ignored the barb. "This housekeeper, this woman was cleaning my office. Out of the blue, she started telling me about these two ghost children that were there in the office. It was pretty weird, but she told me there were two children's spirits around me. It's the Wiley kids, and for a lack of a better explanation, they are haunting me."

MQ puffed out a thick smoke ring, accompanied by a thoroughly Texan accent, "Bullshit!"

I continued, "She said that we, meaning me and those two kids, died at the same time which bound us together somehow. And she was right. If you remember, the shooting which left me clinically dead, was at the same time the Wiley murders took place. She said that in that instant, our souls became intertwined. I survived. I returned to the physical world. They didn't, and in that moment when our souls met, they recognized me as someone that could help them. They want justice. They want me to catch their killer. They want the truth to be told so they can move on to wherever they are supposed to go. They're haunting me."

The smoke ring hovered around MQ's head like a melting halo. "Oh come on, Morris. Spooks trapped in between this world and the next. Bullshit," he repeated. "She must have overheard you talking on the phone. Give me something plausible here."

"No bullshit, MQ. I've never seen this woman before. I don't discuss this case over the phone with anyone but you and never with anyone around. This woman, she's a medium. She stood there and asked the ghost children to tell her what happened, and apparently, they did."

"Did they now? They told her what happened, how they were killed?"

"Kenneth, she told me what happened that day in the Wiley house. Everything she said fits with what we discovered. Aside from her talking to those dead kids, there is no other explanation for how she knew what she knew."

"This is Easter bunny shit," MQ said puffing on his cigar. He craned his neck back, rounded his mouth and blew out two grey doughnuts towards the ceiling. "But I'll play this game with you. You are my friend and confidant, so please, tell me what happened."

"This woman's name is Myra Sutherland. Like I said, she was cleaning my office, actually it was on November 22nd, the anniversary of our murders. How fucking strange is that? Out of the blue, she asked me if I heard them."

"Heard them?" MQ asked.

"Yea. I didn't mention that to you either, but lately, I've been hearing whispers."

I noticed MQ's eyes widen.

"Help me St. Michael, please." MQ said looking up. "Whispers doc, really? You've been hearing voices? Like voices from the other side? Inside your head? What the fuck, are you losing your mind?." He rolled the cigar from one side of his mouth to the other.

"Voices. Worrisome. Yes. I asked myself whether this was my first step toward schizophrenia. I don't know MQ, maybe it is. Maybe I am a whack job. Anyway, the sounds were not exactly speech. At first I attributed it to the tinnitus, but after a few times, I had to acknowledge it was speech. The words were not intelligible, but nevertheless whispers, children's whispers. I've been hearing them for some time now."

"Blessed Mother of Calcutta," MQ said, crossing himself for good measure.

"Yea. You got that right father. So when the cleaning lady asked me if I heard them. I dummied up. She didn't buy my feigned ignorance one bit. And not only that, she said a lot of my problems, the shoulder pain, the tapping sensation, are not entirely organic in etiology. She said they are the children's way of getting me to notice them, to do what they need me to do, to solve the case. My troubles are brought on by ghosts."

"My friend, I can give you a litany of reasons why you have pain and are troubled. You got shot, you have PTSD, you're off the charts with all that Jewish guilt handed down from those dreadful parents of yours, you blame yourself for your failed marriage, you got problems with your own kids, you drink too much and take too many God damn pills. In my humble opinion, none of your problems are otherworldly, and now you're story is that the Wiley children are riding you like a cowboy with spurs. So if all this is true, why don't I have pains urging me on to work this case?

"You didn't die with them, Murph, I did."

MQ's lips pursed. He was quiet for a few seconds while deliberating. "Ok. I'm no theologian or Amazing Randy for that matter, but, I am your friend. So please go on. What did she say happened?"

I gave him a brief synopsis of what Myra had said. While I spoke, MQ chomped on the stub of his cigar. His breathing was heavy and he changed positions frequently. The expressions on his face went from a conciliatory flatness to a mouth gaping wonder.

"It all fits, Murph. Everything she said fits our hypotheses where either Mrs. Wiley did it, or there was a third person."

MQ stood and paced a few steps back and forth. "What are we going to do? Swear this ghost whisperer of yours in at a grand jury. Have her say, 'I promise to tell the truth, the whole truth and nothing but the truth about this circle of fury. I promise to tell the truth about the dead that walk the earth like Cain in Kung Fu?"

"Listen, I didn't tell you about the voices or about Ms. Sutherland because I was hoping for an epiphany from the bowling bag, but we cannot ignore what she said. It all fits."

Sol synopsized through another haze of cigar smoke. "Mr. Wiley comes home and sends the children to their rooms to play. Maybe he goes out to cut the grass. Or maybe he goes to the workshop to re-web that lawn chair. The kids walk in the bedroom to find mommy doing the wild leather and lace thing with someone other than their daddy. And so, they sing the "I'm gonna tell daddy" song. This inflames mommy and/or her boyfriend, who is probably our Detective Patrick. She goes into a venomous frenzy and kills her kids by herself. Or maybe boyfriend lends a little succor, joining in on the mayhem. Somehow, Mr. Wiley discovers the carnage, and ends up dead. Or maybe it is that he catches Frankie and Johnny in the salacious act and the war is on, and during the fight, the kids are collateral damage. Maybe Wiley was so distraught he off'd himself, or more likely, it's a staged suicide. The boyfriend takes off. The bitch hops in the car. She puts on the performance worthy of an Oscar and walks away with her sociopathic life, unencumbered by children or a husband."

"Certainly as plausible as anything else we've come up with," I said.

"So did you ask Jeanne Dixon to identify the boyfriend for sure? He's either a key witness or a co-defendant."

"She could only offer a description, wiry and light hair which fits Detective Patrick."

MQ clapped his hands, "So it's him. Lawrence says that we've got James Patrick's badge and shirt at the scene! And that he was probably doing Mrs. Wiley. I'll bet it's his trace on that plaid shirt. He's our boyfriend, simple as that."

"But if he's still alive, he couldn't have had a hand in the murders of those children. Anyone involved in the murder of Francis Scalini's grandchildren would walk the plank, that is for sure," I said.

"We need to go track Patrick down and see what he has to say! We need to shake that boy's trunk till the truth falls out."

"Slow down there SWAT boy. Let's give this some consideration before we play our hand," I said.

An aggravated voice came abruptly through the door. "Dr. Green, put out that cigar! I can smell it in the hallway. Have you lost your damn mind?"

Like dopers at the knock before the search warrant, we hastily tossed our cigars into the toilet and flushed.

"Sorry Lenora," I said loudly. "I thought the exhaust fan would take care of it,"

Her reply was terse and probably through gritted teeth, "This is a government building. There is no smoking and you know it, Dr. Green. Exhaust fan my ass,"

"I know, it won't happen again, sorry," I said to the door. There was no reply.

"Sorry, Kenneth. $14 for tobacco down the drain."

"No problem doc. Thanks to your poltergeists, perhaps we're finally on the right track. We just need to choose the best route."

So saith Sol.

# Chapter Seventy

The next day I brought in flowers and a tray of sweet rolls for the staff. Lenora looked at me with a wary eye. I put the flowers on the counter in front of her. She grabbed one of the cherry rolls. Apologies were apparently accepted.

As it turns out, the second Myra Sutherland, "something will happen" event, occurred that evening and the price included tragedy for another family.

I'd finished another jam packed day at the clinic. We were into the Christmas holiday season accompanied by an increased patient load in the clinic. Folks wanting medicine refills along with the usual colds, flu, pneumonias and holiday season depressive episodes.

Because of the hectic pace, Lawrence's funeral and his bowling bag, I had only exchanged a few text messages and short conversations with Dr. Classa over the past couple of days.

Margie invited me over for dinner to catch up. She made a platter of three cheese lasagna and a dandelion salad with sliced red onions, tomatoes and basil. Ever the connoisseur of fine fruits of the vine, I brought over a $10 Yellow Tail Merlot.

Over dinner, Margie related the juiciest of traumas she'd seen and I brought her up to speed on the Wiley quest. It was Margie who brought to light the 'something will happen' event.

"Morris, did you hear about the murder-suicide in the city? It kind of reminded me of your case."

"I haven't been watching much news or listening to the talk radio, guess I missed it. What happened?"

"This guy killed his wife, shot her in the chest and smothered their toddler before putting the .38 to his temple and blowing out the left side of his head. The child had Down syndrome, and the story said something about the wife was running off to meet her Facebook lover and had filed for divorce. Something like that. The husband left a note. He was depressed, couldn't live without the love of his life and raise a disabled child by himself. Sad, just so sad."

"Sounds pretty messy. They come to your ER?"

"No. I read about it in the newspaper. It just reminded me of the Wiley thing."

"It's kind of, but really not much like my case Margie. In this one, people were murdered and then somebody committed suicide. No survivors. Like the name implies. You still have the paper?"

"Sure. Over on the coffee table. I think it's on the third page. There's a nice spread with a picture of the family, like one of those taken at a shopping mall portrait studio."

I grabbed the paper and returned to the kitchen table. I read the article, taking special notice of the byline. I leaned back, crossing my arms over my chest and looked up for apparently too long.

"Well, you're doing some heavy duty thinking there detective. What's tumbling around in that noggin?"

"This is a real murder-suicide. Let's say I get the paper to do a story revisiting the Wiley 'murder-suicide' case. Compare it to this one and maybe some others that have happened around here within the past couple of years. Maybe they start off with the question, why is this happening? But we hijack it to our own ends. We get the reporter who wrote this article to contact people who were in the Wiley circle at the time of the murders. They start with Mr. Wiley's parents. Victor and Clarissa will say they never believed their son did it. They will tell the reporter that two detectives from Oakview never believed it either. The story would include interviews with the Goldsteins, Fennelmans, Reznors, and a key player that will make all the difference will be Julie Wiley's parents."

"Really Morris? Maybe you get the friends and Wiley's parents, but you can forget the Scalinis. I can't imagine that a Scalini would ever talk to a reporter about the murder of their grandchildren."

"I'm not so sure Margie. The Scalinis divorced shortly after the murders. Maybe Anthony and Cynthia Scalini cut their daughter off after the murders. Those two children were their only grandchildren. Maybe they didn't believe their son-in-law did it. Maybe they knew their daughter for what she was. Maybe she is dead in their eyes. Maybe one of them will be amenable to talk to a reporter. My guess it won't be Anthony, but the mother. The one that gave the Prozac to her whacked out daughter, I bet she has the guilt. I bet she divorced herself out of the Scalini cesspool because of the murders. Maybe now, since time has passed, she'll tell the truth about what happened."

"Lots and lots of maybes there, but you make a decent point," she said refilling our wine glasses with the last of the bottle. "Parents of murdered children do divorce often enough. I think you've got something there lover. You know what they say, it if bleeds, it leads. There's more than enough hemorrhaging going on in these cases. Why not? Call the reporter and see if they're interested."

"I'll run it by Sol and see what he thinks."

Margie stood up and grabbed my hand. "Let's leave the dishes for later. We have some catching up to do, mainly in the supine position, or others," she said with a wink.

# Chapter Seventy One

caught up with MQ at shift change when I returned to duty. We spoke in the parking lot. A pained expression draped MQ's face as I explained my idea concerning the newspaper story.

"How does media exposure help our cause Doc? No one cares about this. Publicity will only draw the ire of the powers that be. The very same powers that have us in these monkey suits. If we're going to get in hot water, let's go grill James Patrick. That prick knows something."

I held up my hands, "Hold on, Kenneth. Hear me out. The reporter interviews all of Craig Wiley's friends. They all point accusatory fingers at Mrs. Wiley and raise questions about the initial investigation. Her slant on the story is all about the unanswered questions and how it is totally different than the Facebook lover, Down's syndrome murder-suicide."

"Fuck that, doc. If we believe your ghost whisperer, Patrick is our man. Let's find him."

"MQ, we can always butt our head against the wall with him. What do we have to lose if I call Danielle Nicastro at the paper. She wrote the article. She was always helpful when we were in the bureau. She made sure our suspect composites or mug shots made the front page."

"Danielle wrote the article huh?," a sly smile purchasing his chubby face. "We sure had a quid pro quo with Danielle back then. She wrote what we asked her to write. If we needed to put out a story with misinformation, or to garner attention to a case that was cooling off, she was there for us."

"And in return for her help, we always gave her the first heads up when arrests were made. She scooped most of the other reporters thanks to us. We can offer the same deal here," I said.

MQ grinned wide and winked, "And, if you recall, Dr. Green, Danielle is a babe and she liked short, frumpy police sergeants."

"Ok. I'll give her a call."

"You do realize, Morris, that if this were a real news story, something that Danielle would do on her own, she would have to talk to someone at Oakview. She would call them to get a statement about the Wiley case. And you know who she would be referred to, don't you?"

I nodded, "Yea, I know."

"The Chief or Newsham would proudly proclaim that because of the heinous nature of the crime, and as a matter of protocol, the department performed a thorough cold case investigation with assistance from the FBI. The conclusions of that thorough investigation were that Craig Wiley murdered his children and committed suicide. Unfortunately his motive remains a mystery to this day. Doc, the indolent fucks would take credit for our blood, sweat and tears."

"So we make it clear to Danielle that going to Oakview is last on the list and when and if she does, she is to talk to Lt. Hebert."

MQ agreed. "Ok. We'll direct her to the neighbor first, Mrs. Goldstein, the one with the notes, and then the friends, Fennelman and Reznor. We have to make sure her story emphasizes the plethora of unanswered questions. Still, doc, in the end, we'll have press coverage on an old murder case. Then what?"

Then, and granted, this next step is a bit edgy. The reporter contacts Cindy Scalini."

"The friggin' Scalini's! Surely, you jest." MQ blurted.

"No MQ not at all." I spent the next couple of minutes explaining.

MQ shook his head, "Maybe the grandmother has the guilt from giving her daughter Prozac and covering for the murdering bitch. So what. Circumstantial and heresay at best. More than likely, she'll refer all reporters to Chatham Newsham's firm, and the whole thing blows up in our face and we get nada."

"But what if it doesn't blow up? What if she talks? What do we have to lose? How much worse can it get?"

"Listen, Doc, there's no way we'll be able to insulate ourselves from this. When word gets back to the department that Danielle is asking questions, and it will at some point, Newsham and Montileone will assume it is part of our twisted vendetta for being fucked out of the bureau. They will work on firing us. Maybe they'll succeed and I will be forced to take a job as a security guard at Wal-Mart.

I'll be the old man standing outside in drooping uniform pants, smoking a cigarette, a couple days of grey stubble on my face, watching for shoplifters. I'll probably chase some 15 year old African track star carrying a Beyonce CD and drop dead of a heart attack. You will be in your clinic office, making six figures and talking to spiritualist housekeepers when someone will call and give you the news of my death."

"Very nice picture you've painted there, Van Gogh. You're no longer satisfied with your current, comfortable level of misfortune. You've gone onto future pacing your misery. I'm medicating and drinking myself to death, and being haunted by dead children. And you will certainly die a miserable pauper. We certainly make a pair."

"Look on the bright side, Doc, I'll probably be able to get us a ten percent discount at Wal-Mart before my untimely death." MQ patted his jacket. He took two white Macanudo cigar tubes from a pocket and unscrewed both, handing me one.

"Cause for celebration my friend. And we can smoke out here without fear of polluting the compromised pulmonary status of your Medicaid clientele, or being hassled by that rather querulous secretary of yours."

# Chapter Seventy Two

I met with Danielle a few days later at a McMurrays, a copy cat restaurant of a TGIFridays. Danielle hadn't changed very much over the past few years. She had traded her long blonde braids for a tight strawberry perm. She was still 5'10" and one hundred sixty solid pounds of muscle. Danielle had been an Olympic basketball player in the Atlanta games and still played in leagues. Her knees were in pretty bad shape, but she managed.

"Morris Green, I was certainly surprised to hear from you," Danielle said offering a strong hug and light peck on the cheek. "You were rather cryptic on the phone so I have to wonder what you're up to. I heard through the grapevine you and MQ were bounced out of the bureau. Bummer, huh? What kind of political hurricane caused that shake up?" "Same thing we're here to discuss today."

"Oooh, my interest is officially peaked," she responded, wriggling in her chair.

We ordered a couple of beers from a pixie, gum chewing, brunette, all of 21 years of age, whose suspenders were loaded with bling.

"You wrote a story about a murder-suicide in the city last week."

"Oh yea. That was tragic. A cheating woman, disabled kid, old man shoots her, throttles the kid and blows his head off. I got to read the note he left. It was a real tear jerker."

Ever the pragmatist, Danielle immediately followed up with, "What's that got to do with anything? What do you want me to do?"

"I thought you might want to write a human interest story comparing it to the Wiley case. You remember the Wiley murders I'm sure. The only triple murder in Oakview history. And in the course of interviewing certain people for the story, people we can direct you to, you might refresh memories. You might discover something that was missed. Or someone may say something they couldn't or wouldn't say back then. Maybe we'll get a new lead."

Danielle looked puzzled, but took a few notes on her tablet while I spoke. She drained her beer before I had gotten half way through mine.

"I remember the Wiley murders. You and Kenneth worked it over pretty hard, right? But nothing became of it. I remember you guys talking about how fucked up the case was, and how fucked up your department was, and how fucked up the cops who worked the case were, that evidence was intentionally fucked up. But you guys never expanded beyond, well, never beyond fucked up. And now you're saying that working the case got the two of you back in uniform?"

"Yes, that is but one of the bitter consequences that has happened because we tried to solve the Wiley murders. Danielle, if what we have planned works, you will have to use the Richter scale to measure fucked up."

"So, you're still not satisfied with the party line that the father did it and by writing about it, we'll discover who really did it?"

"That's the plan anyway."

"And I guess you have a list of who I'm going to talk to, what I'm going to ask and what I'm probably going to write?"

"I have an outline so to speak, but the article, if you decide to do it, is yours. You can write whatever you want. We just want to help," I said.

"Yea, you're with the government and you're here to help. That's a line of crap. I know you guys all too well. I bet you and MQ will want to know what I've written before I submit it to my editor, but I'm in Morris. It sounds fun and maybe a little dangerous. I've been doing fluff bullshit pieces, museum openings, restaurant reviews. Last week I did a thrilling article on the availability of student loans and grants. That toddler murder/suicide was the first story I've done with any blood and guts in quite some time. A murder story will be fun. Who and what do we do first?"

I gave Danielle the Cliff Notes version of the Wiley cold case and what we had learned after Lawrence's death and the bowling bag. Her jaw dropped a number of times and she uttered quite a few 'Holy Fucks', 'You have got to be fucking kidding me?' and 'Fucking bullshit' as she pecked away on her keypad.

"Interviews should be conducted in a certain order. First the Goldstein's, then Victor and Clarissa, then the Fennelmans and Reznors," I gave her a printout of their addresses and phone numbers, "and then maybe Cindy Scalini."

"Cindy Scalini? Are you kidding me?" Danielle said with widening eyes.

"Nope. No kidding here."

Danielle waved over the waitress and ordered two more beers. She continued to type as I explained the Scalini family connection, including the suspicions I had about my own murder. Her curiosity and interest in the story broadened.

"Dammit, Morris. Murder, organized crime, police corruption, a veritable laundry list of terrific story lines. And I assure you, all of this will remain confidential, protected. Reporter and source protection as far as I am concerned."

"I knew you would treat it with the sensitivity required Danielle. Thank you. I would appreciate you keeping me apprised of what you do, when you do it. Let me know when and where you go to do your interviews. Let me know what they said, and if you are going to meet a Scalini, maybe I could tag along as your photographer, or just sit outside when you are meeting with them. Is that too much to ask?"

"Dr. Green, are you worried about me?"

"Let's face it. We're talking about the murder of two kids and the Scalini family. Organized crime isn't what it used to be, but I suspect Anthony and Cynthia Scalini are not Ricky and Lucy. I wouldn't play them cheap. Let's just take it slow and anticipate what may lie ahead depending on the outcome of each interview."

Danielle shrugged her shoulders as if to say, *'I'm a big girl, I can handle myself.'*

She agreed, though and offered, "I'll set up a meeting with the Goldsteins and Wileys later this week and let you know." Danielle quickly drained her second beer.

"And the plan is to call Oakview PD last if we have to. We get all of our good information first, ok? Oakview last and call Lt. Hebert. He's a friendly on this one."

"Sure thing, Morris. This is going to be fun, a small scale Watergate. I'll be the next Woodward and Bernstein."

"Thanks, Danielle."

"So how is your old partner, the little weeble?" Danielle asked, as our gum chewing bling girl brought another round.

# Chapter Seventy Three

wo days later, at 8am, my phone buzzed as I trudged through a slushy sidewalk and 26 degree temperature, towards my apartment after a miserable four mile run. My Nike's were totally soaked and my feet were numb, closing in on frost nip. I hate the cold. I wonder if those damn Wiley ghosts would chase me down if I moved back to the Caribbean.

It was Danielle. Her voice was effusive and way too loud for my arctic head. "Hey, Morris. So I spoke to the Goldsteins and got some great info. That Beverly, she's a real firecracker. The little nurse kept her notes. Wow! I was also able to talk that George Fennelman guy too. Good historical information. He was really pleased that we were going to write up something about the case. He still feels bad for his dead buddy getting the blame."

My face was stiff and I could not match her enthusiasm or cluttering speech with frozen lips. "They'll be good witnesses."

"I haven't found the Reznors yet, but I'm still looking."

"I'll check for updates in DOR or REJIS."

"Cool. That'd be great, fantastic. I called Craig Wiley's parents and explained that the paper was revisiting their son's case in light of what just happened in the city. I asked if they would mind if I came over and talked to them. Listen to this, Morris. Mr. Wiley was very polite, but in no uncertain terms, he said they had nothing to say and didn't want to discuss it. I asked him how he and his wife were doing. You know, the standard stuff we would ask a victim of a tragedy. I was trying to reengage. He said they were doing fine. They've learned to live with it and that he didn't want to talk about it. And then he said thank you for calling and hung up. He hung up on me. What the fuck? What the fuck's up with that?"

I cradled the phone to my ear as I peeled off soggy clothes in the entryway. "I'm not surprised. They were strange folks. You have to wonder whether they were threatened by the Scalinis and told to keep their mouths shut."

"Or maybe they were paid off. Who the hell knows?" Danielle added.

I pulled on dry sweats and poured a cup of coffee as I began to unthaw. "Let's go on to the Scalinis then. Since we spoke, I ran a Lexus-Nexus public record database search on them. The address and number I gave you is outdated. Anthony lives in Runny Meade Estates, and Cynthia Scalini's most recent address is in the city in one of those new lofts."

"I would bet money that Cindy Scalini knew her daughter's temperament and potential for violence," Danielle said. "She knows something. I bet she does."

"Then we agree Detective Nicastro. Call Cindy Scalini and see if she will sit down with you. Let me know as soon as you find out. I've never met, or spoken with Cindy or Anthony, so I don't know much about them other than what I've told you."

A couple hours later, Danielle called back. "She is willing to talk. I'm meeting her for lunch tomorrow at La Trattoria Italia. It's in the city on Chestnut, great pasta primavera."

"Yea, I know it," I said. "Here's what I think. You meet her for lunch and get her pulse. If she is leaning towards the fact that the official story is wrong, keep her talking about it. Bring her around to what she thinks may have happened differently. Ask for as much detail as you can get, even if you have to promise to keep it off the record."

Danielle's voice became terse, "Morris, you don't have to tell me how to interview or manipulate subjects. I've been doing this a long time."

"I'm sorry, Danielle. It's just that this case is that one for me."

"I get it, Morris. Just trust me. I won't fuck up."

"I trust you. Maybe she knows something Danielle. Maybe the Scalinis threatened to kill her too if she talked. You know, she's not blood Italian or Sicilian, her maiden name was Gerhardt. She married into the family.

"Interesting," Danielle said.

"Now, let's discuss tactics and safety," I said. "How about this? I'll be out in the parking lot before you get there. I'll stay as long as you are there. At some point, go to the ladies room and call me to let me know what she is saying."

"You don't have to, Morris. I'll be fine. If she gives up the candy store, you and MQ can talk to her later in an official capacity. But if you wanna sit out in the lot, it's up to you."

"Man, I wish I had a body wire I could put on you," I said, thinking like a detective.

"Why don't you get one from your tech guy?" Danielle suggested.

"Tech guy? You've been watching way too much CSI. Oakview doesn't even own a body wire. Having the equipment to do the job would, therefore, require that the job be done. As you can tell, Oakview is not in the business of doing the job."

"I'll take copious notes. Don't you worry Dr. Green."

"Thanks, Danielle. You're the best."

"Yes, I am."

# Chapter Seventy Four

I sat in the parking lot and watched as Danielle arrived and went inside. My information said that Cindy drove a new BMW coupe.

A few minutes passed and a black BMW 6, bearing personalized license plates, "FREECIN" pulled on the lot.

"Free or cold," I wondered.

She parked in the handicap space. I was just about to call her a lazy piece of shit, when she got out of the car. I peered through my binocs. Cindy Scalini was rail thin with a gray, pasty complexion. She had a pink breast cancer doo-rag on her head, incompletely covering her baldness. I'd seen them in the clinic, hundreds of times. Cindy was undergoing cancer therapy. She exited the car, and held onto the roof to steady herself, before slowly walking into the restaurant.

"Game on, "I said, fidgeting through a stack of CD's in the glove box. I settled on an old Lou Reed CD.

Twenty minutes later, in the middle of *Sweet Jane* my cell rang.

"Hey, it's Danielle. This is good, very good Morris. It's a fucking tragedy. It's Lady Macbeth. Out, damned spot, out I say! It's a fucking tragedy."

"I saw her go in the restaurant. Cancer?"

Danielle spoke as passionately as she had the day before. "She is terminally ill. She has breast cancer. And Morris, she came right out with it. No bullshitting for this old girl. She said she wanted to get this off her chest before she kicked the bucket. She said she never thought Craig did it. She said he loved those kids more than her daughter ever could. She knows her daughter was involved. She's spilling words out as quick as she can. She said Anthony's family went to great lengths to protect her daughter. It is much more than just the kid's deaths, Morris. It's got to do with the Bullpen, you know that gentlemen's club on the east side. We did a story on it years ago, prostitution, gambling. Anyway, she's rambling about a lot of stuff, I've been taking notes. I hated to leave her. It's like her thoughts are volcanic. They're jumbled and they sputter. But she wants peace, she wants the fucking spot of her grandchildren's blood off her hands. She wants that spot off her hands," Danielle stopped for a moment to take a breath.

I took the opportunity to talk. "She looks bad. I bet the cancer has metastasized. It's eating her up. She's all of 100 pounds. Maybe she has a couple months. I suspect her thought processes are scrambled from the chemo and radiation. I'm surprised she is still driving. We need to get what she has to say PDQ before she dies." I mulled over options. "I'm going to come in."

"Oh man, Morris. I don't know. What if she freaks out? Thinks she is being set up or something, I'm not so sure you should. Are you sure?"

Even though I wasn't, I told Danielle, "I have a good bedside manner. It'll be alright. Go back to her. I'll be right in."

I walked through the bar and into the restaurant, scanning side to side and front to rear. Nearly every table was occupied. Finally I found them at a table in the back of the restaurant. They were talking. I watched for a few moments. It was a give and take, but Cindy Scalini dominated the conversation. In that regard, Danielle was a better interviewer than most cops. She knew that you cannot get a story unless you shut up and let the other side do most of the talking. Too many detectives like to hear their own voices during interviews and never give the suspect enough opportunity to talk and confess.

I approached the table and both women looked up. Danielle stood up awkwardly, her knees banging the table. She grimaced. Her water glass toppled over and she quickly moved her tablet and began dabbing at the puddle with a napkin while I spoke.

"Hello. Mrs. Scalini, I'm Morris Green. I'm an associate of Danielle's and I helped put together this meeting. Would you mind if I joined you?"

Cindy motioned with a purple splotched, skeletal hand for me to sit down. She slid her glasses to the tip of her nose looking over them directly into my eyes.

"Yes, Morris Green, I know who you are," she said, spacing her words. "Detective, and Dr. Green. It's about time we spoke. How nice that the two of you run in the same circle. Please, have a seat, and call me Cindy."

"Ok, Cindy. Very nice to meet you." We shook hands and I sat down. Danielle finished wiping up and took her seat.

Mrs. Scalini spoke with the deep, raspy tone of a lifelong smoker. "Danielle was just beginning to tell me that there was a bit more to this than just a human interest story about my grandchildren."

A vegetable appetizer was on the table between us. She picked up a carrot stick and held it like a cigarette.

"So, what's up, doc?" She said mimicking Bugs Bunny. Despite her troubles, Cindy Scalini apparently had not entirely lost her sense of humor.

"I'm not sure how much Danielle has told you, or what you've told her, but…" Mrs. Scalini interrupted me.

"The name Morris Green was mentioned any number of times over the years. My husband, oh, sorry, my ex-husband, Anthony, may he have a heart attack and die, and my ex-father in law, Francis, may he never rest one moment in peace and burn in hell, they and their lawyers, spoke of you from time to time, and not out of respect or admiration. They talked about you, and your detective partner," she waved the carrot cigarette in the air in small circles. "He had a nickname? MP or MJ, something like that. I, I don't remember some things very well anymore I'm afraid."

"MQ," I said.

"Yes, that was it, MQ. Yes, MQ. I'll tell you what I do remember. I do recall that the both of you were a considerable source of aggravation to the Scalini men, a real pain in the ass, if you'll excuse my French. Good for you, Morris Green. I can't even begin to guess what they paid Chatham in legal fees to keep you from figuring it out."

"Figuring it out?" I asked.

"You know, my mind is, well. I've had a lot of chemo and radiation. I get blank spots, just like time was erased. I can't recall a year here or there, or sometimes what I did yesterday. It's weird."

"Those are very common side effects from the therapy," I said.

"So the doctors tell me, but what I do remember, is that you've spent a lot of time trying to figure out what happened the night my grandchildren were killed, and my ex just couldn't let you find out. I'm sure you suspect that what they said happened, isn't what happened." Cindy Scalini picked up a piece of sliced cucumber, dipped it in the ranch dressing and slowly chewed, struggling with a deep, throaty breath in between bites.

"Cindy, first, let me say that I am so sorry for your loss. It's been a long time, but I know the pain never leaves. It just gets muffled, subdued, by whatever is going on in our lives, but the pain, it's always there, like a river flowing underneath."

"That describes it rather nicely, Dr. Green, and I believe that the, the constant flow of that river of pressure and tension, of me not setting things right, resulted in the cancer. And so, I suppose, I will be the last..." Cindy paused again, and took a deep breath.

I could see she was using her accessory muscles to assist in capturing enough air.

"I'll be the last one to die from what happened that night, Dr. Green. The last one."

"Please, you can call me Morris," I reached across the table and took her brittle hand between mine. I figured she was maybe 7 or 8 years older than me. The cancer had aged her at least a decade. I stared at her face. She had a sallow complexion. Her forehead and cheeks were checkered with multiple coffee colored age spots. Her eyes were dark and sunken, the sclera jaundiced, punctuated with tiny red streaks. I guessed that whatever cancer she was being treated for, had spread to the liver.

"I understand Cindy, really I do. The deaths of your grandchildren have taken a good deal from me, too."

Tears dripped from Cindy's eyes. She dabbed at her cheeks with her napkin.

I began tearing up as well. "I'm sorry, Cindy. This case has been a physical and emotional tempest for me, too."

"Here guys," Danielle handed Cindy and I tissues from her purse.

Cindy was the first to call an end to the grief session. "Enough already. We have some business to discuss. I'm on a ticking clock here. Let's not waste any more time." She sipped water and picked up another carrot stick. "What is it that you think happened, Morris? And tell me the truth. Tell me what you think."

"I can tell you what I believe happened. And this isn't easy to say to you."

I wasn't about to tell her or Danielle that I knew exactly what happened. And that I had received the information directly from her dead descendants.

"I'm a tough old bird, Dr. Green. Remember, I was a Scalini. I can take it."

"I believe that the original investigation was botched intentionally and closed prematurely in order to lay guilt on Craig Wiley. The cold case investigation that MQ and I did was derailed to make sure no other conclusions were considered. And to derail it, it took someone who could reach out and touch someone in the federal government. Someone like the Scalinis," I paused assessing Cindy's reaction. There was none, no indication of surprise or anger. She limply held the carrot stick between her index and middle finger, and sat waiting for me to resume my story.

I sipped some water, and opened the bomb bay doors. "I think your daughter, possibly with the assistance of someone else in the house at the time, killed Taylor and Robbie and then murdered Craig, staging his death as a suicide. Your ex-husband and ex-father-in-law, acted to protect your daughter from prosecution because they considered her a liability.

"I believe that if forced to choose between her own survival and loyalty to the Scalini family, your daughter would choose herself. I think she knew something important. Something that was important enough about the Scalini business that they didn't want her in the position of cooperating with the police to save herself. I'm very sorry, but I believe your daughter may have killed her own kids, and may have had a hand in her husband's death too."

Cindy rested her elbows on top of the table. She put her carrot stick down and began massaging her temples with her fingertips. She sat quietly and continued to rub for a few seconds. She leaned back, sat upright and put her hands in her lap.

"Thank you for your honesty," She said, taking a deep gulp of air in broken strokes. She spoke as she exhaled choppily, "You, are...on track...to some degree," she coughed into her napkin and then continued.

"Chatham, Anthony, Francis, all of them, they knew she was involved somehow. They all knew. Julie has always been a problem and they knew she could be a worse problem, like you said. She knew certain things about the business. She'd done some work for Anthony and knew some things, financial information, business accounts, whatever. And there were other things," she paused, and decided against opening the wound of the exquisitely painful, personal memories of her ex-husband's sexual abuse of their daughter.

"It's always the money, Dr. Green. With the Scalinis, always the money. God damn them!" Cindy coughed several times and spit phlegm into her napkin.

She took another sip of water and resumed. "And Julie is a wild card. She never bought into the family code that goes with being a Scalini. Even after I got divorced from Tony, I still felt bound to certain rules and I couldn't, I wouldn't break them. And if I did, I would pay for it. Except, now, now that I'm dying, it doesn't matter. I'm just doing the right thing way too late." Cindy sipped more water.

"I'm so sorry, Cindy. You've explored all the treatment options? Experimental trials, alternative medicine?"

"Yes, Dr. Green. I have. I've had wonderful doctors. They've fought hard for me, but, I'm done. I am not fighting this anymore. My doctor is just keeping me comfortable. Bruce Hendershott, maybe you heard of him?"

"Dr. Hendershott is one of the best oncologists in town. You're in very good hands."

She sat up in her chair. "Enough about me and more about setting things straight."

"How much do you know about what really happened?" I asked.

"I know enough, more than enough. I found out by accident. You see, Julie stayed at our house the night it happened, and for a couple weeks after. The next day or a couple days after, I heard her on the phone. I don't remember exactly when, but I do remember this. I can't forget it. I wish I could." She sipped more water, licked her lips and continued. "Julie was on the phone in the den. She thought I had gone out, but I came back in the kitchen to get a grocery list or something and I heard her talking."

Cindy closed her eyes, her body melting into the chair. "She was talking to somebody. She was saying terrible things. Just terrible, awful things. I can hear her voice in my mind. I've heard it for all these years."

Cindy shook her head and wiped a few tears from her eyes. Her voice was cracking and weak, not much louder than a whisper. Danielle and I leaned towards her to hear.

"Julie was talking on the phone to this fella, James. She was telling him what happened. I don't know if you know, but James is a city cop. He's on Tony's payroll, has been for years. James Patrick."

"Yes, his name has popped up in the investigation," I said.

"Aside from being a crooked cop, he works with my nephew Vinny in some business things. They make movies, x-rated movies, and according to what Tony says, they make a lot of money. They use the place upstairs at the Bullpen for making the movies.

"Anyway, James and Julie were having an affair. Craig came home and caught them in the proverbial act, and that's what started it all that day. Apparently there was a fight and James smacked Craig in the head with something and knocked him out. He must have left the house before anything happened, because Julie was on the phone with him, telling him what had happened after he left. So he must not have known. She told him that Taylor and Robbie were kicking at her and screaming and fighting with her and calling her names, calling for their daddy to help them. Julie said she chased them into the garage. She said there was a knife in the workshop, a knife and a gun. She said everything went red. She kept saying everything went red James, everything went red."

Tears streamed down her cheeks but she continued. "Julie told him that somehow Taylor and Robbie were lying on the floor and there was blood everywhere. She told him that she didn't remember what happened. She just kept saying it was red all over, and then she was quiet for a minute. I guess James was talking or something. I was standing in the kitchen. I couldn't believe what I was hearing. And when she started talking again, she said she didn't know where she got the strength, but she dragged Craig to his chair and propped him up on a gun and pulled the trigger. She stopped talking again. I guess listening to James. And then she said that she took a shower, put the dogs in the car and drove down to a neighbor's house to call the police."

Cindy paused, cleared her throat, spit into her napkin, wiped her lips and continued. I noticed a pink tinge to the sputum.

"Morris, I was in shock. You can understand. I mean those kids were like mine. They were always at my house. Julie wasn't, well let's just say that my daughter wasn't interested in being a mother. And there I am, and I hear my own flesh and blood saying these things. I didn't know what to do. I left the house and drove for hours. By the time I came home, she was gone, out with Chatham's son, the one that's a cop in Oakview. I just came home and sat down in the kitchen and started crying."

I was processing Cindy's information, the red, the circle of fury just like Myra mentioned, and if Julie was explaining what happened to James on the phone, then Cindy was right. James must have left before the murders occurred. So he was probably not involved in the murders, but he had knowledge of just prior and after. We would definitely go shake his tree as MQ suggested.

Cindy continued, "When Tony came home, I told him. He went berserk, breaking things, expensive vases, knocking over statutes. He put his fist through my microwave door. It was bad. That's where Julie gets her temper, her God damn father. He was stomping around the house. He said she was a crazy fucking bitch and he was going to kill her. It was a good thing she was out with Chatham's son. Tony was going crazy. They were his grandkids, too, you know. I think he…" Cindy started sobbing.

Danielle and I remained quiet, allowing her the time and space she needed to finish.

She spoke through the tears, "I think he loved those kids more than he loved Julie. They were good children, not a spoiled brat, not like she was. Tony said he knew something was wrong. He knew she was lying. But he just didn't want to think that she, that she could do something like that.

Tony said he was going to beat her to death, kill her and be done with it. I called Francis and told him. He told me to keep Tony away from Julie. The old man came over. He and Tony went in the den. A little while later, Chatham came over. They talked for a while. They wouldn't let me in. When they came out, we all went into the kitchen," Cindy closed her eyes. She was almost panting.

"Cindy," I said. "Why don't we take a break."

Cindy Scalini opened her eyes and looked up, first at Danielle, then me. Her red, tear soaked eyes contained a steely focus. "No. No you need to hear this. And I need to tell it."

"Ok, hon, here," Danielle said offering fresh Kleenex.

"I can close my eyes and see it like it was today. Francis, Tony and I sat down at the kitchen table. Chatham stood, leaning against the counter. He looked bad, not at all like himself. Chatham had talked with Julie already so he knew something. That's right, he had already talked to her. He'd come over the next morning, the day after it happened and they spoke alone. And it was later that same day, the day after, that Julie was on the phone. Yea, that's it. I overheard Julie on the phone later the day after. Yea, so it must have been the day after it happened, November 23rd. Fuck this cancer fog bullshit!"

Danielle and I remained quiet as Cindy unloaded.

"Chatham stood there and said that based on what Julie had already told him that he was preparing a defense strategy. Francis said they had already worked out a plan. Tony was pissed off that they hadn't told him about it. Francis said he didn't tell him because he didn't want Tony going crazy, just like he was doing. Francis said it would be ok, that they would take care of it. The old man said, "Don't worry about it. We'll take care of it." He said for me, grandma Cindy, 'not to worry about it'."

Cindy leaned towards me. Her raspy whisper growled in anger. "Our own daughter killed her kids, our grandchildren, his great-grandchildren, and he tells me not to worry about it? I begged them to tell me what they were going to do. I figured they were going to kill Julie. I begged them not to do that. Francis pointed his finger at me and said, "We lost two, we won't lose three." But that was all he would tell me. That was when I decided I was going to get out of this family. It only took me several years, and two cancers, but I got out."

She leaned back in her chair and took a sip of ice tea along with several erratic breaths.

"Anyway, they eventually talked to James and got his story. James didn't have anything to do with the kids. If he hadn't been an associate of ours, I'm sure they would have killed him. I think they hurt him pretty good though, broke his leg or something like that."

Dishes and silverware clinked around us. Other conversations, certainly less traumatic, filled the spaces around the room. Cindy dabbed tiny beads of sweat from her forehead.

Danielle broke our silence. "Mrs. Scalini, I am so sorry, so sorry for your pain and your loss. The burden you've carried so long. Your story is so powerful, so intense. It is,"

"Oh honey, it's not over yet," Cindy said, her voice gaining some strength. "It turns out. Well, let's just say it's a small world. This James guy was one of the city cops the family used from time to time. Did I tell you that already? You know, they had cops on the take all over. Cops who gave Tony and his crew information on drugs and gambling, things like that. The city police, the county cops, all of them. Dr. Green, your police department too. So many Mayors and Police Chiefs with their hands out. The Scalinis had somebody everywhere. Everyone always wanted money and Scalinis paid well."

I nodded, "So we figured. They successfully stifled our investigation at every step. They have considerable reach." I looked over at Danielle who was typing up notes.

Cindy continued, "James was working with my nephew Vincent, at the Bull-pen, the club, a fancy restaurant the Scalinis had opened up across the river. James and Vinny were managing it, and apparently doing a good job. They were bringing in good money from it and some cockamamie movie company they had. I'm sorry, I told you that already. Anyway, the place was a restaurant, but behind the scenes it was all prostitution and drugs. Whores, and stealing and drugs and all that. Like I said, money, it was always the money."

"What did you say happened to James? They broke his legs?" I asked.

"Vincent vouched for him. The BullPen, those x-rated movies, they were good earners. Tony was satisfied that James didn't have anything to do with the kids, that he was in the wrong place, screwing the wrong girl at the wrong time. And it wasn't like they were sneaking around at a hotel. No not anything like that. Julie brought him into her home. She caused it all. So they left him alone and let him be. I mean except for the broken bones."

Cindy paused, as the waiter came by to refill teas and waters.

"I'm sorry Cindy," I said with as much forced empathy as I could muster for a dying woman married to the mob. "What a burden to be living under, it had to be overwhelming. Your choices were keep the secret and keep Julie, or lose, not only your grandchildren, but your daughter as well. Just a horrible situation to be in."

"Exactly. Exactly how it has been for me. But, it was different for Tony and Francis. Sure, they loved Julie, despite the problems that child caused along the way, but it was as much about keeping her quiet, as keeping her safe. Whatever you do, the Scalini's secrets must be kept, the secrets, Dr. Green, and the money.

Something bad happens, and the money could stop. I've got a short time left, and before I go, I have to do this. I have to tell someone this, something that I should have done long ago."

"Cindy, everything you've said supports what we thought may have happened. We developed a lot of circumstantial evidence that supported someone else in the house. We really needed hard, physical evidence to push the case. If there ever was any forensic evidence, the crooked cops involved in the original investigation destroyed it. We never came up with fingerprints, trace evidence, DNA, or anything to implicate Julie or a third party. We can't take this back to a prosecutor without some pretty significant physical evidence. Even with what you have to say, it still boils down to your word against theirs," I said, knowing that I sounded frustrated.

"That is where I think I can help," Cindy said.

"How so?" I asked as a quivering, tapping sensation, like a thick bug crawling under my shirt travelled from the base of my neck to my left shoulder blade. I pushed against the back of the chair hoping to displace the tapping ghost child. Grandma Cindy had no idea that Taylor and Robbie could very well be sitting at the next table.

Cindy continued, "The night I picked Julie up from the hospital she had a pair of jeans on, and a grey sweatshirt. I remember the sweatshirt was turned inside out. You know, I can close my eyes and still see her. Sitting on the couch, arms across her chest, rocking back and forth. I wish that is something the cancer drugs would have erased." Cindy put the napkin to her mouth and belched. She shook her head.

"I'm sorry. Talking about this has me feeling topsy-turvy. My stomach is upset, I guess the vegetables."

"We understand Cindy. Do you want to rest, take a break, talk tomorrow?" I asked.

"We both know that I may not have a tomorrow, Dr. Green."

"You'll have a tomorrow Cindy," I said.

"Oh, cut the bullshit. I just need to get this done Morris, so just listen."

"Yes ma'am." I nodded and glanced over at Danielle still taking notes.

"Julie stayed at our house for a while afterwards. One day I was doing laundry. That sweatshirt she had on, the one she had on that night, when she came home from the hospital, it was still inside out. So I turned it right side out. It was streaked with brown streaks. It was, well, I knew what it was. I'd done my fair share of laundry with blood, either Tony's or someone else's blood. I just knew it was blood. I don't know why, but I, I didn't wash it. Maybe because I knew it was probably from Taylor and Robbie, and holding it, I felt something, a connection. I don't know how to explain it. It sounds sick or bizarre doesn't it? Anyway, I threw it in a cupboard in the basement and kept it there. Occasionally I'd take it out and hold it.

"I still have the sweatshirt. Something told me to keep it all these years. I don't know what or why, Morris. I think my daughter will have a problem explaining how the blood of her children and her husband came to be on her clothes. I guess I kept it for you, Morris. I've watched enough of those cop shows. This ought to be the kind of evidence you need. If you'll follow me to my apartment, you can have it."

A steady, vibrating, electric hum accompanied the bug crawling on my shoulder. I looked at the empty table next to us and winked.

Danielle had more than a human interest story to write. This was turning into a bastardized version of the Sopranos on CSI. We walked Cindy to her car. Danielle gave her a hug and went to her office to start typing up her story. I followed the black BMW.

# Chapter Seventy Five

As I followed Cindy through the afternoon traffic, my mind processed what led us here.

"Taylor and Robbie started their quest for justice and peace with their Grandma. They told her to keep the sweatshirt, to do something with it when the time was right, to help them. Cindy had heard them. She secured the clothing like an insect trapped in amber for this moment. Maybe the children had been responsible for Lawrence's bowling bag too."

Cindy was living in a rehabbed loft building, not far from the hospital complex where she had been receiving her treatment for the past 18 months. It was probably easier to live close, than to have to drive in for her treatment.

Cindy pulled into her garage. I parked on the street, fed the credit card parking meter and waited in the vestibule as a security guard intently watched Judge Judy. We rode up the elevator to the ninth floor. I recalled that this building had been a shoe manufacturing company before it had become trendy to live down here. I hadn't had the opportunity to visit anyone in these newly renovated buildings and was surprised by how nice they were.

"I'm sorry for the clutter," she said as we walked in. "I bought one of the smaller models, only a one bedroom. Not a lot of storage space for things. I bought new furniture and tried to do a little decorating. The rooms are decent sized, not anywhere near what I had at the house. But I didn't think I would be entertaining and I didn't think I would be staying all that long."

The entryway led to a large living room, at least 15 feet wide and twenty feet deep. Our shoes clopped on the dark hand scraped hardwood floors. A glossy white tin ceiling and ornate crown molding flowed from the living room to dining room and kitchen. I noticed an oxygen generator between a wooden, marble topped end-table and a large, overstuffed, white leather couch.

"She's on home $0^2$ Metastasis to the lungs maybe," I thought. "She's right. Her clock is ticking fast."

Cindy said she would just be a minute and disappeared down a hallway past the dining area. I sat on the couch, sifting comfortably into the soft cushions which wafted an exquisite leather smell.

She returned with a paper grocery sack. The top was folded over and stapled. Large handwritten letters in black marker read, "Cindy". She sat down next to me, pulled a nasal canula over her head, and turned the machine on. Her frail shape made no more of an impression into the deep cushions than a shadow.

"I am a little short of breath with all the activity today. I don't usually go out much, but I had a feeling when Ms. Nicastro called that I should talk to her, and look where that led. I'm supposed to take oxygen with me, but it really is too much of a hassle at this point. Damn little bottle and this plastic tubing just doesn't go with any of my outfits," she said with a wry smile putting the nasal prongs in position and taking a few deep breaths.

We chatted for a few minutes about her condition and care.

"Bruce Hendershott and his staff are the best with clinical trials. They've taken excellent care of some of our people from the clinic," I said offering encouragement.

Cindy agreed. "Dr. Hendershott is a genuinely nice man. We've been through a number of surgical procedures, radiation, chemo, chemo-endocrine therapy and an investigational drug trial together. Nothing put me in remission. It was really hard for him to tell me we had exhausted all of our treatment options."

Returning to the task at hand, Cindy handed the bag to me. "Here's the sweatshirt. Except for occasionally holding this bag for a strange feeling of comfort, it is the same as it was when I folded it and put it in here. I know you will do the right thing with this."

I took the bag and immediately was jazzed with another one of those comfortable, warm, charged hums of energy that traveled from my hands to my spine. The children were pleased.

"What do you think will happen if we are able to get Julie charged with the murders?" I asked.

"You mean, what will the Scalinis do? What will Tony do?

"Yes. If it was so important to keep her quiet then, will he still feel the same way? Or are they estranged? What can we expect?" I asked.

"They aren't estranged, per se. Tony still talks to her now and then and, of course, sends her money. He's paid for Spencer Newsham to go out to LA and take care of any problems she has with her temper or finances. Her usual crap. A little while after the dust settled and Julie moved away, Tony and I got divorced. It wasn't an easy time, but I just couldn't live like that anymore, knowing what I knew. And then I got sick. I haven't seen much of Tony or anyone else for that matter. After the old man died, he and his brother, Frank, that's Francis Jr., that's Vinny's father, they still run the family business, but I can tell you, it's different. Frank has always been a little on the slow side, so most of the important business decisions are handled by Tony, and Tony, although he's a hothead and a…" she paused, "Let's just say Tony's no dummy when it comes to business. Over the years, he's gotten them into real estate, the stock market, things like that. The restaurant, the club, the Bullpen was his idea. It's still a going concern, but I understand it's not as much of a part of their portfolio as it was back then. They probably still have some girls working out of there, I suppose."

"The heyday of organized crime and mafia strength is in the past," I said. "Once they started breaking their Omerta and started testifying against each other it seems like they lost steam."

"Don't I know. They were mad as hell when all that Sammy the Bull and Gotti crap was going on," Cindy said. "Just so you know, Dr. Green," she inhaled deeply several more times through her nose for the oxygen and pulled off the canula. "Frank Jr. lives in Reno. I think because he has some health issues, asthma maybe. And that little shit Vinny, from what I hear, he and James are making even better money with their movie company. But I'm rambling, sorry. To answer your question, Tony will not want Julie sitting across the table from any prosecutors. I can tell you that. And it's anybody's guess what the Scalinis will do to keep that from happening."

"We want Julie to face trial, face the consequences, justice to be served," I said, to appease my ghosts.

Cindy looked into my face with a painful resolve. "It's a terrible thing for a mother to say, but I do, too, Morris. I do too." Her shoulders collapsed and it looked as if tears were on the way. Cindy pursed her lips, inhaled deeply through her nose, sat up and charged on. "It's the hardest thing I ever had to not do then, and it's the hardest thing I have to do now. It's the only way at this point."

"I understand."

Cindy scooted to the edge of the couch and pointed a finger at me, "I don't need to tell you, these are vile, mean, violent men. I heard discussions about what to do with you and your partner when you were stirring the pot, looking into it again." Cindy pulled a cigarette and lighter from her pocket and lit up. She took a deep draw and held it in.

"When you were talking to all of Julie and Craig's friends, they had a meeting about you. And I know every one of their friends would have said Craig would never harm his kids. They all would have said what a hothead and piss poor mother Julie was. I know that. And it hurt me. My daughter," Cindy's voice trailed off to a whisper, "What did I do wrong. How did I fail to teach her what it takes to be a mother?" Her voice trailed off as she said, "That fucking Tony."

We sat in silence as the Oxygen generator whirred. I let the quiet go on.

Cindy resumed talking as the haze of cigarette smoke and the past lifted. "And then when you all were working with the FBI. My God, how Tony and Frank Jr. talked. They wanted you and your partner both dead. They wanted to arrange a damn assassination. But they knew better from the last time, the Estrilla thing. You knew about that right? That you were set up."

Confirmation of the known, as MQ would say.

"We suspected, but like your grandchildren's murders, we could never prove it."

"At the time, I was occupied with what happened, the funeral, taking care of Julie," Cindy said, "but later, when the old man learned that Frank Jr. and Tony had sent those Mexicans to kill you and your partner, over what? Over drugs? He sat in my kitchen and read them the damn riot act. 'Omicidio due poliziotti durante attività stupid!' Which means, murdering two cops during a business deal is fucking stupid. If anything, Francis Scalini was a shrewd old man." She cocked her head to the side, "He was basically saying that if you're going to do it, don't do it during our business. Make it look like an accident. But anyway, as you know, they had people take care of the Mexican problem, as he called it. People got paid off to make sure nothing became of it." Cindy put out her cigarette and looped the canula back over her head. "So Frank Jr. and Tony were smarter this second time around and were able to beat you guys without even having to kill you."

"Well, I guess we're grateful for Francis's intervention in this case," I said. "But, even without murdering MQ and me, they were able to hinder our progress every step of the way."

"You were playing against a stacked deck. There was no way you could win. They had everyone in their pocket including your Chief, Chatham's boy, Will. Yea, Will, Will, that's his name. And they had someone at the FBI in Washington DC. Hell, they even had prosecutors at the federal building on the take."

I clutched the sweatshirt bag, and nodded my head, "So we figured."

"Tony always said that your Chief had no balls, and that he was some kind of a nutcase. He said the guy would never take a dime, but he took information instead. Things which made his department look good. Like if Frank Jr. had guys selling a lot of coke or whatever, and there was someone else selling, competition to his guys, whoever it was, they would arrange with your Chief, or another Chief, for the guy to get arrested with a load. No more competition.

"Oakview had that problem with those black gang kids coming into town and selling crack, shooting up the place, spray painting everything. Remember those days? Well, how do you think your department made all those arrests? Tony was feeding the Chief information on where the guys with the most drugs and money were, and having one of Chatham's boys working at Oakview and having James in the city made it easier to do business."

"I hope Chief Montileone and Will Newsham will have a lot of explaining to do in the very near future," I added and wondered whether some of my narcotics cases had their genesis in a leak from the Scalinis.

"Chatham's youngest boy, the one at Oakview police, Will, he was a real piece of work that one," she said. "Chatham told your Chief to put Will on my kid's case. Will first showed up at our house, I think first time he showed up was the night Julie did the TV interview. Chatham was there that night too. He told the TV person what to ask, and she did it. I guess she was in the Scalini pocket too. After the TV people left, he gave Will instructions on what to do next. I heard him talking. Will was supposed to make it appear that Julie was cooperating completely, that she was nothing more than an innocent victim in this thing. I remember him saying, 'Will, keep it simple, 'keep it simple.' It was all supposed to be short and sweet. And Chatham said the plan was to show Julie as a victim. Poor Julie. Poor, poor Julie.

"But, Will spent an awful lot of time with her. It sure wasn't short, but it may have been sweet. He came over and picked her up a couple of times late in the evening and they stayed out for hours. I wasn't sleeping at all, as you can understand. I knew when they came back. And it was late or early the next morning. I didn't know what to think, and I didn't like what I was thinking. Because they came back and they would be joking and laughing. I mean this was right afterwards, Morris. Right after!"

"You thought they were having an affair?"

"Knowing what I know now, yea. She was with James, why not Chatham's son. She was probably using him for something. She was a user. It makes me sick to think about it. Screwing some fat cop while your babies…" Cindy took a few staccato breaths and rubbed tears from the corners of her eyes. "I'm sorry. I get upset pretty easily nowadays. The medicine, I think. He's giving me a new anti-depressant and sometimes it makes me, edgy? Or sadder I think. Or maybe it's just because I'm soon to die, but I guess I should talk to my doctor about this new medicine."

"You really should," I said. "Some of those new norepinephrine and serotonin reuptake inhibitors are unpredictable. I hear the same thing from my patients. Give Bruce a call. He'll get something for you."

"Yea. I will call him later today," she said, hugging a satin pillow.

"So, what happened next, Cindy?" I asked, "Will and Julie are spending too much time together. Please go on."

"Will got in trouble with his father is what happened next. Will and Chatham were over at our house a couple days after. Or maybe the next day. They were meeting about Julie and what to do. I don't know. Maybe it was the next week. I don't remember for sure. But Will gave his dad these papers he had Julie write. I mean it was several pages long. Something like that. Chatham looked at the stack of pages and shook his head and said something like, 'This is short and sweet? This is simple?' And Will said something like he was just trying to do what detectives do, investigate and get statements, do interviews. You have to know Chatham Newsham. He was always a gentleman. Classy, that's the best way to describe him. He goes way back with the old man. I mean 30 years or more. Unlike my ex-father-in-law, Chatham is really a nice man. Classy, in his suits and his speech. A class act that Chatham.

"Chatham hardly ever raised his voice. He didn't cuss very often either, but he did that time. He said something like, 'God dammit, Will. Detectives do those things when they want to solve a crime. We don't want to solve this one! Get rid of all of this bullshit! And don't bother doing anything else. Don't do another God damned thing! Please.' I could tell it hurt Will's feelings, and I don't think he did do anything else on the case because he never came back to the house to see Julie after that.

"That explains a lot," I said.

"Oh, and so you know, Chatham also has a son somewhere in Washington with the Customs department or State Department. These are connected, power-ful, powerful men Morris. I wouldn't play this cheap."

"And we won't. Cindy, would you be willing to give a statement? We could do it surreptitiously, no one would know. We could offer you some protection if you feel you may need it."

Cindy closed her eyes, her lips pursed slightly. She squeezed the pillow.

I immediately realized that what I had just said was totally inane. Her death from cancer was racing towards her like a Tennessee Moonshiner's Ford. What did it matter if a Scalini bullet got there first? Nonsense Morris, you idiot.

"I'm sorry, Cindy, force of habit. Too many years working witnesses as a detective. Thank you for your help and your courage. I hope the coming months are easy for you. If there is anything I can do, please let me know." I wrote my cell phone number on the back of one of my clinic cards. "Call me if you need to talk."

"I may just do that, Morris Green. And you call me and let me know your progress."

"I promise I will."

# Chapter Seventy Six

I was cautiously optimistic as I strode past Cindy's doorman, out onto the street carrying the grocery bag. This was the first piece of physical evidence that could potentially put blood on Julie Wiley's hands. I drove to the clinic.

I called MQ's cell, finding him at home. "Kenneth, I just met with Cindy Scalini."

"I just met with the guy who is going to charge me $3,200.00 for a new furnace. Three grand, Doc. I guess I have to pillage my 401K or the lovely Mrs. Quinn and I wear our coats inside all winter."

"Kenneth, did you hear me? I just met with Cindy Scalini."

"Of course I did. What did the mobster princess have to say?" His tone still a bucket of worry over the price of HVAC.

I outlined the meeting with Danielle, Cindy Scalini and the receipt of the bloody sweatshirt.

"Damn, Doc! Her story is compelling. Confirmation of the known my friend. Some really terrific hearsay. Maybe we can time it right and get a dying declaration from her just as the Grim Reaper makes his appearance."

"Your compassion is overwhelming, Sol."

"Compassion is for you clinician healers. In the meantime we use our forensic skills. We use the video of her wearing that sweatshirt during the interview with Elwyn and Sgt. Himmler to hopefully make a positive identification, an ID that the sweatshirt she wore during the interview, and the one you got from Mrs. Scalini, are one and the same. I would think that any good forensic photo lab can probably do a comparison of unique characteristics, stitching, stains, coloring, et cetera, that maybe there will be enough that they can say the sweater in the video and the sweater we have are probably the same. Have you heard me so far, Doc?"

"Yes, I've heard one hopefully, two probablies and a maybe. You're a real ray of sunshine," I said, my glass rapidly becoming less than half full.

"May I remind you that the last time we got overly excited about our discoveries, all we ended up with was a hangover."

"If they find her hair on it, we'd have some real grit," I said.

MQ countered like a defense attorney. "Mrs. Wiley's counsel, if it ever got to that, could say that their client's hair could have been transferred to the clothing when Cindy did Julie's laundry. And why would she take a shower, and put back on the bloody sweatshirt that she just took off? It makes no sense, Morris."

"I was wondering the same thing. Only explanation I can think of is that maybe when she pulled it off, it was inside out, and when she put it on, in a big hurry, she wasn't paying attention. Either that or it is all part of the ghost children's master plan. In any event, there is no explaining away how the children's blood and the father's blood ended up on the sweatshirt unless it was worn by the killer."

"Agreed. If their blood is on the sweatshirt, that would be a harder sell," MQ said.

How about touch DNA, epithelial DNA? They used it in the Ramsey case."

"Anyone go to jail for the Ramsey case, doc?"

"Right you are, Sol."

"In any event, we need to get that sweatshirt to a lab," he said.

"Back to the state lab?" I asked.

MQ didn't respond to the lab question. He went off on a rant.

"That incompetent ass-wipe Montileone. I guess he assuaged his conscience that taking information from organized crime was somehow less onerous and criminal than taking money. That the quality arrests and media coverage, that made his city look good, secured his job. What a piece of fuck. Fuck him and Newsham."

I heard heavy breaths interspersed between his sentences. He was getting worked up.

"We have got to get those fuckers, doc. They have to pay. For you, for Tom Reynolds, for those kids. They have to go down. And I especially appreciate how we owe our lives to Francis Scalini. Fuck him, too. I'll enjoy the day when I can express my gratitude at his sentencing," MQ said.

"No shit, Murph. We were pretty close to getting executed. And by the way, old man Scalini is dead."

"We can go piss on his grave then. To hell with them all, the whole coterie of criminals."

"Murph, the Scalini's reach extends pretty far. How do you want to handle this? Who can we go to?"

I listened to more heavy breathing. MQ was considering options. He finally spoke. "We need a special prosecutor that cannot be bought and paid for by the Scalinis," he said. "Someone who is willing and able to do the heavy lifting, cut the Gordian knot. Someone who will find a secure lab and pay for the forensic testing. Before it's all over, I want the FBI Behavioral Unit to lose some of its esteemed faculty to a federal penitentiary."

"Quite a wish list," I added.

He continued, "Ironic, don't you think, doc? The corpulent fuck, Lawrence. He was right after all. They probably did kill him."

"Seems that way doesn't it, Kenneth?"

"It does. We cannot take our labyrinthian debacle to the US Attorney's office. Who knows how many of them the Scalinis own. Doc, I would settle for a county prosecutor and a grand jury. Do you have anyone you trust down there?"

"I worked pretty closely with Karen Flavin at the county prosecuting attorney's office. She was the PA that handled a lot of our drug cases. I think she's still at the prosecutor's office."

"Yea, she's still there," MQ said. "She's a lifer, government employee. I saw her in tennis shoes and a business suit walking around the courthouse building not too long ago. Not that I can talk, but she's quite plenitudinous. I guess she was doing the lunchtime exercise and diet routine. Last I heard she was assigned the grand jury and high profile trials now."

"I don't know if you remember, MQ, but I talked to her once about this case back when we had Dr. Rajeda saying the blood spatters were all wrong for Craig to be considered the suspect. She was interested, but after the FBI fucked us, she said the PA's office wouldn't touch it."

"A shining example of motivation by a career employee of a governmental entity," MQ said.

"Karen's a tough prosecutor, I think her interest would be renewed with the additional evidence we have. I remember she put a guy away for life on a murder case without a victim's body."

"Shit, doc, we've got bodies, we've got story tellers, we've got video, letters, CDs, bowling bags. Let's pull 'All right Karen' into our misery."

Karen Flavin had earned the nickname of 'All right Karen' due to her overuse of the words. Karen uses 'all right' in every fifth or sixth sentence. A few years ago, she had a smoking hot body and the 'All right Karen' was a double entendre. More than just a few of her defendants picked up on it and called her "AK" as in the deadly AK-47, fine assault rifle, emphasis on the fine ass.

"I'll give 'All right Karen' a call and set something up. If that doesn't pan out, I guess we could try John Kaltenbrook at the US Attorney's office. He's been prosecuting organized crime cases for a long time and is considered squeaky clean. It's an inheritance with him. His dad was a judge who prosecuted more than one wise guy," I said.

"Fuck the feds. They had their chance with this. We'll get Julie Wiley and Will Newsham indicted by the county grand jury. If Karen wants to bang her head against the federal government wall, that will be her problem," MQ said.

# Chapter Seventy Seven

I called Karen Flavin the next morning and asked her if she had some time available. I was deliberately sketchy.

"I usually have lunch at Panama Jacks, about a mile away from the office. I can get my walk in and eat," she said.

We met at Panama's, a decent soup and sandwich shop. I ordered chili, Karen had a bowl of chicken noodle soup and a salad. Even with a few extra pounds, AK was still a delightfully attractive 40ish professional. She had indigo black, shoulder length hair that was pulled back in a ponytail. I remembered she usually wore it down for court. I was immediately drawn to those oval, smoky grey eyes that hinted of her Asian heritage. AK had Liz Taylor symmetry of her facial features with thick, Angelina Jolie lips and a naturally clear and vibrant complexion. She rarely used makeup except for lipstick. Today her lips were glossy pink.

"Morris, I kind of lost track of you after the shooting, after you left narcotics. What's been going on?"

"Working at the PD, working at the clinic. Same old. And I hear you're doing grand jury and the big cases."

"I've outlasted everyone who moved on to the private firms to make the big bucks. Enough bullshit. All right, so why so cagey about what you want to talk about, Morris?"

"How much do you remember about that case involving the two kids who were murdered in Oakview, allegedly by their father?"

"Hmm, all right, yea. Murder-Suicide. You had Rajeda saying something about the blood spatter being wrong and then the FBI crapped on it. I remember that much."

I leaned forward and lowered my voice. "Karen, here's the thing. We've recently discovered new evidence that was intentionally withheld from the light of day in the initial investigation. This evidence adds significant weight to our theory that the mother was involved in the murders. We have a heretofore, never seen video, of an interview between Oakview detectives and Mrs. Wiley on the night of the murders in which she is caught in a number of lies. She does not look like a woman who was attacked by her husband. We have her written statement which is similarly inconsistent and was never included in the original investigative file. We have a computer disc that indicates someone else may have been in the house at the time of the murders. We've spoken to someone who has alleged that two ranking members of my department, the Newsham Law Firm, a cop from the city and members of the Scalini organized crime family intentionally hid this evidence and misdirected the original investigation and also as well as our FBI cold case. This someone said that one of the Newsham's works for a federal agency in DC and was able to influence the BAU's analysis."

"Holy corruption!" Karen said.

"We've recently received some blood stained clothing that we know the mother wore the night of the murders. She can be seen wearing it during the interview. We'll have to have it analyzed for DNA and trace, but we expect that the blood will be that of the children and possibly the husband. How does she explain that away? We also received a missing GSR test kit which needs comparison to the ammunition used in the murders. We now have a lot of puzzle pieces that we didn't have back then. If I've peaked your interest, I can explain it in detail."

"All right, yes, I'm officially peaked, Morris. Any time you mention putting a case on the Scalinis or Newshams, every prosecutor I know gets a hard-on. The Scalinis have never been dinged badly, and everyone hates the friggin' Newsham Law Firm. John will certainly want to know." Karen said as she wiped a drop of soup from her chin.

"We don't want anyone from the feds involved at this point. Can you understand why?"

"John Kaltenbrook is a good egg Morris," she slurped in some soup. "He's still working organized crime and he's the resident expert. I would trust him if I were you. But, all right, we can bring him in later if you want."

"I don't know if it hit your news radar, but an Oakview cop drove off Bluff road and died. Did you hear about it?"

"All right, yea. A couple Oakview guys were in for a warrant and they were talking about it. Lawrence Johnson, right?"

"Correct. He wrote a letter to me and gave it to his son for safekeeping in the event of his untimely or suspicious demise. The letter directed me to a locker which contained most of the missing evidence. In his letter, he described the Wiley murder cover-up and he implicated Will Newsham from my department, the Newsham Law Firm, James Patrick, a city cop and the Scalinis."

"All right!" Karen said. "Organized crime, murder and messages from the dead. I'm freaking peaking now. Wait a minute, Morris. Then is Lawrence Johnson the source who told you about the Scalini's ability to influence the feds?"

"No, we have two sources of new information. One dead, one alive." I spent the next thirty minutes talking nearly non-stop, covering the Wiley saga from the beginning to yesterday's meeting with Cindy Scalini. I left out Myra Sutherland, the voices and anything else pertaining to my personal messages from the hinterland.

"Listen, AK, because the integrity of this case has been compromised so many times at so many levels, I'd like you to keep this information confidential. The need to know rule applies here."

"All right, but we need to go back to my office and put together a strategy, all right? This has huge implications and complications. We definitely need Dan Block in on this."

"Didn't I read a story that your boss was going to retire in the middle of his term? Some controversy about his affair with someone in the county's accounting office?"

"It was a real mess for sure. Dan started diddling with a perky, 26-year-old auditor named Brittany, working in the collector's office. She suddenly moved to Ohio when the shit hit the fan. He's probably going to get divorced over it. All right, so Dan decided at the last minute to stay for the rest of his term. The scandal wasn't about the affair as much as it was about something funny with the finances in the collector's office. Brittany wasn't involved in any of the irregularities. The investigation determined Dan wasn't taking anything from the collector's office other than Brittany's underwear, and the accounting practices were determined to be sloppy all right, but nothing criminal. Everyone in the office was hoping Dan would retire so some fresh blood could take over. I was even mentioned as a possibility. Imagine that Morris, AK Flavin as the county prosecuting attorney."

"You'd be great Karen."

"Thanks, but, Dan is still here, and I'm not going to be able to get what I need to get done on your case, a case with this much baggage, without him. He'll need to be in on this. He thinks with his dick half the time, but we can't hold that against him now can we, Morris?" She winked one of those devastating eyes. "Dan's a good prosecutor and I trust him."

"Just him then," I said with reluctance.

"So, Morris, are you still separated, divorced or re-married? Did Mrs. Green go by the wayside like Mr. Flavin?"

"Yea, I fucked that up. We divorced long ago. She got the house. I got an apartment, weekend dad duties, child support, the whole megilla. It was really rough on them, especially after the shooting. Anyway, my kids are older and Sheila and I get along ok for the most part. What happened to your hubby, Gary, wasn't it?"

"If you remember, he was a trader. He landed a gig with a New York brokerage firm and chased that dream of big money, all right. All the way to floor of the New York Stock Exchange. I wasn't willing to move. He's been gone about 3 years." She reached across the table and picked up one of my hands. "So maybe we can have dinner sometime? At least now we don't have to look over our shoulders."

"We had some fun didn't we, AK?"

She smiled broadly. "Yes we did. We definitely did."

"Let's get some business done before pleasure. How about that counselor?"

"Certainly, Dr. Green. How soon can you and MQ make it down to my office?"

"I'll call him and see if he's available."

"All right," Karen flipped through the calendar on her Blackberry. "Be in my office tomorrow at 3:00pm."

# Chapter Seventy Eight

MQ and I spent the afternoon at the prosecuting attorney's office discussing the case with AK and county prosecuting Attorney Dan Block in a large conference room. The room was handsomely furnished with a massive teak table surrounded by high back, worn, brown leather chairs.

Dan Block fit the name. A former All-American linebacker from Penn State, even in his early 60's, he has remained a cinderblock of muscle and gristle in a tailored, three-piece, dark brown suit, complete with gold railroad pocket watch. His bulk completely filled the chair at the head of the table.

We brought copies of some of the more recent and pertinent reports in an accordion file and went over the entire case in a chronological fashion. I provided a historical perspective of the public corruption beginning with the Estrilla narcotics caper in which Tom Reynolds and I were targeted for assassination.

Dan remembered the case. "I always thought that there was more to it than just a dope deal gone bad. We'll dust that one off for a second look, Morris." He looked at Karen. She wrote on her legal pad.

MQ went into a discussion of the political maneuvering that resulted in the current Oakview PD staffing structure. He spent a little too much time complaining about how this case fucked us out of the bureau and put him in his current position as midnight shift babysitter. I told them how we had contacted Cindy Scalini using a ruse involving Danielle Nicastro's crime story.

Dan continued, "This sure demonstrates the historical scope of the problem at your department. Years of police corruption, organized crime infiltration. Good God. The fact that one of the premier divisions of the FBI, the BAU and the State Department have been compromised! Incredible, just incredible."

Karen took off her glasses and looked at Dan and then directly at me, "All right, now about Ms. Nicastro. We want to keep this low profile, so no media involvement. All right?"

"Sure. Danielle is an asset, not a liability," I said. "She'll go along with whatever we decide, as long as we promise she can have the story before her competition."

"That's fine. You all right with that, Dan?" Karen asked and Dan nodded.

Dan stroked an imaginary goatee and smirked. "I've had quite enough with the press over the past few months. Morris, you keep Nicastro in line."

I nodded.

Dan and Karen discussed the possibility of the time bars regarding the statute of limitations on the offenses other than murder, and whether or not the federal system had jurisdiction over the murders if they were part of an organized crime investigation.

Dan reiterated the limitations of the case, "We have a real paucity of direct evidence linking Mrs. Wiley to the murders. The chance of making her for the murders is not going to be a cake walk. As far as the sweatshirt, I recommend we use an independent laboratory, such as one of the regional forensic labs. Nothing should go to a county or state lab at this point. Agreed?"

Everyone in the room nodded heads.

Karen had been continually taking notes on a yellow legal pad during the discussion. She had filled three pages with scribbled lawyerese and was working on a fourth.

"Where is the sweatshirt now?" she asked.

"I've got it locked up in my office at the clinic."

"Morris, I'll contact the forensic lab and have one of my staff investigators pick up the sweatshirt tomorrow. When is a good time?" Dan asked.

MQ interrupted, "How about you just let us know where the lab is and Morris and I will take it there. Let's not trust a critical piece of evidence to a staffer, huh, Dan?" His tone was accusatory and implied the obvious. Could Dan Block, and by extension his staff, be trusted?

The muscles on Dan's geometric jaw tightened at the inference. "I'll have you know, Sgt. Murphy," he began, as AK interrupted. "I'll take it myself, all right?" she said. "Problem solved."

Karen changed subjects to lower the tension. She said that she had done some research on the Scalini organization before we arrived. She flipped pages on her legal pad and started a narration. "The Scalinis underwent a little reorg after the elder Francis Scalini died. Frank Jr. inherited the reins and moved to

Reno. Anthony remained here and invested heavily in real estate, the stock market, hedge funds et.cetera, with considerable success. He still has the construction and waste management businesses all over the state. And we still suspect they are involved in money laundering, prostitution and drug trafficking, but the radar pings are significantly less here. The Bullpen continues to remain open as a restaurant and club, and Anthony has a strong hand over the operation that is managed by Vincent Scalini, Frank Junior's son. Despite a number of search warrants over the years, the government was never able to shut down the Bullpen for any length of time. All right, an occasional arrest for promoting prostitution. And those were usually just one of the hired hands." Karen looked up smiling, "No pun intended." She continued, "No one of any stature in the organization was ever officially charged. The prostitutes may still be working there all right, but no real complaints have come in for a year or so. Vinny Scalini and your law enforcement peer, James Patrick have been producing porn flicks for years out of there. A few years ago, there were rumors about snuff films, but we never could determine any truth to it. Once again, no validated complaints, no arrests."

Dan continued, "Our guess is that the Scalinis were, or are, still funneling money through the restaurant, but not any large sums. We've never been notified by anyone from our local banking institutions that they've made deposits over ten grand. They're doing something, just under the radar."

"They've learned how to insulate themselves and avoid scrutiny," Karen added. "And we always suspected that high up, some politically connected folks were running interference for them, someone that offered protection. And now we know that is probably true. All right, in any event, none of the Scalinis have ever done serious jail time."

Dan added. "At some point, we may need to bring in the local FBI for surveillance, wire taps, the usual menu."

"And when you bring the feds in, you bring in more opportunity for them to fuck this up again," MQ warned.

"Agreed. For now, let's keep this between the four of us," Dan said. "Karen and I need your files, all the information, evidence, the documents sent to the NCAVC, all of it. When can you put that together?"

"We'll start working on it tomorrow," I said. "However, we are unable to just waltz into the evidence locker and case file room at Oakview to gather what we need. Fortunately, we do have copies of nearly everything, which we will have to copy for you. Give us a week or so and we should be able to put it together."

MQ and I spun through the revolving door at the Prosecuting Attorney's Office. It was early evening. It had cooled off considerably since we had gone inside. The flags in front of the building were whipping back and forth from the wind.

"I hate this weather. Did I tell you I had to drop three grand on a new furnace?" MQ stuck his hands in his jacket pockets pulling his coat tightly around the tree trunk of his torso.

"So you said. It's always something, isn't it, Kenneth?"

"Murders and furnaces, ghosts and gout, all the same. What is it in Yiddish rabbi? Tsuris?" MQ asked.

"Yep. You are correct Sol. Trouble, tzuris, follows us like a new puppy."

"AK is looking better," MQ said. "She's lost some weight. I noticed she was eye fucking you a few times in there."

"She was not."

"You looked back, too, your testosterone levels were showing, doc."

Sol was right. The detective partner mind meld doesn't only find itself in operation during interrogations.

"Well, we might have dinner sometime," I said and we both chuckled. It felt good to laugh at something.

"You know, if any of this leaks out from AK's office we'll have a three ring circus on our hands. Geraldo, Dan Abrams, Nancy Grace and Greta Van Susternen will be all over this like the fucking Caycee Anthony or Trayvon Martin case. TV vans will be parked in front of Cindy Scalini's building, at the Newsham's law firm, at Oakview. Microphones will be stuck in Chief Montileone's face. Like ants on dropped lollipop, they'll be on us both. They'll swarm at the PD and they'll find you at the clinic. TV vans will be parked on our street for months until the case is adjudicated. I hope Dan Block is in control of his house," MQ said.

"So saith Sol."

# Chapter Seventy Nine

James knew, as soon as he landed on the street after bailing from Lawrence's truck. The crack he felt, and heard, as he hit the ground, was confirmation enough that he'd broken some ribs. Every deep breath and sudden movement was like a burning knife grinding in his chest wall. More pain, courtesy of Julie Wiley.

He hadn't left his house since killing Lawrence, except to go to the corner liquor store for beer, and after placing a call to a pill mill doctor he knew, to the drug store to pick up a prescription for Vicodin. He had only slept the past couple of nights because he took four pills and drank a couple beers before bed. He was able to get about 5 hours of sleep each night before the pain returned.

James wasn't quite awake when his cell phone rang. Vinny Scalini was on the other end.

"What are you doing? Where you been?" Vinny spoke rapidly. "I've been trying to get hold of you. I don't know how many voicemails I left you, you prick."

"Sorry Vinny. I lost my phone. Just found it under the couch."

"I just got back in town after visiting pop in Reno. I checked in at the club and no one's seen you. Where the fuck you been?"

"I'm at fucking home, Vinny. I broke my ribs. You saw me hit the ground when I let go of Lawrence's steering wheel. I can't hardly move. What the fuck do you want?"

"We got a problem," Vinny said.

"I don't give a fuck, Vinny."

"You will pal. It's pretty bad."

"Look, I'm not up to anything right now. I don't give a fuck."

"You better start getting up, lover. Looks like Lawrence kept a bunch of shit from the Craig Wiley case. Evidence, motherfucker. Shit like that. I don't know exactly what yet, but something that should never have been saved."

"What the fuck are you talking about Vinny?"

"Someone from the county prosecutor's office called. Fucking Lawrence left a bunch of papers and shit from my cousin's case in a locker at the fucking bowling alley. Some stuff that Will said was destroyed. Bullshit that may be enough for a grand jury to indict Julie and maybe more. My dad says she's a friggin' loose cannon, and my uncle Tony is pissed off big time."

James slowly reached for the Vicodin bottle and took two with a swig of warm beer left in the bottle from last night.

"Jesus, Vinny. Is this shit ever going to end? It was supposed to be over and done with. First, we have to clean up Will's fuck up with Lawrence. Why don't Tony or your old man make Newsham fix his own mess? Why you and me? Fuck, man, we're running a business, making good money. Now this?"

"Some of this is on you for fucking the bitch in the first place," Vinny said defensively.

"How was I supposed to know she was your cousin. Fuck you. And if you recall, I took my medicine for that, didn't I? I still got a limp and my leg hurts every fucking day, and now my ribs. Fuck it."

"James, listen man, this is serious!" The pitch in Vinny's voice had elevated a notch or two and was edged with nervousness.

James wished he could raise his voice a few decibels higher than Vinny's and give him an earful, but the rib pain precluded any yelling.

As Vinny rambled on about the problems Lawrence was causing from the grave, James thought to himself, "What the fuck does anybody care about that case? Doesn't the Oakview Police Department have something better to do than rehash an old murder case."

In slow motion, James rolled out of bed and stood very cautiously, wincing with each move. "Vinny, she's your family. Isn't she supposed to keep her mouth shut, no matter what? Go to jail, do the time? Your fucking code, all that bullshit."

"She's a crazy bitch. Nothing means nothing to her," Vinny said. "Come on, James, we got to get together on this. My dad said you and I have to take care of it."

"Why us, Vinny? We risked our necks, and my ribs, offing Lawrence because of Will's clusterfuck. Why don't they just call in some talent from out of town and be done with it? Where is she anyway, west coast right? They got people there. Enough is enough, Vinny."

Vinny answered decisively, "We got to go do my Aunt Cindy first, and then we go to LA."

"Your Aunt Cindy, Tony's old lady? What the fuck does she have to do with this?"

"My fucking Aunt Cindy is working with Green and Murphy."

James shuffled into his kitchen, stepping lightly, trying to keep each step from feeling like shards of broken glass grinding into an open wound. He shook his head trying to make some sense of what Vinny meant. "What are you talking about? Green and Murphy."

"Our person at the PA's office says that Cindy told them everything. About you being there, about Julie going nuts."

James interrupted, "Hey, fuck that. I wasn't even there when she killed those kids!"

"About you being there beforehand, you jackoff. About Will and his dad and Spencer, and what they did. Maybe they even know about how you squeezed that super freak from the FBI, and there's no statute of limitations on murder. It sounds pretty fucked up."

"I'm well aware of the law, Vinny. I was part of it for 15 years. And if you recall, we didn't kill anyone. Except Lawrence that is. Fuck!"

"You see what I'm saying. I know it's fucked up, but my dad says we gotta go take care of Cindy and my fucking cousin. We gotta clean it up."

"This should have been done when this bullshit happened. For a bunch of smart guys, Francis, Tony and your dad sure fucked this thing up."

"Well, it was different then, when the old man was still around. I think if my Grandpa had been dead when this happened, my dad probably would have handled it differently. The old man had a soft spot for Julie. I think he felt bad for her cause of how Tony was."

"Yea. She told me how he was a real shit bag, pervert for a father."

"Listen, James. My dad and Tony said they'd take care of you if we do this. You're gonna get a bump. It'll be worth it. So, can you stop bitching?'

"Yea, how much?"

"Enough to make it worth your ribs."

James knew the Scalinis well enough to figure on at least ten grand. He was in the market for a new Harley and the extra cash would buy a lot of chrome. He felt a little better about things.

"How's Tony gonna take his ex-wife getting whacked?"

"My dad says Tony's good with it. She's ate up with cancer anyway and don't have long. And he don't want her talking to anybody. He said it'll be a friggin' mercy killing."

"When?" James asked, sitting down on the couch grimacing and cradling his ribs with his arm.

"Now."

"Fuck, man, I told you, I can't hardly move. I probably should've gone to the hospital," James said.

"Ok. Ok. I'll take care of the Aunt Cindy thing. I got some Oxy 80's, I'll bring to you. You get your bags packed. I'll call you when I'm on my way to pick you up."

"Ok, Vinny, but, dammit, don't bring that toy car."

"Just get ready."

James threw his phone on the kitchen table, "Fuck you, Vinny." He pulled a cold beer from the refrigerator and eased into a kitchen chair.

Vinny was able to catch the door to Cindy's building, holding it open so a large woman and her Shitzu could enter. He wore a bulky coat, sunglasses and a boonie hat that covered most of his forehead and shadowed his face. The security guard didn't even look up as they strolled by. Vinny was unrecognizable even if he was seen on the security cameras.

Vinny followed her in and stood casually with her, petting the dog as they waited for the elevator. He liked big girls as a comfortable change from the skin and bones model types, but she was beyond big, and either her or the dog, or both of them smelled funky, like Parmesan cheese. Vinny was relieved when the fat lady and her little rat dog got off on the sixth floor.

He didn't necessarily want to kill Aunty Cindy. She had always been nice to him. He had spent the night at her and Uncle Tony's house often enough. He'd basically grown up with Julie. She was three years younger and they played together. He wondered how in the fuck Julie turned out to be such a piece of shit. Tony's doing probably, the sick fuck.

Aunty Cindy cooked and wore aprons. He always thought she was more of what a mother should be than his own mom. Aunty Cindy was always baking something. Their house smelled good, like cinnamon. And Cindy was full fig-ured. Vinny wondered, maybe that's where he got the whole big girl thing.

His mom, Marie Jeanette Calandra Scalini, liked to lay at the pool, work on her tan, get facials and manicures. She was Frank Scalini Jr's trophy wife. Marie was top heavy with long, wavy black hair, and always with the heavy, choking, sickly sweet perfume.

Marie shopped almost exclusively in the frozen food section. She burnt up two microwaves. Their kitchen smelled like Mr. Clean rather than food.

Vinny exited the elevator at the ninth floor. Cindy's loft was near the end of the hallway. The hallway was deserted. He put on latex gloves. Vinny took out his lock pick set and inserted the pin in the deadbolt keyhole. Before he could even start to work the lock, the door pushed open.

Vinny carried an AMT .44 caliber 'Bulldog'. A stubby, semi-automatic pistol that easily fit in a jacket pocket. He screwed a silencer onto the end of the barrel. He didn't plan on shooting anyone, but it was better to have and not need, than need and not have. Vinny entered the apartment, stopped just inside the door and listened. He could hear a television from the back of the apartment. Vinny scanned as he walked through the living room, den, and down the hallway towards the sound. The TV was playing in a bedroom on the right side of the hallway.

Vinny's plan was to sneak up on Aunty Cindy, put a pillow over her face and suffocate her. Tony had said she was just a stick figure and it wouldn't take much. He figured he could leave the pillow over her face and he wouldn't have to look at her. He'd shoot her if he had to, but he didn't want to.

He took a quick peek around the corner of the doorway into the bedroom and saw a king size bed across from the door. He could see feet pushing up the covers at the end of the bed.

He listened. He could hear the TV. Jeopardy was on. He couldn't hear anything else. He waited for about two long minutes. He didn't hear any sounds coming from Aunty Cindy. No cough, snore, whisper, breathing, nothing but cold silence.

Vinny crept in the room, staying low to the ground and slid behind a lazy boy recliner. He peered around the chair and saw her in bed. The covers were pulled up to her neck. She was gray and still.

Vinny checked for the pulse in her neck and found none. She was cold. Her eyes were as empty as the eyes of those statutes in the living room. He lifted up the blanket. Her skin was almost translucent, stretched thin over her skeleton. This was not the Aunt Cindy he remembered. He wished he hadn't looked.

He whispered to himself. "Fucking cancer, I'd eat my fucking gun first."

Vinny noticed a half empty glass of water and several pill bottles on the night stand. He looked at the labels. He recognized one of the meds, Morphine Sulfate Extended Release Tablet, 30mg, 60 count. The bottle only contained 4. He wondered if maybe she'd had enough of being sick and just killed herself. It sure made it easier for him. Vinny unscrewed the bottle and took the 4 tablets.

Vinny thought strategically. "If she was talking to the cops, I wonder if she left a note for them."

Vinny searched the bedroom. He looked in all her drawers and desk cubbyholes. He was satisfied there was no note in the bedroom.

Vinny went into the kitchen and rifled through the drawers and cabinets. Nothing.

He went into the living room and there on the coffee table, a pad of paper, a pen, a bottle of Grey Goose and an empty shot glass from the Bellagio.

"The Bellagio, nice."

The handwriting on the note was in large, fancy, girly writing. It was dated yesterday and said nothing more than, "I am sorry. I should have said something long ago. About everything." It was signed, Cindy Gerhardt-Scalini.

Vinny put the notepad, pen and the shot glass in his jacket pocket with the pills. He trotted down the stairs to the sixth floor, took the elevator to the lobby and walked out unnoticed.

# Chapter Eighty

MQ and I started pulling files and copying the crime scene photos for Karen and Dan. We finished early one day and headed to Tom's Tavern for lunch. MQ was off but I had to work the graveyard shift that night. It was lunch, and then black curtains and earplugs for me.

Tom's was a neighborhood bar and grill not far from the university hospital complex. It had been around for at least 30 years and had been frequented by many a student, resident and cop. It featured great 1/3 pound burgers, $1.50 longnecks and $3.00 well drinks.

I called Margie to see if she could meet us. It went to voicemail. She was probably sleeping. I left a message. MQ and I nodded to a few of the regulars at the bar, city detectives who seemed to live at Toms. We settled in a booth and ordered a couple Wild Turkeys.

"We're not far from Cindy Scalini's apartment. That reminds me."

"I don't feel like a social call, doc," MQ said.

"No, I don't mean that. I'll give her a call. Say hello and tell her we're working on the case without giving any specifics. She'd appreciate the update."

A man's voice answered, "Mrs. Scalini's, can I help you?"

"Hello, this is Dr. Green, is Mrs. Scalini available?"

There was a pause followed by muffled voices and then a woman came on the phone.

"Hello, Dr. Green, this is Cathleen, I'm Cindy's sister. Cindy mentioned your name. She said you may be calling. Cindy passed away."

"I'm sorry, Cathleen. I didn't know, I hadn't heard. I met with her last week and I thought she had more time. What happened?"

"We don't know exactly. I came over here and the front door was unlocked. She was in bed, the TV was on. I thought she was asleep at first. We, we don't know for sure, but, she may have taken too many pills. There was an empty bottle of her Morphine on her dresser and she had been drinking it seems. She was in so much pain, so much pain for so long. Ever since…"

She sniffled and paused briefly. "The funeral will be day after tomorrow. We're just a little frazzled right now. I'm sorry. She wanted a graveside service. So, it will be at 11am, at Blessed Sacrament. I can give you directions if you need them." Cathleen said.

My thoughts raced to the heart shaped headstones at Blessed Sacrament, the Scalini family plot. "I know where the cemetery is. Thank you, Cathleen. My sincere condolences to you and your family."

"Thank you. It will probably be a quick service. There aren't many left in our family. Our parents died years ago. We had an older brother, but he died when we were still in high school. There's just me and my husband. Our kids are grown and live out of state. Cindy is divorced. Her ex, Anthony, said he would come and that he was going to call the rest of his side of the family. Ruth, Cindy's mother-in-law, I am sure she will come. They got along well enough. And then there's Cindy's daughter, Julie, but I don't know about her. Cindy hadn't spoken to her in quite some time. I found her phone number in Cindy's address book. She had moved to California, after, well, quite some time ago," Cathleen paused. Maybe she didn't know whether I knew the family history or not.

"I'm quite familiar with what happened Cathleen. Is her daughter coming?"

"I called the number several times, and left voice mails. She never called back. I don't know if she's going to be at her own mother's funeral. It's just sad, really sad. Since Taylor and Robbie died, everything has been just awful for my sister. It would be nice if you came, Dr. Green. Cindy spoke well of you."

"I'm sorry for your loss. Your sister seemed like a very gracious and courageous lady. I'll introduce myself at the funeral."

"Thank you," she said and hung up.

MQ had been listening. "Cindy Scalini dead?"

"Yep."

"Our suspect coming in for her mother's wake?"

"Probably not, they can't get hold of her."

"So how did Carmela Soprano die?"

"They found her dead in bed. Maybe an OD."

"Maybe not. She talked to you and then ends up dead. Scalini goons in play perhaps. You're the grim reaper pal." MQ said sipping his whiskey.

"I don't know, Kenneth. She was terminal, on any number of medications and home oxygen. I am sure she was closing in on multi-organ system failure. She cleansed her soul by giving up the sweatshirt and finally telling the truth. Maybe she just had enough and took a handful of pills."

"I hope for her sake we have a better track record with Karen and Dan than we've had by ourselves," MQ said. "She may have exculpated her conscience confident that we'd be able to adjudicate this case with her information. But there is no guarantee we will be able to, or that any measure of justice will be served. Not by any stretch my friend."

So saith Sol.

# Chapter Eighty One

It was sunny, but only about 35 degrees with a sharp wind on the day Cindy was lowered into the ground. She was to be planted in the next row, directly in front of my ghosts. I purposely arrived late for her funeral and stood about 25 yards to the side and behind the small semicircle of grievers.

I wore a black suit and black overcoat and wrapped a thick knitted wool scarf around my neck and chin. Sheila had gotten it for me years ago, directly from Scotland. They know a little something about shitty weather over there and it had kept me warm longer than she had. I put on sunglasses, a Fedora and kept my head down. I was sufficiently generic looking for a funeral. I doubted that anyone would notice me.

A few of the key players were in attendance. Cindy's ex-husband, Anthony, showed up to pay his respects and Frank Jr. came in, from Reno I guess.

Vinny Scalini was dressed sharply in a black, pin stripe suit and black cowboy boots with silver tips. He had a long legged brunette in tow. She was seductively attired in a black leather dress with a mock turtle neck, replete with stainless studs that looked a lot like a dog collar. The dress may as well have been painted on. She wore a leather jacket that would have been more appropriate for a ride on the back of my Harley than at a funeral service. The woman was taller than Vinny because of the 6" fire engine red stilettos that made her calves scream out for attention.

An elderly woman in a rumpled tan overcoat was stuffed between Tony and Frank Jr. I assumed she was the matriarch, Francis Sr's widow, Ruth Scalini.

Completing a semicircle of front row grievers, stood a man with his arm around an attractive, middle aged women with short curly brown hair. She wore funeral appropriate attire, a black dress and black heels. Cindy's sister, Cathleen, and her husband.

Representing the Newsham Law Firm were Chatham and Spencer Newsham. They stood to the side and behind everyone. Lt. Will Newsham wasn't in attendance and neither was Julie Wiley.

A small gaggle of other folks were there. I saw Cindy's oncologist, Bruce Hendershott, and a few of the nurses that I recognized from hospice care. Bruce and the nurses probably felt like commanders who had lost a soldier in battle.

For some reason, I had expected Ruth Scalini, to be frail, bony and dark haired. An old, brittle Italian woman, hunched over with osteoporosis, walking with a cane. Ruth Scalini was not at all frail looking. She was old, probably in her eighties, but she was anything but frail. Ruth Scalini was stocky as a draft horse, probably 175 pounds, and every bit of 5'8". A maroon scarf covered her head. She wore black knit, fingerless gloves over her stubby fingers. Her long gray hair was braided down her back and extended nearly to her waist. Thick calves and ankles extended below the drab, beige overcoat that was one size too small. She was wearing black running shoes. I could just make out the "N" for New Balance. A large brown canvas sack hung off one of Ruth Scalini's chunky arms.

Because of the wind and my tinnitus, I could barely hear the service. They were at the end as they all recited the Lord's Prayer. The priest said a few words, shook hands with the family and it was over. Everyone mingled a few minutes around the gravesite. Frank, Tony, Vinny and Vinny's brunette walked back towards a black limo, chatting and smoking. The Newshams headed to a silver Jaguar. The limo and the Jag pulled away.

At the gravesite, Dr. Hendershott and the nurses all shook hands with Ruth and Cathleen. Hugs went all around. Bruce spoke with them for a few minutes. Another hug and the nurses strode towards their cars.

I took off the hat and sunglasses and approached. Dr. Hendershott spotted me. "Hi Morris. You knew Mrs. Scalini. Was she a patient of yours at one time?"

"No, just an acquaintance."

"She was a truly strong and courageous woman. She fought it every step of the way," he said.

"I got the same impression. Is there going to be a postmortem or tox screen to determine how she died."

"No. She's been through enough in life. I signed the death certificate and I don't really care whether she accidentally took a few too many morphine sulfates."

"I understand, Bruce. Sometimes I think Jack Kevorkian may be onto something."

"In my business, you don't know how many times I wonder the same thing. Take care, Morris. See you around." We shook hands and he walked towards his car.

Cindy Scalini had been through enough. She had carried the guilt of what she had allowed her husband to do to their daughter, and what her daughter had done to the children. It had eaten her alive.

I understood completely how she could find peace in death. There had been any number of times I looked into the narcotics cabinet at the clinic considering the path I had taken and the tornadic damage I had done to those that loved me. When the lack of sleep due to the nightmares, the relentless tapping shoulder pain, the headaches, the whispers and the depression were overwhelming, I occasionally thought how easy it would be to go to sleep, end the pain. I was not nearly as strong as Cindy.

Cathleen and her husband were heading towards the vehicles. I introduced myself and spoke briefly with them, offering my condolences.

Everyone had gone from the gravesite except Ruth Scalini. The only car remaining nearby was a mint condition, silver, mid 1970s Mercedes 450SL.

"Odd that she would drive herself, rather than ride in the limo with her son," I thought. "I guess the Scalini's have their own issues."

I remained off to the side at a safe distance. The cemetery was quiet with a comfortable stillness. I watched as Ruth stood at her husband's grave. She pulled a bouquet of silk tulips and roses from the canvas bag and arranged them in a hole at the base of Francis's stone. She pulled out another similar bouquet, arranging them on the double stone that Robbie and Taylor shared. Her bulky frame squatted and bent over. She kissed the top of their headstone. I could see her lips moving, but could not hear her.

"Is this another one of those 'something will happen' events that Myra Sutherland meant?" I wondered. "Maybe I'm supposed to meet Mrs. Scalini. Maybe she knows what Cindy knew. Maybe she has something for me too."

Ruth Scalini pushed herself upright with a loud exhalation. She sobbed, and rubbed tears from her cheeks with the palms of her gloves.

I looked around. Everyone was gone, the coast was clear. I walked over to her and offered her a handkerchief. "Here, it's clean. A new suit, a new hankie."

"Thank you. Thank you very much." Her voice was raspy but soft, flavored with the old country. She dabbed her eyes and handed the handkerchief back.

"You can keep it Mrs. Scalini."

"That's very nice of you. And you, you are?"

I hesitated, not knowing exactly what the name Morris Green might mean to her. Her son had wanted me dead, and her husband spared me. "I'm Morris Green, an acquaintance of your daughter-in-law. At one time I was a detective involved in the investigation of the deaths of your great-grandchildren."

Ruth studied my face and then looked directly into my eyes. Her plump cheeks were wrinkled and there were crags and fissures in her forehead and around the corners of her mouth, but her eyes were exceedingly clear and bright. They were dark, green emeralds, somewhat hypnotic, like Margie's.

"Detective Green, yes, yes, I've heard your name," Ruth said. "It's been awhile though, hasn't it?" she said, continuing to peer into me.

Her unblinking gaze was uncomfortable and I shifted a little to the side. I extended my hand and we shook.

"I'm sorry for your loss. I only recently met Cindy," I stopped mid-sentence. The hum, the vibration, the electric ghosts, like a centipede with 100 icy needles for feet were crawling the familiar route from the base of my skull down my spine, where they began tapping my left shoulder blade like a conga drum. My eyes became moist.

"Of course the children would be at Grandma Cindy's funeral, why wouldn't they?" I thought. I sniffled a few times. Ruth handed the handkerchief back.

"Take this detective. Please, you take this," she resumed staring at me. "I know you're very sorry for my loss, and thank you, thank you for thinking of them, and spending so much effort in trying, in trying to figure out what happened that day. If you spoke to Cindy recently, perhaps she, perhaps she…" Tears rolled into several of the wrinkles of her cheeks and we did another handkerchief handoff.

She continued after blowing her nose, "Cindy and I were still close, even though she left the family. She was divorced from Tony, but we had a bond, we did, the two of us. We married into it, into the Scalini family, and we shared the sacrifices for many years." She blew her nose again and waved at the long gone limo.

"You see how much attention my son gave to his wife here at her funeral, how long he stay here. Disgustare, pietoso," Ruth closed her eyes, shook her head and sighed heavily before continuing to speak, "As soon as Father said the last words, off they go in their big black car, the bigshots. And that Vincent, that girl. Non appropriato."

Mrs. Scalini dabbed her eyes and continued. "I visit Cindy in the hospital when they were trying these different treatments. Her passing, her passing, her passing is a blessing. She suffered so much."

I took her gloved hand, covering it with my other hand, preacher style. "You're right, Cindy was a very strong woman, and at least now she has some peace."

Ruth nodded.

"I know this is not a good time, Mrs. Scalini, but at some point, I need to talk to you about Taylor and Robbie." I rolled my left shoulder and arm around in hopes that the tapping would settle down.

Ruth Scalini cocked her head and craned towards me. After an awkward pause, a hint of a smile appeared. "They use to come to me. My Taylor, especially my beautiful Taylor. We were so close. My kids, my beautiful kids," she glanced over at the headstone and then her eyes bore through my skull. "Parlano voi. Vengono a voi. They speak to you. They come to you, don't they, detective?"

Ruth gripped my hand firmly, rhythmically squeezing it. She was still speaking. I could see her lips moving but I had lost everything she said after, "They come to you, don't they, detective?" The hushed voices filled my ears with echoes that stirred the air. A soft whoosh in which I heard, and could understand words for the first time. The children were whispering, "Meeemaaah, Meeemaaah."

The blank look on my face must have read like a blinking no vacancy sign.

Ruth patted the top of my hand with her other hand.

"Detective, Detective Green?"

"I'm sorry, Mrs. Scalini. I kind of zoned out for a second, I'm so sorry." I shook my head to clear the voices. "You were saying that they come to you. Whew, it, uh, threw me."

"Oh yes, Detective Green, my kids, they used to come. Nei miei sogni, in my dreams. In my dreams we would be walking in the park, each one holding my hand like we used to do. The dreams were so real. It was, it was like they were with me, right there, in the park. We would take off our shoes and walk on the grass. The smell of the honeysuckle so sweet. I would ask what happened, why? And then they would leave, walk away into the trees. I wished I could dream forever. Sometimes, I wish I could be with them again. Robbie and her, vivo di nuovo. The dreams would always wake me up in the middle of the night. I don't know how to describe it, but when I woke up I felt tingly all over, all over, and the honeysuckle, it filled my nose, even after I woke up. I felt that same electricity while I was holding your hand and I smell the honeysuckle right now." She sniffed in deeply. "Molto strano, isn't it, Detective Green? Molto strano, very strange."

"Yes, Mrs. Scalini, very strange. What, what did the kids call you? Did you have a grandma nickname?"

"They called me 'Meema', and Francis 'Peepa'."

I shuddered as if to shake off a cold, damp breeze. "I heard that, just now. Their whispers. Did you hear them? And the electricity, I feel that. I have Mrs. Scalini, I have for quite some time now."

"I know. It's them, detective. They visit you now." The rubor in her face had made way for a doleful emptiness. "I wish they would come back to me. I come here. I come here and I talk to them. I hope they hear me. I come and talk to my Francis. Now, I come and talk to Cindy, too."

Ruth fished a pen from her bag and wrote her number on the back of a grocery receipt. "In a couple of days, you call me, Detective Green. I want to know about what my kids say to you."

"I will. I will definitely call."

"Thank you, Detective Green. You keep listening and you tell me. You tell me what my kids say."

"I will, Mrs. Scalini. I promise."

"I know you will. And please, you call me Ruth." She turned and waddled towards the Mercedes.

The vibration and hum, the shoulder tapping and the voices abruptly stopped like a faucet being turned off. It left me with a warm, comfortable feeling much like the initial wave of a high dose of Oxy.

"The little ghosts are going with Meema. Good. I hope they stay with her for a while."

A stream of thoughts pushed their way out like someone had yelled fire in the theatre. "I have to get the sweatshirt out for AK to take to the lab. I've got clinic hours this afternoon. I've got to work at Oakview tonight. I gotta pack for my trip. I told Sheila I would stop by and look at Jake's term paper. Yet here I am at a Catholic cemetery for the funeral of a fucking mobster's wife. I don't even remember the last time I was at the Jewish cemetery to visit any of my relatives. I am a real piece of work. Yes you are Morris Green, a real piece."

I leaned against the silver maple next to the kids' graves. I took a long pull from my flask as the gravediggers approached to lower Cindy's box into the ground.

# Chapter Eighty Two

MQ and I left a copy of the complete Wiley file with AK Flavin. It seemed like a repeat of our doomed effort with FBI Agent Sasha Lenhart.

As promised, I called Ruth Scalini a few days later. She invited me to come to her house for coffee and a parlare, a talk.

Ruth and I shared the ghostly visitations. Hers were pleasant dreams of walking in the park and the sweet smell of honeysuckle. Mine were various versions of unwelcome prodding and pain. I decided to use my visit with Ruth to trap her granddaughter.

She appeared to live modestly in a 1960s era, brick, two-story home. There was a separate two-car garage with its own driveway to side of the house. The house was located on a secluded cul de sac surrounded by mature 60 foot hardwood trees. It was at the most, 2500 square feet, and the lot was no more than an acre or two. In the sixties, the area would have been far suburbs bordering on rural, but over the years, it had become over developed. It was now surrounded by strip malls, big box stores and auto dealerships.

I surmised that she and Francis had lived there the entire time he was busy building his criminal empire. Francis and Ruth Scalini had not internalized the materiality their sons had. Francis probably chose to invest his fortune in the growth of the business, rather than the trappings of success.

Mrs. Scalini answered the door with a warm smile and a firm handshake which was pleasantly devoid of an electrical charge. Perhaps the children were busy haunting some other poor bastard today. She was wearing a worn denim apron over a pair of orange knit slacks. A brown, marled Cardigan hung loosely over her shoulders.

My nylon gear bag was slung over my shoulder and she gave me a puzzled look. Inside was my laptop, a 9mm pistol, and a few other investigative tools I thought I might need.

"It's my laptop," I told her. "I might want to type up some notes as we talk."

She nodded and led me through the entry way, past the living room into the kitchen. I detected the familiar, stuffy smell of a grandmother's home.

The kitchen table was covered with a red and white plaid tablecloth. A silver candlestick with a white tapered candle, still wrapped in cellophane, was placed in the center of the table. There were four high-back, wooden chairs around the table. A blue and white patterned china cup and saucer were placed in front of two of the chairs.

"Please sit, join me," she said, pouring me a cup of coffee.

Ruth laid a small china plate of pastries in front of me. "These are sfogliatelles, delicious, just delicious, my kid's favorites."

The name of the Italian pastry rolled smoothly off her tongue.

"I haven't made these since they passed. Sfogliatelle, it means many layers. The shell, light and crispy is stuffed with baked ricotta cheese and pieces of candied fruit. Eat," she prompted, pushing the plate closer to me.

"Thank you, Mrs. Scalini." I took a bite. "Marvelous. I can see why they loved these."

"I have more in the refrigerator, if you like Dr. Green."

"So you know I'm a doctor, too?"

"Oh yes. I know quite a lot about you."

My eyes narrowed, not sure what she meant and how she meant it.

"It's ok, Dr. Green. That was before. When the police were looking, but they are different now, things are different now."

"Yes, the investigation involving the deaths of your great grandchildren is no longer a concern to anyone in law enforcement."

I lied. I wasn't going to tell Mrs. Scalini we were in the process of developing probable cause for an arrest warrant for her granddaughter. I took another bite of the pastry, chewed and swallowed allowing her time to process. She didn't respond.

I continued, "Well, no one in the police department cares. I still do though. Your kids latched onto me. At the cemetery, you were spot on. Like you said, they come to me."

"I know. I felt it. I just wish…" she paused and took a sip of coffee changing her train of thought. "Should I be calling you Detective, or Dr. Green?" she asked with a broad smile, and continued. "A doctor and a police officer. Two jobs, you must have been very busy, very busy, kind of like my Anthony. Did you know that Tony, he went to college for business?"

I shook my head no, and finished off the first sfogliagtelle. They were clearly addictive.

"Oh, he was plenty mad about having to go to school, plenty. Most of his friends weren't going to college and Frankie Jr. wasn't going to college. He was going right into the family business. It's just as well. Frankie, he's non cosi brillante, not very book smart. But Francis made Tony go to college, four years, right after high school. Tony, he was so mad about it. So mad that Frankie got to go right into the business. You see, Francis, my Francis wanted Anthony to have an education. He wanted Tony to have a choice. That maybe he could do something other than, what he do. And my Tony, he graduated with a business degree from Illinois State."

She grinned and held her head up proudly. "And for a year or so, he took a job as a manager. A manager at a plastic manufacturing company. It was a good job," Ruth paused, and ran her index finger around the rim of her coffee cup.

"But at the same time, he was working for his father in the evening, to make extra money. He ended up quitting the plastics company and going in with his father anyway," she shook her head as she spoke.

Mrs. Scalini paused, pursed her lips and puffed out words burdened with a heavy regret, "I wish he had stayed at the plastic company, made a different life for himself. Oh, well, acqua...water under the bridge. Things would have been different for him. E por noi. E por noi. And for us," Ruth said, shaking her head a few times. She took a sip of coffee.

"I know. I wish I could go back. I'd do a few things differently," I said.

"You have children?" Ruth asked.

"Two, a boy and a girl, about the same age as..." I stopped and changed course. "I know if I had to do it over again, I would do things differently. I would have spent more time at home with them, and less time chasing, whatever it is I was chasing."

"I know very well what you mean," she said nodding her head. "Time, it goes by faster. It goes by faster, the older you get, Dr. Green."

"So, my kids come to you. What do they say? What do they want from you?"

"They want peace, so they can move on to the other side, to God to Heaven, who knows? It sounds weird saying it out loud. Your great-grandchildren have been urging me to find some kind of closure for them. For lack of a better description, they've been haunting me to solve their case and bring their killer to justice. It wasn't their father."

Ruth looked puzzled, but she didn't immediately ask who it was, if not Craig. She was more interested in my haunting.

"I miss them so much. I only wish they would come to me again, even if it was just dreams. How is it they come for you?"

I didn't know why, but like Myra Sutherland, I felt comfortable telling Ruth the story. I spent the next several minutes devouring another sfogliatelle and a refilled coffee cup, while I explained the circuitous route in which Taylor and Robbie Wiley made their way into my life. I told Ruth about being shot on the same day as their deaths, the tapping, the shoulder pains, the voices and dreams. I didn't tell her that my death was her son's doing. Mrs. Scalini's interest became amplified when I got to the point in which I spoke about the spiritualist, communicator with the dead.

"This woman, she, she sees my kids. She sees them like they, like they are here with us?"

"Yes, she can see them as if they are in the room with us. She can speak with them, but the communication is telepathic. She feels their thoughts. At least that's how I understand it. What she said, what the kids told her, it all fits with what our investigation found."

Mrs. Scalini was peering into her coffee, circling the rim of the cup with her finger again. She looked up and reached across the table taking both of my hands in hers. "So, you tell me what happened, Dr. Green? You tell me who it was did it."

My initial reaction was to reflexively pull back and avoid the jump start jolt or the electric hum that, to this point had been absent, but she held firm and looked directly at me, "It's been a long time Dr. Green, a long time to live with this."

She squeezed my hands tighter and continued, "We knew Julie was not, Julie was not telling us the truth. From the first night we knew. We did not want to believe it. We did not want to believe, that she, that she could have done anything like that to, propria carne e sangue, her own flesh and blood. It was a nightmare, Dr. Green, the worst time of our lives. To have something like this happen. Incubo terribile."

Mrs. Scalini let go of my hands and stood up suddenly. She took the empty pastry plate and her cup and saucer over to the sink counter crossing the kitchen. Her back was to me when she resumed speaking.

"Julie told us about having another man in the house, and how Craig, how Craig caught her and that he went crazy. And how Craig tried to kill her and the man, and how she got away. And that she could not save the kids. That Craig, Craig, he killed the kids."

I went over to the sink and stood by her. "Mrs. Scalini, Cindy never told you about the phone call she overheard?"

"No. What phone call? What did she tell you?"

"The call where Cindy overheard Julie talking to someone the day after it happened. The call where Julie was talking to her boyfriend. Talking to the man that had been at the house on the day of the murders. The phone call where she overheard Julie say that she did it. That she snapped and killed the kids, and then she killed Craig. Cindy didn't tell you?"

"No, no, no," Ruth dropped the dishes in the sink. The clatter of broken dishes rang in the kitchen like a thunderclap. She turned to face me spewing sentences like machine gun burps. "Cindy never said anything about that, never. Non verrei che, never like that. That Julie did it all? Never. Francis, he said, he said it was Craig who went crazy, and that Julie, well Julie, she did something. She did shoot Craig. And that we had to protect her because of that. I don't want to believe that Julie…"

I interrupted her. "Cindy told me that your husband and son knew what really happened. They knew the boyfriend was there. They knew him. He was someone working with Vinny. Francis and Anthony found out that this boyfriend left before the murders. That he had nothing to do with the deaths of the kids. So they just broke his legs or something like that to teach him a lesson. That's the only punishment anyone ever received for the murders of Robbie and Taylor. Apparently they kept you in the dark about everything, Mrs. Scalini."

Ruth put a hand on a chair back. She was putting the pieces together and sat down slowly.

"I'm not making this up, Ruth. This is what Cindy told me. She said that your family just could not bear losing Julie as well. That your husband said, we lost two, we can't lose three."

Ruth's head nodded, the denial and surprise were making way for the truth. She knew those words were her husband's. She looked up directly at me. Tears rolled down the corners of her eyes following the deep creases and dripped onto the tablecloth.

"I knew something. I felt something was wrong, Dr. Green. What was going on then, what they were telling me, that it was, it was not right. Francis and Chatham, they spent a lot of time with Julie. I heard them tell her, 'You have to say this, or you have to act like this. You can't say this or you must not say that.' They made up a story for what happened." She sniffed and coughed a few times and then became eerily quiet.

We sat at the kitchen table while the stillness filled the room. After a minute or so, Ruth broke it as soundly as she had the dishes.

"Francis, maybe he knew, but he never tell me. He just say that what they were doing, was for the best. After we got through the funerals, my Francis, he stopped singing. He changed, he became quiet, a quiet man, very quiet. He stopped laughing, stopped singing. Then he went to sleep and he never wake up. I knew something it wasn't right."

Mrs. Scalini stood up, got a new saucer from the pantry and returned with two more sfogliatelles. She put the saucer in front of me, smiled and sat back down. "I felt so bad for Craig's parents, but what else could I do, what else could I do?"

I went off as quickly as a firecracker without a fuse. I screamed in thought so loud, I was sure Ruth could hear. "You knew something wasn't right? What else could you do? You could have called the police. That's what you could have done. Your fucking, criminal, slimebag husband knew your granddaughter was involved. Your piece of shit son knew his daughter slaughtered his grandchildren. It was your blood for Chrissake! So you're husband became morose and didn't want to sing anymore. Too fucking bad.

"Your granddaughter was a sociopathic butcher, yet you said nothing. All because you all were afraid that she would sell your family out to save her own ass. You are all worthless pieces of shit, every one of you. You could have given Craig's parents, and those great-grandchildren you claim to love, some mother-fucking peace. That's what else you could have done. And if you had, I wouldn't have been plagued by your God damned kids!" I wondered if the words hadn't leaked out, but Mrs. Scalini showed no reaction.

My thoughts skidded sideways to a stop to avoid a confrontation with the old woman. Having her as a adversary, was not in my plan. "Mrs. Scalini, I wish things had been different, but they weren't and we are where we are."

"Dr. Green, you tell me, you tell me what that woman, the one who talks with my kids, what she said. You tell me how my kids died."

I took the opportunity to give Ruth a chunk of wooden cross to carry. Cindy died as a result of the one she had carried since the murders. I felt it only fair to burden, "Meema" Scalini, who baked pastries and bought silk flowers for handsome gravesites while her daughter-in-law suffered. Ruth's comfortable life was sponsored by the Scalini criminal canvas of misery. It was time she was dealt in.

Using what Myra said and what our investigation suggested, I described a chaotic bedroom bondage scene. How Craig and the kids walked in on Julie tied to the bed having sex with another man. How the two men fought and Craig was injured. How the boyfriend fled the scene, leaving Julie in the house alone, with her confused and frightened children, and what she had done to them.

Unfortunately for me, the medical examiner's report and the autopsy pictures ran like a hologram in my memory, whenever I happened to think of them. I closed my eyes and found it an easy task to read directly from the translucent paragraphs of Ajay's report, paging in front of me. I narrated the pathologist's descriptions of Robbie's evisceration and Taylor's multiple skull fractures. I described the loose bowel and stomach contents, the multiple gunshot wounds and the exposed brain matter.

Ruth sat in silence.

Finally, I got to the last paragraph of Taylor's autopsy report, "Four superficial, puncture wounds measuring 6mm in length, and 4mm in depth, were noted in the soft tissue over the victim's abdomen, directly above the umbilicus. Neither of these injuries penetrated the dermis."

I opened my eyes and made eye contact with my coffee and pastry host. That captivating glimmer was gone from her eyes. They were bloodshot and rung with tears.

"Ruth, these wounds, these little 6mm nicks, are more like a scratch than a cut. You see, Taylor had sustained a mortal head wound from the machete blows. She was dying and exhibited what we call agonal respirations. In layman's terms, a death rattle. The brain involuntarily makes a last ditch effort to supply oxygen to the body by deep breathing. Taylor was taking in her last, few gasps of air. I suspect that, seeing her daughter breathing, Julie didn't know if Taylor was still alive or not. So, she poked her with the tip of the machete."

I picked up my fork and prodded the crust of the pastry in front of me. "Like checking a piece of meat to see how well done it is. Julie stuck the tip of the knife into the skin over Taylor's stomach, making those little puncture wounds. Taylor didn't respond. She was well done."

Ruth covered her face with her apron and wailed. I spoke louder and faster. "Satisfied that her children were dead, your granddaughter left them on a cold, concrete floor in an ever expanding pool of their blood. Then, she propped Craig up in his recliner, leaned him over the barrel of a shotgun and pulled the trigger. At least that part of your husband's story was accurate. Julie did kill Craig.

"Craig's head exploded all over the living room. Julie would have been covered in Taylor, Robbie and Craig's blood. The blood, the innocent blood of her family, your family, swirled down the drain as she washed up. Julie put her little pooches in the car, and drove away to call for help."

Ruth Scalini dropped the apron from her face. Her eyes were glazed over and she was pale. Her face and forearms glistened with moisture. She slumped forward, her ample chest and abdomen melting onto the kitchen table. I reached forward and supported her shoulders to keep her head from smashing the last of the sfogliatelles. They really were delicious. I pushed the plates to the side and lowered her torso onto the table.

She was panting with a respiratory rate of about 40 breaths per minute. I checked her pulse. It was fast, slightly irregular, but otherwise strong. I let her lay on the table for a few minutes and watched her breathing slow, while I monitored her pulse. She spontaneously regained consciousness and sat up.

"Mrs. Scalini, Ruth!" I said loudly. "You fainted. Are you all right?" I was still holding her wrist, checking her heart rate. She pulled her hand away, lifted her apron again and dabbed the moisture from her eyes and face.

"Non sapevo! I didn't know! No one ever told me. I didn't know it was like that. No one ever told me."

"You needed to hear that and feel that. Can you even begin to imagine what it was like for those kids? Confused, terrified, the blistering horrific pain, and your family, the Newsham Law Firm, all of you, you protected a sociopathic monster."

"Please, Dr. Green, please no more, no more of this."

"Those kids were frightened Ruth. They were hurting, calling for help. Maybe they even called for their "Meema", as they were being butchered. But no one came."

Mrs. Scalini continued her pleas for me to stop.

"The sudden and horrific manner in which they were murdered ripped their souls away. They became phantom energy forms, frightened little children ghosts, that were left to wait in the dark, alone, calling for someone."

She interrupted again, putting her hands over her ears, shaking her head, "What could I do? Per favore, per favore, Please, no more, no more of this, please!"

"Frightened little children, alone in the dark. They are calling out for help, and they're still calling. You felt it at the cemetery. They're still calling. And you know who they call Ruth? They call me. Your precious kids, they call me. Not you! They keep calling me!"

Ruth Scalini wept, and between sobs, she asked, "What can I do, what can I do?"

Grammar. The little difference in verb tense can make a big difference. Just maybe, my plan was working.

Ruth had gone from 'What could I do?' to 'What can I do?'

"I'll tell you what you can do. You're going to help Robbie and Taylor. You're going to help me. We're going to make a phone call. You're going to call your granddaughter."

# Chapter Eighty Three

R uth Scalini wrung her hands. "Dr. Green, I don't know if I can reach Julie. She don't answer her phone. Tony, he called Julie the day her mother died. She say she would come. She no come. He called her that day. He called her the next day. He called her, he left messages. Julie, she never call back."

Mrs. Scalini continued to talk as I attached an in-line telephone digital voice recording adapter to her phone. "Julie, she is like that. Even with me, she is like that. She may not be home. She don't answer her phone. Who knows what? Who knows what she will do?"

"Ruth, we don't know what she'll do, but if she answers the phone I want you to be ready. What we want her to do, is to tell you what happened."

Ruth's hands were trembling. "What can I do? She won't talk to me."

I put a hand on top of her shoulder. "You can do this, Ruth. It's the right thing to do. For you, for Cindy, for Taylor and Robbie, for Craig, for Craig's parents, even for your husband, so he can rest in peace, too. You can do this. You can make this right."

I took out a notepad from my bag and choreographed the phone conversation for Ruth. I wrote a playbook of bullet points in large letters for her to follow. I hoped Ruth would follow my directions better than Will Newsham followed his father's.

- Talk about the funeral, small talk, like who Vinny brought, the girl in the red heels.
- Tell her that you put new flowers on everyone's graves.
- Ask her why she did not come in for her mother's funeral.
- Let her make excuses for not coming in.

- Interrupt her while she makes excuses.
- Tell her you know.
- Tell her you know what happened.
- Just before she died, Cindy told you.
- Tell her Cindy told you about the PHONE CALL WITH THE BOYFRIEND
- Accuse her of DOING IT. Keep telling her "I KNOW JULIE"
- That Cindy told you. "I KNOW WHAT YOU DID JULIE"
- Keep accusing her of doing it.

"Remember Ruth," I said. "Your job is initially to ask questions, get her to talk, let her do most of the talking, then follow the script."

I turned on the recorder and picked up the telephone. "This is Morris Green, Oakview PD, it is Thursday, December 14th, 1655 hours. I am accompanied by Ruth Scalini. We are at her home, 6235 Bluebird Lane. We are placing a call to Julie Wiley in Santa Monica, California."

I dialed the number and handed the phone to Mrs. Scalini. Five seconds passed.

Mrs. Scalini looked up with a surprised grimace and wide eyes, "Hello, Julie, it's grandma." She listened for a minute, running her fingers over her hair with her free hand.

"The service for your mother, very nice. Father St. Onge, he did it. I'm sure you remember him." She paused and listened.

"Your father and uncle were there, Vinny, he came. He is so flashy now. Mr. fancy suit. He brought a girl, in a leather dress with red high heels. Disgustaro. Dressed like that, red high heels at a funeral. Makes me so mad." Ruth listened briefly again.

"Your aunt Cathleen and her husband Steve, they came." She paused, listening again.

"Don't you miss your family here, Julie? How come you don't come? Everyone they ask me, where's Julie? Where's Julie?"

She listened briefly.

"I say, I don't know, I say, maybe she's sick. But I don't want to lie."

She listened for about half a minute.

"Your mother, she suffered so much. You couldn't come in to say goodbye?"

Ruth pursed her lips as her granddaughter was speaking. She closed her eyes and rubbed her temple. Julie was delivering pain. No surprise there.

"I know, Julie," she said with a voice hardened by years of pain. "I know the two of you couldn't get along. I know."

Ruth's eyes closed as she listened. Finally, she spoke through pursed lips with determination, "And now, I know. Now I know why!" she paused to catch her breath. Her voice became stronger. "Your mama, on her deathbed, just before she take her last breath, she told me what. She told me she heard on the phone. She heard you talking with that man, your boyfriend. How you said you went crazy, you snapped. Avete fatto."

Ruth pulled the pin on the flash grenade and stuffed it through the phone line. "You did it! How you did it! Why would you do it, Julie?" Her voice crumbled as she nearly whispered, "My kids and Craig, too. How could you?" Ruth began to cry. Throaty sounds of anguish went into the phone.

The flashbang had detonated. Julie's voice was loud enough that I could hear it.

"That bitch! That nosy, snooping bitch listening in on me. She should have kept her fucking mouth shut. She should have taken it to the grave. God damn her!" Julie stopped abruptly.

Ruth recoiled, in a jerky motion, pulled the phone away from her ear.

I could hear clearly as Julie screamed at Ruth, "My mother didn't know shit grandma. She didn't know what the hell she was talking about. She didn't know a God damned thing!"

Ruth straightened up in her chair. She looked at the notepad, wiped away the tears from her cheek with the back of her hand. She followed the script and quickly intervened. "Your mama, she heard. She told me. You were on the phone. How you snapped! Snapped, that's what she said. You snapped and did it. And how you put Craig in that chair. I know now. I know, too. Your mama, she didn't take that secret to the grave. She told me. How could you?"

"Craig and his precious angels got what the fuck they deserved. My mom didn't know a fucking thing, grandma, and you don't know a fucking thing either!"

A dark shadow of hurt enveloped Ruth's face. This was not the little girl who played Candyland and dominoes in this very same kitchen and loved the sfogliatelles she made. That girl had been replaced by some malevolent creature.

Ruth became pale again. The knuckles of the hand holding the receiver blanched, as she gripped it tighter, putting the phone back to her ear. "How could you do such a thing. Oh my God. Your own blood, Julie."

She sobbed into the phone. "This thing, it is what killed your mother, not the cancer. She knew, she knew all this time. It killed her, and it took my Francis, it broke him." Her head listed to the side, as she laid the phone on the table.

Her eyes took on that thousand yard stare and she seemed like a silhouette now. Julie must have hung up as I heard a dial tone.

I picked up the phone and spoke into the receiver, "End of conversation between Julie Wiley and Ruth Scalini. This is Morris Green, December 14th, the time now is 1701 hours." I turned the recorder off.

I spent a few minutes doing my best imitation of consolation. I attempted to assuage the torment Ruth was going through, but my heart wasn't in it. For many years, the Scalini family benefited from the pain and suffering of innumerable people. The chickens had come home to roost.

I replayed the conversation to catch the parts I had not heard. Ruth said she didn't want to hear it again.

"Too fucking bad," I thought and hit play.

Ruth's double chin hit her chest as she listened.

I heard the front door open.

"Ma, hey, who's car is that out there? Ma?"

Anthony Scalini ambled in. His black London Fog flapped open, and a cold breeze accompanied him into the kitchen. Ten years ago, my police reflexes would have had me on my feet, preparing for a confrontation. Older, slower and medicated to the max, I was still sitting at the kitchen table when the big man entered the room.

It took Anthony a few seconds to process the situation of a strange man at his mother's table.

"Who the fuck are you?" He looked closer as his neurons connected. It only took a few more seconds. "I remember you. Green, fucking Detective Green, right? What the fuck are you doing here?"

"What the fuck is he doing here, ma?" Anthony said, looking over at Ruth as he continued searching his brain for an explanation.

I watched his hands. He was not reaching into his waistband or his pockets for a weapon. So far, so good since I didn't have a gun in my waistband. It was in my bag, a significant tactical error.

"Ma, what the fuck is going on here? Ma!" Anthony yelled, stirring Ruth from that desolate place she'd gone.

"Dr. Green, he came to talk to me about Taylor and Robbie. He knows, what happened. He knows what Julie, what Julie did. Cindy told him before she die," Ruth said as she began sobbing.

For a fat man, Anthony moved quickly. His stubby arms stretched out and connected with my chest, pushing the breath out of me and knocking me backwards. The chair and I fell back to the floor with a loud thud. My head, and the back of the chair grazed an old pie safe on the way down. The thud was followed by rattling and breaking glass from inside the cabinet.

"Dio dannazione, Anthony, my Lladros are in there, and some of your grandmother's china," Ruth said, paying little attention to my worsening situation. The old woman, who was a sinking ship two minutes ago, was now, very concerned about her chachkas. What a fucked up family they really were.

Anthony stood over me yelling something in Italian. I assumed it included a description of what was to be my painful demise.

I rolled to my side to get up. Anthony kicked me in the gut with a polished and pointy black shoe tip. The blow finished the deflation process completely, leaving me gasping and gagging, flat on the floor.

The woman who I had just emotionally prosecuted, intervened on my behalf. "Tony, stop! Si sieda, stop! He came to help, to help me understand. I ask him to come. Si sieda, sit down, Tony and listen! You listen to me now! Sedere. Sit!" Her voice was surprisingly strong and forceful.

It was as if the coiled spring inside Anthony had played out. Little Anthony must have listened to his mother, and thank goodness he still did. He stepped back from me, turned and grumbled something unintelligible. He threw his overcoat over a kitchen chair and took a seat.

I had gotten to my hands and knees and was concentrating on breathing without vomiting. I retched a few times. Ruth picked up my chair and then helped me into it. I bent over at the waist and breathed deeply, in and out.

All this time, the digital voice recorder spewed out Ruth's conversation with Julie. The sudden quiet in the room let the phone call take center stage.

"Your mama, on her deathbed, just before she take her last breath, she told me what. She told me she heard on the phone. She heard you talking with that man, your boyfriend. How you said you went crazy, you snapped. Avete fatto. You did it! How you did it! Why would you do it, Julie? My kids and Craig, too. How could you?"

"That bitch! That nosy, snooping bitch listening in on me. She should have kept her fucking mouth shut. She should have taken it to the grave. God damn her!"

"Holy Christ! What are you doing, Ma? What the hell are you doing? Taylor and Robbie are dead. Cindy just died and you're bringing this all back up?"

Anthony returned his attention to me. "And you, motherfucker, who the fuck you think you are coming to my mother's house causing her grief?" He leaned over the table, his face less than a foot away from mine. He grabbed my lapels pulling me up.

"Anthony, you stop! I said stop!" Ruth said, pulling her son's hands off me. Anthony sat back in his chair, huffing, his fat jowls shaking.

"I asked Dr. Green to come. I ask him. He found out what happened. Cindy told him. I ask him to come. He told me what Julie did. How it happened. We called Julie. You heard it, now I know," she said striking the table with her fist.

Ruth turned, picked up a carafe from the counter and poured her son a cup of coffee. She placed the cup and saucer in front of her son. "Now, you sit, drink some coffee. You listen to him."

"How the fuck do you know what happened, Green? How do you know to call my daughter in LA? What do you want?"

Ruth Scalini gave me a glass of water which I sipped. The water soothed my throat, diluting the remnants of the stomach acid that I had nearly puked up. I had come perilously close to losing the sfogliatelles.

I kept my hand on the glass in the event I had to shove it into Anthony's face.

"I spoke to your ex-wife just before she died. She knew what happened. She overheard a conversation that Julie had with the boyfriend. She told me about Julie and James Patrick and what happened that night. She gave a written statement, a formal dying declaration. It was notarized. It's going to go in front of a judge." I said, more like a lying declaration on my part.

I hoped he would buy the lie that the truth was out and soon to be acted upon by the law, and that people, other than me were aware. Anthony was clenching his fists as I spoke. I pushed my chair slowly back from the table to increase the distance from him. I needed to get to my pistol in the bag.

"Mr. Scalini, I met with your ex-wife just before her death. She cleared her conscience. She told me what you knew, or at least strongly suspected, that your daughter is a killer and probably a sociopath. She didn't care about Taylor or Robbie and certainly not about Craig."

I paused, as Ruth looked over at Anthony, neither speaking a word. "Cindy provided confirmation of what we suspected. We all suspected your daughter was involved in the murders somehow and that there may have been a third party in the house."

I slowly scooted towards my bag and the pistol. I thought, "Fuck it. I'm throwing the Hail Mary just like Lawrence. I just hoped it would work out better for me. I gritted my teeth and glared at Anthony, switching a hard gaze to Ruth and back to Anthony.

"You won't be so lucky in protecting her this time. This time the media circus will follow all of you like the snakes following St. Patrick out of Ireland. Since the

OJ trial, the Menendez brothers, Jon Benet, Caycee Anthony, Trayvon Martin, it's a different world out there for suspected murderers, especially involving children. This case will become fresh and new once again. The networks will park their trucks outside this house and every other Scalini location including the Bullpen. The feds will be all over this. You may not suffer as much as I have with this fucking case, but you'll suffer, I guarantee it."

Anthony straightened up in his chair and stood. His jaws clenched and I saw his knuckles blanch. Apparently, Francis Scalini's son did not take kindly to threats. He reached into his pants pocket.

It was like Jorge reaching into the gym bag.

I leaned back, thudded against the pie safe again and rattled the china as I reached under the table inside my bag, blindly searching for my 9mm.

Anthony's hand came out with a small stainless semi-automatic which he leveled at my head. "Bring your hands up on the table now, motherfucker!"

With my eyes on Anthony, I was still scratching inside my bag searching for my weapon. "Dammit Morris, what a worthless tactical piece of shit you've become," I thought.

"I said bring those hands up now, Green! You ain't talking to nobody about this, especially no prosecutors," Anthony growled.

I put both hands on top of the table.

Anthony glanced at his mother. "Go in the other room, Ma! Now!" Anthony commanded. Ruth got up quickly and left the kitchen.

"Think, Anthony, think," I said. "You're gonna get a world of pain when your daughter eventually goes down, but you didn't kill those kids. You want to add the murder of a cop to it? The prosecutor's office and my department, they all know about this. They know I'm here. Is your daughter worth doing a life sentence or worse? If you off me, you'll be the media darling of the month. Whether or not she confesses or makes a deal or not. So, now what?" I asked, stalling, looking around the room for an out.

"Now is when you shut the fuck up. Get up. We're going downstairs."

"Anthony, think about this."

"Shut the fuck up and get up."

As I stood up slowly, Anthony backed away, removing any opportunity for grabbing at him or the gun. With a wiggle of the gun, he motioned towards the basement door, behind and to my left.

I heard the shots, and jerked as if I'd touched a live wire. I should have dove for cover, but that would have required reflexes long subdued by drugs and vodka. I was frozen in position.

I saw Anthony's torso jerk, and lurch forward. It seemed in slow motion. His belly jiggled as he fell to his knees. His left elbow banged on top of the kitchen table. Plates clattered and bounced as if on a trampoline. Coffee spilled onto the tablecloth, spreading like ocean tide, turning the white squares brown. Anthony slumped and fell forward onto the same spot of floor I had just vacated. The back of Anthony's white shirt turned to red, the blood leaking out onto the floor.

Behind him, Ruth was standing with her right arm extended, holding a blue steel, snub-nose revolver in her hand. Smoke was still wandering out from the barrel.

Ruth did not look up. Her voice was bland, monotonal. "Basta abbastanza. Enough is enough. I know why Julie turned out the way she did. Tony, he did things. He did bad things to that girl. My son. I knew. I said nothing. Tony, he made Julie do things. I knew. Cindy, she knew too. My son."

She shook her head slowly, tears dribbled from her puffy cheeks onto her apron. "I have my grandchildren's blood on my hands and now my son's. You go, Dr. Green, you go now!"

In much the same gun wiggling motion as her son had just used, she pointed towards the front door of the house.

I grabbed the digital recorder off the table and stuffed it in my bag. I made it as far as the living room when I heard another gunshot.

I jumped behind the couch and proned out on the hardwood floor, my heart bounding. Finally, I pulled the pistol out of my satchel. I laid there for a few seconds slowing my breathing, trying to gain some semblance of control. My face was next to the floor vent. I felt the furnace kick on. Dust bunnies twirled on the floor under the couch. No other sounds came from the kitchen.

I crawled out and leading with my pistol, peaked around the corner. Ruth Scalini's body lay across her son's, her forehead on the floor. The blood from the hole in her right temple oozed onto the linoleum. A finger wide stream of red flowed towards the expanding pool of blood from Tony's wound. I watched as the mother's blood joined the puddle of her son's, the two bodies silent and still. The furnace turned off. It got very quiet.

I went back to the living room and sat down on the couch. The plastic covering on the furniture crackled like dry twigs underfoot. My side was becoming stiff, a result of Tony's punt into my ribcage. I pulled a flask from my bag and gulped down a couple ounces of Stoli. It burned.

I rested on the couch a few minutes collecting my thoughts. "It must be something in the Scalini's genetic make-up that sanctioned the cancellation of the blood line as a solution to problems. The list of people to whom I owe my suffering just got shorter. It was too bad the rest of the players weren't in the kitchen today. *Death Wish* Grandma Ruth could have dished out justice as expeditiously as she had sfogliatelles. Then, my little goblins would have been able to cross over to their permanent spiritual home. I could have gone on with whatever life I had left to live without the haunting. The tape is damning. Julie Wiley bared her black soul. She'd come close, but she had not said that she killed those kids.

"Unfortunately, Cindy and Ruth Scalini, both potential witnesses for the prosecution, were now dead. I considered my options. I should call 911, then Karen Flavin and MQ. Just like any good police officer who had witnessed a murder-suicide would. The media circus would begin immediately.

"Or, I could wash my coffee cup, spoon and plate, wipe down whatever I touched, and get the fuck out of there. Sooner or later someone would find mother and son. There would be plenty of speculation until the forensics told the tale of an actual Scalini murder-suicide. In the interim, we'd have time to get the DNA and trace evidence from the sweatshirt and the GSR testing to indict everyone."

I stepped over the bodies, avoiding the blood. I took my saucer, coffee cup and spoon, rinsed them with hot water, dried them with a paper towel and replaced them in the cupboard. I wiped down the table where I been sitting, my chair, the pie safe, floor, couch, and anything else I thought I may have touched. I worked my way out of the house, wiping surfaces with the towel. I peeked out the living room windows. Tony's car was in the driveway, parked next to mine. I pulled Ruth Scalini's front door closed softly and wiped the brass handle with the towel.

I peered up her street. I scanned telephone poles and light standards for traffic cameras. There were none. There was no activity on the street. No witnesses to say that there had been any visitors to the Scalini home other than Tony. I pulled away from the curb slowly.

My side was starting to swell and burn. I rifled through my glove box and found some Percocets, took two with another swig from the flask. By the time I had gotten home, I wasn't shaking anymore.

# Chapter Eighty Four

poured a double White Russian, went into the bathroom and took off my shirt. It was torn, streaked with dirt, and damp from fear and sweat. I inspected my side in the mirror and grimaced at the softball sized, angry, purplish red welt just below my ribs.

I washed it off and put a dab of Betadine ointment on the scrape, taping a Telfa pad over the seeping plasma. I slipped on a clean shirt and made another drink. My cellphone rang.

"Morris, it's me," MQ said, his pitch higher with each word. He was either drunk or happy and my money was on the former.

"What. What's up, Kenneth?"

"I bring fortuitous tidings."

"What? Already?" I said hesitantly, wondering how the word about the shooting got out so fast.

I sat down slowly, leaning away from the bruise, still contemplating on what to say and do.

MQ continued, "Morris, I have AK on the phone. I'm going to conference you in. I want you to hear what she just told me. Hold on."

A few clicks and MQ returned to the phone. "Karen, Doc, you both on?"

"I'm here," I said.

"Me too, Kenneth," Karen said.

"Go ahead counselor, please bring the good doctor up to speed."

"All right, Morris, so, listen to this. Remember Dan said he wanted to use an independent lab for the analysis, all right? But I just had the feeling that if it went there, well, it was just a gut feeling that something would go wrong. So, I told him

I took the sweatshirt to the regional lab, but I took the sweatshirt and the GSR kit to our county lab."

"For Christ sake Karen!" I broke in loudly. "I don't need to hear this bullshit right now. We talked at length about this. The county lab was at best incompetent and probably corrupt. Who knows if the Newshams or the Scalinis have a mole there now? What the fuck!" I was about to question Karen's prosecutorial abilities and loyalty, when she cut my tirade in half.

"Green, zip it! I have a source at the county lab, someone I know I can trust. My sister-in-law, she works there. All right? So, I pulled a few favors and had them rush through the analysis. I have the DNA results, just got them today."

"Tell him already counselor, tell him," MQ said with as much salivation in his tone as a dog standing over a plate of bacon.

"Both of the kids, and the husband's blood, are on the sweatshirt. They are doing the trace analysis on some long strands of blonde hair now and I expect we'll probably find that the hairs are Julie Wiley's and if we're lucky, maybe there will be some of James's hair, too. All right, so for a woman who said she didn't see her kids, and had no idea what happened, she has some explaining to do, don't you think?"

MQ added, "And our good ole boy Derrickson is personally taking charge of the gunshot residue testing. He says they will have the comparisons between the powder compositions in about 72 hours. I trust the boy, don't you, Morris?" MQ added.

"Yes I do. I'm sorry, Karen. Sorry I jumped your shit. It's just been one of those days."

"It's all right. You can make it up to me," she responded.

The centipede wearing ice picks for shoes returned to my shoulder as airy murmurs whirled around my ears. Apparently the Wiley children were conferenced in on the call, too.

"What now, AK?" I asked.

"We'll get the GSR results which will be additional cause to implicate Mrs. Wiley, and/or James. Then, grand jury next week. All right, we've scheduled the jurors for at least two consecutive days. I want this thing going, as soon as possible. I'm pushing everything else back. We're going to get some indictments next week. A passle of indictments, all right? A passle meaning when the paddy wagon comes all the girls go. I mean all the Newshams, Scalinis, all the girls. Next week, Thursday morning 10am. I'll need you and Murphy. Be in my office on Thursday at 9:00. Sergeant Murphy, don't be late."

"Have I ever let you down, AK?" MQ asked.

"Yes you have. On more than one occasion, you've arrived late, or with a buzz on. Don't fuck around on this one, all right!"

A sheepish MQ said, "HUA," softly. "Early and with nothing on my breath but Crest."

"I have to go out of town on some personal stuff, help my sister," I said.

"Your sister get divorced again, Morris?" AK asked.

AK and I had been through one of my sister's debacles when we were a thing.

"Yea, but I will be back by Wednesday afternoon. If either of you need me for anything, or anything happens, just call my cell."

"All right, I will see you both next Thursday. Travel safe, Morris."

# Chapter Eighty Five

Dan Wolfe had been in town for a couple of days on business. He and Will spent the night at the Hilton, after closing out the Parasol, a club out in the suburbs. Dan was already up and had started making coffee when Will's cell phone rattled.

Dan handed Will the phone. "Sorry, Will. I tried to be quiet, but it doesn't seem to matter, does it? The damn thing keeps going off."

Will opened his eyes and smiled at Dan. "Thank you. I'm sorry if it woke you."

"I've been up for an hour. Just watching you sleep, making coffee, the usual," Dan said.

He brought over a cup of coffee and put it on the nightstand. Will's beefy thigh stuck out from the covers and Dan gave it a little slap, furthering Will's drift towards waking up.

Will looked at the number on the screen. "It's my father. I better get this."

Chatham Newsham answered. "Jesus Christ, Will. I've been calling your cell phone and leaving messages. Don't you hear your phone? Don't you answer your calls?"

"I'm sorry, dad. I had it on vibrate and didn't hear it. You sound irritated. What's wrong?"

"You need to come to the office right now!"

"What? What's wrong, dad?"

"You need to come to the office right now, Will!" Chatham Newsham's tone was clipped and stern.

Will had heard this voice before. It was something serious, laden with concern.

"What's wrong, dad?" Will asked sitting up, reaching for the coffee. He pulled the sheet over his legs.

"Just get over here. Right away now, Will, don't screw around."

"What's wrong, dad? Is it mom? Tell me."

"Your mom's fine. Get up, get dressed and get over here, now!"

"Jesus. Ok. Do I have time for a shower at least?"

"God damn it, Will. No, you don't have time for anything but getting to the office right now!"

"Ok, Dad, Ok. I'm on my way. I'll be there in thirty minutes. Is that quick enough?

"Make it twenty!" Chatham Newsham hung up the phone.

Will washed his face and brushed his teeth. He'd brought a change of clothes and pulled on Khaki Dockers and a green cashmere knit sweater.

He gave Dan a kiss on the cheek and apologized. "Sorry to rush off. I'll call you later."

Will looked at his phone display. "Oh shit, my battery is about dead. Damn it. Call me at work later and let me know what time your meetings are over."

"I'll be tied up all morning. If I get finished early, I may want to catch a flight home tonight rather than tomorrow. How about dinner and a ride to the airport?"

"You are just so needy," Will said as he closed the door behind him.

Will walked into the Newsham Law Firm, giving a quick wave to Louise. She looked up at him. Her face was taut and anxious, like she had been constipated for days.

The first thing Will noticed when he walked into his father's office was how dark it was. This time of the morning, the blinds were usually wide open. The view from his father's tenth floor, corner office, overlooked the grass tennis courts in the park. To the left of the courts were several massive, interactive stone sculptures for kids to run through and climb on. His father enjoyed watching the tennis players or the children play while he worked.

This morning, the only light was a pink and yellow glaze coming from the rose Tiffany lamp that sat on his father's desk. The lamp had been on that desk for as long as Will could remember.

The lamp's geometric rows and segments of precisely measured panels of orange, white and green, surrounded the red namesake flower design. It was a gift from his mother. The story was that Chatham had finally settled a case of some significance and mom used almost all of the fee dad had earned to purchase the antique lamp.

Seven year old Will would fold a piece of paper over and over in a special method until it formed a dense triangular package which could be used as a football. The Tiffany lamp had a two-stem base of patinated bronze legs. Will and his brothers used the legs for goal posts, flicking field goals, playing on their father's huge desk while waiting for him to finish whatever it was fathers did at their offices. The fact that the lamp was worth probably $80,0000.00 was of no consequence to them, or their father. The big desk and lamp were interactive, much like the stone sculptures and Chatham liked watching his boys play.

Chatham Newsham stood in front of the closed blinds. His back was to Will and he had not noticed Will enter. Chatham Newsham was not wearing his suit coat. Despite the dim lighting, Will could see sweat bleeding through the back of the starched, powder blue shirt. His father never sweated. Will felt a chill. Maybe something happened to one of his brothers, something bad.

"Dad," Will said.

Chatham Newsham turned. His face was unnaturally pale. He looked sick, heart attack sick, Will thought.

"Shut the door, son," Chatham said with the same ominous tone he had used on the phone.

"What's wrong dad? Are you alright? You look bad. What's going on?"

Chatham massaged his temples, moving his fingers to the back of his neck, still rubbing, trying to relieve some of the tension. "I got a call from a source at the county prosecutor's office. Jesus, Will. The Wiley case. They've got enough to indict you, me, Montileone, Anthony Scalini. It's not good, son, not good at all."

Consistently self-centered, Will whined defensively, "Me? What do they have on me? I haven't done anything."

"They have enough."

"What could they possibly have? Nothing. There is nothing to have on me," Will said as he slumped into one of the dark, maroon, tufted lawyer's chairs across from his father's desk.

"What are you so worked up about dad?"

"For Christ sake, Will. Jesus, Mary and Joseph. Will, Will, Will," Chatham said, his head shaking, his voice weakening and trailing off with each successive utterance of his youngest son's name.

"What? What? What do they have? We took care of all the loose ends. That thing is old news."

Chatham came around his desk and stood over his son. Color was returning to his face as he spoke.

"They have Julie Wiley's Miranda form along with the video of her interview with your detectives the night of the murders. They have that mammoth, hand-written bullshit story she wrote for you that I told you to destroy.

"They have something about computer discs with information from the Wiley's home PC and they have some clothing, a sweater or sweatshirt that Julie was wearing that night, and it has DNA evidence on it. God Damn it, Will, the prosecutor has it all. What the hell, son, what the hell! You told me you got rid of all of that!" Chatham was standing directly in front of his son, his arms crossed over his chest. Not only had the rubor returned to Chatham's face, he was becoming scarlet.

Will sat up in the chair, interlaced his fingers and rested his chin on them.

"Aw shit, I gave everything to Larry. I told him to get rid of all that shit. Damn him. I guess he didn't do it."

"You guess he didn't do it. You guess? Fuck!" Chatham raised his arms up in the air, shaking them towards the heavens like a country preacher. "Apparently, upon Lawrence's accidental death, all that shit somehow made its way to Morris Green and Kenneth Murphy, who promptly took it to the PA's office."

Will interrupted, "What are you talking about? Green and Murphy aren't even detectives anymore, you know that. They're not relevant. They've been dickin' around with this case forever and it's never gone anywhere and it won't now either. I'll get with Vinny, we'll handle it."

"Shut up, son! Oh, it's much worse than just that Will. Lawrence wrote a letter, a letter about how we covered up the Wiley murders. About..." he paused, closed his eyes and shook his head. "Hell, Will, about everything, every damn thing."

Will was silent. The tumblers were starting to click in his head. Larry had made good on his spurned lover promise.

"I'm sorry, dad. I trusted Lawrence. He told me he..." Will started to explain, but Chatham cut him off.

"Damn it, Will. You trusted Lawrence? Trusted Lawrence? And you expected him to trust you, too, didn't you? Bullshit, son! I'm not blind or stupid. I know what's been going on in your household. And I wasn't blind or stupid back then when those kids and their father were killed. I remember what you were doing then. You treated him like chattel. You were selfish and petty. You were busy at the time thinking only of yourself, and Julie Scalini's ass, but I didn't care who you fucked, or who fucked you, or that you were wasting your life with that God damned police department. You told me you took care of it, not Lawrence! You said you took care of it! What the hell were you thinking? This is a God damn time bomb son, and it's going to go off very soon."

Chatham Newsham did not swear often. The words were particularly vulgar and felt like bites taken from Will's flesh.

"I'm sorry, dad. What, what can we do? What's going to happen, dad?

Chatham Newsham paced briefly and then sat down behind his desk.

"Once a grand jury hears all of this, they'll indict Julie for the murders of her children and husband. It sounds like James may sustain some damage too. Hell, he may even work a deal and testify. I don't know if they have enough to win a conviction or not, probably not. That doesn't matter right now. This firm, and the Scalinis have been a thorn in the prosecutor's side for years. They will go out of their way to indict us for obstruction of justice, corruption and complicity in the cover-up of the Wiley murders.

Once they have Julie in custody, it will all be over. She'll cooperate with them to save herself. That has always been our concern. She'll give up you, me, the firm, the Bullpen, everything. It could very well open up the Estrilla case and all the cooperation we've had with Chief Montileone and the others over the years. And your Chief, since he's never had any testicles, he'll fold. It will be very, very bad for us."

Chatham paused and took a few deep breaths before continuing. "Listen, son, I know Anthony and Frank Jr. very well. Neither of them have Francis's calculating, calm temperament. I've already spoken with Frank Jr. and given him a briefing. We're going to have a sit down with Anthony tonight, but I am much afraid they may strike out in anger and start eliminating liabilities. You see what they did with Lawrence, don't you? Green and Murphy are walking dead men, that's a given. They may come after you and Montileone. They may have Julie killed, their own flesh and blood. Hell, they may even put a contract on me and burn this place down."

"Fuck the Scalinis!," Will yelled. "They're not the only ones that can pull a trigger."

Chatham stood up from behind his desk and glowered at Will. "God dammit, son. You've never killed anyone, and you don't have the killer instinct. Stop bullshitting and acting like you're some kind of Clint Eastwood character. Stop lying to yourself. Just stop it!"

Will cringed from the painful words his father spewed.

"Son, can you even begin to understand the hurricane that will follow the indictments? What if they find out the whole story behind that FBI agent's sexual transgressions, and how we blackmailed him. And how Mark helped us find out who, at the profiling unit, was assigned to the Wiley case. Mark's career at the State Department would be over. Dammit, Will, our life, your life, will be chum to the media sharks. Everything is about to change."

Will dry heaved into the wicker trash basket.

"Oh Jesus," Chatham said as he came from around the desk, knelt next to his son and put his arm around his shoulder. They stayed in this position for several minutes until Will gained some composure. Chatham handed Will his handkerchief,

"Here son, I know you don't have one."

Will's eyes were wet and his voice weak. "Dad, I'm sorry. I'm sorry. I figured Lawrence did what I told him. He never said a word all these years. I don't understand how…"

"It doesn't matter at this point. I'm sending you out of town for now. Time has a way of diluting drama. Spencer and I will take point on our defense initially. That is if they don't send someone after us right away. I've already retained additional counsel and security for us. Maybe after the initial blitzkrieg of indictments and the spectacle of it all calms down, you can come home. I just don't know at this point, Will, and I'm not taking chances. Call Chief Montileone and tell him a family matter came up. Tell him you have to go out town for a few days. Sound normal. I don't want him to suspect anything. They'll probably arrest him within a week anyway, but he's not my concern right now, you are."

Chatham pulled out a brown leather satchel from under his desk and handed it to Will. "There's ten thousand dollars in here, along with an e-ticket and your passport. I have a limo waiting downstairs for you. He will take you directly to the airport. You are on the 1:15 flight this afternoon to LaGuardia. You have a hotel reservation at the Weston in Times Square booked under your mom's maiden name. Check in and wait to hear from me. I'll call you at 6, NY time. Go directly to the airport now. Don't go home, don't go to the police station. Whatever you need, toothbrush, clothes, whatever, buy it at LaGuardia when you get there. Use cash, no credit cards. I want to limit your paper trail. I'm making international flight arrangements for all of us just in case. Got it?"

"But, I need to…" Will stammered.

"No, son! You don't need to do anything, but what I just said. Please, Will. Just do it."

They hugged.

"I love you, son."

"I love you, too, dad. I'm really sorry."

"I know. Now, go. I'll call you tonight."

Chatham picked up his phone. "He's on the way down. Yes, straight to the airport. Thank you."

# Chapter Eighty Six

**W**ill closed the office door behind him and shuffled past Louise who looked at him with the face of a lost Bassett Hound. A black Lincoln Limo with windows tinted beyond legality waited in the garage. The driver stood by the rear passenger door. Will was still dazed and drained.

"Hello, Mr. Newsham. It's been quite a while." Kostaki Koulakis opened the car door and watched as Will just stared at him as if he had spoken in his native Greek.

"Please, sit, sit," Kostaki urged with sweeping hand motions.

Will poured himself into the seat. His head was a blender of what ifs, and now whats, swirling at 1000 RPM. The car started moving through the morning traffic. He grabbed a bottle of Evian from the shelf, took a long drink and splashed some on his face and around the back of his neck.

After a few minutes he spoke, "Kos, I need to stop by my house before we go to the airport."

"Mr. Newsham said I take you straight to airport. No stops. Your father was very clear on that."

"It will only take a minute. I have to pick up, uh, the charger for my phone."

"He was very clear. Directly to the airport."

Will took a hundred dollar bill from the satchel and handed it through the partition.

"Kostaki, to my house. I'll just run in and run out. Dad will never know and you get a C note."

"Very well, Mr. Newsham."

The back seat of the limo may as well have been a wooden church pew. Will squirmed, sat straight up, slumped, leaned forward and rocked back and forth. His legs were alive, bouncing up and down on his toes. He drummed on his knees and the seat. Every now and then Kostaki turned his head around and looked.

"You all right, Mr. Newsham?"

"Yea. Fine. Just peachy."

Twenty five minutes later the limo pulled into Will's driveway. Will punched the garage door opener code. He slipped in between the bass boat and his personal vehicle to reach the kitchen service door. He wondered if he'd ever be able to take his boat out on the lake again.

Will went into his bedroom and found his charger on the nightstand. He grabbed one of his military back packs and threw a few shirts, trousers and underwear in the bag. The real reason he wanted to come home was to grab a piece.

He opened the nightstand drawer and took out Lawrence's Taurus .38 five-shot revolver. He opened the cylinder. It was loaded with hollow point bullets. It couldn't hurt to be armed in New York, irrespective of whether or not his world had gone to hell. He would stop by the UPS store and mail the gun to the hotel.

Will came out of his bedroom. Vinny and James were standing in the hallway.

"Shit!" Will yelled in a tenor's range. He dropped the backpack. "You scared the shit out of me, Vinny. I guess you guys heard."

Vinny raised his Glock and neatly fired two shots.

"Fuck, Vinny. What the fuck," James said as his back thudded against the wall, knees buckling. He slumped to the floor. A single magnum round from Vinny's .40 calibre pistol ripped into James's chest. A few raspy gurgles accompanied another 'What the fuck?' as James's chin, hung to his chest. Blood seeped from the hole in his chest and he exhaled his last breath of life.

Will ducked back in the bedroom. He started to speak, but found it difficult. He felt sick like his stomach was swaying in a hammock during a Tsunami. His green cashmere sweater was wet and clinging to his belly. The beige Dockers were turning red. His legs gave out. Will fell back against his dresser and slid down to a seated position on the floor. He listed to the left struggling to keep from sliding prone.

Vinny stepped in the doorway assessing his victims and the expanding pools of blood. He made eye contact with Will and shook his head, "Sorry, Will, no loose ends. You shoulda never trusted Lawrence like that. Look what I had to do to James. Now, I gotta go do my cousin because of you. You stupid faggot fuck," Vinny said, raising the Glock at Will's head to tie up the last, loose end.

Will held Lawrence's .38 against his hip and angled the barrel upwards. He squeezed the trigger. The bullet struck Vinny's throat, tearing open his trachea and his right carotid artery. Vinny's blood sprayed onto the wall with big droplets streaking down towards the floor like a bad painter's drips. Vinny dropped the Glock and clutched his throat with both hands. He made a few shrill, strident sounds as he tried to breathe. He slumped to his knees, and collapsed over Will's legs, unable to do anything else but die.

Will struggled to move from under Vinny. He grunted and sobbed in a staccato rhythm as the last few ounces of blood spurted from his macerated right renal artery. He slid to the floor onto his back one arm over his head, the other clutching the hole in his abdomen. The two men were posed in much the same fashion as two dead children who were found in a workshop years earlier.

A short time later, Kostaki Koulakis went into the house looking for Will. He would tell the story of this day many times.

# Chapter Eighty Seven

Patty Reznor put on her best blue jeans and a bright cotton shirt. She bought the shirt just last week, specifically for her trip. It was yellow with a green and orange floral pattern on the shoulders and chest. It was her favorite, because it had pearl snaps for buttons, just like the shirts her mom used to wear.

After Mike died, Patty moved into a group home. The residents suffered from a variety of conditions, many with autism spectrum disorders. There were others who had suffered a brain injury, stroke or had various levels of mental disabilities. They were all allowed to care for themselves to the extent they were able. Several walked or were shuttled to local businesses and sheltered workshops where they washed dishes, stuffed envelopes or stocked shelves.

Patty's doctors found a combination of medications that stabilized her depression. Aside from the side effect of a little hyperactivity and confusion, with time she had become quite functional.

She was still thin, but had put on a little weight and was nearing 105 pounds. She kept her dark hair short for low maintenance and rarely wore makeup, but today Patty put on some eyeliner and blush. She wanted to look her best for her trip to see Beverly.

Beverly Antonacci had been Patty's roommate at the group home. They had become friends as the layers of their dysfunction dissolved. After nearly a year living together, Beverly suffered a small stroke and moved home to Anaheim to be close to family. The two friends stayed in touch, and now Patty was going to visit Beverly and they were going to go to Disneyland. Patty thought of the roller coasters and funnel cakes, the magic castle, the ocean and going to the beach.

Patty methodically packed her yellow canvas backpack, following directions given to her by her mother, seemingly a hundred years ago. First she packed her shoes, stuffed with socks to save space. The matching yellow, nylon draw string bag containing her hair brush, toothbrush, toothpaste, her medications and what little makeup she brought, were packed next to the shoes. She tucked her underwear along the edges of the backpack and laid an extra pair of slacks, another pair of blue jeans, two pairs of shorts, a one-piece swim suit, two collared, yellow knit shirts and three yellow T-shirts on top.

Yellow was her favorite color. Her therapist said that was a good color to have as her favorite because it was sunny, bright and happy. Patty zipped up the case. She looked out the window checking for the cab. It was raining. She grabbed her umbrella, put on her favorite yellow raincoat and her yellow cap. She looked like the Morton's Salt girl.

Patty Reznor rode quietly in the back of the taxicab as it headed towards the airport. This was her first trip out of town since everything had happened. Upon arrival, she paid the driver, slipped on her backpack, hurried through the rain into the terminal and took her place in the security line.

She felt kind of jumpy and shaky. It was different than the usual edginess she experienced as a result of her medications. She even felt a little nervous. This was particularly odd since she probably had more air miles than anyone in the long security line.

A tall, middle-aged pilot with snow white hair, confidently strode past the line pulling his black rollerboard carry-on behind. He showed his credentials to the security personnel and disappeared.

Then, as had been occurring with increasing frequency, a memory from Patty's past life returned like an ocean wave rolling gently up the beach. Ever since the doctors had weaned her off of the heavy anti-psychotic medications, memories had been smuggling into her consciousness, hitchhiking on something she saw or felt. This time it was the handsome pilot acting as trigger.

She closed her eyes and thought of her father, so tall and thin, standing there smiling in his pressed, dark blue, pilot's uniform, the gold braids on the sleeves and the gleaming white shirt.

He always wore his dark blue hat with the shiny brim. It was so shiny, she could see her reflection in it. When she was little, Patty referred to the hat as his 'ice cream man's cap'. Her father would always laugh when she called him the ice cream man, and sometimes, on the way home from the airport, they would stop at a Dairy Queen for a Dilly Bar.

She remembered how she and her mother would always sit in first class. They would read the magazines together. Patty always sat next to the window to watch the clouds.

Sometimes, the stewardess would motion for her to come up front into the cockpit. This was way before September 11, 2001 when flying was fun.

Patty would look at all the gauges and dials with amazement in her eyes. Her father would explain the purpose of each dial. She would look out the windshield into the brilliant blues, the prismic hues of the sun, the thick white blanket of sky below them. She felt like they were in heaven. Maybe they were.

Then a memory of Mike, the other tall and thin man in her life, crept into her consciousness. There he was sitting at his desk in that glass walled office at the car dealership. His spindly arms and twig-like fingers pushing a pen and a stack of papers across his desk toward a prospective buyer. He had that Snidely Whiplash smile. She thought of her life with, and without him. He had stuck by her through the worst of it. The hospitalization after Craig's death. The inpatient and then outpatient treatment. The endless tests, doctors, medications and counselors. She thought of Mike. Poor Mike, who had gone through a series of sales jobs as he attempted to manage a seriously ill wife and a cocaine habit that eventually took his life.

A faint smile came over Patty's face as her thoughts turned to the warm sand, sunny weather and the beaches she and Beverly would find. The man behind her in line bumped up against her. Rather abruptly, she left the beach and returned to the stark, sterile grey and hard tile floor of the airport.

Her hand quivered as she held the postcard of Disneyland that Beverly had sent, asking her to come visit and providing directions to her house. It was a picture of the Magic Kingdom, the fireworks, and a smiling Mickey Mouse in the upper right corner. She concentrated on the picture. Patty planned on standing in the same place the photographer stood to watch the fireworks and take her own picture.

The chubby woman in front of Patty took a plastic tray from the stack next to them. She put her shoes, jacket and purse in the tray. Everything matched the woman's shirt and pants, all purple. The chubby lady's clothes brightened up the line of gray trays containing overcoats and laptops waiting to go through the x-ray machine.

"She looks like an eggplant," Patty thought.

The purple lady walked through the scanning machine. Patty stood watching, still wiggling, but not as nervous.

The TSA officer spoke to Patty, "Ma'am, please remove your shoes and jacket, put them in one of the bins."

Patty stared at him without saying a word. He repeated the request. It finally registered.

Patty slipped off her tennis shoes and her shiny, yellow rain slicker and put them, along with her umbrella in the tray as instructed. She pushed the tray onto the conveyor belt followed by her yellow backpack. She walked through the scanner and showed the TSA officer her postcard. He smiled, "Going to Disneyland are you?" Patty nodded. "We are. My friend Beverly and me. And we're going to the beach and probably shopping too."

"You have a wonderful time and say hello to Mickey for me," the officer said.

Patty put her shoes on, grabbed her bag and followed the eggplant lady.

"I'm a little yellow banana and she's a big, purple eggplant. A banana and an eggplant going to California." Patty whispered to herself.

The two pastel women boarded the plane.

# Chapter Eighty Eight

Leaving town with the grand jury so close was a two edged sword. I had just witnessed a murder-suicide, so my absence and the distance away from the incident would be good. However, I wanted to be around to make sure MQ and I had all our ducks in a row.

But, I had promised my sister Carol that I would help her move, again. She was moving to Santa Monica from the Hollywood area and had already rented a truck and trailer. She and her new boyfriend had taken off work for two days. I was committed.

Carol's history was predictable. Husband-boyfriend-divorce-husband-boy-friend-divorce-husband-boyfriend-divorce. It was a consistent pattern as Carol sought the love she didn't get as a child, or so her psychobabble therapist told her.

I called MQ as I filtered thru the long airport security line. "I'm on my way to my sister's Murph. I tell you, I have no business going now. I shouldn't be taking the time off. We should be together, prepping for next week."

"Let not your heart be troubled, doc. You know the facts and nuances of this case as well as anyone. I took a couple personal days off and I am doing nothing but reviewing Wiley files. I'm not going back to work until the indictments are handed down and they take Montileone and Boy Wonder away in cuffs. Don't get all ferklempt rabbi. Relax, get a little sun, run on the beach. Find some hot babe. Do something exciting so I can live vicariously through you."

"Right. I'm a real swinger, Mr. Party, that's what they'll put on my headstone," I said, cradling the phone with my shoulder. I put my laptop in a tray and lifted my carry-on onto the conveyor belt. "I swear MQ, this is the last time I'm moving my friggin' sister. At some point, she has to get her shit together and settle down. She's no spring chicken anymore for Chrissake."

MQ immediately recognized the absurdity before I did. "Morris, may I remind you that your gestalt is far from settled. You take a variety of prescriptions for God knows what, chased down your gullet with brand name vodka. You suffer from audio hallucinations and are currently being haunted by dead people. Yet Carol has to get her shit together?"

"Game, set and point well taken."

"Travel safely, doc. Give me a call if you need to talk."

I stuffed my carry-on in the overhead compartment and settled into the aisle seat in Row 14. I had scanned the Wiley file to pdfs and decided to review a few on my laptop during the flight.

As I settled in, I was jarred by another traveler as she went past my seat. A skinny woman in a loud, yellow rain slicker. Her equally blaring bright yellow backpack slammed into my left shoulder. Not even an "I'm sorry," or "Excuse me."

The woman juggled her things into the overhead compartment and sat down behind me. Over the next few minutes, there was more jostling and bumping transferred through the seatback. I felt like I was in a horse and buggy and we hadn't even lifted off yet.

I leaned into the aisle, turned around and gave her a "Please settle down" look. She smiled back with that faraway "I'm not right" stare that I'd seen on clinic psych patients, or the homeless after donating a dollar. I gave her a tight lipped smile in return.

They hadn't yet made the announcement to turn off phones so I called Margie. "Hey girlfriend. I just wanted to call and tell you that I wish you were here sitting next to me. They've got me sandwiched between this smoking hot, Swedish film star Ulla, and her twin sister, Viveka, and this flight has free Jaegermeister shots."

"Hi, Morris, so, you're in an aisle seat and no one is sitting next to you, huh?"

"Yea."

"I wish I could be there with you, too, babe," she said. "Sun and surf sounds much more fun than shootings and stabbings, but I must work. I have this really high maintenance boyfriend. He has so many issues I have to deal with, it's really too much to even discuss on the phone."

"I'm so sorry for you. Anyway, if history is a marker for the future, this won't be the last time I have to move my sister. Maybe you can make the next trip and help me. I'm not getting any younger and her refrigerator is not getting any lighter."

"Well, be careful and don't hurt yourself old timer. Did you at least take a pair of swimming trunks so you could get in some beach time?"

"I've got some running shorts and I plan to get in some miles on the sand. Other than that, I have a lot to review for the grand jury. Which I hope to do at the beach while stuffing limes into multiple bottles of Corona."

"I will be so glad when you are finally free of this case, and all of those monsters have their well deserved, wooden stakes sticking out of their chests. Maybe we can both get a good 8 hours sleep, uninterrupted by ghosts, trains or Harvey Keitel. It's been a long time coming. I am so happy for you that the end is near. Happy for us too."

I started to agree, but heard a pinging noise over the phone.

"Oh shit! God dammit, anyway," Margie said. "How rude. I gotta go, Morris, someone just coded. Be careful. I love you."

Click.

I powered down my phone for the flight.

I closed my eyes and settled back in my seat as the plane climbed. A murmur of unintelligible words marched through my head as a muscle cramp under my left shoulder began to annoy me like a hangnail. Apparently, my visitors travel the friendly skies. A double Stoli on the rocks manicured the discomfort away and stifled the voices.

Margie said she loved me. It sounded so natural coming out of her. I think I love her, too. She's perfect, and yet I wonder what resuming something with AK would be like. I reached into my pocket and swallowed a Xanax bar, hoping it and the alcohol would temper the self reproach I was feeling.

Thankfully, the yellow girl calmed down, too, and the remainder of the flight was uneventful.

# Chapter Eighty Nine

Carol picked me up at the airport and the work began right away. I spent the next two days packing, loading, schlepping and unpacking in the heat. I kept my mouth shut about Carol's current boyfriend, Ryan, the 40ish, multifunction printer/scanner/fax machine salesman. The guy reminded me of George Fennelman. He exchanged Fennelman's speech dysfluency of overusing 'like' with 'Dude'. I heard Ryan say far too often, "Dude, am I right or what?" By the time we finished at the end of the second day, I wanted to shove a printer cartridge down his throat.

I had decided to stay an extra day and do a drive-by of Julie Wiley's condo. I wanted to make sure of the address, get a description of the property and identify any vehicles. In the event arrest warrants or search warrants would be issued, any additional information I could garner would be helpful to AK and the California cops. Plus, I wanted to catch a glimpse of her if possible. I wanted to lay eyes on the woman responsible for the hell I'm living in.

Rather than couch surfing at my sister's with the 'Dude', I had checked into the Marriott hotel on the beach in Santa Monica. With my sister safely tucked away in her new place, I returned to the hotel. It was dusk, but still comfortably warm, 78 degrees with 80% humidity. They expected temperatures in the mid 80s for several more days. I changed and went for a five mile jog, 2 ½ miles out and back along the beach. I slowed to a walk at the end of the run as I reached the cobblestone drive under the canopy in front of the hotel.

"A hot one today, no?" one of the valets asked.

I nodded, still catching my breath and continued on into the hotel. I glanced at my watch. It had taken me 55 minutes. "Fuck me, 11 minute miles. I may as well get tennis balls for the bottom of my walker. What a crock of shit."

I boarded the elevator, stepping in between a family of five. They gave the sweaty old man some space. I showered, put on a T-shirt and jeans and headed for the bar. I ordered some tasty stuffed mushrooms and a grouper sandwich for dinner from a chiseled waiter. I supposed he was a Brad Pitt stand-in, waiting tables while waiting for his big break. I watched sports and news on the 20 televisions surrounding me.

I pulled up Margie's number in my contacts a dozen times, but hesitated punching the call button. She loves me, warts and all, and that is saying something. Nevertheless, I decided there was just too much on my plate right now. I will delve into relationship issues after the grand jury. Morris Green, the master switchman, successfully avoiding an emotional commitment.

I drank alone until just after midnight and gave Brad a $30 tip. My plan was to get up early, grab a rental car and head out to find my murderess.

Thanks to the vodka and an Ambien, I overslept. I yawned, pried my eyes open and looked over at the clock. I jolted up like a fireman. "Holy shit, 11 'o' clock? How can that be? I never sleep late!"

The sun glared loudly through the tinted window and I winced at the beautiful beach scenery less than a ¼ mile away. I pulled the drapes closed and sat back on the bed, trying to massage the fog and headache out of my temples. After a few minutes, I reopened the drapes and hurriedly rifled through my bag for some clean clothes. It was near noon when I called the concierge desk to arrange for a vehicle.

A pleasant woman with what sounded like an Australian accent answered, "I will transfer you to the car rental desk, hold please." I flipped the TV on while holding and found a local station.

They were airing an exclusive 'On the Scene' story about a dog left in a car in the California heat. There were images of a Silver BMW coupe parked in a shopping mall lot, the rear driver's side window broken out. Waves of heat rolled off the asphalt parking lot. A ticker on the bottom of the screen listed the noon temperature as 89 degrees. The owner of the Beemer was apparently in the mall shopping.

A morbidly obese, Hispanic woman with dirty sweat rings on her shirt and a toddler on her hip was being interviewed. She had apparently called 911. "I don't know how anyone could leave a leetle dog in a car in thees heat. There is no excuse for something like thees. I pray to Jesus it will be ok." She crossed herself.

The reporter, sweat beads popping on his forehead, spoke to the anchor at the station, "Don, this is really a dramatic story. Our News First van was in the area when we heard the call on our scanner, dispatching the police to the scene. We were here when the police broke into the vehicle to rescue the little thing. Here's how that went down."

I sat on the edge of the bed, and sipped a bottle of the hotel's Evian that I would probably be charged 6 bucks for. "A dog in a car is breaking news down here? Must be a pretty slow news day."

I was about to change channels when the news crew's video showed the officers punching out the rear window, opening the BMW and removing the listless pooch from the backseat.

"Holy shit. They must really like their dogs down here. If I would've ever busted out a window to get to a dog, there'd have been hell to pay. Montileone would have had a fit. Don't these guys have Slim Jims to pick door locks?" I continued watching.

"I'm happy to report that the pup has come around," the reporter said. "We gave it some of our bottled water. The little fella really drank it up. Don, the police checked the vehicle's license plate," the reporter read from his notepad, "The vehicle belongs to Julie Wiley, one of our own residents of Santa Monica. We were still here when Mrs. Wiley returned to her car and this is what happened."

I focused on the television, wondering whether I had actually heard what I thought I had heard.

The camera zoomed in on a woman walking towards the news crew and police. She was carrying two pink plastic shopping bags.

I wondered what Julie Wiley looked like now. I was hoping that she had become a slovenly, stringy haired, trailer trash looking piece of shit. I was as wrong as Bernie Madoff. A stunningly sexy body with long blonde hair tied in a pony tail approached the scene. Her face was partially obscured by large Hollywood style, white framed, oval sunglasses. But as the camera zoomed in, I recognized her immediately.

"Well I'll be damned!" A burst of electrical buzz oscillated down my arms and legs like a cracking bullwhip. I fell back on the bed catching my breath and heard the whoosh of bleating voices, "Maaaaama, Maaaaama." The words were as recognizable as anything coming out of the news reporter's mouth. The children were close.

I turned on my side to see the TV. Julie Wiley was wearing a white spandex top and red nylon, workout pants. I could tell by the definition in her arms, the flat stomach and crisp cheekbones that she was no stranger to Pilates or spinning classes. Clearly, her physical appearance had not suffered as a result of the murders, and why should it? The death of her kids was no more of a bother to her than breaking a heel on a pair of her shoes.

I watched the drama as the police officer approached her and asked her if the BMW was hers.

"What's the problem?" she asked, and then noticed her broken window. "What the 'bleep' did you do to my car? Are you 'bleeping' crazy or something?" She stomped around the car, continuing to scream obscenities that were censored with more bleeps.

The officer explained that her dog was nearly dead due to the heat. She continued to yell at the officer. "I was only in there five minutes, this is 'bleep'!"

"Maaaaama, Maaaaama," the kids said.

The camera panned on a small crowd of shoppers that had gathered. The officer politely asked her to settle down. "Ma'am, I've been on the scene for nearly 15 minutes, long enough for us to get in your car, rescue your dog, revive it and wait for you to come out. Please settle down."

"That's 'bleep'. Who's going to fix my window? What's your 'bleeping' name?"

"Ma'am please settle down," the officer requested.

"What the 'bleep'! You busted my 'bleep' window!"

"Ma'am, please settle down and lower your voice. If you don't relax I will have to cite you for peace disturbance."

"You break into my car and now you're going to 'bleeping' cite me? I don't think so buddy. I want to see your boss. Get your 'bleep' damn supervisor here right now! This is 'bleep'."

The camera returned to the reporter.

"Don, a lieutenant arrived and asked us to stop filming at that point. The pooch has been taken to the shelter to be checked by a vet. Mrs. Wiley was given a summons for peace disturbance and animal endangerment. She'll have her day in court. From Westfield Century Mall, this is Chris Martinez, back to you at the station."

I laid back on the bed. My mind wandered to Bev Goldstein's notes. To the story about what had happened at the Oakview Baskin Robbins when Julie Wiley swung her purse into a woman's face in a similar incident.

"Maaaaama, Maaaaama, Maaaaama, Maaaaama," the call from my specters resumed and became louder than the television. I'd heard enough from the little bastards. I sat up on the edge of the bed. "What the fuck do you want? We're gonna put your mother on death row and clear your father's name. What the else do you want from me?"

"This is the car rental desk. I'm sorry. What did you say? Sorry for the wait, how can I help you?" The voice on the phone startled me back to discussions with the living.

# Chapter Ninety

While I was still asleep due to the Ambien, Patty and Beverly had eaten a breakfast of frosted Pop Tarts and orange juice. They had packed a cooler with soda, summer sausage, cheese, crackers and fruit and were going to spend the day at the pier and the beach. Beverly and her mom had gone to the store to pick up some sun block.

The flat screen in the living room was on. A news crew was reporting a disturbance at a shopping mall. Patty's attention locked onto the TV as she watched, her mouth agape.

A shadowy glaze came over her. She leaned forward, craning her neck towards the TV. She recognized the woman. The news reporter hammered the spike into Patty's brain when he identified the dog owner as Julie Wiley of Santa Monica. Patty continued staring at the TV. She didn't see the next story on a land development scam.

As had happened at the airport when the pilot walked by, a film reel of past events, long lost to her conscious mind, started playing a memory.

She was at Craig's house, standing on the landing, holding Craig's phone. He had forgotten it at her house and she was dropping it by. She felt the confusion as she saw Julie Wiley propping Craig's head on the barrel. She flinched as the explosion from the gun surprised her. She saw a misty curtain of pink and red envelope the man who loved her. In an instant, her memory of that day, the day that had been buried for so many years, returned intact, clear and succinct. "Julie killed Craig, Julie killed my Craig."

On the day it happened, she had become a blank slate of nothingness. And she had stayed that way for such a long time.

Patty stepped out onto the porch, leaned over the rail and vomited. Strawberry Pop-Tart and orange juice blanketed the pebbled walk below. The memories triggered a migraine headache and Patty laid down on the guestroom bed and pulled the covers over her head.

While in bed, her mind's projector continued to display memories long repressed. Chronological newsreels of her life returned. It was a series of visions, each moment, a picture of who she was before it had happened.

She remembered her trips with her parents, wearing a beret, posing in front of the Eiffel Tower, her wedding to Mike in the city park, huddled under the shelter, the loud pinging from the raindrops on the metal roof.

She saw Craig. Their very first meeting when he'd come over to visit Mike. She watched as her relationship with Craig matured, from friends, to confidants, to lovers. The memories washed over her like warm Kodachrome waves. She loved caring for Craig. They shared so many dinners when Mike was away. He helped her with the dishes. She helped him in dealing with the misery Julie dished out. She remembered their talks, their lovemaking, his tenderness and understanding. The solace he said he found with no one else but her, Patty Reznor. She was someone to Craig, someone important to him. He was her soul mate, and she was his.

Finally, she watched Craig's murder again. Patty's body tetanized, every joint fully extended. She screamed but no sound came forth. With open, cavernous eyes, dark as obsidian, she watched Craig's murder over and over. The curtain of pink froth enveloped Craig as his head exploded.

She recognized the day that Craig, her true soul mate died, as the pivotal event that led to her decline into the darkness. It was the event that stole her love and her life. It stole her chance for the happiness that her parents had shared with her, the happiness she felt with Craig. The monster, the killer, was a thief too.

In the quiet darkness of the room, she thought to herself, "She took my Craig. And she took away his children too. Yes, she took away the children. She's a monster." Her fists clenched and she beat the bed. "A monster."

Patty was angry and confused, "Why had Julie done that to Craig and Robbie and Taylor? She killed them all. How could she do that? Why would she do that? Why Craig? Why Taylor? Why Robbie? Why me?"

She had no answers, other than that Julie was everything the bible says is bad. She is evil, wicked and cruel. The monster is everything the bible says is bad. Julie Wiley was the beast that killed the man who loved her and the children he loved. Julie was no different than the heart attack that had taken her father and the heartbreak that had taken her mother. Julie Wiley was a disease, a monster. She was the devil.

The seizing muscle contractions subsided and Patty rolled to her side. She clutched the pillow to her chest assuming a fetal position. She rocked back and forth on the bed. Her chest heaved as she wept uncontrollably. Tears splotched her pillow. For the first time that she could recall, she was able to feel the loss. She was able to grieve. Patty wept for Craig, for Taylor and Robbie and for herself.

The shaking and sobbing became hiccups. Patty's choppy breaths finally slowed to an even mechanical pace. She stood, stretched her arms out wide and took a deep breath in, exhaling slowly. She looked at the damp and wrinkled pillow she'd hugged for comfort, and the rumpled blanket and comforter. She looked down at her shirt, stained with red jelly and orange juice. Patty spoke out loud, "What a mess I've made." Her voice sounded different.

She shook her head, something was quite different. She didn't have the usual foggy, dull, drab medicated monotone and she felt electric, excited, and somehow fresh or cleansed, like she had gone down to the river in a white robe and been baptized by a preacher in the name of Jesus. She didn't feel the weight of anxiety brought on by having to endure another day.

The squeezing pressure in her head that she had grown accustomed to every morning was absent. She felt a clarity. She felt light and clean. Something had changed.

She looked in the mirror and spoke to her reflection. "Patty Reznor, you have a purpose. You have something to do."

Patty went into the bathroom, got a drink of water and then took a shower turning the hot water on full blast. By the time she finished, she was all pink and tingly. Her skin felt warm and somehow safe, like when she put clothes on right after they had come out of the dryer. Even after she dressed in a pair of jeans and put on her favorite yellow and white shirt, the country one with the pearl buttons, even after she dried her hair, she still felt a comfortable buzz of energy and excitation traveling up and down her spine.

Patty made several phone calls until she had gotten the information she wanted. She went into Beverly's kitchen and got what she needed. She packed and went out to the street. A cab pulled up.

Patty pushed her backpack across the back seat and got in. She told the driver the address. He looked into the rear-view mirror and they pulled away from Beverly's house.

The air in the taxi was a familiar swill of stale, musty odors thick as syrup. She sniffed in deeply and closed her eyes. A picture of that room in her basement formed. Mike had a weight room with black vinyl benches, barbells, racks of dumbbells and several blue, rubber floor mats. He had a baseboard heater and would turn it on high in order to sweat. A smile crossed her face as she recalled skinny Mike, flexing his muscles in the mirror. He was so skinny, you could see each muscle. She remembered when Craig would come over and work out. She would peek in and watch them. They lifted weights without their shirts. She felt a warm glow as she remembered Craig's bulky muscles and smelled that familiar fetid odor that slipped through the crack of the basement door and filled the cab.

The drone of the taxi's engine was soothing. She looked out the window as they past strip malls, tall apartment buildings, restaurants everywhere and then onto one of the widest highways she had ever seen. The driver sped up, switched lanes back and forth and mumbled strange words she didn't understand as motorcycles passed by them, only inches from her window. He honked his horn every couple of minutes. They exited the highway and drove down streets with too many stoplights to even count. Each intersection seemed almost the same to Patty. There were stores everywhere. Some had impressive neon lights and huge mirrored windows with parking valets in red or black vests standing outside, while others were gilded with iron gates and shabby people leaning against the walls smoking cigarettes. But everywhere, it was crowded on the street, people were on the move, either walking, jogging or bike riding.

Patty's thoughts turned inward, "I am a nobody. I have no one now. Mom and dad are gone. Mike is gone. Craig, who I should have shared a happy life with, is gone, taken by a cruel woman without a heart or a soul, a devil who took the children I should have had with my Craig. Julie Wiley, Julie Wiley, Julie Wiley, Julie Wiley, Julie Wiley, Julie Wiley, Julie Wiley, Julie Wiley Julie Wiley, there is no room for her anymore. This world is too crowded. She is rancid, evil. No room for the evil disease she spreads. No room for Julie Wiley, Julie Wiley, Julie Wiley, Julie Wiley."

The dark skinned cab driver turned back to her, "What did you say? I did not understand you?"

"How much longer is it?" Patty asked.

"Not far miss, 10 minutes."

Patty took out her spiral notebook of wide- ruled paper she used to chronicle important things. Patty started writing as the cab drew nearer to Julie Wiley's.

To whom it may concern:
My name is Patty Reznor. I live at the Circle of Hope, 11327 Warwick Circle in Montgomery Heights. I work for Mr. Schrader at the closet rack company. I have

killed Julie Wiley. It had to be done because she is the devil. There is no room for her. She killed Craig Wiley. I saw her do it. I saw her. Craig and I were going to be married, raise his kids Taylor and Robbie, and have our own children and buy a nice house and a new car and go on trips to far-away places like my mom and dad did, and live to be old together but Julie Wiley ruined that. She is the devil. She killed Robbie and Taylor too. I am sure of it. This all happened in Oakview. The world will be a better place now that she is dead. I have no one anymore and I will find Craig when I die. Which might just be today.

Patty Reznor

Patty closed her notebook and returned it to her backpack.

The taxi passed through the open gate of the complex where the monster lived. There was no one in the guard shack. Patty told the driver to stop just past the monster's home.

The cabbie opened her door. She paid her fare and gave the driver two twenty dollar bills for a tip. He nodded his head and mumbled something that sounded like thank you.

Patty turned without saying a word. She walked around looking at the brass numbered addresses on each of the identical, pastel townhomes. She stood in the breezeway of a yellow and tan stucco two story. The front door was flanked by tall palm trees. She looked up and down the street. It was eerily quiet.

All the windows of the townhome where she stood were closed and the blinds were drawn. She took out her cell phone and called the number directory assistance had given her for Julie Wiley. An answering machine picked up on the fourth ring and a chipper voice responded.

"Hi, this is Jules. I can't get to the phone right now. I know you know what to do, so do it after the beep. Bye Bye."

# Chapter Ninety One

I put on a black Under Armour T-shirt and running pants and checked out of the hotel. I threw a bag with my camera and binoculars onto the front seat of the rental car. I headed towards the highway winding my way in and out of traffic. I'd taken my morning cocktail of pain meds and anxiolytics and yet the vibrating drone in my shoulder did not abate. Apparently, Robbie and Taylor were along for the surveillance, perhaps to catch a glimpse of their mother and killer. Fortunately, they had shut the fuck up and their whispering calls for Mama had stopped.

I parked in a spot about 50 yards from Julie Wiley's front door. I took out the 10x42 high powered Bushnell binoculars that I had told DEA were lost. I began writing a description of the condo when a taxi pulled up front.

The driver opened the door and a woman in a yellow raincoat exited, holding a yellow backpack. I focused the binoculars and recognized her as the rude, whacked-out passenger sitting behind me on the flight.

"What the hell?" I said out loud to my passengers.

The woman walked to Julie Wiley's condo. She stood facing the front door, her back to me. She took a cell phone from the back pack and apparently called someone. It was a very short conversation. She returned the phone to the bag in less than a minute.

"This woman knows Julie Wiley and we were on the same plane? How bizarre is that?"

The woman turned the knob but the door did not open. She ran her fingers on top of the door, felt underneath the mailbox and behind the porch light, apparently looking for a key.

She turned obliquely, offering me a profile. Her lips were pursed and she began tapping her chin with her index finger.

At that instant, while I watched, another memory washed ashore for Patty Reznor.

She and Craig were sitting on the couch in her den, their bare feet up on the coffee table, ankles over ankles. Mike was away on a sales conference. Craig had come over to get away from Julie. She rested her head on his shoulder. He was venting.

Craig had so many complaints about his wife, her selfishness and her unwillingness to take care of the kids. She wouldn't cook, couldn't cook and wouldn't clean house. Everything that Patty was willing to do for Craig, Julie was not.

"Patty, I tell you, she forgets her house keys at least once a week. Once a week she locks herself out of the house. The place is such a pit, it's no wonder she can't find a fucking thing, excuse my language. So I have to stop doing whatever I'm doing and go let her in the house. I finally bought one of those fake rocks. You know, it looks just like a rock, but has a compartment inside for a key, and you know what? She left the damn rock with the extra key inside the house one day, and locked herself and the kids out the next."

I watched as the girl in yellow picked up a brown and white softball sized rock next to a palm tree just to the left of the front door. She fumbled with it, put it back on the ground next to the tree and then turned to the door. The front door to the condo opened a few inches.

She slipped off her backpack, bent over and unzipped it. She pulled out something that glinted in the sun and laid it on the ground. I focused the binoculars on a large, wood handled, butcher knife.

She put her backpack on and picked up the knife. Then she turned facing the street, facing my direction. She held the knife in her left hand. She stood erect, both arms down at her sides, as if standing in formation awaiting inspection. She looked up and down the street slowly, mechanical, robotic.

I zoomed in on her face. Her lips were moving, but I could not make out the words. I knew that face and paged through the few memory banks that still were operational. It finally came.

"What the hell? That is Mike Reznor's schizoid wife, Patty, Patty Reznor."

My faithful Centipedes with needle sharp cleats crawled around my neck and shoulder blades. The children were interested but still not vocalizing.

Patty Reznor slowly looked up and down the street one more time and then pushed the door open and went inside Julie Wiley's condo. The door closed behind her.

I turned to the vacant passenger seat and spoke, "Ok, so, a mentally disturbed Patty Reznor, armed with a butcher knife is lying in wait for your mother. It doesn't take Matlock to figure out that nothing good is going to come out of this Hitchcockian set up."

I uttered my third, "What the hell?" as a silver BMW pulled up and parked in front of the condo. The car was missing a rear window.

The driver remained in the car. She was looking at herself in the rear view mirror and talking on her phone. After a minute or so, she got out. Julie Wiley stood next to her car continuing to talk on the phone. She talked, laughed and crouched down to look at her reflection in her driver's window. After a couple of minutes she slipped the phone in her purse. She removed two shopping bags from the back seat. Two quick horn beeps and the BMW lights blinked on and off. She walked up to her condo and juggled the bags as she unlocked her front door.

I pointed at the passenger seat like a drill instructor, "I want your mother to go to jail just as bad as you do. I want her to pay dearly for leaving you to wander around in the netherworld. I want an indictment and a conviction. I want to be there when they stick her in the arm with that needle. I want to watch that bitch struggle to take her last breath. I want justice to be served, too. I don't know what the fuck is going on, but murder by Patty psycho does not come close to my plan for a suitable resolution. That is too good, too quick and too easy for your fucking mother. She is not getting off that easy."

The centipedes stopped marching.

# Chapter Ninety Two

Patty was inside the home of the woman who had stolen her life. She took off her backpack and laid it in the entryway closet. She looked around while she waited for evil.

The entryway's pink walls were bordered at the ceiling with a light green, floral patterned wallpaper that flowed into the kitchen. Framed prints with beach themes including images taken at Venice, Malibu, Manhattan and the pier at Santa Monica lined the hall.

She stepped into the kitchen. It was open, airy and uncluttered. The floor was laid in glossy black and white ceramic tile squares. The kitchen walls were light lavender with a satin white wainscoting below. A row of six stainless track lights were directed onto a large kitchen island with a dark, granite countertop.

There wasn't a crumb of food on the island. There were no dirty dishes or even a glass in the sink. Patty noticed the stainless double-door refrigerator. The face of the fridge was vacant. No pictures, no magnets, no notes. It looked sterile.

She walked down two steps into a great room. The entire room, walls, ceiling and carpeting was white. There was a wet bar in the far corner with a counter top just like in the kitchen. In front of the bar were three clear, plexiglass bar stools with white leather seats. A large picture of two martini glasses tipped towards each other hung on the wall behind the bar.

Patty walked over to a dark red brick stone fireplace on the far wall of the living room. It was topped with an ornate white marble mantel and supported by marble columns with lion faces carved into them. On top of the mantel were two large stainless steel candle holders, each with a tapered 10" white candle. A small silk floral arrangement with peonies and hydrangeas in a white wicker vase was placed between the candlesticks. Patty stared at the mantle and chewed on the inside of her lower lip. She tucked the knife into her belt, pirate style, and took one of the candelabras off the mantle.

Patty's thoughts carried her back to the mantle at her parent's house. It was always topped with pictures. Pictures of her dad in his pilot's uniform, of her mom and dad at their wedding. There were pictures of past vacations to Italy, France, St. Thomas, of her as a ten year old in her girl-scout uniform, of Jackie, her favorite yellow lab, long gone. She saw the pictures of her and Mike at their wedding, and another of them standing in front of their newly purchased house.

She was not surprised that there were no pictures of Taylor, Robbie or Craig. Patty mumbled to herself, "The devil cares for no one but herself."

She walked through the living room towards the steps that led upstairs when she heard the front door open and then close. She froze, held her breath and heard the sounds of shopping bags crunching on the counter. Then she heard a closet door open.

Patty quietly crept into the kitchen. Julie Wiley was standing partially inside the closet.

"Now whose backpack is this?" Julie asked.

Patty squealed as she brought the heavy candlestick down on top of Julies head. It was a bit awkward since Julie was a few inches taller. The strike was a hard, glancing blow rather than a direct hit. Nevertheless, it partially tore off Julie Wiley's left ear which now hung by a meaty thread next to her jaw.

Julie emitted a high pitched grunt and then fell to her knees, face forward into the closet and collapsed on top of the yellow backpack. Patty watched her for a moment. Julie was still.

Patty stared down at the thief who had stolen her life.

"I have to get my notebook so I'm going to need my backpack, Julie," Patty said to the body. She bent over, grabbed both of Julie's ankles and dragged her out of the closet. Julie groaned and coughed once. Patty pulled her backpack out from underneath the body. Julie rolled onto her back.

"We reap what we sow you devil," Patty said, shaking her head and pointing her finger at Julie.

Julie's eyes were closed. She moaned several times. Her white spandex top was turning red..

Patty went into the kitchen and returned with an elaborately etched, 40 oz. lead crystal pitcher filled with water. She slowly poured it on Julie's face, essentially waterboarding her.

Julie gagged and coughed as she sucked water into her lungs. Her head rolled back and forth trying to get out of the stream. Patty held the pitcher above her head with both hands and let it go. The heavy pitcher struck the right side of Julie's face, gashing and crunching her fashionably high cheekbone and then cracked into shards on the floor.

The water and the pain stirred Julie. She rubbed her eyes and propped herself up on her side, inadvertently leaning on broken glass, slicing open her right elbow. She shrieked in pain and anger.

Julie felt the blood and fleshy pulp that had been her ear, hanging down on her cheek She looked down at her red shirt and then up at her attacker. A familiar red rage was developing. The blood from her elbow rolled down her forearm into her hand. She wiped her bloody hands on the front of her shirt.

"Who the fuck? What the fuck, you fucking bitch!" Her voice was garbled due to the fractured maxilla. She sat up and focused on the woman standing over her.

"Patty Reznor. Jesus. Fuck! What the fuck are you doing here?"

She cleared her head with a few shakes. "You fucking bitch!"

Patty slipped the butcher knife from her belt.

# Chapter Ninety Three

peered up and down the empty street. It was quiet. No one was out except an elderly woman working in a small garden and her back was to me. I put on the jacket of my running suit and pulled the hood out of the zippered collar. No sense in having my face on any surveillance tapes, should there be any cameras. I strolled casually across the street, hoping to look inconspicuous. Sure, in 85 degrees, a guy in dark clothes and a hoodie might not look out of place. I went for it anyway.

I made my way to the front door of Julie Wiley's condo and reached for the door, but stopped.

"Fuck, I need gloves. You ass, Morris," I whispered to myself and looked up and down the street again. Except for the old woman it was still quiet.

I reached into my pockets and felt latex. I had a couple pairs of gloves in the pockets. I guess I must have worn the jacket to a crime scene at some point. I put gloves on and listened at the door.

"Patty Reznor. Jesus. Fuck! What the fuck are you doing here? You fucking bitch!"

"You took away my life. You are a monster. You stole the happiness I was supposed to have, like my mom and dad. You stole my Craig, not yours. Not yours to take. Mine, my Craig! You, whore, devil's concubine! Evil, murderer of children! Evil must die."

"I'll fucking kill you bitch!" Julie screamed.

While I picked up the fake rock and fumbled with the hidden compartment, Patty reared back with the butcher knife to deliver justice.

Julie Wiley grabbed the handle of the broken pitcher lying on the floor next to her thigh. A diamond shaped piece of the pitcher was still attached to the handle. She swung it, slashing Patty's left calf with the razor sharp glass. Patty screamed and stumbled back. Julie took the opportunity to get off the floor. She stood awkwardly, panting like a boxer in the 10<sup>th</sup> round, leaning in a crouch against the wall.

Patty lurched forward, unable to bear weight on her left leg. Hopping on her good leg, she slashed out with the knife and let out a high pitched shriek like an Apache attacking pioneers.

Julie stood up and swung with an outstretched arm as Patty approached. This time the glass shard raked across Patty's throat cutting deep through blood vessels and tracheal rings. Blood spurted across the hallway. Julie lost her grip on the pitcher handle and it flew across the room.

I opened the front door and saw a scene that was every bit as gruesome as any *Saw* movie.

"Police. Don't move!" I yelled.

I couldn't travel with a weapon, so I was unarmed. The order had little weight.

Patty Reznor's blood sprayed a jagged line across my jacket. She was falling towards Julie with the butcher knife still intent on its mission. I stepped in and grabbed her wrist and twisted the knife out. Patty fell into me, grabbing for anything to hold onto as she wheezed and gurgled.

A crimson Julie sprung from the wall and grabbed for the knife. "Gimme that. I'm going to kill that cunt!"

The three of us fell to the floor and I ended up on my back, Patty lying across my lower legs. Julie Wiley on top. She was on the offense leaching onto my wrist that was holding the knife.

"Gimme that, I'll kill you, you prick! I'll kill that bitch!"

I gripped the wooden stock of the knife tightly with my right hand as she tried to pry my fingers away.

"Stop. Police. Stop fighting!" I yelled as she continued to wrestle for control of the butcher knife.

I doubled up my left hand and delivered an old fashioned haymaker which struck her remaining right ear and jumbled her broken cheek. It stunned her and she rolled off Patty and me.

Patty Reznor's neck bubbled red froth. Her eyes closed as she gurgled a few unintelligible words. She was a few seconds away from death.

I rolled to my side and slowly stood. I was leaning forwards towards the kitchen counter, when I heard what sounded like a rabid screech owl behind me.

Julie Wiley jumped onto my back and before I had even the inclination to react, she whacked the top of my head with something that felt like a baseball bat.

The momentum of her weight bent me over the kitchen counter. I pushed back with all the energy I had in my quads and we both went backwards across the hallway, smashing against the wall, crushing in the drywall. I heard cracking sounds that were not just building material.

We fell to the floor and I crawled away from her. To my surprise, Julie Wiley was still conscious and on the move. Her face was streaked with blood and fury. I had dropped the knife and she was crawling towards it grunting and mumbling.

I stumbled and walked awkwardly on my knees towards the knife and was able to beat her to it. I grabbed the knife and in a halting motion, stood up. My head felt like it would explode.

"Stop moving!" I said. "Stop right now! I'm a police officer!"

"Fuck you!" Julie Wiley growled and continued forwards rising from her knees to a crouch. Wet, deep and guttural indecipherable words came from her mouth.

I stepped back, once again, leaning against the kitchen counter.

She let out another nails on the blackboard squeal and leaped towards me like a lion after a gazelle.

I side stepped her this time and she slammed into the edge of the counter. She slipped on blood and fell on her back, landing on several large shards of the broken pitcher. A stifled groan came out among the gasps for air.

I jumped on top of her, straddling her hips to pin her down.

"You're a dead…man," she said, gasping for air.

"I've been dead a long time because of you."

Taking the same intra-cardiac injection path I had used as a paramedic years ago to save lives, and the same one I used to murder Daniel Gonzalus, I stuck the butcher knife into Julie Wiley's chest, upwards under her left costal arch, directly into her left ventricle.

Her eyes widened. She gasped several uneven strident breaths. Blood trickled from her mouth and nose. A few more wet gurgles emerged, and then she was still.

I crawled away from the two dead women, my mind wobbling like a broken gyroscope. I stood up slowly, I was dizzy, my vision was tunneling and I felt like I might pass out. I turned on the cold water from kitchen faucet and stuck my head under the water. I heard them.

"Maaaaama, Maaaaama, Maaaaaama, Maaaaama."

The room abruptly turned ice cold. An Arctic glaze of frost appeared on the windows above the kitchen sink and on the mirror above the fireplace. The water from the faucet froze solid. Ice crystals formed on my face. I could see my breath. The blood on the floor became solid, black ovoid pools which cracked like thin ice on a lake. The entire building shuddered. The thundering roar of a train passed in front of me. Inside one of the cars was a man flanked by two children. The little girl raised her right hand as they passed. It was not a wave as much as an acknowledgment. I understood. They'd crossed.

The noise diminished and the room returned to its climate controlled temperature of 74 degrees. I turned the faucet off and looked over at the stove's digital clock. It read 3:00 pm.

"I'll have to tell Myra Sutherland that there may be something to the 3 o' clock hour."

Despite a mild concussion, I felt refreshed, clear and energized. It was akin to snorting the best cocaine on the planet. I rotated my head and moved my left shoulder around. They felt fantastic, like I could throw a 95 mile per hour fastball in the strike zone with ease. I have to say that being released from the grasp of ghosts is better than any orgasm I ever had.

I surveyed the carnage and considered what had just happened and what would surely follow. There weren't too many options.

"I don't want any part of this. I was never at Ruth Scalini's and I was never here either."

I looked at myself in a large oval mirror hanging in the living room. There was a large hematoma just above my right ear. My hair was matted wet with blood. I felt the small scalp laceration from which blood was seeping.

I took off my jacket and T-shirt and stuck my entire head under the kitchen faucet. I rinsed the blood from my hair and neck. I applied pressure to the scalp laceration with paper towels for several minutes and it stopped bleeding. I finished washing up and dried off with more paper towels.

I found a half gallon bottle of Clorox under the sink. I poured some down the kitchen drain, flushed it with several minutes of water and then washed the sink, faucets and countertop down with bleach and wiped them dry.

Even if the cops pulled the plumbing traps, any evidence of my blood was long gone, and if they were anything like the Oakview PD, they probably wouldn't pull the trap anyway. No need, this looked like a cat fight between these two women that had gone horribly wrong. Piss poor police work got me into the children's murder and probably keep me out of their mothers.

I found Q-tips in the bathroom, wet them with nail polish remover, and scraped under Julie's nails in the event she got a part of me during our tussle. I took hold of her still warm hands. I scratched Patty's arms with Julie's nails leaving red lines from Patty's elbow to wrist depositing Patty's skin cells under Julie's nails, just like a cat fight. I wrapped Patty's bloody hand around the handle of the knife and then let it go limp.

I examined the floor for bloody shoeprints, handprints or any other evidence indicating someone other than two women were involved. I wiped down all the surfaces I might have come in contact with and wrapped everything I used inside my jacket. I found a Dodger's baseball cap in the closet and pulled it over my forehead. I peeked out the window for any traffic. A car or two passed by every few minutes. The old lady was gone and there were no other pedestrians.

I closed the front door and took off my gloves. For the second time, I drove away from a house in which two fresh dead bodies lay.

Like Kostaki Koulakis, one of Julie Wiley's inquisitive neighbors or maybe the maintenance man for the complex would have their own story to tell.

# Chapter Ninety Four

By the time I returned home, the news of the deaths of Oakview police Lt. Will Newsham, former city police officer James P. Patrick, as well as Vinny, Anthony and Ruth Scalini had made the leap from local to national news. All the talking heads spun the story with interviews of everyone they could find. Even Dan Wolfe, the city planner from Marietta, was interviewed for his 15 minutes of fame.

Everyone speculated on reasons. Through tight lips, Montileone promised a full investigation. John Kaltenbrook from the U.S. Attorney's office made references to the resurgence of the most violent organized crime activity in decades and the potential infiltration into law enforcement circles.

MQ and I spoke several times during my first couple of days back from California. His opinion was quite simply, "Fuck them. Now, let's get the bitch." The mayhem in Julie Wiley's condo had yet to be discovered, so I readily agreed with him, "Fuck them. Now, let's get the bitch."

I called Sheila when I got home to check on the kids. I filled her in on Carol's latest boyfriend and the move. She wasn't so interested in my sister's romance. She wanted the low down on the Newsham and Scalini drama. "I wanna know what is going on Morris. We lost you to the machinations of those bastards and I want to know, really know, what the hell is happening."

She was right, I owed her an explanation. At least one that was better than what was on MSNBC.

"The whole story is going to come out after the grand jury indicts some folks. We start grand jury tomorrow. The whole megilla, Estrilla, the Wiley murders, organized crime, all of it."

"And the results of the grand jury are secret. At least that's what you always have told me, Morris. So you're going to keep this close to the vest like everything else?" Her tone was acerbic and reminded me of how we communicated back in the day.

"No, no I'm not. You're right. You of all people deserve to know. Here is what the jurors will hear. Montileone, Will Newsham, James Patrick and the Newsham law firm have been conspiring with the Scalinis for a long time to control narcotics, prostitution and God knows what other criminal activity in the city and county. They have other cops, other police chiefs, some mayors, even some feds in their back pocket. This has been going on for decades. They were the ones that set up Tom and me."

"Wait, Jesus Christ Morris. Are you telling me that you're finally going to be able to prove that Montileone and someone in the department were involved?"

"Yep. Our snitch on the Mexican case, a big black guy named BB was working with the Scalinis. I figure Patrick and Will Newsham heard about our case and told BB who we were. They had BB play us like a cheap violin, or so the saying goes. He gave us what he knew we wanted, a Mexican source, and we took the bait. With us out of the way, no one else was looking at the heroin trafficking that closely. BB is looking at additional attempted murder charges now, so he's cooperating fully. He's got a lot of stuff on the Scalinis, Newsham, Montileone and Patrick."

"So how did the murders of those two children and their father and your shooting figure into all the killings that happened just now?"

"It's a convoluted soap opera Sheila. So, on the very same day I was shot, Mr. Wiley caught his wife, Julie, in bed with James Patrick. In the mayhem that followed, Julie Wiley killed her kids and her husband. Patrick took off and apparently wasn't involved in the killings. And if you will recall, Julie Wiley is old man Francis Scalini's granddaughter. At the time, she was felt to be a liability to the organization if she was arrested.

"Kenneth and I found the proof that she did it and the Scalinis and Newshams covered it up to protect her and keep her mouth shut. In the course of the investigation, we exposed corruption and conspiracy that goes all the way to the FBI in Quantico and the State Department in Washington DC where Will Newsham's brother works. It's going to be a real circus around here for awhile."

"Oh my God! Those sons of bitches. I hope they all burn in hell. So, what happens next?"

"Karen Flavin, MQ and I will lay out the story to the grand jurors. They will indict anyone who is still alive."

"Oh, that Karen Flavin, huh? Your paramour," Sheila asked with an underlying riptide of hurt and weariness from long ago. I didn't know she knew AK and I had an affair during those last few years of our terminal marriage.

"Yea, that Karen Flavin. In any event, it's coming to a close."

"So it's all going to be over soon?"

"I hope so."

"Me too, Morris, me too."

"It's been a rough road. I am sorry you had to go down it with me."

"Water under the bridge, Morris. Anyway, if you're free this weekend, Jake, Olivia and I are going to the lake house. The kids want to cut down their own Christmas tree and dad says he's picked out a couple for them to look over. You wanna come?"

"Yea, with all that's going on and the trip to Carol's, I'd forgotten the holidays were so close."

"If you wanna bring your friend you can."

"Awkward?"

"Not at all, Morris. The kids have been telling me about her, the ER doc. Jake and O like her. They say she's really nice, and funny, too."

"I'll check with Margie and let you know. It sounds fun."

"I love you, Morris."

"I love you, too, Sheila. And I'm sorry for all of this."

"Just try to make it to the lake this weekend. The kids would love to see you and so would my folks."

"I'll call you Friday."

Before I could put the phone down, it immediately rang.

"Green here."

"It's Karen."

"Hi, Karen. I was wondering if you were gonna call. We ready for tomorrow?" I asked, acting with as much enthusiasm as I thought was expected.

"You sitting down, Morris? I got some news, some real news, all right? Hot off today's presses."

"Yea, I'm sitting, go ahead."

"They found Julie Wiley dead in her Cali condo in some kind of bizarre home invasion attack. She'd been dead several days. At least that's what they're saying right now, all right. The killer was Patty Reznor. Name sound familiar?"

"What the hell? What happened now? Patty?" My voice rising with counterfeit surprise.

"Yes sir. Patty Reznor."

"Yea, sure, Patty Reznor. She and her husband were friends of the Wiley's, um…" I paused for effect. "Mike, that was her husband's name. Mike Reznor. MQ and I interviewed them both. She was out of it, major depressive disorder if I remember correctly." I waited for a response. I could hear papers shuffling.

"Yea, all right. That's right, here it is. Husband was Mike Reznor. He's also dead, but not recently. He had a heart attack a few years ago."

"So, Patty Reznor off'd Julie Wiley?" I asked, and added, "That makes three generations of scumbag Scalinis dead in a week, a pretty good start. So what happened? Did she make a statement, tell why she did it?"

"Get this Green, Patty Reznor's dead, too. Looks like they killed each other in some crazy fight, but Reznor left a note, all right. Patty Reznor wrote a note."

"What the fuck?" I answered with legitimate surprise.

"They found her backpack there, and inside it was a note. She put in this note all about how Julie Wiley killed Craig Wiley. That she witnessed it, all right. That she knew Julie killed the children, too. She wrote that it happened in Oakview, so the local coppers called Oakview PD. Lt. Hebert took the call. He checked with MQ who referred them to me here at the PA's office. I've been on the phone with LA County Homicide the past couple hours. I guess MQ will be calling you pretty soon. Act surprised if you want him to think he's giving you the scoop."

"Sure, sure thing AK."

"Morris, they faxed me a copy of the Reznor note. I have it here in my grubby little hands. It's some rambling crap with satanic references, all right, but it seems that back at the time of the murders, Patty Reznor and Craig Wiley were having a big time love affair. She must have known all this time that Julie was involved in the murders. For whatever reason, she waited this long to take her revenge. LA County is working the case as a home invasion and murder. They'll be following up on Patty Reznor's work and psych history over the past couple years to figure out the details. What the fuck about sums it up in my book, all right."

"AK, all of our players are dead. Now what?"

"Not everyone Morris. We're going forward. The grand jury is still on. We are going to lay out a story for those folks as good as anything John Grisham ever wrote. All right, we may not be able to fully explain all of it, but we'll get damn close. By the way, the lab came up with DNA from skin cells in those shoes you guys seized."

"The shoes with the solitary drop of blood on them,"

"They're James Patrick's shoes, alright. My guess is he was there when it happened, and left in a hurry, barefoot. We can figure that he wasn't wearing those shoes if he had a hand in the murders of those kids since there's only one drop of blood on them, and there weren't any barefoot prints in the crime scene photos, plus he's dead anyway. All right, with the forensics we have, and now this Reznor note, we can weave a telling tale of conspiracy, murder, organized crime, narcotics, public corruption and some freaky sex club extortion bullshit. Since we don't have to worry so much about convicting anyone for the actual murders, we go after the remaining scumbags."

"Sounds like a good plan, Karen."

"Thanks Morris. As far as I know, Chief Montileone and Chatham Newsham aren't dead. Yet anyway. And neither is Vinny Scalini's father, Frank Jr. And there are some targets in the DC area, too. We still have some breathing bodies to take to the woodshed. Kaltenbrook has called me a half dozen times, all right. I kid you not, I bet he's had an erection since all this has gone down. He smells the blood and wants in bad. There are some conspiratorial fish to fry, and we damn sure intend to pan fry some of those bastards. The Scalinis and Newshams are weak now all right, with the deaths of their sons and daughters, and we're going to exploit that advantage."

"I'm on board, AK. I'll see you tomorrow."

# Chapter Ninety Five

Margie and I were both off work the night before the grand jury was set to convene. We'd spent the day together at her place, reading and napping. I had successfully avoided any serious relationship discussions. We woke up about 4 pm. Margie made some dinner, I poured us a cabernet. We were through the dinner and bottle by 5:30.

It was about 22 degrees outside with a stiff wind out of the north. Her loft was a bit drafty, so I flicked the switch on the gas fireplace and turned the blower on low. It was getting comfortably toasty. Margie was in blue jeans and a Scrub top, doing a crossword. I had on sweats and a T-shirt and was reviewing the file once more. We were each leaning on opposite arm rests of the sofa and our legs were pretzeled.

"Why don't you give it a rest, Morris? You're prepared. You're ready."

"I'm reading these things that I did, but so much has gone on since then. It's like all this happened to someone else."

"I wish it had Morris, I really do."

"I mean, these reports are just a small part of the story. What's on these pages is really nothing compared to the bullshit that really happened. It's been a living hell, you know?"

"Morris, you've woken up in my arms drenched in sweat, screaming, tachycardic, as close to psychotic as a functional person can be. I think I have a handle on your hell."

"Maybe not so functional. I may have crossed that fine line of sanity a time or two."

"Oh, you mean when you talk to dead people?"

"Uh, you knew? You knew I was possibly closing in on schizophrenia?"

"You were a dream talking son of a bitch, Morris. You had conversations with those two dead children. You'd call them by name, Taylor this, Robbie that. You'd tell them you and MQ were doing your best, and sometimes you weren't so nice, Morris. You'd say things like, stop tapping me you little bastards, or get off that fucking train you shits and leave me alone. You were pretty hard core sometimes."

"Why didn't you tell me, make me take more medication or something?"

"That subconscious life and your daily reality are so complex, Morris. The PD, the clinic, Sheila, Jake, Olivia, your sister, these murders. I didn't want to become another actor in your drama for you to have to explain yourself. So, I let you handle it and for the most part, you did, and we can both see daylight ahead can't we? And you know, what I said is true. I'm really in love with you, like the real kind, like the, this is it kind, but you are so hard to read. You are so God damn closed sometimes. And with all this going on, I don't want to add to the load, but I don't know where you are with me. Sorry, I'm fucking rambling. I do that when I get nervous, and I didn't want to engage in anything this heavy right before the grand jury. I'm sorry, honey."

"I don't want you to apologize or be nervous, Margie. I want to let you in. I want you to be part of my life. I do love you. You are everything I wish I could be."

Margie untangled her legs from mine and leaned over, stretching out the full length of the couch, lying on top of me. We started kissing and rolled onto the shag rug in front of the fireplace.

# Chapter Ninety Six

The grand jury was composed of 16 citizens. All right Karen took three days to paint the canvas of the Wiley case for them. In addition to MQ and me, she called Elwyn Bryson, Officer Davidson, Sally Sunderman, Alan Derrickson, Ajay, Triple T, her sister in law from the county lab, and Tom Reynolds. Tom and I gave our recollections of the shooting.

AK brought in BB from prison. He was doing 18 years on drug and gun charges stemming from our heroin case on him. He was looking at life if he was wrapped up in the attempt murder on our lives. He was happy to get out of jail for a few days to testify. BB filled in the blanks about Estrilla, the Scalinis, the Newshams, and their connections to the drug trafficking, Mexico and what had led to the ambush on Tom and me."

The 16 jurors indicted Chief Montileone, Chatham, Spencer and Mark Newsham, and Frank Scalini Jr., on acceding to public corruption, conspiracy to hinder prosecution and conspiracy to commit murder. Mark Newsham was immediately placed under administrative suspension by the State Department. His passport and credentials were taken. FBI Supervisory Special Agent Daniel Oromando was indicted on public corruption. The day after being released on bond, Oromando was able to flee the country and is believed to have gone to South America.

At the first opportunity, Chief Montileone spilled his guts. Turns out he had kept a notebook, in that crow's nest he called his office, in which he kept track of all the tit for tats between he, Chatham Newsham and the Scalinis, including dates, times, arrests and personnel involved. It was all in there. Kaltenbrook had that woody for weeks.

Chief Montileone made bond. It looked like an accident when he was struck by a city bus while jogging and died of massive internal injuries at the scene. We all wondered whether a Scalini may have given him a little push or the old man just wanted to avoid going to the pen.

The Newsham Law firm hired outside counsel from New York and continued to battle the charges. I followed most of the trial in the paper, rather than showing up in person. Sometimes it seemed as much of a circus as the OJ or Blago trials.

Chatham Newsham's stroke occurred in court during an appeal hearing in April. Margie had switched to dayshift and was working in the ER when they brought him in. She called me, after she called the code.

"Hey, lover. You'll never guess who is four paws up in one of my ER cubes?"

"I don't know. Elvis?"

"Smart ass. You know as well as I do that Elvis is poolside at his posh mansion in upstate New York. Nope. One of your remaining nemesi, if that is the correct plural for nemesis. Chatham Newsham. He stroked out in court. It was a massive head bleed. DRT baby, dead right there in the courtroom really, but they scooped him up and brought him here. We worked him for about 35 minutes. We were short-handed and even I had to do a little CPR. I'm sore as hell. The asshole caused your back to hurt in life, and mine in death. What a prick!"

"Jesus, Margie. They are dropping like flies. Montileone steps in front of a bus and now daddy Newsham is dealt the ace of spades. Holy shit!"

"One by one, so it seems. It's Hitchcockian, Morris. Very cool. So, what are you doing?"

"I'm at the clinic today. It's been a COPD and asthma day for some reason. Must be the pollen. I'm finished at 7. How about I come over to your place and take care of that sore back? I have pretty good hands."

"I know you do, you mind reader. See you tonight, my love, gotta go."

AK and I never did hook up to rekindle a lusty affair. We both got busy with our other lives and decided to let the past stay the past. It's probably for the best. Margie and I are serious about our relationship. She expects and deserves exclusivity, and Dr. Classa is the type of woman who would have kicked both our asses.

I hung up and considered how the past few months had been so different from the last several years. The tapping, the voices, the nightmares, were turned off like a faucet following Julie Wiley's death. I half expected one last dream. Harvey Keitel at the controls of the train with Taylor, Robbie and Craig Wiley standing on the platform of the caboose as it streamlined up into the clouds of God. I guess that kind of schmaltzy thing only happens in the movies.

516

I weaned down the narcotics gradually. I haven't pilfered pills or forged prescriptions in a long time. I'm only taking Percocets for headaches and a couple of Xanax per day to manage the devils that still linger around me. I am hovering at a fifth of Ketel One on the rocks about every two weeks.

MQ and I received Board of Governors Meritorious Service Awards for Valor and Certificates of Recognition from the FBI and the US Attorney's Office in a public ceremony on the courthouse steps. The US Attorney's Office also gave Tom a letter of appreciation for his work on the case. It was a nice touch. He accepted the letter standing on two computer operated C-legs. He reminded me of Lieutenant Dan from Forrest Gump.

Lt. Hebert became Chief Hebert and promoted MQ to Lieutenant in command of the Investigations and Intelligence Division. I was promoted to Detective Sergeant in charge of the bureau. I rotate between day and evenings, coordinating my three shifts a week at the clinic with my police schedule. The rush and run of adrenalin remains the one dysfunction I am unable to shake.

I talk and or text with Jake and Olivia about every day and with Sheila a couple of times a week. As more of the people orbiting the Wiley case died, the better my life became.

Chatham Newsham's death took the wind out of Mark and Spencer's sails. The two sons took a proffer with John Kaltenbrook and named names, dates, places, and actions of corrupt agents throughout the FBI and the State Department. A wholesale cleansing took place over a few months as various US Attorney's offices around the country gained indictments and prosecutions. Spencer and Mark each received 25 years which will be done in solitary due to death threats from the remaining Scalinis.

Frank Jr. and the Scalini organization tied the government up with legal wrangling maneuvers. Frank remains free on an ankle bracelet and a five million dollar cash bond.

# Chapter Ninety Seven

I was charting at my desk the first week of the new year when Myra Sutherland stopped her housekeeping cart in front of my office. She leaned her bony shoulder against the door frame.

"Dr. Green, from what I been reading in the papers, things certainly did come to a proper conclusion don't you know?"

"They did Myra, and you deserve some of the credit."

"Not at all, Dr. Green. This was all you, and those kids. Who, by the way, are on the other side with their father, thanks to you."

I came around my desk. "No, really. Thank you so much for helping me." I extended my hand and when we shook, I pulled her to me and gave her a hug. Myra laughed and hugged me back.

"You've certainly become the friendly one," Myra said as we stepped apart.

"I just want you to know how grateful I am for what you did, how you helped me. How you helped us."

"It was just supposed to be, Dr. Green. I just played a small part."

"We'll have to agree to disagree on that. You finishing up soon? I would love to take you to lunch."

"I've one more floor to do, but I'd be delighted."

"Ok, come on back here when you're done. Any place special you'd like to go?

"Someplace quiet. We've got to discuss the other one."

"The other one?"

"You know, the other one. The other spirit trapped in between. She's still here," Myra said, pointing towards the corner of my office.

I glanced over at the empty corner. "Oh, for Chrissake. I don't have any unsolved murder cases. Damn, I forgot all about that."

"She didn't forget about you, Dr. Green."

"It's a she, is it?"

"Yes, a woman."

I deflated and leaned against the opposite door frame. "I don't know if I'm up for anymore of this justice for the dead work."

"Now, you don't have to worry. Everything will be fine. I'm pretty sure the best day of your past, will be the worst day of your future, Dr. Green, but we can talk about that over a corned beef sandwich. How about that?" Myra pushed her cart up the hallway and turned the corner.

I walked over to the corner and stared at the empty wall, "Who are you and what do you want?"

End